A Whisper and a Breath

The Riehse Eshan Series, Book Two

ADELAIDE BLAIKE

Copyright © 2022 Adelaide Blaike

All rights reserved.

ISBN: 9798365255883

CONTENTS

Author's Note	i
Map	iii
Genograms	v
Translations of common words	vii
Recap of the series so far	ix
Chapter One	1
Chapter Two	10
Chapter Three	15
Chapter Four	22
Chapter Five	27
Chapter Six	35
Chapter Seven	42
Chapter Eight	48
Chapter Nine	54
Chapter Ten	60
Chapter Eleven	65
Chapter Twelve	71
Chapter Thirteen	79
Chapter Fourteen	93
Chapter Fifteen	99
Chapter Sixteen	105
Chapter Seventeen	113
Chapter Eighteen	120
Chapter Nineteen	128
Chapter Twenty	142
Chapter Twenty-One	151
Chapter Twenty-Two	159
Chapter Twenty-Three	167
Chapter Twenty-Four	174

Chapter Twenty-Five	183
Chapter Twenty-Six	189
Chapter Twenty-Seven	197
Chapter Twenty-Eight	203
Chapter Twenty-Nine	217
Chapter Thirty	223
Chapter Thirty-One	232
Chapter Thirty-Two	248
Chapter Thirty-Three	256
Chapter Thirty-Four	263
Chapter Thirty-Five	276
Chapter Thirty-Six	287
Chapter Thirty-Seven	300
Chapter Thirty-Eight	308
Chapter Thirty-Nine	323
Chapter Forty	336
Chapter Forty-One	358
Chapter Forty-Two	372
Chapter Forty-Three	376
Chapter Forty-Four	382
Chapter Forty-Five	389
Chapter Forty-Six	394
Chapter Forty-Seven	399
Chapter Forty-Eight	402
Chapter Forty-Nine	406
Chapter Fifty	408
Chapter Fifty-One	410
Chapter Fifty-Two	414
Chapter Fifty-Three	417
Chapter Fifty-Four	421
Chapter Fifty-Five	425
Chapter Fifty-Six	428

Chapter Fifty-Seven	432
Chapter Fifty-Eight	435
Chapter Fifty-Nine	438
Chapter Sixty	443
Chapter Sixty-One	446
Chapter Sixty-Two	450
Chapter Sixty-Three	453
Chapter Sixty-Four	456
Chapter Sixty-Five	459
Chapter Sixty-Six	463
Chapter Sixty-Seven	467
Chapter Sixty-Eight	470
Chapter Sixty-Nine	474
Chapter Seventy	477
Chapter Seventy-One	480
Chapter Seventy-Two	484
Chapter Seventy-Three	488
Chapter Seventy-Four	492
Chapter Seventy-Five	497
Chapter Seventy-Six	505
Acknowledgements	511

A WHISPER AND A BREATH

AUTHOR'S NOTE

While some of the practices and languages in this book share similarities to real cultures, this is for fictional entertainment purposes only and (many) changes have been made to suit the story told. As such, nothing in this book is intended to be a reflection or commentary on any real culture or person, alive or deceased.

> Please note that this book contains internalised and externalised homophobia (including on religious grounds), misogyny and gendered abuse, attempted sexual assault, references to child abuse (non-sexual), character and animal death, elements of dub-con, mild BDSM, anxiety/panic attacks, and suicide. One of my ARC readers would also like to add: 'might have hurtful words from an asshole character against the LGBTQ+ community' (he really is an asshole). This book is intended for mature readers only, and reader discretion is advised.

A WHISPER AND A BREATH

MAP

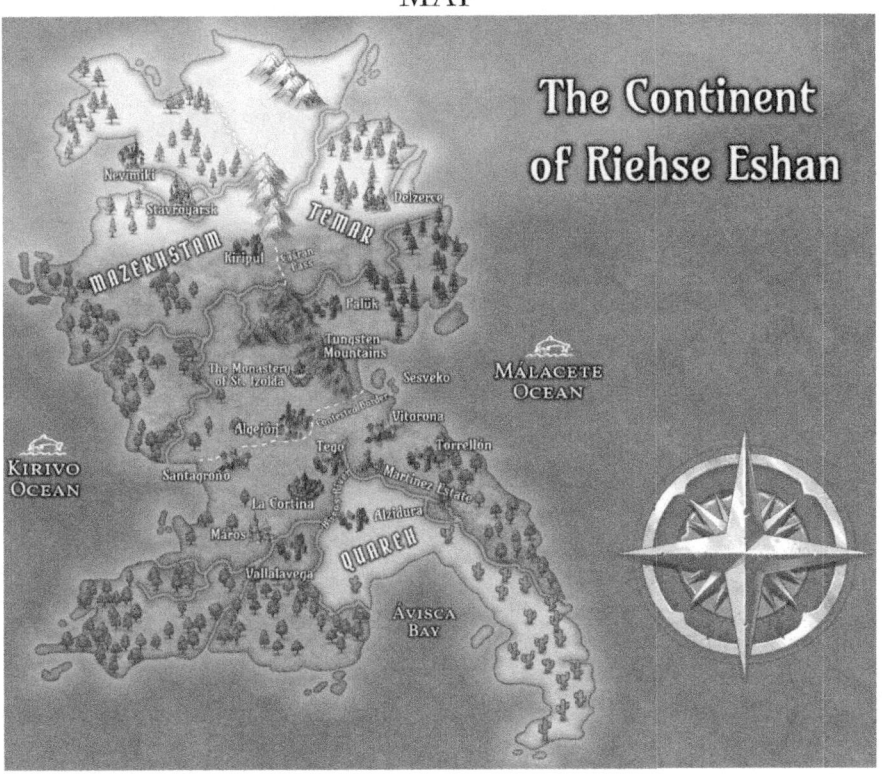

A WHISPER AND A BREATH

GENOGRAMS

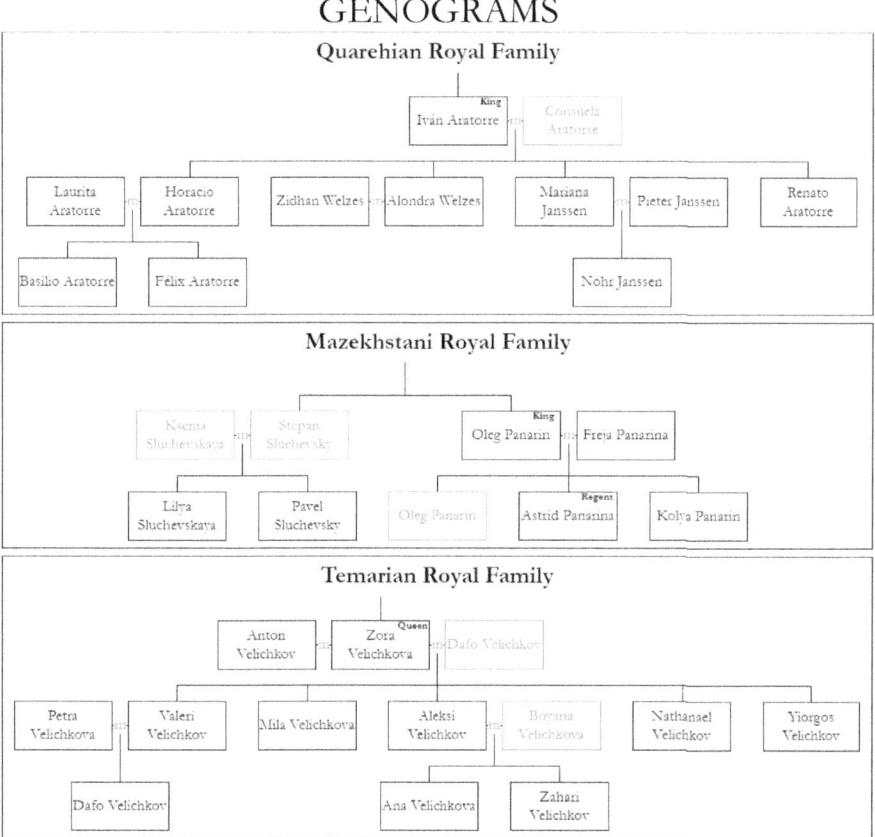

Quarehian Royal Family

- King Iván Aratorre — Consuela Aratorre
  - Laurita Aratorre — Horacio Aratorre
    - Basilio Aratorre
    - Félix Aratorre
  - Zidhan Welzes — Alondra Welzes
  - Mariana Janssen — Pieter Janssen
    - Nohr Janssen
  - Renato Aratorre

Mazekhstani Royal Family

- Ksenia Sluchevskaya — Stepan Sluchevsky
  - Lilya Sluchevskaya
  - Pavel Sluchevsky
- King Oleg Panarin — Freja Panarina
  - Oleg Panarin
  - Regent Astrid Panarina
  - Kolya Panarin

Temarian Royal Family

- Anton Velichkov — Queen Zora Velichkova — Dafo Velichkov
  - Petra Velichkova
    - Dafo Velichkov
  - Valeri Velichkov
  - Mila Velichkova
  - Aleksi Velichkov — Boyana Velichkova
    - Ana Velichkova
    - Zahari Velichkov
  - Nathanael Velichkov
  - Yiorgos Velichkov

A WHISPER AND A BREATH

TRANSLATIONS OF COMMON WORDS

<u>Quarehian</u>
Ahora – Now
Apúrate – Hurry up
Bárbaro – Barbarian (*pequeño bárbaro* is little barbarian)
Cabrón/malnacido – Asshole or bastard
Cobarde – Coward
Dios – God (*por Dios* is oh my God/for God's sake, while *Dios mio* is my God)
Eres hermoso – You're beautiful
Gato montés – Wildcat
Gracias – Thank you
Hijo – Son
Idiota – Idiot
Lo siento – I'm sorry
Mi amor/cielo/sol – My love/sky/sun
Mi querida/querido – My dear or my darling
Mierda – Shit
Naranja – Orange (fruit)
Por favor – Please
¿Qué? – What?
Sí – Yes
Señor/señora/señorita – Mr/Mrs/Miss

<u>Mazekhstani</u>
Blyat – Fuck
K chertu eto – Fuck this
Khorosho – Fine
Konchaj bazar – (roughly) Stop talking/shut up
Moy dorogoi – My darling
Moy knyaz – My prince
Nyet – No
Otvali – Fuck off
Svoloch – Bastard

Please note that occasional foreign words which are used when the characters are permanently speaking that same language are included solely for creative impact. Any errors in translation are the author's own and are apologised for in advance.

A WHISPER AND A BREATH

Recap of the series so far

Mat: *(bows) Zdravstvuyte,* reader.

Ren: He means hello. Mat, they probably don't speak Mazekhstani. Just talk normally for five minutes, okay?

Mat: 'Normally'? What is that supposed to mean?

Ren: It means speak in Quarehian. You know, the native tongue of Quareh, the finest of the three countries on the continent of Riehse Eshan? *(preens)* You may have heard of it.

Mat: I've done more than *heard* of it. I was captured by it when its stupid prick of a prince decided to kidnap the northern country's princess and ransom her in exchange for one of its occupied cities.

Ren: I'm ignoring the fact you dared to call me stupid, and choosing to instead focus on the brilliance of my plan.

Mat: *(snorts)* Yeah? How's it working out for you?

Ren: It *was* a brilliant plan. I just didn't count on some idiot ruining it by sacrificing himself for the Princess Astrid. While she was crowned Regent following her father's unexpected coma, that self-same idiot was rewarded for his troubles by getting thrown in my palace's cells.

Mat: The cells. *(shudders)* Don't remind me of those.

Ren: I don't know how many thousands of people have been sent down there over the years, and they were…*mostly* fine, but-

Mat: Except for that prisoner with the Voice you executed.

Ren: You know as well as I do that the Voice can command instant obedience, including compelling the victim to commit suicide or murder. I had no choice. But you're interrupting me, as per fucking usual. I was trying to point out that your delicate northern self was almost dead within two weeks down there. That's damned inconsiderate of you, Mathias Grachyov.

Mat: That's not my name.

Ren: I know that. I also know that you're a Blessed liar who had us all believing that you were the son of Mazekhstam's Commander Grachyov so we'd try to negotiate your release in exchange for Algejón's freedom. You ended up making us all look like fools.

Mat: You achieved that all by yourself, *prince*.

Ren: *(makes an indignant noise)*

Mat: I suppose I'm lucky that your healer saved me from both fever and death. Starling is far more talented with her gift of the Touch than any other of the magically-enhanced Blessed I've ever seen.

Ren: You know how you could find yourself even luckier? *(runs fingers up Mat's arm)* Say yes to me.

Mat: For a horny, flirtatious prince who has slept his way through half the palace and has his pick of lovers, you're strangely obsessed with getting me on my back. I've told you before. I'm not interested.

Ren: *(winks slyly)* You clearly are.

Mat: I'm *not*. I can't be. In my country, lying with another man is both criminal and sinful. As much as I might want…

Ren: Yes, *mi amor?*

Mat: *(clears throat)* Nothing.

Ren: As I said. *Liar*. I'll get you to admit the truth eventually, Mathias. After all, you're stuck in my company day and night, once I realised the only way to protect my valuable hostage from an unfortunate death was to keep him at my side. Where I go, you go. Be that political events, dinners, my bedroom…

Mat: You really never stop hoping, do you?

Ren: Never. Although I didn't realise you'd be *quite* so annoying. I gave you a guard uniform and told you to shut up and pretend you were one of them. But could you do that?

Mat: It's pretty obvious I'm not a guard, Ren: I look nothing like you southerners. And your guards are all twice my size! Jiron's *arms* are thicker than my entire torso.

Ren: *(seemingly not listening)* You could not. You just had to go causing problems with every little issue you saw-

Mat: *Little issue?* Are you talking about the horrifically deep-rooted misogyny that has embedded itself in Quarehian culture, leading to the daily oppression and abuse of thousands of women and girls? Or maybe you're talking about your own callous indifference towards the brutality of your father's reign? Perhaps you've forgotten how you laid open my back with a belt?

Ren: Because you put my best friend Alta in danger with your stupid, judgmental, northern *idiocy*.

Mat: Your best friend who is also your betrothed. Why did you never mention that?

Ren: It never came up. *(waves a casual hand)* Besides, talking about my future wife with the man I'm going to fuck felt like a mood-dampener, somehow.

Mat: Are you deaf? I am not going to let you fuck me.

Ren: Mmm. Say that again.

Mat: I'm not going to let you-

Ren: Yeah, again, but drop that ridiculous *'not'* word that keeps appearing in there.

Mat: You're impossible.

Ren: You almost did let me, remember? That time you stuck your annoyingly perfect nose where it didn't belong and discovered my father and Comandante Moreno had been...well.

Mat: Physically abusing you since you were a child? *(snarls)* Your father dares call himself a *king*?

Ren: Well, he stabbed the last one who had no heirs to replace him, so right of succession and all. But I'm talking about us that night, *mi amor*. How you let me make you come, and you were so beautifully responsive and desperate and-

Mat: *(flushes)* Shut up. That was a mistake, and I told you never to touch me again.

Ren: I know. *(sighs)* And I've been good, have I not? I haven't touched you once. Or twice...I don't know, there might have been occasional brushes against you, a tiny bit of wistful staring, but nothing like *that*. Even when that stupid emissary from Mazekhstam, the real Mathias Grachyov, arrived at the palace and almost made you cry.

Mat: I wasn't *crying*.

Ren: Come on, you know you can't hide anything from me. I worked out who you are, remember? Prince Nathanael Velichkov, son of Queen Zora Velichkova of Temar, kept in Mazekhstam since you were a child as a political hostage to stop war breaking out again between the northern countries. A damn fine liar with a damn fine ass. *(pauses)* And a decidedly less fine brother.

Mat: You don't get to talk about Valeri after what you did! Using me as leverage to force him to surrender to you? Do you not already have enough Temarian princes in your captivity?

Ren: And once again, you prove how utterly devastating you are to my plans, Mat. I have to admit, I didn't expect you to get the upper hand in that little encounter, nor use your new gift of the Sight – don't think I didn't notice that, you asshole – to help your brother escape the Dios-forsaken island we found ourselves on. And now he gets to sail away on a fucking ship, and I'm standing here on Sesveko looking like an idiot.

Mat: I-

Ren: And it's raining, Mat. *Raining*.

Mat: You think *you're* hard done by? I had to give up my freedom for Val's, and then your guard started pummelling my face in-

Ren: Well, you did have a knife to the throat of the charge Jiron has dedicated himself to protecting for the last thirteen years. And made him watch.

Mat: Did you expect me to ask him to close his eyes first?

Ren: Might have been polite.

Mat: I'll remember that for next time.

Ren: Next time? *(winces)* Maybe next time forget the knife and just go for the kiss you gave me afterwards, yeah? That was nice. *Real* nice.

Mat: That's what you're focusing on right now?

Ren: Mmmm.

Mat: Are... are you just going to stand there as Jiron hits me?

Ren: No. I'm telling him stop.

Mat: *(rolls eyes)* Clearly not very loudly.

Ren: How the fuck would you know? You're too busy getting your *face pummelled in*.

Mat: I think the very fact that I am is evidence enough.

Ren: *(sighs)* He does appear not to be listening to me. I'll be right back.

A WHISPER AND A BREATH

Chapter One

Ren

"Jiron!" I yelled down the sea-sprayed dock between us. "Stop!"

I knew he'd heard me. The waves crashing into the rocks were loud, but not so much that my voice wouldn't carry to him only a few feet away. The rain had eased from its pounding torrent of earlier, now no more than an incessant nuisance.

And yet he didn't stop. For the first time in our entire lives, Jiron deliberately disobeyed my order.

Fuck.

His fist continued to come down on Mathias' jaw, and he held down the man's wrists with his other hand to stop him fending him off. Not that Mat could have done so: Jiron was several times the size of his slender frame, and the northerner looked pitifully tiny beneath him. It would have been difficult to watch even if I didn't care for them both, but as it was, it was *agonising*.

The giant brought his wrath down again and again on Mat's beautiful face, its only reprieve when he directed his attention to sinking his heavy fist into his abdomen and ribs instead, and Mathias' groans turned to pained whimpers.

"Jiron!"

And yet still Mat struggled, trying to pull free or curl up to protect his stomach and head. But there was no escaping Jiron, no hiding oneself from him, and my guard was utterly ruthless as he conveyed his fury to the man beneath him.

"Stop, damn you! Jiron!"

I ran down the dock towards them, hoping to Dios I wouldn't slip on the wet boards, and yanked at Jiron's arm as he pulled back for another blow.

It was if I'd tried to stop the wind, or the waves crashing into the dock supports beneath us. My hold on him did nothing, and I felt the vibration through my fingers as his knuckles collided with Mat's face once more.

"For fuck's sake, Jiron! I'm ordering you to stop!"

I let go of him and instead slapped him hard across the face. It felt like smacking stone and did less to him than it did me, but to my relief, my guard finally fell still.

"You're out of line," I snarled. "I told you to fucking *stop*."

I tugged at his arm again and this time he let me pull him upright, rising with his usual gentle grace despite the white-hot anger I could see in his eyes. Mathias slumped bonelessly at Jiron's feet, blood streaming from his nose.

"Jiron."

My guard pressed his hands to my biceps and lifted my boots an inch up off the dock as if I weighed no more than a chair, moving us back onto not-so-dry land and into a shaft of moonlight so he could inspect every inch of me. By the Blessed, I usually adored being stared at and felt up, but this intense examination was something else. Yet for his sake, I suffered through him prodding at my arms and lifting the hem of my jacket to check I hadn't suffered any mysterious and fatal wounds to the gut, but when he pried my eyelids back, I slapped irritably at his hands until they obediently withdrew.

"Why the fuck would I have a concussion, Jiron? I'm fine."

He cupped my face instead. Amber gaze dropping to my chin and his top lip curled back into a silent snarl, my guard grazed his thumb under my jaw. When he pulled back, I could see it was glistening crimson before the rain snatched the blood away.

Mat's knife had left its mark.

I'd felt it happen when he kissed me, but it was only now Jiron had drawn my attention to the wound that it started to sting.

"I'm *fine*," I repeated, but Jiron still hadn't spoken. Neither had Mathias, although his persistent attempts to push himself up to his elbows were being thwarted by Luis, who had taken Jiron's place at the northerner's side. The guard watched on with folded arms and an expression that was feigning stoicism but coming across as closer to *concerned* as Mat winced and spat out blood onto the sodden planks of the dock, an arm wrapped around his stomach.

Mathias glanced up, catching my gaze, and a quick frown marred his perfect features – along with so much fucking blood – as he caught sight of my chin. And then his wide-eyed look turned to the ocean as he searched the waves.

I didn't bother. Velichkov and his people were gone, as was my hope of using the Temarian heir to leverage Algejón's release while keeping my father's eyes off Mathias. We were back where we started: one stupid, extremely fucked northern bastard in the hands of one very attractive southern prince...who was also extremely fucked. Either Mat's – *Nathanael's* – life could secure our city back from the north, in which case I'd be forced to give him up in exchange for the freedom and safety of thousands of my people, or it couldn't. And if the latter proved true, somehow I doubted that my father and Moreno would let such a failure go unpunished, for either me or Mathias. By the time the king and his Comandante were done, I'd be a bleeding wreck and Mat, as a useless hostage, would be well and truly dead.

I didn't know which was worse.

Dead, obviously. Dead was far worse. But the idea of having to let him go tore painful strips from my soul, and I knew it was irrational and jealous and possessive, but I didn't *care*.

For that man over there, choking on his own blood and yet still offering Luis a withering glare as the guard put his boot on his shoulder to keep him on the ground, had too much of a hold on my heart. He may have been rash, stubborn, and annoying as fuck...but he was also loyal, clever, and unendingly compassionate. *And* rash, stubborn, and annoying as fuck.

What can I say? I enjoy a challenge.

I also enjoy being an asshole.

"Red suits you," I told him, striding back over to my northerner and sensing Jiron tense at my back. "Is there anywhere you're *not* bleeding?"

"No idea." Mathias rasped, and then held up a limp hand as if to stop me moving any closer. "That's not an invitation to check, Ren."

Now there was a thought. If my hostage was at risk, it would only be proper to ensure he wasn't too badly injured. An examination just as thorough as the one Jiron had given me, only with less clothes to be really sure, and-

Don't touch me again. Please, he'd begged me that night. *I can't do that again.*

I came to a stop. Too far away to hold him in my arms like I wanted to, and too close to avoid counting every gash Jiron had inflicted across his face. His bottom lip was split in two places, his top, one, and his right cheek was cut open. It was clear he'd have bruises all over his face tomorrow, and his nose was still trickling blood, as was his temple. When he grimaced at me, I could see his teeth were stained crimson.

I swallowed.

From the way Mat was holding himself as he lay limply on the dock at Luis' feet, Jiron's fists had done a number on the rest of his body too. I could only pray that my oldest guard had shown his usual restraint even while lost in his fury, and that no permanent damage had been done.

Or Jiron would find himself in twice as much agony in turn. I shot him a look to communicate exactly that, and my guard dipped his chin in silent acknowledgement before moving down to the far end of the dock where I'd last seen Velichkov and his damn boat. If it were anyone else, I might have been worried they'd try to throw themselves into the churning waves to escape my wrath, but I knew Jiron too well to expect such a foolish, cowardly act from him.

"Luis," I said. "Let's get out of this accursed rain, shall we?"

Mathias let out a devastating noise as Luis bent and folded him into his arms; a kind of half-whimper, half-pained hiss, and half – because Mat wasn't the type of man to let himself be constrained by mathematical rules as petty as how many halves were in a whole – half-growled curse.

"I can walk," he snapped, looking tiny when cradled against Luis' chest. He lifted his fingers to prod gingerly at his jaw.

"Sure you can," I agreed. "With Dios knows how many bruised ribs, blood dripping into your eyes, up a narrow, wet cliff path…in the middle of the fucking night."

"And with bound hands," Jiron added as he returned to us, and when Mat opened his mouth, probably to say something stupid like point out how his hands were free, Jiron grabbed them easily and secured his wrists with rope. The same fucking rope that had previously held his brother's boat to the dock, and which he'd cut to grant Velichkov his freedom. Jiron had a cruel sense of humour.

Mat made an irritated sound, either at the irony or the indignity, but Luis held him firm with one arm under his back and the other both supporting and pinning his knees as Jiron gave him no opportunity to fight him off, having the knots yanked tight within seconds despite the rope being wet. Mathias let loose at both of them in pissed off Mazekhstani, and I raised an eyebrow.

Jiron had given him advance notice of his intentions, which was downright kind for the huge man. Maybe, despite him punching my future husband's face in, he did have a soft spot for the northerner after all.

Fuck. *Husband?*

Where the hell had that come from? That was way too intense a thought, even for me. Of course I wanted Mat in my bed, and with that edible body of his – I still hadn't seen much of it, but my fantasies had filled in the gaps nicely – I'd certainly be up for more than once, which didn't happen with every person I got intimate with. But marriage? That was far too hefty a commitment. And impossible. He was an enemy prince, and I was already engaged, and…and…and I was sure I would come up with a convincing reason eventually why even *thinking* that word was a terrible idea.

"I'm not going anywhere, Jiron," Mat snarled, finally returning to Quarehian so both guards could understand him, although I was pretty sure that his cursing needed little translation. "You saw to that, you prick. Do you see another boat hanging around?"

"You threatened my prince. Hurt him," Jiron said to him in a low voice. "I will not allow you a second opportunity."

"Inside," I interrupted. "*Ahora.*"

To my relief, Luis moved away without a word. And I felt even greater relief when Mathias held his tongue and didn't taunt the guards like I knew he wanted to. Perhaps even he realised how dangerous that would be in this precarious moment.

"Jiron," I muttered as the others began their ascent up the cliff, and he was at my side in an instant.

"Yes, my prince?"

"Your actions were unacceptable," I told him quietly, ignoring the lump in my throat at seeing Mathias hurt. At feeling helpless to stop it happening. "I will not tolerate disobedience from you."

"He had a knife to your-"

"And backtalk? Fuck, Jiron, I thought you were better than that."

He swallowed, and in all his years at my side, I'd never once seen that expression on his face. Shame? Regret?

The huge man went to one knee at my feet, head bowed in submission.

"My apologies, Your Highness. I did defy your order. I have no excuse."

"No," I agreed. "You don't."

His shoulders tensed, and it was obvious he wanted to point out the blood on my chin again, but he remained silent as his professionalism returned to him.

"Should I expect this from you in the future?"

Jiron's head shot up at that, and he set that finely sculpted square jaw of his as he worked through the last remnants of his ire.

"No, my prince. Of course not. I am *yours*."

"And what exactly am I supposed to do with you for that little outburst?"

"Punish me how you see fit," he said immediately. The hesitation came with what he said next. "Just please...please don't send me away from you."

I raised an eyebrow, and his throat bobbed as he swallowed again.

"Please, Ren. I couldn't bear to see you hurt and not be there to protect you."

"Sentimental fool."

"Perhaps," Jiron admitted, and the faintest wry smile tugged at his lips. "But I've grown far too fond of that young prince I was assigned to fresh out of training to let him loose in the continent without me at his side."

"For my sake, or that of the continent?" I asked.

"Quite assuredly both."

I hid my own smile. "Jiron."

"Yes, Your Highness?"

"Will Mat be okay?"

"Yes, Your Highness. I did not cause any lasting damage. He will hurt for a few days, is all."

I let out a breath at the surety of his words. Despite tonight's slip, Jiron was too good at his job for me to ever doubt him. And I sure as fuck wouldn't ever dismiss him from my service when he was the only reason I was standing here at all, having saved my life on far too many occasions to even be able to count, let alone bother doing so.

Eyeing the man at my feet, I bit my lip, suddenly able to see the humour in what he'd said before.

"Punish you as I see fit, Jiron? Are you sure you're prepared for what that might *mean*?" I gave him a heated look to ensure he understood my implication.

A third swallow. Dios, the man was fragile today. One little knife had caused so much destruction to us all.

"If that is what my prince wants," Jiron said carefully, although it was clear it wasn't what *he* wanted. He'd never shown any interest in the type of play I engaged in with some of the others, Lord Lago included, and if I was honest, I was lucky Jiron ever let me take him at all. He wasn't a natural bottom, submitting to me merely because it was the only way *anyone* could have me whatsoever, but it wasn't what he enjoyed. It grated at me each time we fell into bed together, and I'd vowed more than once to find a better way to make it work between us so I felt less guilty about him having to ignore his preferences for me, but no fantastic idea had yet struck. Maybe Mat could use that Sight of his and tell me what brilliant solution I would think of in the future to save me the hassle of having to actually come up with it myself.

Mat.

I glanced up and spotted the small figures of Luis and Ademar reaching the top of the cliff, Elías joining them with his bow strung across his back. Unless they'd tossed the bastard into the sea while I wasn't looking, Mathias was fine.

"What I *want*?" I asked the man silently kneeling at my feet. "What I want is to know that you won't hurt him again."

My guard dipped his chin. "If that is your order, Your Highness, it will be obeyed."

"*This* time."

He didn't rise to the bait.

"And if you order me into your bed or your ropes as punishment, I will obey that too." His eyes bore up into mine, his mouth drawn into a tight line.

"Oh, for fuck's sake, Jiron. I was joking."

"I wasn't."

"Hey," I said. "Don't go thinking you get to choose your penalty for your disobedience."

Bowing his head again, he spoke to my boots. "That is your honour, Your Highness."

"Actually, it's Mat's," I said, struck with the idea. "Considering he's the one who suffered from your extremely rare misbehaviour, he can decide the consequences for you in return."

Jiron looked up at me. If I'd expected him to argue against giving the man whose face he'd just beaten to a pulp the power to choose his fate, I wouldn't have known him at all.

"Of course, my prince. Except for-"

"Except for the ability to dismiss you as my guard," I agreed, and he relaxed at that. I nudged him with my foot. "Now, get up off your knees. Mathias got carried up that treacherous slash in the rocks the Ivanovs have the audacity to call a *path*, and I don't know why I shouldn't warrant the same treatment."

Jiron rose to his feet and scooped me into his arms in the same fluid movement. I lazed back, crossing my ankles, and grinned up at him luxuriously.

"I could get used to this. Perhaps I'll have you carry me everywhere from now on, Jiron."

The position certainly came with its own perks. I ran a hand over his wet shirt up the planes of his chest, feeling his pectoral muscles tighten as he shifted me in his arms.

He glanced down with an amused expression.

"Please don't distract me, Your Highness. If I slip, we're both dead."

"Then don't slip," I said.

That order, he obeyed.

*

Chapter Two

Mat

"You're unusually quiet," a voice said, and I turned my head to find Ren stepping through the open doorway to the bedchamber, scrubbing at his long, rain-drenched hair with a towel. He pulled a face as he looked at me. "And you're still dripping blood everywhere, I see. Why haven't you cleaned up?"

I returned my gaze to the fire. While a small one had been lit in my room, Ren's allocated quarters on Sesveko had a massive fireplace that stretched half the width of the back wall. The flames licked ferociously at the air, heating my face even as the rest of me remained frozen under my wet clothes.

Ren clicked his tongue. "I asked for a bath. I know you like those."

"I'm fine," I said shortly, although to my aching body, a bath sounded absolutely perfect.

"Well. After being entreated to five different excuses from various Ivanovs about how that would take several hours to arrange – again, water availability cannot be the fucking problem here – I had them send up some bowls and cloths instead. And it doesn't take your gift of the Sight for me to *see* that they have arrived and you have not touched them. Do you have a preference for being covered in blood? It does make you look rather dashing, but…"

"Ah," he said in realisation as he circled around to face me, the fire at his back. "That's just rude."

I ignored him, feeling warm wetness trickling down my cheek, and Ren sighed.

"Ad, why the fuck is he tied to the chair?"

Ademar frowned from his position near the window, where he'd been glaring at me for the last ten minutes. "Your Highness? Mathias attempted to kill you."

"*Did not*," Ren and I both muttered at the same time, him decidedly more cheerily. He shot me a wink.

Ademar tried again. "We're just taking precautions, my prince."

"There's no need. He's not going to hurt me now it's over."

The guard made a noise of frustration. "Your Highness, you can't know that for sure-"

"It was to save his brother, Ad. Wouldn't you have done the same? I'd like to think I would have for mine. Hopefully with half the blood and twice the dramatics." Ren waved a careless hand. "Untie him so he can wash."

Ademar moved into my field of view, obediently pulling a knife from his belt and cutting through the knots of rope.

"Now leave."

"Jiron said he had to be watched at all times."

"Hmm," Ren said. "I assumed when I hired you five years ago that you had all your faculties intact, Ademar, but apparently I was wrong. For if you can listen to Jiron speak and instead of that big brute's growl you hear an indescribably sexy prince, then there's *something wrong with your fucking hearing*."

"It's still a sensible idea," the guard protested, and Ren gave a short laugh.

"When have I ever been sensible? *Out*."

The prince all but shooed Ademar through the door, slamming it shut on both his and Luis' concerned faces. I snorted, shaking off the ropes with no small amount of discomfort and making my way towards the bowls of warm water laid out on the table. Ren watched my every wince with a keen glint in his gaze.

"I don't suppose you'll let me...?"

"Not a fucking chance," I told him, pressing a cloth to the cut above my eye. The blood soaked it through almost immediately.

"I'll be gentle," he purred in my ear, and I tried not to flinch. I hadn't even heard the bastard move. "Unless you *want* me to hurt you, and then I'll oblige."

I turned around. "Really? You don't think Jiron did enough damage tonight?"

Ren gave me a languid smile. "I'm talking about hurting you in the way you'll enjoy, *mi amor*." He plucked the cloth from my hand, washed it out, and dabbed it to my stinging cheek. And my *not a fucking chance* must have sounded as hollow to my ears as it clearly did to his, because I let him.

"No one enjoys being hurt."

He snickered at that, but his brows were drawn down into a frown as he stroked the blood away from my chin and drew the cloth across my broken lips, as carefully as he had promised.

"A shame he had to ruin your mouth," he murmured, and this time it was not the cloth but his thumb that brushed against my bottom lip. "It kisses as passionately as it speaks."

I scowled and batted his hand away. "We're not talking about *that*. It was a-"

"Don't you dare go on about that 'mistake' shit again," Ren interrupted, shooting me a reproachful look. "Or I'll beat it out of you so hard you won't be able to form *words*."

I eyed him, startled, and tried to ignore the way his sharp, suddenly dominant tone sent a rush of unexpected heat through me.

"You and Jiron deserve each other," I told him, and spat blood into one of the empty bowls.

"Don't be like that. Unless you truly believed Jiron would have run you through with his sword, you knew you'd survive whatever happened. And yet you still kissed me." The prince shrugged, his eyes alight with mischief. "That has to mean *something*, Mat."

"It means I got caught up in the moment," I said.

"Oh, I know. You had a knife to my throat for over ten minutes without incident, and yet you let it slip at the very last second?" He fluttered delicate fingers over his chin, which he must have cleaned of its own blood before he returned to his room. "*Very* caught up, I'd say."

"Well. I'd say I'm sorry, but I'm not."

Ren sighed and turned away. "You're an idiot to have gotten involved at all. I would not have hurt your brother."

"No, just held him hostage like you have me."

"Exactly. If I had the Temarian heir, no one would have cared about Zora's fourth child."

I scoffed. "Charming."

"I didn't mean-"

But whatever he had meant, the knock at the door silenced him.

Ren cleared his throat. "Yes?"

Elías slipped through the door and dropped into a bow. "Your Highness," he said. "The Ivanovs have posted sentries on the cliffs as you requested. They'll report if they see anything that…how did you put it? 'Threatens the neutrality of the island'? I'm not sure how you kept a straight face, my prince."

"With great difficulty," Ren agreed. "Have they mentioned the Temarians' absence yet?"

El nodded. "Yes. They asked if we knew anything about it."

"And you told them…"

"Our prince was out for a walk to expel the frustration of the day's trade talks when one of our party slipped in the mud and was injured on the rocks," the guard recited casually, glancing at me with such an innocent look that I was forced to reassess everything I knew about the man. He seemingly wasn't as honest as his young, clean-shaven face made him seen. "We didn't see anything of any Temarians. Whatever could have happened to make them leave so abruptly? The Ivanovs don't think that the north is *up to something,* do they?"

His expression was a perfect balance between eager and utterly sarcastic.

"I don't know which of you I trust the least," Ren drawled, glancing between me and his guard. "Why do I attract the company of such excellent liars?"

"Well, if we ever pay you a compliment, at least you can be sure it's utter bullshit," I said, but El didn't smile. Instead, he dropped his gaze to the floor.

"Your Highness, I'm sorry. I missed-"

"El. Even if you'd killed a man for every arrow you loosed – or a woman," Ren added hastily, glancing at me as if expecting me to start objecting about his gendered language when he was talking about murdering my fucking people, "it wouldn't have made a difference, not with what happened. In fact, it would have probably made tensions worse."

Worse. *Heh.* Val was going to be pissed, and I didn't want to be in Ren's boots when my brother finally caught up to him. Which I had no doubt would happen eventually; my stubbornness was a family trait.

"But we didn't-"

"You all did your jobs. You followed orders, *mostly*," Ren said, glancing at the door where I knew Jiron would be waiting, "and kept me alive, which is all I've ever asked. Now go. I can't believe I'm saying this, but three's a crowd. I'm about to get Mathias naked and I don't want you making him shy."

Elías' eyes flickered to mine in confusion, as if wondering if his prince was serious about laying with the man who had just held a knife to his throat. I gave an exasperated shake of my head, but he just dipped his chin and left in silence.

I glanced at Ren to chide him for his words, and immediately regretted it. His shirt was already off, the wet material draped over the crook of his arm, and he was busy kicking off his boots.

"Oh, for fuck's sake, asshole."

Turning away, I felt my face heat, and I tried *not* to replay that singular image of him undressing over and over in my head. And then I didn't have to, for it was replaced by one showing even more skin as he walked past my line of sight entirely naked, clothes and boots in his arms. My cock hardened in an instant.

I groaned and closed my eyes, but the sight was burned into my vision and I expected I'd be seeing it for a *long* time. "No. One desperate kiss does not equal a full fucking invitation, okay?"

A soft laugh hit my ears. I felt warm fingers curl at my neck from behind, and then Ren was tugging at the fur coat my brother had given me, trying to ease it from my shoulders.

Oh.

*

Chapter Three

Ren

Mathias tensed at my touch. "Back off, Your Highness, before I give Jiron a real reason to hurt me."

I clicked my tongue as I dragged off his furs. "Mat. I don't know what terrible fashion choice inspired you to don this monster, but I can practically still hear it growling at me."

"It's weather appropriate."

"If your clothes weren't already sodden underneath, I might agree with you. But you're freezing, and you're shivering. You need to get yourself and your clothing dry, and you can't do that while it's still on you."

He turned around under my hands, a startled expression on his face. For someone normally so naïve when it came to affairs of the bedroom, Mat had a remarkably dirty mind.

"What?" I asked innocently. "Did you think I was undressing us both for a different reason?"

I waved an arm over at the fireplace, where I'd draped my own wet clothes over the unmatched chairs to dry them out. Servants, my ass. I was perfectly capable of looking after myself. Although my coat looked a *little* too close to the flames…

I wandered over and yanked its chair back, just as an ember sparked into the space it had been sitting.

See? Perfectly capable.

Mat was biting his lip, glaring my way and seemingly trying very hard not to lower his eyes from my face.

I laughed. "I'm not going to fault you for looking, *mi amor*. Although I'd prefer you wait until I warmed up, just in case the cold is…acting unfavourably towards me."

"It's not," he muttered, and then hissed in an annoyed breath, crimson flushing across that gorgeous ivory skin of his. Fuck me, I didn't know how he had any blood left in his face to blush, but I'd never get tired of that sight.

I tossed his coat over another of the chairs before the damn thing could return to whatever beast form it had held before a Temarian had killed and skinned it.

"Your turn," I encouraged, and dug my bare toes into the rug. "I want you on the floor in front of the fire, stretched out and naked, so I can use my tongue to dry you off."

I paused for dramatic effect, then shot him a grin. "Did I say *dry?*"

Mathias' eyes flashed with colour, one blue and one gold, and he swayed on his feet.

"Hmm," I said, when his eyes returned to normal. "Did you See yourself doing what I want for once?"

"No," he retorted. "I Saw your hair catching alight."

"That's not-"

I yelped when I felt a lick of heat behind me as the fire flared, and stepped neatly away before the flames could get close.

"Thank you for saving my second favourite part of me," I said grudgingly, gathering the long strands of my dark hair over my shoulder to keep them safe. "Perhaps you can now turn your attention to the first?"

I watched with unrestrained delight as he removed Ademar's jacket and his boots. And then with utter fucking frustration when he didn't go any further.

"Nathanael," I said. "I'm being serious. You'll catch another fever if you leave your clothes on."

"I am not undressing in front of you, Ren. You'll take it entirely the wrong way."

"I'll turn around."

"I'm sure you will. And then right back around again. I don't trust you one inch."

I raised an eyebrow. "As you pointed out, I have far more than one inch to spare. Trust those *many* other inches instead."

Mat scoffed.

"I know you're stubborn, but this is ridiculous. You're going to make yourself sick because you're incapable of seeing sense. Is that what happened down in the palace cells?"

He ran a hand over his face, wincing as he caught the injured skin. "I want a blanket."

"Of course."

I fetched him two from the bed. No one could accuse me of not being generous. Particularly when I then proceeded to turn around and didn't even *attempt* to peek at my northerner behind me as he peeled off his wet shirt and trousers with small noises of pain, even though there was a perfectly reflective surface on that jug there, and that brass handle there, and-

I closed my eyes.

It seemed like an eternity before Mathias finally cleared his throat. I peered over my shoulder, trying to stifle my laugh at the sight of him wrapped neck to toe in blankets as if the fact that I was used to at least seeing his bare throat and forearms had to now be remedied.

"You're one of a kind," I said, amused.

Wandering over to the bed, I slid under its remaining covers. I didn't offer to share. It was clear what his answer would be, despite the fact that it had been *him* who kissed me down at the dock, when he could have just run. I was too tired to think that through, but with Mathias' obstinacy and frigid northern upbringing, it would take more than a casual comment to get him tucked up in here with me.

He settled himself carefully on the rugs in front of the fire, and even if half of my fantasy had come true, my tongue apparently wasn't getting anywhere near him tonight. I wondered if it was the lack of available chairs or his pained ribs that was preventing him from taking up his usual spot in an armchair at the furthest corner of the room from me, but that was answered by his sudden intake of breath when he shifted to lie down.

"He's yours," I said, staring up at the shadows that danced across the cracked and mouldy ceiling. Fuck, this place was a mess.

"What?"

"Jiron. For what he did to you. I've told him he's on your mercy." I lounged in my own blankets, enjoying the feeling of being dry once more even if the material was scratchy and frayed. "You may return each one of the blows he inflicted on you, if you like."

"I'm not going to hit him."

I pulled a face as I watched a spider crawl along one of the bed posts. "Probably wise. I fear I broke more than one of the bones in my hand just slapping him."

Mat was silent.

"So go order him to take a long swim in the freezing ocean," I suggested. "Tell him he has to walk home backwards. Or if your head hurts too much to be creative, there's always *la Cortina's* stablemaster and his nine tailed whip."

"I am not sentencing Jiron to a flogging!" Mat hissed, the scorn clear in his voice. I glanced over to find him staring at me from his position on the floor, the fire's flames reflected in his eyes.

"Then how would you have him punished?" I asked. He shook his head.

"I wouldn't."

"You do know he just beat the shit out of you, right?"

"He was protecting you." Mathias narrowed his eyes at me, but the stern effect was quite ruined by how he snuggled his chin down into his blankets. I'd never wished to be a threadbare piece of cloth before, but I sure was now. "And you fucking knew I'd say that, didn't you?"

I shrugged, returning my gaze to the cracks in the ceiling. One of them would be better termed a fissure, but I doubted the Ivanovs were taking complaints when the alternative was sleeping out under the stars...and Sesveko's seemingly never-ending rain.

"You dote on that man," Mat accused. "Why tell Jiron I would be responsible for his punishment if you knew I'd never deliver one?"

"Because *he* doesn't know that," I pointed out. "Let him stew for a while."

"Or I could change my mind and take you up on your bluff."

He wouldn't. Mathias was the most forgiving person I'd ever met, unnaturally so. The things I'd done to him, and yet he just…shook them off. Personally, I'd have my enemies boiled alive in hot oil if I had the opportunity. And if there weren't any flesh-eating eagles nearby that I could use instead.

"Is there anyone you would actually take vengeance on, if you could?" I asked.

Mat's response was immediate. "Your father and the Comandante come to mind."

Yet neither of them had ever laid a hand on him. Did he give their names because of Alta, because of Astrid? For all the disparaging comments they'd made about women, and their roles in keeping men at the top of the Quarehian hierarchy?

Or for what they'd done to *me*?

I feigned a yawn, suddenly uncomfortable. "Well, no one's disagreeing with you there. Goodnight, Ma…Nathanael."

"You can call me Mat," he said quietly, but when I glanced over at him in surprise, his eyes were already closed.

—

It didn't take me long to match his slowed breathing, but my sleep was far from restful. Angry wolves chased me into towering waves, the snout of a bear grew from Mat's fur coat and bit at me, and I fell into a bed of knives that sliced and cut at every inch of my bare skin.

With each strange new scene, the fear they inflicted paled when compared to the inexplicable sensation of loss and loneliness that came from traversing the dreamscapes alone.

When my eyes next opened, the fire had sunk low into smouldering embers, and the pale glow of dawn seeped through the window. A noise drew my attention to the floor, like it wasn't already heading in that Dios-damned direction of its own accord, and I sucked in a breath as I realised Mathias was shivering in his sleep, the blankets still up around his chin but clearly not doing anything to keep out the chill that had infected his body.

I'd fucking told him.

I should have given him more blankets. I still had a couple on the bed, and I could have gone without if needed, and-

His teeth chattered, and his eyebrows scrunched further as if the cold was physically paining him. And then I remembered that it was more than cold he was dealing with, and if the dark shadows I could see stretched across his face were actually the bruises I'd anticipated, he was sure as hell not feeling particularly good right now.

Fuck. The pain, I couldn't do much about. I'd already begged the Ivanov family for relief, but they'd told me they had nothing to hand, and any herbs that could have been useful grew only on the mainland.

But the cold?

I slipped out of bed and laid another blanket over Mat, moving slowly so as not to wake him. Yet this close, I couldn't help but reach out and run the back of my fingers down his uninjured cheek, and Dios help me, he was still *freezing*.

Before I could think about it, I'd ducked under the blankets and stretched out behind him where he lay on his side, pressing my chest to his bare back. His skin felt like ice, and I willed my own to heat him up, rubbing my hand up and down his arm to warm it with the friction.

By the Blessed, his whole body was still impossibly cold, and I should have gotten someone to keep the fire going, asked for more furs, and-

Mathias stiffened against me.

Oh, fuck, fuck, fuck.

This was the fault of my sleep-addled brain, because if I'd been thinking straight and not affected by that crazy nonsense wreaked in the first few seconds after waking abruptly, I would never have done such a stupid, thoughtless thing.

Don't touch me, he'd said.

And I'd fucked that up.

"I'm sorry," I whispered, those wholly inadequate words echoing around the room. I peeled myself away from him – *what the fuck, Ren?!* – and dropped my hands to the floor to push to my feet, flushing with self-loathing and humiliation. How could I be so-

"You're already here, you impossible man," Mat muttered. "Just keep your hands to yourself."

I stilled. "You…want me to stay?"

"I want to get some sleep without feeling like parts of me are going to be lost to frostbite," he said quietly. "Hands. To. Yourself."

Scarcely daring to breathe, I settled against his back once more, careful to keep my fingers no lower than his elbow and my hips twisted away as I pulled his cold body closer to mine.

And the feeling of him settling back to sleep in my arms, his breathing gradually evening out as his skin warmed against my own, was the best fucking thing I'd ever felt in my life.

*

Chapter Four

Mat

It may have been the pain in my ribs that stirred me from sleep, but it was the prince I found wrapped around me that kept me from returning to it.

My heartbeat raced. It hadn't been a dream.

I'd known I'd been inviting trouble when I stopped him from leaving, but the heat he'd brought with him had been impossible to resist when I couldn't stop shivering no matter what I'd tried, and-

I was making excuses.

Last night, I'd kissed him, and this morning I'd let him into my bed. Naked. By the Blessed, I could only be thankful I couldn't feel certain parts of him pressed up against me, because I was on the last frail threads of my self-control here.

I'd long given up on trying to convince myself I didn't feel anything in Ren's presence, but letting it get even this far was unacceptable. Was I completely fucking delusional? Had I forgotten all the terrible things that awaited me if I gave into what was quickly becoming the worst — and the most tempting — idea of my entire life?

Fuck, I'd seen men die from the punishments delivered upon sodomites; commoners and nobles alike. Even royalty wasn't immune from the consequences of that crime. And those that survived the floggings had to then endure the continued shame of public condemnation, the church's vicious attempts to correct their wrongful lust, and the stain on their immortal souls.

Diverse sexual relations might have been an acceptable practice in the south, but they lived to their own blasphemous rules. I wouldn't be here forever, if Sesveko even counted as Quareh, and when I returned north, what then? Would they be able to tell how close I'd come to sinning?

Maybe not, if I made sure to keep things as they were before. Continue to share a bed with Zovisasha or Lilia, perhaps ensure we were deliberately caught in public one time so no one would have any reason to doubt me.

Live a lie, like I knew I was capable of.

Even if that made me sick to my stomach. Even if my cock wilted at the very thought of having to get busy with one of them, the pure exhaustion of pretending to be interested and hold onto that long enough to finish us both off...

Oh, fuck. I'd never had a high libido, but I'd *managed*. And now Ren had gotten me confused, and the idea of getting naked with a woman was doing less for me than even usual, and I was going to murder the bastard for everything he was doing to my head, and fuck me, why was it that I was now thinking of him that my cock was deciding to take an interest? The feeling of him at my back was just too damn comforting, as was the way his chin rested against my shoulder, and his warm arm around me, holding me close, and it all felt far too natural and-

Yep, I needed to get up. *Now*.

I shifted out from under his arm, tensing when Ren's breathing abruptly shallowed at the movement. But despite me having clearly woken him, he didn't say anything. The prince continued to feign sleep to do me the courtesy of allowing me to slip away without having to confront whatever the fuck this was.

And that made it worse, because there was no justification for such a thing other than that he was doing it to be nice to me. And I could deal with Ren being cruel and flirtatious and callous and arrogant, but *nice* always left me off guard.

Holding my breath, I extricated my leg from his and rolled up onto my knees, hoping I could get dressed before he-

"Blyat!" I swore, grabbing hold of the blankets and tugging them with me as I fell backwards with a pained shout, accidentally bringing all three and exposing Ren's naked form on the floor.

The prince did crack an eye at that. But I was too busy staring at, and trying to keep myself covered from, the other four men in the room.

"What the *fuck* are you all doing here?" I snapped, my heart pounding at their sudden appearance. Had I really been so caught up in my head that I hadn't noticed them standing there?

"We were wondering why His Highness had not yet woken," Luis said.

"It's mid-morning," advised Elías.

"He's normally up early," Ad offered.

We all looked at Jiron.

"Yes," was all he said.

I glared at them, attempting to get my breathing under control. "And that takes four of you?"

"Not usually," Luis drawled.

"But we were all ready to leave," El pointed out.

"So we thought we'd wait where we could keep an eye on you both," Ademar said.

"Yes," said Jiron.

He gave me a pointed look, and I flushed, hitching the blankets around me higher.

"It's not what it looks like."

I should have gotten those words branded on my forehead. It would save having to speak them so often.

"It sure is," said Ren happily, and entirely unhelpfully. Rolling over onto his back, he tucked his hands behind his head in a vision of satiated male indulgence.

I extricated one of my blankets and tossed it over him, wincing as the movement made my ribs ache.

"I'm surprised you were not in too much pain for such activity," Jiron said to me in a wary tone, and there was a dark look in his eyes that suggested if I wasn't, I soon would be.

"I told Mat I'd be gentle," Ren drawled, not exactly untruthfully, once he'd freed his face from the blanket. My aim hadn't been the best, and the parts of him I'd actually wanted covered – because they were both distracting and not helpful to the conversation at hand – unfortunately remained free.

"Fuck off, the both of you," I said to them. "Actually, make that all five of you. I knew Quarehians were perverts, but this is excessive. Maybe knock next time?"

"We did," Luis said.

"Several times," El added.

"You were clearly too...*exhausted* from last night to hear us," Ademar said with a smirk.

"This morning," Ren interrupted before Jiron could offer his singular word of wisdom to the mix, and I closed my eyes. Blessed save me from the bragging of ego-inflated princes.

"...we need to meet with the militia on the mainland," Ren continued, and I cracked my eyelids open again to find him getting to his feet and reaching for his clothes. "I'd like to be at Vitorona by mid-afternoon, and spend the night at Lord Martinez's estate. Ad, make sure a message is sent ahead to his household by any rider the militia can spare."

"Vitorona?" I asked, trying to manoeuvre my own trousers on while remaining covered by the blankets. "The village that was found burnt to the ground with only a single survivor?"

"Yes," Ren said. "The child was allegedly raving about demons. Moreno's mundane story of brigands does not account for that, nor why a random settlement with no strategic importance or resources would be targeted with such ferocity." His face darkened. "And then there's what Alta said to me before we left."

I remembered her words. *It's about Vitorona. Ren, my father was...* she'd started to say, her eyes wide and terrified, and then Moreno himself had arrived and she hadn't been able to continue.

Had the Comandante been involved in whatever horrors had befallen Vitorona?

I grabbed Val's fur coat and Ren let out a breath. "Sure I can't convince you to leave that atrocity behind, Mathias? We're travelling south; you won't need it."

"I'm keeping it," I told him. It was the only thing that I had to remind me of my family.

Jiron snatched the coat out of my hands and I lunged for it, but he batted me away easily as he ran deft fingers along its edging.

"You'd know if I had another knife stashed away," I said sourly. I'd be stabbing at least one of them with it.

"Would we?" Ren asked. "Because I'm pretty sure you could hide a whole pack of wolves in that thing and still have room. Is that why you northerners are so fucking irritable all the time, because you're always heaving around heavy and shapeless clothing that offends any sense of fashion?"

I eyed him. If he thought his laced shirt with its frilled cuffs and his fitted turquoise coat would do anything at all to protect him in the true north, then I was willing to dump him in the snow and watch him freeze within minutes.

"Speaking of wolves, would you really have had El shoot Wolf last night?" I accused him. "That shit's just cruel."

Ren's hand shot to his heart in feigned horror. "Of course not. I love dogs."

I frowned. "I'm pretty sure he's a wolf."

"*¿Qué?*" The prince's brows furrowed in mimicry of mine. "No. That's just his name."

"Yeah, I think that's why Val called him that."

Ren closed his eyes. "*No.* I outrightly refuse to believe that anyone could have a pet wolf and be unimaginative enough to name it *wolf.* Even your brother."

I pressed my lips together and took the coat back from Jiron as he held it out.

"I don't know what to tell you."

The prince just shook his head. "And he's going to be king one day. *Dios nos salve.*"

God save us.

If He didn't damn us first.

*

Chapter Five

Ren

"We're not going to make it to Vitorona before nightfall."

The words made me wince. Not because they weren't true, but because they were *audible*.

I shot their speaker a glare. "Yes, Luis, I'm well aware. Jiron told me hours ago, although he had the decency to do it *silently*."

Mat's chin lifted from where it had been awkwardly resting on his chest, late afternoon sunlight filtering through his hair and giving it a mesmerising bronze glow. It was difficult to tell through the dark rainbow of bruises that adorned his face, but he seemed paler than even his usual porcelain self and the fingers that were twisted in Viento's reins held no colour at all. And it wasn't due to the fresh ropes that once again bound his wrists as a result of my guards' paranoia, as I'd sniped at them enough while they were tying him to ensure the binds were as loose as they could be without slipping from his slender wrists.

I exchanged another conversation with Jiron in nothing but a shared glance. This time, his message was a further apology.

Damn him, he was meant to be the rational one, the composed one! I was the person who got fired up and angry and put us into dangerous situations that Jiron had to get me out of. For him to have done what he did to Mathias...before last night, I wouldn't have even believed him capable of losing control like that. I'd underestimated the depths of his devotion to me.

Or I'd underestimated the northerner's ability to get under our skin.

Mat shifted in the saddle, and his furrowed brows belied how much pain he was in, even if he hadn't uttered a word of complaint in the hours we'd been riding. His resilience continued to astound me. Setting his jaw when he found all of my guards watching him, he caught my own gaze.

"Because of me," he said flatly.

Oh, *mi amor,* I thought. Everything's because of *you*, these days. My every waking moment is consumed by either your presence or the memory of you, and it's really fucking inconvenient.

"We could have ridden faster," he pointed out, his words both unnecessary and wrong.

Because by the Blessed, a lame cow would have moved swifter than us. But I hadn't taken into account his bruised ribs when laying my plans this morning, and I'd be damned if I was going to subject him to a day of hard riding with the discomfort he was already suffering. We'd moved to a canter only a couple of times, and when he looked like he was going to pass out on the second, I'd quickly put a stop to any thought of a third.

"We could have," I agreed. "But the wind gets my hair all tangled."

I patted it where it was tied over my shoulder. A braid would have been more practical for riding, but the man beside me made odd protests every time I attempted to have it plaited, and I'd given up trying to work out why.

I'd also given up wondering if the 'why' I was ignoring was *why* he didn't like it styled that way, or *why* I cared what he thought enough to appease.

"You don't need to lie, Ren."

"No. You already do that enough for the both of us, *Nathanael*."

"We're not on schedule because you don't want to hurt me."

I saw Luis' eyes narrow and gave them both an airy laugh. "Of course I want to hurt you, *mi amor*. One day, I'll show you quite how much."

Mathias' face and neck coloured, and thank fuck for that. He looked almost human again.

"But on my terms," I told him. "Not Viento's."

The horse nickered and I looked at El. The siblings had grown up in northeast Quareh and knew this area better than the rest of us, even if they'd spent the last few years at my side. "Are there any settlements between us and the village that we can rest in for the night?"

He shook his head. "No, Your Highness. We'll have to find somewhere to sleep out in the open once we cross the canyon."

"Which is…"

"Right past those trees." He nodded up ahead where a cluster of birches hid the winding road from view.

Mathias clicked his tongue, settling back into the saddle as he squeezed his legs around the horse, and Viento took off into a gallop towards the trees. Jiron, whose hand had shot out to catch his reins, pulled back at a shake of my head, and we all urged our own horses to follow.

I grinned, partly due to the exhilaration of properly riding once more, and partly because my boy was more of a masochist than I'd thought if he was going to push himself through pain like that.

Those few seconds, with the warm glow of the dying sun on my face, were the lightest I'd felt all day.

And then we reached the trees and slowed back to a walk at the sight of the massive fissure ahead, and it all came rushing back. The horrors we'd find at Vitorona, and the unknown threat of whatever had caused an entire village to be wiped out. How I'd sent the militia off to the Mazekhstam border this morning, knowing many of them might not make it home alive. Even if we weren't officially at war with the northern country, the regular border skirmishes made it a risky place to be.

And then there was Temar, and what my attempted capture of Valeri Velichkov might mean for Quareh. Fuck, that was an act of war in itself, and much like the gamble with the plan to kidnap Princess Astrid of Mazekhstam, it wouldn't have mattered if it had succeeded. If we'd held their heirs, we'd have held their countries, and we could practically have set the terms of their submission.

But also like the plan to seize Astrid Panarina, it had failed. And the reason for both losses was seated six feet away from me, silently bearing the painful cost of his latest interference, but that was no comfort to what it could mean for my country. How would Velichkov retaliate? There was no doubt in my mind that he *would* – such insults could not go unpunished without appearing weak – but surely he wouldn't dare to act while I still held his brother?

Mat had become more than leverage for Algejón; now he was protection for all of us. The only thing that could save Quareh from Temar's fury.

And currently that great saviour was doubled over in his saddle, clutching at his head.

"We cross there," Ademar said, pointing at something, but I didn't take my eyes from Mathias.

"No," my northerner gasped, finally straightening. His voice was hoarse. "That way lies death!"

Luis snorted, and even El cracked a smile.

"Your dramatics are beginning to rival the prince's," Ademar told him irritably, and snatched at Viento's reins. "Come."

Mat tried to tug them back. "No! There's a raiding party further along the road, on the other side of the canyon. They're going to ambush us!"

My guards all began to make various disgruntled noises of objection, disbelief and consolation, but I held up a hand.

"What happens?"

"Your Highness, you can't possibly-"

"He does have the Sight, Luis," I told him. "We ignore it at our own risk."

"But you can't believe he's actually going to tell the truth. Not after…with who he is," Luis hissed as he shot a dark look at Mathias, who pulled a face at him. Slumped on his horse, bound, beaten and bruised, he looked nothing like the royalty he was. But then, Nathanael Velichkov had grown up not in his own palace where he would have been honoured and respected, but as a ward of a foreign country that didn't give a shit about him, but only what assurances his presence could give it.

And those conditions hadn't raised a prince, but a fierce and contrary man who had been repeatedly let down by the world and yet still fought to see the best in it. Stavroyarsk didn't deserve him. *I* didn't deserve him.

But I'd be damned if that meant I'd be giving him up.

"An arrow through the eye," Mat said to Luis with a sneer. "That's your fate." But he swallowed, telling me that he liked that idea a lot less than his cool tone indicated.

Or so he was making us believe. Fuck me, an asshole who could lie as well as he did was impossible to trust.

Ademar clicked his tongue. "Bullshit. You're scheming, *bárbaro*."

"Describe it," I ordered.

Mat closed his eyes. "There's five or six of them."

"We can take-"

"They get off a volley from their archers before we even see them," Mat continued over Ad's protests, his voice pained, but firm. "Luis and El go down immediately, and even though Jiron throws himself in front of Ren, the prince still takes an arrow in his gut."

Jiron stiffened at that, his eyes grazing the tree line on the canyon's opposite side.

"Who are they?"

Mat's shoulders lifted and then dropped in a drawn-out, exhausted shrug. "I don't know. They're dressed in peasant clothes, and their weapons are unremarkable. But their skin..." He chewed at his lip. "I think they're northern."

"This deep in Quareh?" Luis exclaimed, his voice rising in pitch. "I'm with Ademar. This is nonsense."

But I didn't think so. If Mathias was lying, he would have told us our would-be attackers were Quarehian. It would have been far easier to believe.

"Where does it happen?"

Mat dragged his eyes to mine. They held none of their usual fierceness, just a type of weary frustration. "I don't know. I think I...I think I die soon after Elías does."

He wore a pained expression as he held up a hand to the side of his head again, and I remembered that some of the Blessed who had the Sight felt every physical sensation their vision selves suffered.

Ad snorted. "Convenient."

"The trees, Nathanael," Jiron said gently. "The ground. What did you See?"

Mat's eyes widened fractionally at the sound of his real name on the man's lips, or perhaps it was Jiron's belief in his vision.

"Um, still birches, but thicker, denser. Some of them have been partially burnt, but I expect a long time ago as they're growing fresh shoots.

There's...there's a stagnant pond to the right of the road, a large flat rock at its centre?"

I looked to Ademar, who had fallen still.

"I don't know about the burnt trees, but the rest of it is accurate," he admitted. "Maybe five miles up the road once we cross."

"The fire happened after you left, Ad," his brother said. "A summer blaze." El set his jaw as he nodded at me. "We can stay on this side and cross at the next bridge twenty miles up, but the path won't be as clear as the road. It will be slower."

"Then slower it is," I said, drawing on Miel's reins to direct her off the road and onto the track that ran along the edge of the canyon. The fissure stretched a dozen yards wide, and I could now see down into its depths, where thick foliage tucked itself around a small stream. Nothing like the raging torrent of water that must have once flowed through here to have cut the land in half.

"Your Highness..."

"I rather like your eyes the way they are, Luis, without any arrows in them," I told him. "Don't you?"

"...yes, Your Highness," he said stiffly, and trotted his horse past me to retake point at the front of our group. Brave, considering the fate Mathias had just described for him.

"Speaking of eyes," I drawled, pulling Miel aside Viento. "Shall we talk about how your Sight is in Aratorre colours?"

Mat eyed me with suspicion. "What?"

"Each of the Blessed's abilities manifests through colour on the relevant sense while they're using it. I'm sure you've noticed?" I thought about the green and red sparks that coated Starling's hands when she was using the Touch to heal, and the blackened tongue of...

No. Not thinking about that here.

When Mathias inclined his head warily, I grinned. "Well. Then tell me why your eyes turn gold and navy blue."

He rolled his eyes. "They don't."

"Mat, I was three fucking inches from your face when you went into a vision last night on Sesveko. I know what I saw."

He faltered, looking at me as if trying to spot the joke. And when he didn't, those self-same eyes widened.

"What? How?"

"Fate has a wicked sense of humour, it seems." Oh, this was far too funny. I'd tried to bind him to my family by gifting him a guard's coat of blue and gold, yet his gifts had seen fit to take it one step further. "How long have you had the Sight?"

He glanced down at his tied hands before ruffling them in Viento's mane.

Go on, Nathanael Velichkov. Lie to me again, I dare you.

"I don't know," he said eventually. "I only had one vision before coming to Quareh."

"And what was that?"

"You."

I sucked in a breath, not having expected that answer at all.

"You and me," he added, and oh, that just sent delicious waves of warm contentedness through me that soothed those possessive urges I was starting to be consumed by lately. He'd Seen us? Before I'd ever laid eyes on my little wildcat that night in *la Cortina's* throne room, he'd been thinking of me?

"What were we doing?" I asked, trying to keep my voice even.

"You were..."

He couldn't seem to finish that sentence, and it gave my imagination all sorts of wicked ideas about what his Sight had shown him.

"Let me guess," I purred, just to help him along a little. "I was giving it to you good?"

Mathias visibly flinched, and yanked at Viento's reins to pull him up short, guiding him in behind my own horse instead of beside her. Sure, the path was narrowing treacherously, but if he was up for sharing a little leg room, we'd have managed for a while longer.

Mierda.

This morning, I'd almost convinced myself his kiss had meant something. But it seemed that was merely the result of a vivid imagination and an inflated ego, and I had plenty of both.

*

Chapter Six

Mat

I was trying to recall my vision of the ambush in case there was any clue embedded in it as to who those people were, but it was a different future that kept coming to mind. The one I'd Seen over and over again back in Mazekhstam, yet convinced myself was a hallucination or a recurring waking nightmare, because why the hell would I ever find myself in Quareh? Why would a foreigner address me as Mathias, a name that wasn't my own?

But now that those things were far too real to me, the rest of it no longer felt so fanciful. The bloodied handprint across Ren's face, the wind tearing at his loose braid.

The fucking knife he had embedded in my gut.

I'm sorry, Mathias.

Sorry? If he was truly *sorry*, why by the Blessed Five had he stabbed me? Why did he stand there without care, watching impassively as my insides abandoned me and blood gushed from my abdomen? Why did he turn away without even having the decency to stay with me as my body failed from what he'd done?

I knew Ren could be cruel, but I couldn't imagine a situation in which he would ever kill me. Not cold-blooded like that, with no guard or the king in sight. The only time I'd ever seen him be so ruthless had resulted in the death of the prisoner in the cells, the one he'd told me had the Voice…

Oh, fuck. *No.*

Was *that* why he would do it? Why there wouldn't be a trace of remorse on that beautiful face of his as my guts splashed onto his boots?

Because to have the Voice was condemnation without exception, execution without trial. The people of Riehse Eshan had suffered too much at the hands… the *tongues,* of those with that particular sensory gift, for it to be anything less than a guaranteed death sentence. For an individual to hold the power to Tell another to do *anything,* be it to take their own life, that of their loved ones, or tear apart the babe at their very breast – fuck, that had been a difficult tale to hear recounted all those years ago – was not an ability that any of the three countries of our continent would accept. It was one of the few things that seemingly united them, that unceasing intolerance for any member of the Blessed granted the Voice rather than any of the other four sensory talents.

And if I had it…it would more than explain why Ren had decided to decorate the terrace of *la Cortina* with my blood.

But I apparently had the Sight. And I'd never heard of anyone bearing two gifts before, so there was no way I could be-

Viento reared beneath me without warning, and the reins slipped through my loose grip. I'd have fallen clean from his back had my ankles not been tied to the stirrups, and a pained grunt left me as my bruised torso was wrenched backwards by gravity, my bound hands making it difficult to right myself. A horse screamed, a horrific, terrified noise, and I could only pray it wasn't mine. And then there was yelling and the sound of metal on metal, and a firm hand scooped under my back to shove me bodily forward onto Viento's neck as his front hooves returned to the ground.

I got a mouthful of coarse hair and horse sweat, and coughed it up as I tried to lift my head to see what was happening, but my tied wrists were caught underneath me and any leverage I achieved was undone by Viento's brisk movements as he danced around, further unbalancing me.

"*Quieto,*" I hissed at him, begging him to still, but the horse listened to me as well as he had done for the last three days or so, which was to say, not at fucking all.

Around me, I could hear screams and further clashes of swords, and not being able to see the danger was absolutely terrifying. I dug my elbows into the horse's neck as I crawled my hands upwards, whispering apologies to Viento even as I cursed him, and I finally pushed myself back into my seat to find pure fucking carnage. Luis' horse was thrashing on the ground on its side with an arrow in its flank, its former rider fending off a hooded man bearing down on him from his own horse. El was on the other side of the path, ducking around trees and under low branches as he pulled his bow back and shot two of the pale-skinned attackers in quick succession; one with a clean shot to the heart, the second with a slower acting yet no less fatal hit to his neck. Another man already dangled limply from his saddle, an arrow protruding from his cheek.

And Jiron was in the thick of it all, his sword slicing cleanly across the chest of one foe even as he brought it up to block a second, and by the Blessed, the man was fast, even while seated on horseback. He was huge, and I knew from personal experience that meant he was impossibly strong, but I hadn't expected him to be so graceful in his movements. It just didn't seem fair that one person could be all of that, his skill clear in every elegant swing of his blade that travelled no further than it needed to in order to achieve its purpose. Efficiency, power, and utter fucking beauty in both, and his opponents never stood a chance.

As Luis' mount gave a final dying shriek, he stabbed up at his own foe, pulling him from his horse and finishing him off with a slit throat from his knife.

Something nudged my knee and I glanced around in alarm only to find Ren at my side, his eyes narrowed as he watched the chaos unfold before us. Ademar had a protective hand pressing down on the prince's shoulders, forcing him into the same position over Miel's neck as I'd been in, keeping his head down and his charge's body shielded with his own even as he guided his horse between Ren and the desperate rush of the dying man with the arrow in his neck who knew he had nothing to lose.

Ad lifted his sword with one hand to block his strike but was forced to let go of Ren to prevent the blade from slipping. Both our horses shied backwards with a squeal as the metal clashed only a foot from their faces.

And then Miel's heavy warmth abruptly disappeared from where it had been resting against my leg.

I threw my tied hands out to the side where Ren had been, desperate and horrified. They met only empty air, and I lunged again, catching Ren's outstretched fingers even as his horse scrabbled for purchase at the edge of the cliff, her back hooves already doomed and her front skidding on the loose clumps of grass.

"*Miel!*" Ren yelled, tangling his other hand in her mane as if he could keep the weight of a thousand-pound horse from the embrace of gravity, and there was neither breath nor time to chastise him for such *stupidity*. All I could do was hold onto his fingers tighter as Miel's heavy form was dragged the final few inches over the edge and she disappeared from sight.

Viento and I took Ren's full weight with a shared grunt, and I barely had time to be thankful that the prince's feet hadn't been caught in his horse's stirrups before he slammed into Viento's flank with a cry.

I threw myself to the left, wrenching his arm up over my shoulder, and because some stupid fucker had decided to bind my wrists together this morning, I could do nothing to adjust my grip or grab him properly. Ren's yell of pain cut through me, but if the prick was screaming, he was still alive, and I tightened my fingers around his, refusing to let go.

And then his other hand was at my knee, and then my elbow, and my shoulder, and I finally eased my hold on him as he climbed up my aching right side to swing his leg over Viento and seat himself behind me. The horse stepped sideways from the edge with an indignant whinny, and Ren buried his face between my shoulder blades, hissing out a single, broken word.

"Dios."

And then another.

"Nat?"

I heaved in a ragged breath, wishing I could do more than just sit there, but adrenaline and the ropes held me in place. I couldn't even twist around to look at the prince, my ribs screaming in pain at the very thought.

All I could do was focus on how his knees were tucked behind mine – good, he still had two legs – and his arms were wrapped around my waist – hands were fine, even if the fingers on his left weren't quite closing properly – and his irregular breathing rasped against my neck – hopefully that accounted for the rest of him?

"Ren-"

Movement, in my periphery, and Viento tossed his head as a final attacker bore down on us from nowhere with a drawn blade. I saw Elías twist in his saddle, raising another arrow to his bow, but it was too late. The man was already at our side, his sword swinging down, and fucking hell, the northerner was going to take both me and Ren out in that single strike.

He was so close that I could see the spittle flying from his mouth as he brought his blade through the air, and everything that wasn't the man pressed behind me felt freezing cold as if death had already found its mark. Ren's arms tightened around me, but there was no time for either of us to do anything at all: any action that wasn't already in motion would happen too late to make a difference.

And then the sword met our throats, pain and pressure and red and cold and Ren-

"*Dios.* Nat?"

I gasped as I surfaced from the vision we'd just died in, the vision that was less than a second from coming true for real. I yanked on Viento's mane when I couldn't find his reins, making him *move,* just a fraction, just enough to save us from the steel that I knew was hurtling towards our necks, and *there* – the man was already there, too close, but too far? – and the sword was coming down and-

An arrow speared through the man's open mouth as his head separated from his body with the flash of Jiron's blade, and Ademar grunted as he diverted the still-falling sword into the grass with his own, cascading it away from me and Ren. Luis had hold of Viento's bridle, tugging him away from the edge of the canyon, and fuck, was it finally over?

The silence told me it was.

I turned my head and the prince's mouth crashed against mine, our kiss messy and wet and probably entirely indecorous considering all the dead men surrounding us.

But although it may have been born from desperate relief, it endured with something much more, a lasting moment of warmth and rightness and *Ren,* and fuck it, if death could stretch its fingers so close to us so easily, what did propriety even *matter?* What did any of it matter?

And then I realised that the wetness tasted like salt, and drew back to find tears running down Ren's face.

He swiped at them angrily.

"Miel," he muttered, and El peered over the cliff's edge.

"Look away, Your Highness," the man said gently, drawing the final arrow from his quiver.

Ren set his jaw. "Do it."

Elías barely seemed to aim before the arrow loosed from the bow, thwacking into something below with a distant thud. The prince's breathing stilled.

"You," Luis snarled, catching the collar of my coat and dragging my face down to where he stood at our knees. I cried out as the movement pulled at the painful parts of me, my legs bending awkwardly where they were still tied to the saddle. "You told us they were on the *other fucking side of the canyon*!"

"These aren't the same men as I Saw," I gasped, fresh pain lancing through every Blessed inch of my bruised body. "I didn't know there was a second ambush!"

"Luis," Ren said quietly from above me, his hands trapped around my waist while I was almost bent in two.

After glancing up at his prince, the guard let me go, albeit with obvious reluctance. Ren yanked me back upright against him with as much care as Luis had used to pull me down, and I cursed at them both for the rough treatment.

"If the horse hadn't randomly reared, we'd have had a far poorer outcome here than what *el bárbaro allegedly* saved us from over there," Ademar said, dismounting with Jiron and moving to stand by Luis. He also didn't look particularly impressed with me, and to be honest, I was disappointed in myself. Why would my gift show me one attack and not the other?

"It wasn't random," Ren said, reaching around me to pat Viento's neck as he spoke fondly of him. The movement pressed him closer against me, and I could feel an unfamiliar hardness against the small of my back. I tried very hard not to move, staying utterly fucking *still*. "He must have heard something. He threw us out of position for their archers, and Luis' horse was the closest the volley got to any of us. Mat, if you keep wriggling like that I can't be held responsible for what I do next, and I don't think Viento will be best pleased with either of us."

"If it wasn't for Nathanael, your *poorer outcome* would have had our prince dead at the foot of that cliff," Jiron growled, smacking both Luis and Ademar around the back of their heads simultaneously. The look of outraged humiliation they shared made my shoulders heave in silent amusement, and Ren groaned indecently into my ear as the movement jostled me against him.

"Two ambushes?" Ad asked with suspicion, stepping neatly aside so Jiron couldn't hit him again. As an elite soldier dripping in the blood of his enemies, I guessed that had been more than a little damaging to his pride. "Out of all the roads and paths in Quareh, we're expected to believe that two northern raiding parties happened to slip across the border and be waiting for us on the same afternoon?"

"I don't think anyone considers it a coincidence," Ren said shortly. "Check the bodies and see what you can find."

"Apologies, Your Highness. We should have left one alive to interrogate."

"If you had, I'd have been rather tempted to tear him apart in Miel's name," the prince spat, and then let out a sigh. "It's fine. There wasn't time."

"We could still take prisoners from the other party, across the canyon."

"We'll send any men Lord Martinez can spare when we reach his estate tomorrow, and see if they were stupid enough to hang around. But I'm not having any of you fumbling around in the dark trying to subdue another half a dozen armed men." His chest heaved against my back. "If there's no bridge for miles in either direction, we're as safe here as we're ever going to be. Find this group's camp. I'm fucking starving."

Ren's words sounded fake to my ears, full of feigned disinterest and insincere malcontent. Even his flirting had been half-hearted. But I didn't want to call him on it in front of his guards, not when Miel's death and the closeness of his own drew the prince's breath out in short, harsh huffs. His anger and misery were palpable.

Unable to reach for him, I dropped my head back against his in silent acknowledgement, and he sighed into my hair, muttering words too quiet for even me to hear.

*

Chapter Seven

Ren

It was the quiet that got me, an eerie silence that never belonged in a village square. But the settlement's merchants that would once have filled it with cries were dead, its men and women butchered, and even its children were nothing but blackened corpses in the mud.

I'd expected a massacre to have a stench to it, but any scents the fire had pulled from its caress of the bodies and homes of Vitorona had long been snatched away on the wind. And the shrivelled husks of the villagers could almost be mistaken for burnt trees, if one didn't try too hard to blink away the rain from one's eyelashes. So it was the quiet, really, that was the most disconcerting thing.

A hardness formed at the back of my throat as the inhumane shapes at my feet coalesced into a family, with the two larger figures wrapped around each other in an embrace and a smaller black lump only a couple of feet away.

Raiders, Moreno had blamed it on. He'd said the village had been discovered under a layer of ash, and that part of the story seemed true at least. There were several sets of footprints across the blackened ground; the heavy, sure tread of soldiers as they moved from house to house, checking for survivors.

But only one person had survived this tragedy, a child who had fled to the nearest town at the time of the attack, and I intended to speak to him next. Because I couldn't fathom why raiders, either northern or native, would do something like this. Raiders took food, money, women...they didn't wipe entire fucking settlements from the face of the continent. Why would they destroy what was essentially a renewable resource for them to steal from later?

And the numbers they would have needed to pull this off...with the bodies strewn across the square, most bunched up together as if they'd been gathered for the market or entertainment, how had the attackers managed to kill all of Vitorona without the villagers taking more than a few steps to flee? I was pretty sure that if I saw a bunch of heavily armed thugs coming towards me, I'd be legging it.

Not that anything would get through Jiron. He'd been his usual unparalleled self yesterday evening as he took down my would-be murderers with nothing less than ruthless efficiency, and perhaps more importantly, he hadn't bought into Luis and Ad's far-fetched suspicions about Mat's involvement in the attack. Jiron was back to thinking clearly after his fuck-up in Sesveko, and even if I'd had to shoot him a couple of glares to stop him chastising himself about almost losing me over the edge of the canyon, it hadn't prevented him from taking charge when everyone else was either too exhausted or strung-out from the fight to do more than follow orders.

And so while the other guards had been tasked with setting up a perimeter and a watch roster, Jiron had fussed over me, pulling me from Viento and setting my dislocated fingers, ensuring I ate and then tucking me up in one of the tiny one-person tents we'd found a couple of miles down the road. A tent I'd insisted would actually fit two, or even *six* people, I was feeling that generous, but had been steadfastly ignored by all of them, which was downright fucking rude.

And what had been even ruder was the weather, waking us just before dawn with sheets of freezing water that were twisted by the wind in all directions as if it was even less sure of itself than Mathias was certain he was straight.

Rain that had eased throughout the day but not entirely let up, and it still quietly dribbled down my face as I stood in the remains of Vitorona. It was warmer here, the village being much further south than Sesveko, but I couldn't help eying Mat's fur coat with a newfound appreciation as he wandered from body to body, gazing down at them with such aching sadness in his expression that it physically hurt.

"Anything?" he asked in a solemn voice as he reached me, and I shook my head.

"Just another family. Killed in each other's arms, for fuck's sake."

Mat's mouth twisted in anger and he muttered some choice words in Mazekhstani that had naturally been the first I ever learnt in his language. What child would choose knowing how to politely ask what day it is, when they could learn how to curse like a sailor instead? Although, the royal tutor hadn't *quite* seen it the same way.

I frowned down at the bodies at our feet again, noticing something new.

I'd been wrong before. The couple wasn't embracing.

I tried to crouch down in the layer of ash, stopped by Mathias' hand catching on my arm. And then *he* was caught by a hand on his own.

"Let go, *bárbaro*."

"I have a name, Ademar," Mat retorted, although he obediently released me to allow me to drop down to the filthy ground. "Two of them, in fact. *And* a title."

"That I sharn't be using," Ad said from behind me. "Don't touch His Highness."

"Touch me all you like," I murmured, but the suggestive words were no more than reflex as I peeled one of the corpse's blackened fingers back. They disintegrated under my own and Mat let out a noise of disgust, but I was more interested in what lay beneath. A singed square of metal which was tapered on one end. The blade of a hatchet, its wooden handle destroyed in the fire, still embedded in the ribs of the other body.

"What the fuck?"

"Is that one of the raider's weapons?" Mathias asked, peering down over my shoulder. I shook my head.

"No. At least, I don't think so. I think...I think that one killed the other one with it," I ventured, pointing at the two bodies. "Look how they're touching, like he, she, whatever, is bracing himself for the blow."

Mat crouched beside me, drawing an annoyed noise from Ademar's throat, but if he thought he could keep my northerner from me, he needed to reconsider his love for breathing. Although that was nothing compared to the fuss all four of my guards had put up this morning when I had prevented them from waving a single loop of rope in Mathias' direction, telling them that none of *them* had stopped me from going splat at the bottom of a ravine, and I wasn't going to let such brave declarations of love be rewarded in such a way. And then Mat had loudly complained about how *no one was saying anything about love*, and Luis about how *there's such a thing as a long con, my prince*, and Elías just shrugged because he was fantastically chill that way, and Jiron had hefted Mathias onto Viento and then roped his reins to his own.

Because damn it, I hadn't specified that Mathias' *horse* couldn't be tied up, just the man himself.

Mat had seemed more impressed than irritated at Jiron's ingenuity, shaking his head and shooting me an amused grin over the man's shoulder that made my heart race.

But watching Viento's indignant snorting and stamping at his treatment had just made me think of Miel and how she'd have taken it with more grace. She'd been the most willing horse I'd ever owned, and the knowledge that I'd never hear another of her soft nickers or feel the gentle brush of her nose across my cheek had kept me stubbornly fighting off more angry tears the whole morning. Thank fuck for the rain wetting my cheeks and keeping us all silent as we rode, Luis and I on horses taken from our attackers.

But as miserable as the journey had been, I'd have taken it over the destination if given the chance. Because this shit was soul-wrenching. There had been nearly a hundred people living in Vitorona according to the latest census and tax records, and now what was left?

One scared boy.

Ademar finally gave into his curiosity and knelt with us, hitching in a breath as his eyes flickered between the corpses.

"¿Qué?"

"Look," he said, running his fingers over the burnt rib cage and digging his nail into each groove in the bone he found. "This one was stabbed or struck, what, two dozen times?"

"This one too." Mat pointed at similar markings on the other body, only the slightest of pained winces on his face telling me that he was still healing from Sesveko.

"They stabbed each other? Over and over again? For what purpose?"

Both men gave me equally bewildered looks. Ad shuffled over to the child's corpse, and while I didn't want to look, I heard his words clear enough.

"Same here. If this is the case for all the others, this would have been a fucking bloodbath."

Ademar swore, but rarely, and the curse brought my head up.

"Check the other bodies for weapons."

Ademar passed on the message to the other guards and all six of us roamed the square, wincing as we brushed off ash and lifted limbs, snapping them more often than not. But Moreno's men hadn't seen fit to give these people a proper burial, and there wasn't enough of us to do differently. I just kept Dios' name on my lips as I offered a muttered prayer for each corpse I came across, the sheer *number* of them unfathomable.

An hour later, we regrouped at the edge of the village, dusty and solemn.

"All of the bodies show signs of repeated trauma." Luis confirmed what we'd all discovered. "There's few clean cuts among them."

This wasn't raiders. Expert soldiers they generally weren't, but even raiders knew how to kill quickly. And they certainly didn't have time to hack at someone with an axe twenty times and still keep the rest of their victims from running away in the meantime.

"No corpses of anyone other than the villagers," Ademar added. We'd looked hard for any sign of strangers, but if any of their attackers had died in the assault, their bodies had been removed by their comrades.

"And the weapons that killed them are mostly missing," said Jiron, his jaw clenched. We looked down at those we'd been able to find: the single hatchet blade, two short knives, and a twisted piece of metal that looked like a masonry tool.

"Which, if some of them went crazy and killed each other like this all suggests, makes no sense."

Mat's eyes were on mine, worried and wide. "We found each of these hidden beneath bodies," he pointed out. "They were missed. Someone cleaned the village out, tried to make it look like an external force rather than death by their own hands."

"But didn't care enough to get rid of the bodies entirely?" I asked.

"I suspect the fire was intended to cover up the evidence, Your Highness." Elías' face was grim. "I doubt they expected someone to pick through the mess as we've done."

Jiron exhaled. "The footprints of the Comandante's men don't lead to every corpse," he noted. "The weapons must have been removed before the fire."

Fuck. For it to have been Moreno would have been too neat, wouldn't it?

Or maybe not. It still wouldn't have explained what had happened, why these villagers had carved each other up. And I was beginning to suspect only one thing would.

"We going to Torrellón," I said quietly. "I want to speak to the survivor."

*

Chapter Eight

Mat

The survivor was dead.

It was what we'd been told when we first arrived in the town that neighboured the now ex-village of Vitorona, ash still lingering in our hair and mouths. It was what had been variously hissed, murmured and gossiped at us in Torrellón's taverns when we started to ask around, Ren in borrowed clothes from Ademar and all of us having removed our royal guard jackets to avoid drawing attention to ourselves.

And it was what had been sullenly repeated by the thin, cracked lips of their local healer when we knocked on her door, right before the old woman slammed it in our faces.

So I was pretty fucking confused why, instead of staying at the inn we'd booked under false names and an even falser story, we were now sneaking back to her house through Torrellón's narrow streets.

"Because," Ren said, when Jiron finally halted us in the shadows long enough for me to ask.

I thought he was going to leave it there, but he shot me a grin, his teeth flashing white in the darkness. "I know when a woman gives me a *'come back after dark and don't let anyone see you'* look, Mat, and I've never refused one yet."

Behind the prince's crouched form, Elías appeared just as bewildered as I was, but he didn't seem as inclined to question. We'd left his brother and Luis back at the inn to keep an eye out for anyone who might be looking for Ren just in case the ambushes on the road had been part of something bigger, and to avoid drawing attention to us as we crept through the streets like criminals. Personally, I thought Jiron's giant bulk and my foreign appearance was enough to attract the eye in any event, but both Ren and Jiron had refused to let me out of their sight.

So as jealous as I was of the others getting to put their feet up in front of a fire and drown themselves in cheap ale, I didn't have much of a choice but to follow Ren in whatever ridiculous scheme this was. Although, I would admit it was much more fun than being cooped up in the palace all day with the scheming and simpering of courtiers all wanting a piece of their prince in one form or another.

We slipped from shadow to shadow until we reached the door of the healer's home, Ren giving it a sharp rap with a hand that looked far too bare without all his usual rings. Jewellery that, if worn, would undermine what he was attempting to do with his plain clothes in hiding his wealth and status, although it hadn't stopped him grumbling as he was forced to pull them from his fingers. He'd insisted that he keep the leather cuff on his wrist and we'd all shrugged, because it was his Blessed plan in the first place and he could have kept his rings in place for all any of us cared.

We stood in silence for a long time with nothing stirring from inside the house, making me thankful for the warm night air and the rain long having ceased.

I blew out a breath. "Looks like your secret dalliance had better plans than you tonight," I told the prince, and he gave me an offended look over his shoulder just as the door swung open.

"Señora," Ren murmured, and although I expected her to shut it on him again, the old woman stepped back and waved us inside, a harried expression on her face.

"*¡Apúrate!*" she hissed, and we all hurried up as commanded, Jiron having to hunch his shoulders and duck his head to fit through the tight doorway. We found ourselves in a softly lit kitchen, with a snoring man in the corner who didn't even stir from where he was seated near a table with various medical implements on it that reminded me of Starling's surgery back home.

Home? That was...that was obviously the wrong word. Permanently thinking in a second language had apparently messed up my head.

"Where is he?" Ren asked, brushing his long hair from his face with an impatient swipe. The healer glanced at the snoring man and the prince waved a dismissive hand. "Not your husband. The boy who survived Vitorona?"

Yet the woman shook her head, retreating into a corner of the kitchen where she picked up a knife.

El tensed at my side, his hand falling to his sword, but she only used it to peel a half-skinned potato with brisk, efficient movements. Offering a plaintive meow, a tabby cat wrapped around her ankles, giving the falling peel a haughty sniff and throwing us an even more derisive look.

"He's dead, ain't he." It was an answer, not a question, despite her odd phrasing.

Ren paused. "Truly?"

The healer inclined her head. "*Sí*," she confirmed, and when she looked back up at us all, her eyes glistened wetly in the candlelight. "I buried his body. I expect they imagined the rumours would start flowing if they just made him disappear."

"Who are 'they'?" I asked.

Her gaze narrowed on me and she didn't answer.

"It's okay," Ren said, and it was nothing like his usual *'ignore him'* mantra that he shot out around me that I blinked. "You can answer him."

The healer pushed her tongue into the side of her mouth. "The soldiers, Your Highness."

Neither El nor I let our surprise show, willing to continue the deception, but Ren's stunned reaction gave him away entirely.

"You're not supposed to know that!" he chided her indignantly, and I rolled my eyes at his inability to hold a lie. Although I suppose when he'd first confronted me about not being Mathias Grachyov, I'd been similarly backfooted. I could have blamed it on my almost dying earlier that very night, but there's something about being called out with such confidence that always makes you falter, no matter how good your disguise.

And Ren's was not very good at all. He still moved with the arrogance of a prince used to people getting out of his way, and we'd almost found ourselves in a fight when he'd pulled that shit on a group of mercenaries in the tavern. It had only been Ademar's quick thinking that had saved us from drawing the exact type of attention Ren had been trying to avoid – the local law enforcement kind – as it was clear Ren was never going to apologise to them for his pushing in line even if it would have solved all of our problems.

Me, I'd been happy to sacrifice him to their wrathful fists for the greater good of whatever secret mission we were supposedly on, but somehow that hadn't even been on the list of possibilities. So we'd left Ademar buying them a round of drinks and bonding over old war wounds, and escaped back into the streets with a fuming prince and an *almost* exasperated Jiron.

"Sorry," the healer rasped now, not sounding it at all. "But it was too shitting obvious who you were. Why d'ya think I made sure the neighbours saw me send you away earlier?"

Ren was insistent. "What happened?"

She set down her knife with a sigh. "The boy was found on the streets and brought here to look after. Told the local soldiers so they could investigate whatever 'appened in Vitorona to have caused him to flee here, and instead it's *us* that gets the old visit in the night."

"They killed him?" I asked, my voice rising in anger, but she just shrugged.

"Not in front of me, in any event. They said they just wanted to question the boy about the incident, told me to scarper while they did. When they finally left and let me return to my own bloody house, he was alive. By morning, he wasn't."

"Poison?" Ren asked, and I glanced at the bottles and instruments adorning the room.

Shouldn't she have been able to prevent it if it was?

"Magic ain't about waving your hands and making shit disappear, boy," the old woman snapped, and I turned to find her glaring at me. "It takes a long time to heal someone. Hours, normally, if not days. Don't you go judging what you don't know nothing about."

I held my tongue, but my eyes found Ren's. So she had the Touch, but an incredibly weak version of it, by what she was saying. Starling could likely cure the effects of a poison in seconds.

"What did he tell you, before they got to him?"

The healer sucked on her teeth. "Ain't that the question? Exactly what those soldiers kept asking me, too. What did he tell you, María? You sure about that?" She fixed Ren with a glare and jutted her chin out when she next spoke. "He didn't tell me nothing."

I watched her carefully. Double negatives and incorrect phrases of speech were often used by liars who wanted to claim honesty if they were ever questioned on it. But the woman's poor Quarehian, despite it being her native tongue, suggested that *not having told her nothing* was exactly what it appeared at face value.

The prince moved closer to María, Jiron close at his heels. The cat hissed at them both.

"Por favor, señora," Ren said, holding out his hands in the universal gesture of peace. "I am trying to discover what happened to that boy and his poor family. Anything you can share would be appreciated."

She scoffed. "No royalty cares what happens in these parts."

"He does," I told her quietly, and Ren's startled gaze flickered to mine. "Trust him."

"Trust?" She all but screeched the word. "If they find out I've been talking to you, I'm done for too. You all need to leave. You shouldn't have come back here."

"María," Ren insisted, but the cat clambered up her dress and dug its claws into her bony shoulder, snarling at the prince. He gave it a scornful look of outrage, as if he couldn't believe that something wouldn't be falling over itself to love him. "I know the boy spoke of *unos demonios*."

The healer shrugged, still shooing us backwards. "Demons. They say that's what he screamed when he was first picked up in town. But the boy was deaf and darn near mute by the time he crossed my threshold. He didn't utter a Dios-damned word to me in the two days he was here."

Ren exhaled, drawing a hand down his face and jerking his head at the door. We filed out more sombrely than we'd come.

"Your Highness." María's raspy voice halted Ren as he crossed the threshold, and he glanced past Jiron's protective stance to where the old woman stood, her face twisted into a bitter grimace. "I didn't lie to them soldiers. The boy didn't say anything to me."

She held out something pale out to him and he took it. "But he didn't communicate in words. This is the only one that isn't just a page of solid black charcoal."

He looked down at whatever it was, and then back up at her with a question on his lips, but the door slammed shut on us all.

The prince let out a long breath. "Fuck."

He glanced at each of us in turn, and then eventually held out the piece of parchment to me. I unfolded it, tilting it to catch the moonlight, and the others peered down over my shoulders.

"It's not proof," Ren spat, "and it won't convince my father. But it's enough to tell us that Moreno was there that day." His mouth drew into a thin line. "Whatever killed those people, the Comandante knows the truth about it all."

I frowned at the childish drawing on the page. Lots of stick figures overlapped in a bizarre floatation of bodies, and at first I thought the boy had drawn the aftermath of the massacre. And then I saw the smiles, drawn so widely that they spilled out of the circles indicating their faces. These people were alive.

At the heart of the crowd were the only two figures that were given any greater detail than single-lined arms and legs. One was padded out in all black, lines of long hair extending down past his head. It could have been a thousand different Quarehians, Moreno and Ren included. But the boy who had survived Vitorona only to die shortly afterwards in Torrellón had coloured the other character with significantly more care, and the red and black lines of her dress were familiar. Perhaps it wouldn't have meant anything on its own, but Alta's words about Moreno the day we left *la Cortina* came rushing back to me, as did the anguish on her face.

She'd seen something happen there. She knew her father was responsible.

And with the village's only survivor dead, that left Alta the sole witness to whatever the Comandante had done that day that left a hundred Quarehians slaughtered.

*

Chapter Nine

Ren

"We could have kept going," Mathias muttered darkly as we ascended the manor's wide stone steps and I breathed in the fresh twilit air wafting through the open windows on the second floor. Anything was better than the smoky, sweaty stench of the dining hall we'd just left. "I would have happily ridden all night had I known that was what awaited us as an alternative."

"We wouldn't have reached *la Cortina* before dark, especially with my horse losing its shoe."

"I wouldn't have cared," he retorted. "Luis? Ad? Would you?"

Neither of them answered, but I could feel Ademar's fuming scowl on the back of my neck that told me he was even more disgruntled than Mat.

I shouldn't have made the guard accompany me to the dinner, but I'd already sent Jiron off when we arrived at Lord Martinez's estate earlier that afternoon, and I certainly wasn't letting that pig of a noble catch sight of Elías. El was under strict instructions to stay out of sight, although perhaps I needn't have bothered, as Martinez hadn't seemed to recognise Ademar. Maybe there were enough years behind their altercation for the lord to have forgotten the siblings.

Or maybe it was Mathias' sufficiently distracting self that had kept Martinez's attention from the guards at my back. Because while the lord went off on his usual rants about the various uselessness of women, servants, and daughters who couldn't even find themselves a husband, Mat had smiled from where he stood against the wall, nodded as if he agreed with the whole tirade, and started tossing insults at him in Mazekhstani.

It had been difficult to keep a straight face as Mathias continued to hurl derision his way, accompanied by a revoltingly fake smile that evidently confused Martinez just enough for him to not immediately demand Mat be disciplined for speaking out of turn. And by the time the man overcame his pride about not understanding a damn word my northerner was saying and asked me to translate, I'd managed to gulp down enough wine to not feel guilty about feigning exhaustion and excusing us all to bed.

"But Your Highness! Assuming my sorry excuse for a butler has bothered to prepare it for us, I was hoping we could take a cigar together in the parlour?"

"If he can walk that far without choking on his own vitriol, I'll happily ram a cigar in more places than down his mouth," Mat had muttered, eying him with distaste even as he kept the sickeningly sweet smile in place.

"We've been travelling for days," I'd said to Martinez instead. "I wish to retire for the night."

"It's the dry pheasant that has upset you, isn't it? My prince, I cannot apologise enough. I'll have the chef flogged for the insult, if I can work out which of the fucking half-breed peasants he is."

"If anyone's a *half-breed,* it's him," Mat had mused. "Do your people normally mate with cockroaches, or should I be asking how closely his parents were related to each other?"

Lord Martinez had ground his teeth and glared at Mathias, perhaps finally cottoning on to his indecipherable taunts. "Your Highness, if you could please-"

"Leave?" I said. "My pleasure. I would hate to get in our beneficent host's way in his own home. I'll see myself to my rooms. I assume they're prepared for me?"

"I...yes, sire," he'd said, deflating. "It was done two days ago, as that was when that dumb bitch told us you'd be arriving."

"Fuckwit," Mat had snapped, not even bothering to be creative anymore.

"I don't expect you'd be talking about your wife," I'd said to the lord through fury barely more restrained than Mathias', "considering that's the message I'd had sent to her."

And damn it, if only it had just been his wife here. I'd gotten unlucky with Martinez himself at home: he got underneath my feet enough while in *la Cortina* that I hadn't expected him to be at his estate when we arrived. But no, apparently I hadn't prayed hard enough to Dios recently, because instead of a bunch of silent servants who could have just shown me to a room for a night, I was greeted by the lord's nasally simpering and the obligation to take a fucking meal with him.

"I should have just smacked the asshole," Mat muttered now, and I shot him a fond look.

"Not that I wouldn't have loved to watch that, Nathanael, but without provocation Martinez would be well within his rights to order worse on you in turn."

"He's a disgusting, intolerant grub who revels in the misery of others and is incapable of speaking without abusing or vilifying someone. What more provocation do I need?"

"If you get him to hit you first, that would help," I suggested with a grin, wandering down the long hallway to the royal suite of rooms that all nobles held ready in their homes for an Aratorre visit. The floorboards creaked beneath my boots. "Then I'd have no choice but to call it a duel between two lords, instead of an assault on a noble by a foreigner."

"I'm pretty sure he hit me," Mat said instantly. "Luis?"

Luis frowned. "He was nowhere near you."

"I saw it," Ademar offered, and him and Mat exchanged conspiratorial smiles.

I waved them apart, although the fact they weren't growling at each other for once cheered me immensely. "Not when he had half a dozen servants to support his side of the story, you didn't."

Mathias rolled his eyes. "So remind me again why you wanted to stop here for the night rather than just finding a nice ditch somewhere to sleep in? It would still have been far more pleasant than his company."

"Reasons," I told him dismissively, letting Luis slip through the bedchamber door to do whatever it was that guards did when they insisted on going into unfamiliar rooms before me. A quick wank, perhaps, or to pocket the silver?

"Reasons. Multiple?" asked Mat.

"Yes."

"Is that one of them?"

I followed his gaze through the cracked door, where a highly attractive ass peered back.

I hummed appreciatively, nudging the door wider with the toe of my boot for a better view. As Luis peered behind tapestries and under cabinets with his hand on his sword hilt — odd fucking places to keep the silver, in my opinion — Mat and I watched the servant smooth down the bed sheets with over-exaggerated, deliberate movements, her back almost fully arched as she took advantage of her thin dress to show off each one of her gorgeous curves beneath it.

"You're drooling," Mathias snapped at me, and then raised his voice. "And you're not fooling anyone, señorita. This room was readied two days ago."

The girl turned towards us, twisting her hips in a way that should be illegal considering what it did to my cock. Fuck me, she was stunning. Wavy brown hair starting to come loose from the braid wrapped around her head, sultry bedroom eyes, and the fullest lips I've ever seen. Lips that looked…vaguely familiar.

"Your Highness," she purred, sashaying her way over to me and putting herself in that far too tempting spot between too distant to touch and too close to avoid making me anything but fucking ravenous for her. "It's so good to see you again."

Hmm. Maybe more than vaguely.

Her gaze dropped below my belt then, her pink tongue darting enticingly over her bottom lip. Mat stiffened at my side, and damn it, he was distracting me from the perfection in front of us. I should have just ignored him, like I was so good at ignoring people who were inconveniencing me, and yet I was all too annoyingly conscious of every move he was making.

The girl gave my trousers another heated look. "I see you haven't forgotten me."

Her name, I absolutely had. But I could now remember my own teeth sinking into those lips, and the exquisite noises I'd been able to pull from her as she'd ridden me to blissful heights. On the bed, the lounge, on the floor, on the bed again…by the Blessed, she'd been insatiable.

And now she was in my face, eyelashes fluttering and breath warm against mine.

"My prince. Be my king again for the night?"

"Luis," I heard Mat snarl. "If you're clearing the room, don't forget to remove the fucking temptress."

"That's just Abril," Luis said. "She kept the prince company last time he was here."

Cold air hit my face despite the warmth of the night, chilled by the disappointment of there being any space at all between me and the pretty creature that had been abruptly yanked away from me and was now held in Mat's grip.

"*Out*," Mathias told her firmly, pushing her through the antechamber's doorway and into the corridor. She made as if to duck back inside, but he blocked it with his body. Bless him, he was trying very hard to make himself look larger than the skinny northerner he was. Scarier, too, if the deep growl in his tone was anything to judge by.

"Aren't you meant to be working?" he snapped.

Abril's shoulders dropped at that, and all the seduction drained from her body. It was the saddest sight I'd ever seen. "Until nine, sir."

"Then get to it."

Mat watched her walk away, keeping a suspicious eye on me too, and I pulled a face at him.

"You really know how to take the fun out of an evening, you prick."

"You'll survive."

"Just," I conceded, although my cock vehemently declared its disagreement. Fuck, it had been far too long since I'd last gotten laid. "Seeing as it's already past eight o'clock now."

Mathias rolled his eyes and moved past me into the bedchamber just as Jiron arrived in the antechamber with El in tow. He gave me a look to let me know he'd been successful with what I'd tasked him to do, and I nodded. That was one less burden on my conscience.

"Clear," Luis announced, emerging from the bathing room attached to the bedchamber, as mine was at home. Few nobles had the same bathing facilities as I did back at the palace but Lord Martinez was one of them, and *that* had been one of the reasons I'd elected to stay at his estate, because I knew how fond Mathias was of baths.

Even though I'd quickly washed before dinner I headed for it now, pulling off my coat and not caring where it landed. I didn't think there was water hot enough on the continent to scrub away the memories of the last few days, but by the Blessed Five, I was going to try.

*

Chapter Ten

Mat

I sighed as I snagged each piece of the prince's clothing from where he'd tossed it to the floor, laying them all over the end of the bed. If he'd travelled by carriage to his trade talks, he could have had a whole wardrobe spare, but on a borrowed horse carrying nothing but food and water, accompanied by four guards without a servant in sight, this was all Ren had to last him back home. We'd washed our clothes as best we could in Torrellón last night, but while *well-used* was fine for those of us in guard uniforms, his expensive coat and trousers were starting to look more than a little battered, and his shirt was more crease than fabric. Not that the dishevelment didn't suit the prince in its own way. It gave him a dashingly roguish look that had caused my traitorous eyes to cling to him more than once, but it was nothing like the put-together appearance he maintained in his court.

Movement behind me caused me to turn. The guards had been speaking together in low tones as they compared their thoughts on the risks of the estate and figured out their roster for the night, but now Jiron was making his way towards me.

"I was going to…" he said, trailing off as he waved a hand towards Ren's clothes on the bed, and I shrugged, suddenly embarrassed. It wasn't my damn job to clean up after the prince, and I didn't know why I'd bothered.

"I can throw them back on the floor for you to sort if you'd prefer?" I offered, and Jiron gave me an amused look that quickly sobered. I fidgeted, uncomfortable under his cool gaze.

"So, little one. You're a royal," he said after a long moment, and the other guards perked up at that, wandering over to us as if that had been permission to finally address the revelation I had dropped on them at Sesveko. It wasn't lost on me that this was the first time since that night that Ren wasn't present, the sounds of splashing water muffled by the bathing room door.

I lifted my chin. "It doesn't seem to have made any difference to you four," I said coldly as they formed a menacing semi-circle around me, still feeling the soreness of my ribs and the chafed skin at my wrists.

"Because we don't give a shit who you are," said Ademar, his eyes hard. "Someone hurts our prince, and we'll put them in their place no matter their rank or title."

If only that were true.

I bit down on the words I wanted to say, knowing they'd only lead to questions. These four men may have been damn good protectors to Ren, but even they didn't stop his father's and Moreno's abuse. Largely because Ren had hidden it from them for years, whether due to his pride or in a valiant attempt to protect them.

"Ren threatened my brother," I said instead. "Under the guise of peaceful trade talks, he tried to capture the fucking heir to the Temarian throne. What did you expect me to do?"

Luis let out a short laugh. "We certainly didn't expect you to pull a Dios-damned knife on His Highness," he responded, but he almost sounded entertained. Maybe enough time had passed for him to be no longer bothered by it, but there was still some darkness lingering in the eyes of Ademar and Jiron. "We thought you were all bark and no bite, *pequeño bárbaro.*"

"I'm only *little* when compared to you four brutes," I hissed, offended. "When do you even have time to work out?"

"Whenever we're not on duty," El said, flicking his long hair over his shoulder. I'd rarely seen it unbound, and it transformed his smooth face into that of a younger man.

His brother reached out and squeezed my bicep, ignoring my attempts to bat him away.

"I remember having arms that thin once," Ademar teased.

"I don't," said Jiron.

"Yeah, I was five years old. Did your muscles get lost in the snow somewhere, tiny northerner?"

"Fuck off," I told him, and wrenched my arm from his grip with no small amount of effort. "I'm the same size as Ren."

"Yeah, but he's a prince."

"So am I," I reminded them, offended by their snorts of laughter. Fuck, they were annoying.

"Perhaps we should curtsey," drawled Luis, earning himself a rare grin from Elías.

Ad gave me a sly wink. "Princes don't normally beg and kneel in dirty kitchens for hours on end. I'd have enjoyed that far more had I known who you were at the time." He shook his head in disbelief while I flushed with humiliation at the reminder. "A fucking Temarian prince."

"One who takes a beating too well," murmured Jiron, and the others fell silent at his words. He cocked his head, watching me intently. "Almost as if it's not his first."

I shifted, uncomfortable. I didn't know that there was a way to take such things *well*, but it had been instinct to try to protect my head and relax the rest of my muscles so it wouldn't hurt as much. And yes, I'd learned that from all the times I'd been hit and kicked by the other children back in Stavroyarsk, but I sure as shit wasn't going to be telling any of the prince's guards about that.

"Mathias is good with pain," drawled a familiar voice from behind Jiron's bulk, and he shifted to the side to allow Ren, a towel at his waist, into the line of men caging me against the wall. This ganging-up bullshit was getting old, fast.

"No," I said flatly. "I'm not. Don't get ideas."

"I'm getting ideas," said Ren.

I sighed and pushed between El and Luis. I figured they were the least likely to stop me escaping to a less crowded part of the bedchamber, and apparently I'd guessed correctly. "Have you left me any hot water, or shall I proceed to drown myself in a cold bath?"

"If you'd wanted heat, you could have just joined me in mine."

I didn't bother dignifying that with an answer, heading to the bathing room as the guards starting fussing and muttering behind me about their postings.

"No," Ren grumbled, and I paused, glancing over my shoulder to find him face to chest with Jiron as the prince did his best to look suitably fierce despite his shorter height. "I told you all those years ago, I'm not having a room guard."

I snorted at that, and Ren grinned without looking in my direction.

"With the obvious exception," he said.

Luis groaned. "But this room is only on the second floor. You're going to make one of us stand below your window all night again to ensure no one tries to get to you that way?" At Ren's nod, the guard's shoulders dropped. "Which of us-"

"Seeing as you volunteered, Luis," Ren purred sweetly, dropping his towel from his hips and wandering over to the bed. I hastily diverted my gaze, but none of the others seemed bothered, and damn it, reactions like that were how he managed to wind me up so easily. Even now, I could see in the corner of my eye that the prince was watching me with a cruel smirk, pleased he'd garnered a response.

I needed to not respond at all, to treat it as I'd have dealt with any disrobing man in Mazekhstam. Just an ordinary thing, as mundane as taking breakfast or going for a walk. Not something that could make me flush each fucking time I saw his smooth chest, his bare legs, his exposed cock...

"I'll do it," Jiron said, and my lips had already pushed back into a snarl, ready to tell him to *back the fuck off,* before sanity caught up to me and I realised he was talking about taking guard outside and not about getting his huge hands on *moy knyaz,* my prince. "The rest of you, rotate through the night but keep El out of Lord Martinez's sight when he goes to bed."

There it was again. Those references to a history between Martinez and Elías, some secret I wasn't privy to but apparently the rest of them were, as they all nodded solemnly.

"Do us a favour, northerner," Ademar tossed back at me as they left the room. "Try to escape tonight, won't you? It would be a shame for your face to ever actually heal, when watching it get beaten in is so much more fun."

I made a rude hand gesture, and he smirked.

"Don't you dare," Luis snapped at me, as if it had been *my* idea. "After nearly a week on the road, our patience is extremely thin, Mathias. Uh, Nathanael."

"Mathias," Ren corrected from where he was sprawled out on the top of the bed, not a single Blessed blanket covering his naked body. His hands were tucked behind his head, ankles crossed and eyes closed, as if he planned on sleeping like that. As if I'd be able to even *think* about sleep while he was like that.

"It's who he is to anyone outside of the six of us," he continued. "Understand? The last thing I need is Moreno interfering in my negotiations with Queen Zora. Let him go chasing his own tail."

I blew out a breath, my arousal at the sight of the prince abruptly doused by the reminder of who I was to him. Nothing more than a political hostage to be used to bring my country to its knees for Quareh.

I pushed my way through into the bathing room, its floor glistening wetly as if Ren had decided to expel the entire contents of his bath across the tiles, and closed the door on the other men just as I caught their final exchange.

"Ademar? I know it's going to be difficult for you, but that means you have to stop."

A confused pause. "Stop what, my prince?"

"Bowing and deferring to Mat all the time. You're going to give us away."

I heard the guard's soft snicker. *"Yes,* Your Highness."

*

Chapter Eleven

Ren

"I'll get the door," Mat said as he emerged from the bathing room still disappointingly clothed, and stomped past the bed. I blinked up from the book I'd found on the bedside table – a tedious collection of Riehse Eshan ballads – not having heard a knock.

But just as he reached the door, it arrived, two heavy thumps that told me Jiron hadn't yet retired outside to his lonely post below my window. I was surprised the guard hadn't gone along with letting Luis get dumped with the task, but maybe he was craving space. The five of us practically lived on top of each other, day after day, and it became more than a little claustrophobic at times.

I tossed the book to the floor as I settled more comfortably on the bed, listening to the murmur of voices and looking forward to the uninterrupted hour or two of stress relief that my poor balls so desperately needed. I hadn't instructed my men to stop Mathias leaving the room this time, and if he'd Seen the knock, he probably knew what it meant even if he hadn't checked the time.

But Mat passed back across my line of sight, heading back to the bathing room with a towel folded over his arm, and I frowned at the main bedchamber door that was once again closed.

"Um," I said, because this wasn't supposed to be how it went. "I thought I heard Abril's voice?"

"You did," he confirmed, disappearing into the bathing room. The sound of running water ceased a moment later, and I heard him let out a contented sigh.

He loved his baths almost more than he loved me.

Almost.

"So where is she?" I demanded, surprised when Mat's head appeared around the door frame to grin at me. Grin! Like an actual upturned mouth, the type of expression I'd kill to put on his face more often.

It was also suspicious as fuck. I peeled my hands out from behind my head and pushed myself up to a seated position on the bed. "Nat?"

"Gone," he said. "I told her you were exhausted from the day and there's only a certain amount of times a man can get it up."

"Well that's not true," I pointed out. "Jokes aside, Mathias, where's Abril?"

"I'm not joking. I sent her away."

I stared at him. Unless he was planning to offer himself up in her stead, which didn't seem particularly likely, there was no possible explanation he could give to soothe my aching cock. But I asked it of him anyway. "For the love of Dios, *why?*"

Tugging on the collar of his coat where the gold band lay, my northerner gave me a wicked smile, all teeth and bloody heartlessness. "I'm taking my duties as your room guard very seriously," he said. "Who knows what malicious intent any of your…*numerous* lovers may have towards you? A knife in the heart while you're distracted, and where would you be?" He drew a finger across his throat and made a dreadful cinching sound.

"They're frisked before they-"

"And then of course there's the trail of angry spouses you're leaving in your wake as a result," Mathias mused. "Any one of them might decide to act to protect their marriage bed. Really Ren, in the interests of your safety, the only option for you is abstinence. I can't believe I was lax enough as your *guard* not to have insisted on it before."

"Abstinence," I repeated slowly, horror flooding through me. "No fucking way. You think you can-"

"I think I already have. Goodnight, *Your Highness*."

He slammed the bathing room door and I narrowed my eyes at it, allowing myself the brief indulgence of a fantasy where I followed him through it, shoved him down over the edge of the bath, and fucked his infuriating ass until he was *pleading* for Abril to divert my attentions from him.

And then I climbed out of bed and stalked towards the other door in the room, wrenching it open.

"Your Highness," Elías exclaimed, surprised. "Are you feeling well? Mathias said you were-"

Having confirmed that Abril was well and truly missing from the antechamber, I cut him off with a wave of my hand. I couldn't send someone after the servant now; it would look desperate. And I wasn't going to admit that Mat hadn't been acting on my orders. Appearances were everything, sometimes even with my guards, and they couldn't know I'd lost control of him.

If I'd ever even had it.

"I just wasn't feeling that particular dessert tonight." I gave my guard a lingering look, my painfully hard cock making my eyes catch on his long legs framed so perfectly by his trousers. I was horny and I was frustrated, and there was only one way to ease both problems. "El, will you join me instead?"

Good luck to Mat on trying to scare *him* away on the fucking nonsense he was spouting. Abstinence, seriously?

Elías' lips tightened. "No thank you, Your Highness. I'm on duty."

"I can change that," I said carelessly, and El's abrupt intake of breath was mirrored by his brother's where he was standing on the other side of the doorway. I briefly closed my eyes and then looked between my guards, berating myself.

"I meant swapping your shifts," I corrected. "Elías, you know I'd never remove you from my retinue."

"I know," he said stiffly, and I turned to Ademar.

"What about you? I know you usually prefer pussy, but-"

"Not usually," Ad said with a faint smile. "Always."

I clicked my tongue in disappointment, although I knew it had been a long shot. "One of these days I'll get one of you on your backs. Preferably both."

I wandered further into the antechamber, snickering at the identically disgusted faces the siblings were attempting to mask. "I didn't say at the *same time*, for Dios' sake."

Ademar hissed out a terse breath.

"Jiron! You don't have to stand outside if you're guarding me from my bed."

I threw myself down onto the lounge beside his huge bulk, tossing my knee over his so he could get a good look at what I was having to deal with. "Entertain me?"

"Not tonight, Your Highness," Jiron said to me with an amused look. "It's a double shift, and you are not exactly restful."

I sighed, nudging my bare leg higher up his trousers to rub against his cock in case I could persuade him to change his mind. He just chuckled, and I transferred my attention to Luis as he entered from the corridor with a platter of leftovers.

"Luis," I murmured softly, patting the seat next to me. I spread my knees wider and rolled my head against the back of the lounge, trying to hide my desperation with lazy indulgence. "Come join your prince, won't you?"

He froze at the sight of me and glanced at Jiron as if for assistance, eyes wide. "Uh…"

"Don't worry about him," I crooned, drawing his attention from Jiron. "He's just a boring old man who would rather stand out in the dark than have any fun. But you and I, Luis?" I gave him a decadent smile. "We're going to have *lots* of fun."

"His Highness is in a wicked mood tonight," Jiron warned. "You don't have to say yes."

I narrowed my eyes and pulled my leg back from his, pressing my toes to his ass to kick him off the lounge. Jiron stood smoothly, making it look like it had been his intention all along, and made his way across the room as he pulled off his shirt. The sight of his bare muscular back only made me more pissed off at whatever *idiota* had forced him to stand outside all night.

Oh wait. It had been me.

Jiron snagged a fresh shirt from his bag, catching my eye with a knowing look – that *I know you were watching me* smirk he sometimes liked to pull when he was feeling particularly brave – before he dragged it on and glanced at Luis. "But if you do agree, be prepared. I doubt he's looking to be kind to whatever poor soul ends up beneath him."

"Uh, maybe another time, Your Highness," Luis stammered out, and I shot a hateful look at Jiron before throwing my head back and glaring at the ceiling.

"Well *someone* better let me fuck them," I snarled, and the distinct lack of offers filling the subsequent silence only riled me up further. Jiron was right, as he usually was: after the dual disappointments with Abril, whoever I brought to my bed tonight was not going to have it easy.

And then the guard chuckled. "Perfect timing as always, Mathias," he called loudly as he departed into the corridor, and I dropped my chin to find Mat having appeared in the doorway of the bedchamber, already dressed and drying his hair with a towel.

"What?" he asked, confused when the others echoed Jiron's amusement with their own low laughter. He narrowed his eyes and glared at me – keeping his eyes firmly above my neck – as if their nonsense was *my* fault. "Ren, what are you all-"

"Goodnight, my prince," Ad said with a sly smirk. "Sleep well."

"Hmm," I said, annoyed and still not having found what I needed, but unable to do a damn thing about it while they were all being so incredibly boring. And I couldn't exactly start wandering Martinez's estate begging for a bed companion. That shit looked desperate.

Appearances are everything, I reminded myself, following Mathias back into the bedchamber and slamming the door on Ademar's smug expression. As worked up as I was, I could surely survive it. One more night and we'd be back at *la Cortina*, and then I'd be spoilt for choice with who I wanted to get me off.

Oh but fuck, if only my guards' taunts were accurate and I could take Mat right now. I'd tie him down so tightly, he wouldn't be able to *breathe* without my permission, and then I'd make him feel the full depths of the restless irritation he'd caused me until its aching marks eased from my body and transmuted to his. He'd bruise beautifully, I expected, every place my fingers landed blossoming into colour, and I let myself imagine how loudly I would make him scream.

To be Temarian meant he'd never been touched in so many delicious places, certainly not by any man before me. Would his eyes widen when I found them with my fingers? Would he let himself surrender to the pleasure, or would he writhe and curse, fighting it to the bitter end as he did everything else?

"Ren," Mathias said, and my cock twitched at the mere sound of his voice. Fuck me, thinking of anything but sex was impossible right now.

His cheeks flushed, telling me that he'd noticed the effect he'd had on my body. It seemed the bastard had snuck a look without me noticing, and no part of me minded that *at all.*

"Say my name again," I demanded, leaning back against the closed door and palming my aching cock. "Only with more desperation, and a *lot* more lust."

"*Ren!*" he snarled at me in outrage, and I let my eyes drift closed as I wrapped my fingers around my length and gave it a few quick tugs, my harsh breaths quickly falling into the same rhythm as my hand.

"Not quite what I meant, but it's surprisingly still working for me."

"For fuck's sake. Stop touching yourself while I'm right here!"

I cracked an eye. "What about touching you instead?"

"*Konchaj bazar, svoloch!* Get into bed and cover yourself, *now.*"

The dominance in his voice had me shutting my mouth and sliding under the bed's blankets before I knew what I was doing. I could admit that it was hot as fuck when he went all bossy, but not in the *bedroom.* Not only had Mathias denied me Abril's sinfully hot body, *twice,* but now he'd stopped me from even taking care of myself.

I couldn't think clearly enough through the ache in my groin to know how or when I was going to make him pay for this, just that I *would.*

Nathanael Velichkov was going to remember this night for a very long time.

*

Chapter Twelve

Mat

Across the semi-dark room, tucked up in his bed, the prince gave a forlorn sigh that was half a hiss and half a groan. The restless noise caught my ear where I was curled up on the lounge, stirring me out of the sleep I'd just started to drift off into.

A moment later, he did it again.

I wet my lips, debating if the idea of him jerking off with me in the room horrified or thrilled me, and hating that I even had to ask myself that question. But as I strained to listen more closely, clearly resolving that question with the *wrong fucking answer*, I realised my mistake. He wasn't trying to get himself off. The rustle of blankets was the result of his attempts to get comfortable, and the sighs were of irritation, not pleasure.

"You alright over there?" I snapped, pleased that my tone didn't sound as breathless as I felt.

"You are not permitted to complain when it's you that put me in this state," Ren growled, and I felt a momentary pang of guilt. I hadn't *intended* to give him blue balls, but I wasn't going to stand around and let señorita bat-my-eyelashes crawl all over him either. Fuck, didn't he have standards? She'd barely said *hello* before she was attempting to play hide and seek with his cock.

It's Ren, I reminded myself. *Of course he doesn't have standards.*

"Don't tell me one girl got you so worked up."

He gave a dramatic sigh from his bed. "*No*, Mathias. It's been over a week since I last played with anyone, and oh yes, that anyone was *you*. And perhaps your memory is fuzzy from how hard I made you come that night, but you might recall you didn't exactly reciprocate. My cock has never felt so neglected."

I squirmed in my own makeshift bed, the guilt hitting even harder. I'd pushed him away after that terrible fuckup, and it hadn't occurred to me that I'd left him unsatisfied. I'd just been so angry and humiliated over the fact I'd let him touch me at all, and I'd hardly been about to return the favour.

Maybe I should have been nicer about Abril.

I frequently complained about Ren coming onto me, and yet I'd stopped him from seeking release elsewhere. I was surprised he hadn't yet called me out on the hypocrisy, but even the *thought* of someone else getting their hands all over him made me irrationally furious.

I was so messed up. And it was becoming too Blessed hard to work through it by myself, without it affecting him as well.

"There's really been no one since?" I asked, not sure why it mattered to me. If I didn't want him, who cared if I was his latest or not?

I cared. I cared so fucking much.

"Nat. Where I go, *you go.*" Ren sounded irritated. "Have you seen me fucking anyone else? That old healer? A couple of seals on Sesveko, perhaps?"

I rolled my eyes.

"Maybe I should have accepted Velichkov's invitation to suck me off under the table during our trade talk," Ren mused, and I was relieved that his words had regained some of their usual playfulness. "I was put off by his sullenness because fuck knows you bring enough of that to my life, but maybe he'd have looked more attractive with my cock down his throat."

"That's my brother you're talking about," I reminded him with distaste. "And if you're hallucinating *invitations* from straight-as-an-arrow Valeri Velichkov, you really are out of it."

"It was all in his eyes," Ren told me, and I could practically hear the grin in his voice as he continued to tease. "The things they asked me to do to him, Mat, you wouldn't believe. He's almost as depraved as you."

"He's not."

"You're right. You're much worse. The things *your* eyes beg for make even me blush."

I glared over at his indistinct mound of blankets. "Go to sleep, Your Highness."

"I would love to. But you sent my exercise away and now I can't."

"You keep whining and I'll help you out with that little problem," I warned.

"Please."

"I meant I'll knock you the fuck out, Ren."

He laughed, a soft chuckle in the gloom. "You're welcome to try."

The challenge sent a delicious thrill through me that I stamped back down.

"Right. And you're hoping I will, so you have an excuse to inflict blows back on me tenfold. I'm not falling for it."

"No retaliation, I promise."

I eyed the darkness dubiously. "You're just going to lie there and let me smack a prince of Quareh into unconsciousness?"

"I have no intention of *letting* you do anything."

My pulse roared in my ears at the sheer arrogance of him, but there was blood pumping to somewhere else too, and both parts urged me to take him up on his offer of getting closer. And it was stupid and terrifying, but I had lain awake for hours on this lounge before sleep had finally started to beckon, the first time I'd truly had to myself since Sesveko, as I worked through various images and tried to process what it all fucking meant.

Ren, his face only an inch from mine and lit up with satisfaction as he stroked me into ecstasy that night I'd discovered what his father and Moreno had been doing to him.

Ren, anger and disdain dripping from his voice as we fought in the throne room about how he hadn't saved the little girl who'd been sold to a neighbour for a handful of goats.

Ren, and how he'd held me so gently as I shivered through our night on Sesveko, careful to keep his hips turned away so he wouldn't accidentally press his lower half against me.

Ren, tears running down his cheeks as he silently cried over the death of his horse, and again, hurriedly wiped away, when he saw what had been done at Vitorona.

And Ren, sprawled naked on the lounge in the room next to this one in a vision of masculine nonchalance, legs spread, head cocked, and lips pulled into a devilish smile that promised giving into the temptation he posed would be *magnificent*. It had felt like a different Nat that stood before him, clutching my towel between whitened knuckles because they'd ached to reach for him instead, knowing it wouldn't lead anywhere good.

But in the dark, my mind half-blurred from sleep, *good* felt like far too much of a relative concept.

Another memory crept into my mind, and it was even clearer than the others, despite it not holding any visuals at all. Just a feeling: an indescribable, horrific, agonising sensation of *loss* when Miel had slipped off the edge of the cliff with the prince on her back, and again when the blade of that stranger's sword had met our necks.

I'd said fuck it then, hadn't I? What had changed? My future — my *life* — was far from certain, and Ren had many enemies. What did tomorrow matter if it never even came?

Swallowing, I shucked off Val's fur coat that I'd been using as a blanket, and let my bare feet drop down to the rug. Ren watched me silently as I closed the distance between us, offering none of his usual snark or coarseness.

And then I was by the side of the bed, looking down at him and how his loose hair splayed out over the pillow, how his blanket lay up to his neck, how his lips curled into a small smile that suddenly looked so vulnerable.

Oh Ren, you beautiful bastard. What have you done to me?

I put a knee on the bed, my hands coming to rest on the blankets by his shoulders…

…and then I was pressing my lips down onto his.

He hummed happily at the contact, and the vibration sent heat through my body, dropping me down even closer to the man beneath me.

My tongue sought entrance to his warm mouth and he granted it eagerly, deepening our kiss and allowing that sinful taste of citrus and saffron to flood every inch of my fucking soul. Ren started to move beneath me but I had him pinned by his own blankets, trapping his arms by his sides so that I could live in this moment of perfection of just Ren and *me* and Ren and *everything*, and my thoughts turned hazy as I forgot how to breathe.

The kiss wasn't like what we'd shared at the base of Sesveko, or again on Viento's back after the ambush. Those had been hungry, sure, but also desperate and terrified. This was something new, something beautiful and raw and tentative, but even as I thought it, it turned rougher. His tongue now fought mine for dominance, taking as much as he was giving. He growled against me, his body tensing where I held him down.

This was perfect. It felt so *right,* in a way nothing had in a long time, and *fuck me,* I was kissing Renato Aratorre?

The prince worked a hand free of the blankets and trailed it up the back of my neck and into my hair, the gentle caress making me shiver.

I felt his lips curve into a grin against my own a second before his fingers tightened in my hair and he ruthlessly yanked my head back, exposing my throat. Then he buried his face into my neck, biting and kissing, and making me groan shamelessly at the bittersweet attention of his mouth.

"Let's get something straight, Nathanael," Ren whispered into my skin while he held me in place with a single merciless hand, forcing my back to arch as he freed his other arm. "*You* do not pin *me* down."

He emphasised the words with a sharp nip to the base of my neck where it met my shoulder and I hissed at the bite of pain, my fingers fluttering up to his wrist at the back of my head.

"I thought I just did, asshole," I murmured, and Ren drew back, his eyes flashing in delighted surprise. Had he actually expected me to go submissive for him now he had me in his arms? I may have given in to weeks of confusing-as-fuck desire by coming over here to kiss him, but that did not mean for one Blessed second that I was giving in to *him*.

I took another moment to admire the man beneath me who lazed back on his pillow with his cocky smirk restored, his hand knotted in my hair to keep me where he wanted.

And then just as he started to speak again, I caught his wrist and twisted it outwards, careful where I placed my thumb to ensure I would both have the leverage I needed, and to avoid breaking anything. I was pretty sure that promises of *no retaliation* didn't extend to snapped bones, at least not from where the prince's guards would be concerned.

Ren let out a startled cry at the pressure and loosened his hold on me. I lifted my hips to allow him to roll onto his side, the body's natural reaction when its arm was forced in such a direction, and I'd only just released his wrist when his other elbow shot out and caught me in the ribs.

The same spot he'd watched Jiron hit me three nights ago.

"Prick," I hissed out on the sharp breath that left me as I fell onto him, and Ren's sadistic laugh in response sent delicious waves of heat through me, as did the prince's squirming as he fought to get the rest of himself free of the blankets. I kicked out at his knee now that I knew we weren't abiding by gentlemanly conduct, causing him to curse, and he grabbed my shoulder only for me to duck under his arm. We rolled across the bed in a heated tangle of limbs and grasping fingers, the prince eventually finding his way on top of me like the stubborn bastard he was. It was only when the blankets dropped from his chest onto mine that I remembered he was naked underneath them.

Ren, his grin telling me that he hadn't forgotten any such thing, took advantage of my distraction by snagging the front of my shirt and yanking my face close to his.

"Oh, Mat," he purred, his tongue running up my abused neck and soothing some of what he'd done to it. "You're wearing far too many clothes for this bed."

"Just because I kissed you doesn't mean I'm letting you fuck me," I told him firmly, and I knew the words were unromantic but if we were *getting things straight,* that was an important one. I wasn't ready for...that. Could one ever be truly ready for having a cock up their fucking ass? Didn't it *hurt?*

"We'll see," he said, all tease, and then his expression became carefully sober. "So what does it mean for you?"

I hoped it was dark enough that he couldn't see me flush. I swear I did it more in a single hour in Ren's presence than I ever had back home.

The thought of the north — and more importantly, the thought of what the north would make of *this* — made me try to pull away.

But the prince had a tight hold on me, his arms curling around the back of my neck and tugging me up to meet him once more. Our lips collided for a second time, no less hungry and frantic, and I knew I was making pathetic noises as I kissed him, but I couldn't fucking help it. His mouth was warm and welcoming and soft, yet also fierce and demanding. It was a contradiction that I'd only ever found in Ren, and I absolutely adored it.

"Don't think," he murmured, separating his lips from mine to deliver the words. "Just say whatever comes into your head."

"Taste," I breathed with relish, rising up onto my elbows to chase his mouth and bring it back to where it belonged. On mine. "I like how you taste. Like…oranges."

His amusement shook his shoulders, his brown eyes filling with silent laughter. On impulse, I caught his bottom lip with my teeth and bit down, hard.

Ren tensed and dove forward. I found myself flat on my back again, his fingers curled around my wrists as he pinned them to the bed above my head.

Oh, fuck. If the way my cock was thickening in my trousers was any indication, I liked that. I liked that a whole lot.

And it made no Blessed sense considering my life was currently full of people either tying me up or holding me down, but there was something about this moment, just me and him, no politics or guards, that gave it a whole other meaning. Something strangely, incredibly arousing.

"I'm not sure you're getting the point here," Ren told me, his dark hair fluttering down around his head to tickle my face and curtain us from the rest of the world. "Causing pain is also *my* prerogative. Learn your place, Mat, before I put you in it." But his tone was teasing, his breath catching on the spirited words, and I had no intention of listening to a fucking thing he was saying.

Mostly freed from the blankets, his bronzed skin on display as he knelt over me, I expected he thought he was in the stronger position. But while I was shit at holding off his skilled guards and didn't know the first thing about weapons, grappling was far more familiar to me.

I hooked my feet behind the prince's bare ankles and widened them, causing him to fall face first onto my chest with a spluttered curse as his knees were taken out from beneath him. But the bastard recovered quickly, and my efforts to catch his arms turned into a wrestle that was doing far too many wonderful things to me as he took every opportunity to torment me with his tongue, both with coarse insinuations and playful licks at every inch of my exposed skin he could reach.

Yet his efforts distracted him and I finally got us both onto our backs, Ren on top of me, with my feet curled around his legs to keep him in place. I had one of his arms twisted behind his back and trapped between us, and the other pinned beside him, holding him tight.

The prince wasn't going anywhere.

I let a grin break out across my face while he couldn't see me.

"Yield," I said.

*

Chapter Thirteen

Ren

It wasn't *quite* the position I'd had in mind when it had become clear that this wasn't just a delicious dream and Mat was actually here in my bed. It didn't even make the top hundred imagined positions, if I was being honest, but that was because all of those involved him being underneath me in a way where I could actually *touch* him.

Spread out on top of his body without being able to reach him or even myself was a torture unto itself, and if it was anyone else, maybe I'd have felt vulnerable with me naked and him clothed, splayed like a prawn stretched out on a fork. As it was, it was…different.

Good different though, and I was finding that a lot with Mathias. It was a thousand new experiences I'd never had with anyone else, and despite my plans for us, none of it ever happened in the way I expected.

All I could do was make sure to ruin *his* plans just as thoroughly.

Including *mi gato montés* thinking he could dominate me – *me!* – with his surprisingly skilful hands and far too much fucking smugness in his voice as he demanded my surrender.

"Yield."

Oh, Nathanael. Watch and learn.

"Hmm," I murmured, rubbing my bare ass against his groin and making him groan wantonly in my ear.

His hands tightened around my arms, and everything in me rebelled at the restraint. I hadn't been joking when I'd told him I didn't do being held down. I had enough of that when my father made me submit to Moreno's floggings…

Stop it, Ren. Stay in the moment. Focus on the sexy northern prince beneath you.

I wondered if Mat wished he'd gotten undressed now, because the barrier of his clothes between us was distressingly agonising.

I let myself slump back down against him, going limp. "Fine. I give in."

Mathias let out a satisfied hum and let go of my arms and legs as he relaxed his guard.

Idiota.

I immediately rolled over and pinned him and his wrists down like before, in the position that had made him go all delectably wide-eyed and breathless. This time, I made sure to straddle his hips and tuck my ankles beneath his shins so he couldn't pull any of those clever moves on me again.

"Hey!" Mat protested as he struggled against my hold on him, his indignance making him so fucking endearing. "You yielded!"

I leaned down to suck on the lobe of his ear, and he bucked against me. I sank my teeth in as punishment. "So?"

"So you're a fucking cheat, Renato Aratorre!"

I laughed and didn't deny it. "I play to the stakes."

"I should have learnt my lesson long ago in trusting you, it seems. Let me up."

"I don't think so," I said, biting his ear harder until I drew a gratifying yelp from his mouth that I smothered with a kiss. Fuck, he made beautiful noises. "Not until I get what I want."

"And what is that?"

I gave him a broad smile, loving the way he was still writhing beneath me as if obstinate determination alone would earn him his freedom.

"Your clothes."

Mat stiffened in surprise. "What? They're already yours, you asshole. It's a guard uniform."

Pressing my mouth to his neck to stifle my laughter sent vibrations through us both. Dios, his naivety was something else. I should almost feel bad for trying to ruin such innocence.

I lifted my head. "Your clothes, Mathias, *off you*. I want you to undress for me."

Uncertainty flickered in his beautiful blue-grey eyes, and I kissed away the furrows that formed across his forehead.

"Stop frowning, *mi cielo*. I will not fuck you."

He relaxed at that, although whether it was because of the assurance or the new pet name that had struck my tongue without warning, I didn't know. But although I should have left it there, I couldn't resist teasing him further.

"Not tonight, at least."

Mathias scowled again, giving his pinned wrists another sharp tug as if such a thing would dislodge me. But I had my hands on my gorgeous northerner at last, and I wasn't letting him go so easily.

"Do we have a deal?"

He fell still, but it felt less like surrender and more like he was settling in to wait me out. I growled at his defiance, rubbing myself against him for the friction my poor, aching cock so desperately needed. If I'd thought it hard before at the idea of Abril in my bed, that had *nothing* on what it was like now I had Mathias beneath me.

Oh, if only I didn't have to be so careful with him. If I wasn't scared of pushing him too far, I would have let loose my most creative self in retaliation for all the shit he'd dared to pull just now instead of letting me take charge like he knew he wanted to. The idea caused me to let out an obscene moan as I rocked against his hip, the roughness of his trousers making it all the more intense in my sensitive state.

"Fuck, Ren, you're not just going to…"

He trailed off, staring at me with huge eyes as my breaths hastened into harsh pants.

"I may," I admitted. "By the Blessed Five, I'm already so close, Mat, and your edible self is not doing a damn thing to help me pull back."

"These are my only clothes!" he hissed, looking alarmed at the prospect of me coming all over him while he lay there fully dressed, even as the same thought brought me even closer to the edge.

I wasn't normally so fragile. It had been a long time since I'd fucked up and let myself come too early, but it seemed that nine days of *abstinence* and a sexy northerner in my arms were my absolute deprivation limit, and I had very little control left.

"Fine," he ceded through gritted teeth after a few moments, and although it should have killed the mood, it didn't, because it was *him*. Sulky petulance was just Mathias all over, and I didn't know why I found it so hot, just that it was.

I released him and he slithered free from the bed, shooting me a glare before reaching over his head to tug off his shirt. His ivory skin seemed to shimmer in the dim room, marred only by the bruises around his abdomen that Jiron had left him, and his smooth chest couldn't be called muscular, yet was still gorgeously defined. I couldn't wait to explore him with my hands and mouth, to learn every inch of him and what he liked.

Mat's scowl darkened and I bit down on my tongue before I could ruin this by pointing out the obvious, being that he could have played by the same lack of rules as me and not done a damn thing to hold to his promise once I'd let him go. Yet regardless of what honourable traditions I'd ignored – and would quite happily keep on doing, because honour was just something else that could screw you over – we both knew he would do the opposite to what I had done, *just because*.

He'd argue with me about the colour of the Dios-damned sky if I'd dared to utter such a statement, and I adored him for it.

I leant back against my pillow and took myself in hand, watching with rapt attention as Mat's fingers fluttered across his belt fastening and trouser ties. And then he paused, eyes meeting mine.

He had a choice. He always had a choice with me, and I'd made sure he knew that. I teased and I flirted, and I may have felt him up more than once, but I *never* took more than that without permission.

So when I now growled 'I told you I wanted it *off*,'' and he obeyed me, pushing his trousers down to let them pool at his feet? That was all him.

And fuck me, *all* was so beautiful I could have wept. I settled for a deep groan instead, increasing my pace as I watched Mathias' shoulders hunch awkwardly as if he was embarrassed by how hard he already was, or how his cock swelled further under my gaze, a slight natural curve to it making my mouth water with pure fucking need.

Yet my own body demanded release, and the sight of him without a single shred of clothing between us at long last brought me there, a final stroke sending me over the edge and into blissful oblivion. The results of my climax draped hot and thick over my stomach.

I shuddered, taking a long time to come down. My limbs felt heavy and content, and maybe, finally, I could get some damn sleep.

But first.

I opened my eyes to find Mat at my side. He was holding out a towel, his trousers already laced back up. His shirt was still missing, which was something, but quite clearly *not enough.*

"Mothering me," I said dryly. "Very sexy."

He shoved the towel into my hands and I obligingly cleaned myself up, not taking my eyes off him and those stupid trousers.

"I don't know why you bothered getting dressed," I drawled. "I'm only going to drag those back off you."

Mathias looked up, startled. "You just came," he mumbled, and aww bless, that adorable flush was back in his cheeks as he spoke of such things. "There's no way you can already be …"

He trailed off, and I laughed, rising from the bed. "No," I agreed. "But you helped me clear my head, which means I can now turn my attention to *you*."

Taking a small step backwards as if he'd heard that as a threat and not a promise – and maybe it was a little bit of both because it was *me* – Mathias wore an expression I couldn't quite read. Maybe nervousness, definitely interest, and something akin to…surprise?

"You have a gorgeous body," I told him, both because it was true and because it seemed like he needed to hear it. "And we have all night for me to work out what it likes best. Trust me?"

I crossed the distance between us and took him into my arms. Kissing Mat had rapidly become my favourite thing *ever* in this last half hour or so, although I was sure I would find many more favourite things in the next. But fuck, this was a good one. He made wonderful sounds as I caught his lips with my teeth, or his tongue with my own, little moans of want and demand that I swallowed down like air. For a man who engaged in surly silences so often, he was so fucking *loud,* and I couldn't wait to see what other noises I could draw out of him.

My hand slipped underneath his trousers as it had done that first night he let me touch him back at the palace. Praying he wouldn't pull away, I palmed his hard length and he let out a gentle whine. Hiding that beneath clothes was *criminal,* and I told him so.

"Hmm," he murmured, mocking me, but that faint little hum did terrible things to the health of my heart. Pressed together as we were, I felt it throughout my entire body, and by fuck, I wanted him to do it again. Preferably with his mouth wrapped around my cock so I could feel the vibrations against the most sensitive part of me.

I licked my suddenly dry lips. Mathias was right: I'd just come, and I should *not* be needing him again this soon.

"Your safe word is *naranja,*" I told him, remembering what he'd said about me tasting like oranges and wanting to torment him with that fact a little longer. And it was perfect: my favourite fruit for my favourite northerner.

I watched him frown and mouth out the syllables of the word. The way his eyes widened in realisation a moment later, the soft little 'oh' he breathed out, was the most adorable sight I'd ever laid eyes on, because of course my uptight little Temarian had never played with anything requiring a safe word before.

"All you need to do to make me stop is say it," I confirmed, knowing from his expression that he'd worked it out, but needing to be sure. "No matter when or why, okay?"

Mat huffed out a breath. "Ren-"

"No," I interrupted, cutting him off. "I intend to be rough with you, and I need to know you'll use it if it gets too much. And if you can't speak, you can use your hands or feet to tap out, either on me or the floor or whatever. Three taps."

"Why wouldn't I be able to speak?" he asked, alarmed, and I tried not to laugh, because really, if he thought that was the worst of what was coming his way, he was an innocent little flower who should be kept away from me at all costs because I was going to fucking ruin him. And that thought had me running my hands all over him, touching the man I really had no right to make a claim on but unable to resist the temptation of doing so.

"Show me," I murmured, peppering kisses down his jaw. As I took a breath to explain what I meant, realising I'd spoken without clarification, Mathias tapped his fingers against my arm. Three times, in quick succession, and fuck, as naïve as he could sometimes be, the fact that he was so in sync with my thoughts at times like now was intoxicating.

I gave him a heated look, drinking him in. "Perfect. Now be good for me, Nat, and take what I give you."

I slammed my mouth to his, delivering a kiss that was more teeth than tongue, feral and demanding and exactly what we both needed. He moaned so sweetly when I pulled away, nipping and teasing at his lips, and his eyes had darkened with lust.

I reached for his chin, grabbing his jaw hard enough to bruise. I needed to lay claim to what was *mine,* and wanted my boy to know that now I had him, I wasn't ever letting go.

Mat hissed from the pain and foolishly attempted to pull from my grip. So I caught hold of his jaw again, rougher this time and not taking no for a fucking answer.

And then I paused. This was new to him, and I should be more careful.

"Naranja?" I asked meaningfully, but he gave me a tiny shake of his head, all the movement I allowed him as I held him in place.

"Did you hear me say it, you asshole?"

I hummed happily and pushed at Mathias' chest, ruthlessly shoving him backwards onto the lounge where he'd been sleeping. His bare shoulders slammed hard against its thinly cushioned back as he fell into its embrace, and he watched me prowl closer with his lips slightly parted and his cheeks flushed. It was an obscene sight, all wanton heat in his gaze, and it made me wonder how quickly I could take him apart.

And then I'd do it again, more slowly. And again.

"Eres hermoso," I said, telling my northerner again how beautiful he was as I sank to my knees before him, unable to believe this was finally happening. That I had permission to fucking *touch* him. I kissed his inner thigh, letting the warmth of my breath soak through the fabric of his trousers, and his hands came up to tangle in my loose hair. He didn't pull it, but he wasn't

gentle either, and shivers shot up my spine at the feeling of his hands on me. Mat matched my contented murmur with gentle noises of his own.

Softness curled beneath my fingers as I ran my hands up the outside of his legs, and I eyed the fur coat spread beneath his ass with no small amount of amusement. Was I petty enough to ensure he came all over his brother's gift? Fuck yeah, I was.

I pressed a gentle kiss to his hip, just above the line of his trousers. I sank my teeth into his skin in the same place and Mat cried out with a half mewl, half gasp that echoed around the room, bucking against the firm hold I had on him.

I licked at the bite, lavishing the sore spot with attention, and feeling his body gradually settle under my hands and mouth once more.

"Fuck, why is this…?"

I lifted my eyes to his. "What, *mi cielo*?"

Mathias was silent, chewing on his bottom lip with heat in his gaze. I knew what he was on about, but it was far more enjoyable to drag it out of him.

"Say it, Mat."

"Why is this working for me?" he whispered, and I snickered softly against his bare stomach even as his words lit a fire inside me. Because it was certainly working for *me,* and while this was what I'd always wanted to do to him, was what I needed to satiate my own desires, it was still making me unbelievably happy that he was letting me hurt him without running screaming in the opposite direction. I grabbed one of his hands and licked at his palm for no reason other than to surprise him, and his delighted little laugh was all I wanted to hear for the rest of my fucking life.

Correcting the heinous mistake he'd made in getting half-dressed, I unlaced his trousers and freed that exquisite cock of his for the second time tonight. It was erect and waiting, still so perfectly hard for me. The thought that I could do that to him made my heart pound with elation.

"It's been too long, you and I," I told it fondly, and Mat's snicker turned into a groan as I licked at the slit, my tongue moving to explore his crown with firm, slow strokes. He threw his head back, his grip on my hair tightening.

"Ren. *Fuck.*"

I continued to lavish attention on him but made sure it was on my terms, not letting my lips or tongue move down any further than the head of his cock. And as I'd expected, my northerner was a greedy bastard at heart.

"More," he growled, trying to thrust into my mouth, but I stopped him with a hand splayed across his stomach. Did he still not understand who was in charge here?

"No you don't," I told him firmly.

Mathias let out a pitiful whine, trying to reach for me, and I jerked my head out of the way.

"Ren, you prick."

"Oh," I said, amused. "We're going to keep mouthing off, are we?"

His retort was breathless, but somehow still sardonic. "Did you expect any differently?"

I tried not to smile. He'd learn soon enough that as much as I might put up with most of it normally, while we were playing I intended to punish him for every scrap of insolence he dared to dish my way.

"Spread your legs for me," I ordered, and when he didn't immediately obey, I glanced up at him, injecting the dominance into my tone that the brat deserved. *"Now,* Nathanael."

Perhaps he'd intended to refuse, to continue with his usual game of making everything as hard as fucking possible for me. But whatever might have been going on in his head was seemingly overruled by his body, as by the time I'd finished speaking he'd already complied, his knees widening to give me better access.

I growled happily, dipping my head beneath his erect cock to take his balls into my mouth, the edge of his trousers rubbing against my cheek. Mathias gasped and shuddered against me, pleading for more in two languages.

He was so perfect. And in this impossible moment, he really was mine.

"Mat?" I asked, lifting my head as I was struck with an idea that was going to bring the man before me to fucking *ruin.* "Will you let me-"

"Shush," he said unexpectedly, stiffening under my touch. I looked up to find his gaze dancing around the room and landing on things that, annoyingly, weren't me. "Did you hear that?"

"No. I want to-"

"I definitely heard something," he said, his voice losing all of its husky arousal, and I cursed mysterious, inopportune sounds in every language I knew.

And then a scream cut through the air, desperate and angry and *hurting*.

We both stared at each other, his grey-blue eyes boring into mine with horror, and then we were moving, climbing off each other and scrambling for the door. I was forced to pause long enough to grab my trousers from where they'd fallen to the floor, yanking them on to provide me with the minimum decency required for wandering the Martinez estate when I knew there were children around. But the precious seconds it cost me allowed Mat out of my sight, and he was already gone by the time I made it to the antechamber.

"Your Highness, Ademar is already-"

I ignored Elías' protests and ducked into the corridor, spotting Mat and Ad halfway up it as they peered into closed rooms. My guard had his fingers locked tightly around one of Mathias' wrists, but they both seemed to ignore that fact as they used their free hands to systematically open doors. I caught up to them, my bare feet padding down the plush rugs of the hallway and trailed by El, just as they opened another.

We all stared at the child on the other side of it, one hand wrapped around a stuffed bear, the other fisted in her nightdress. She stood awkwardly in the middle of the room, eyes flitting between us.

Mat hissed in a breath. "Are you hurt?"

Little Lady Martinez stared at him in terrified silence, either his pale skin or shirtless state making her tremble. I stepped past him and dropped to a knee in front of the girl, offering her a wide smile. I couldn't help my lack of shirt either, but I was hoping my obviously Quarehian appearance might help settle her.

"Alva," I said gently. "Was it you who screamed?"

The eleven-year-old shook her head and lifted her free hand to point to our right, immediately scampering into her bed and tucking up underneath the covers. By the time I got back to my feet, only El waited at the doorway for me, and I emerged into the corridor just in time to see Ademar release Mathias' arm and push him roughly to the side before slamming a booted foot into the door at the end of the hallway. It crashed open at contact.

"Did you at least try the handle first?" I asked, but both men disappeared through it without a single glance back in my direction. Feeling like someone needed to remember who was the Dios-damned prince here with all the work I was doing chasing other people around, I followed to find Ademar standing just beyond the broken door with his hand on the hilt of his sword, a half-naked woman bleeding from her face on the bed, and Mathias standing over a fourth figure who was grunting in pain and clutching his groin.

Ah.

"Your Highness!" gasped the man on the floor when he'd finally drawn in enough air to breathe, and I didn't need to look at his face to recognise his unpleasant whine. "*El bárbaro* assaulted me!"

"*El bárbaro* doesn't care," Mat snarled, giving him a hard kick in the side. Without boots, it might have hurt, but I expected Pablo Martinez's hefty bulk absorbed most of the impact. "What the fuck were you doing to her?"

"She's my wife!" the lord yelled up at him, indignance etched into every one of his quivering jowls.

Mathias scoffed, slamming his fist into Martinez's face when the man tried to rise. It was quite nice to watch him on the *other* side of a brutal beating for once.

"You sick fuck. You think that gives you the right to hurt her?"

I cleared my throat, knowing that there was hurt and then there was *hurt,* and all too conscious of how delicate that balance could sometimes be. Yet I also knew Pablo Martinez, and I doubted he'd been engaging in anything as consensual as what he'd just interrupted in my own room.

"My lady," I said to the woman on the bed, politely averting my eyes as she pulled her gown closed over her chest. "My apologies for the intrusion. We heard a scream."

"I fucking *told you* to be quiet! Now you've gone and disturbed His High-"

Martinez's hands shot to his throat as Mat hit him in it.

"Your Highness, I witnessed the whole thing. Lord Martinez struck Lord Grachyov without provocation," Ademar told me, letting go of his sword hilt. "It seems he wished to commence a duel."

"I did no such thing!" spluttered Martinez. He pointed an accusing finger at Ademar. "He's lying!"

"He is *not*," El said scornfully, laying a hand on his heart as if in horror. "Look at the bruises on Lord Grachyov's face! How hard he must have been hit!"

Those fucking two. I hid my smile and glanced back at Lady Martinez. Her word didn't mean shit legally and we both knew it, but that didn't mean I didn't want to hear what she had to say.

The woman didn't support my men's lies, but neither did she correct them, gazing back at me with a hard expression and blood running freely from her temple.

Good enough for me.

"You," Martinez snarled, his finger moving to Elías in trembling accusation. "Don't I know you?"

"*Pablo*," I cut in. "How fortuitous I find you awake. I was just coming to inform you of your new assignment."

Five faces turned my way with equally confused expressions. They needed to learn to keep up.

"My militia," I said. "They're new, inexperienced, and in dire need of a noble's leadership. Naturally, I thought of you. You'll find them a couple of dozen miles south of Algejón." I gave him a broad grin. "If you reach a city occupied by bloodthirsty northerners who want your head for a ball in a game of *lapta*, you've gone too far."

Lord Martinez gaped at me even as Mat sniggered at the visual.

"Well?" I snapped. "Do you intend to keep your prince waiting?"

"You want me…to…to lead your militia?"

"That's what I said."

"N…now?"

"Fucking yesterday, Martinez," I growled. "Get going before I decide to allow you your duel with Lord Grachyov."

With a fearful look at Mat, who narrowed his eyes at him, the lord pushed himself to his feet with no small amount of effort and waddled from the room. His barked yells for his servants faded as Mathias moved over to the woman on the bed and gave her a deep bow in the stiff formality of his people.

"My lady," he said, and then faltered. "My apologies if I've caused you additional strife. I'm finding I have a tendency to do that."

Oh, hell to the fucking yes he did. But I couldn't fault him this time — we'd all rushed in here at the sound of her screams, even if Mat had taken it a gratifying step further. I wished I could have done more than send Pablo away, but in Quareh's eyes, he hadn't done a Blessed thing wrong.

Lady Martinez still didn't say a word, but to my surprise, she held out her hand to Mathias. He glanced at me, and then took it.

At the sight of the blood now soaked through the collar of her dress, I ordered El to fetch the estate's healer, whoever they may be, and hoped they were the kind that was Blessed. And then when the lady of the house folded herself into my northerner's arms, her limbs starting to tremble and her breathing harshening, I told Elías to also advise Jiron he now had two windows to guard, because I could see where this was going.

Mathias was good at comforting injured souls, his gentle compassion unrivalled by anyone I'd ever met. My own back sparked with memories of his tenderness, even if I was trying hard not to think about how that night had turned significantly more...interesting. Which meant something needed to be done about his half nakedness to ensure it didn't repeat itself here.

I strode over to the wardrobe and yanked out one of Martinez's huge shirts, tossing it over Mat's bare shoulder. He dutifully released the woman long enough to pull it on, rolling up the sleeves half a dozen times before his hands could even be seen, and then he wrapped her back up into a quiet embrace as she started to shake against his shoulder. I could have had someone fetch his own clothes, but I had hoped that having him look pathetically drowned in one of her husband's shirts would be an appropriate antaphrodisiac for the Lady Martinez.

But although Dios knew how, Nathanael Velichkov somehow managed to pull even *that* off, the hem below his knees and folds of material hanging off his thin frame in a way that should have been entirely unappealing, yet made me want to order him back to my room and fuck him in it.

"Leave the door open, Mathias, so my guards can see you," I told him quietly, walking away as I left half my heart in that room with the shattered door.

*

Chapter Fourteen

Mat

I'd not been in the best of moods this morning, somewhat tired and more than somewhat pissed off at the absent Lord Martinez. I was beginning to suspect that Ren had done the abhorrent beast a favour by sending him away so suddenly last night, because when the healer arrived and the full extent of Lady Martinez's injuries became clear, I'd been ready to throttle her husband with his own shirt.

It had been a delicate balance of looking and not looking, the horror of the bruises and cuts hidden below her dress drawing my eye to places that were not appropriate, but I was prevented from leaving by her fingers still entwined in mine. The estate's healer, a tall man only a couple of years older than me, drew sparking yellow and blue fingers across the woman's wounds with a tight, resigned expression that told me he'd been required to do this before, and Lady Martinez watched him work with a dull look that spoke of embarrassment long having left her.

He'd insisted on healing my own bruises before he left, and while his Touch felt more distant and awkward than Starling's warm glow of magic, he was apparently talented enough to have sensed the remaining injuries to my ribs and pull apart the folds of my shirt to heal those too.

I'd tried to thank him but he'd brushed the words off, slipping through the open door and leaving me with a woman in my arms whose silence had eventually transformed into quiet sobs, and then steely determination as the sun rose.

We hadn't said a word to each other all night. I'd held her as she cried, held her as she picked up the pieces of herself and reforged them afresh, and then she'd held me in turn as my exhaustion took over and I fell asleep against her for a short while, her hands stroking my hair in such a motherly way it was almost painful in its reminder of what I'd never had.

When my eyes had opened to the chattering of caged birds greeting the dawn from the corner of the room, I found she had regained the rest of her strength in both body and mind, and was busy fussing over my mussed hair even as she shooed me from her room to dress for breakfast.

The woman hadn't wept for what had happened last night, I knew that. From the sight of her abused body and the reaction of the healer, a few hits to the face were nothing for the Lady Martinez. I expected her tears were for her whole life, of what she'd wanted but never had, and I hoped that now her husband was gone, at least temporarily – although I'd be speaking with Ren about that – she might be able to regain control of it. But Quareh would make that as difficult as its oppressive, misogynistic self knew how.

It only occurred to me now as Ren and I descended the manor steps after a breakfast to which neither her nor her daughter had appeared at, that I didn't even know the lady's name.

But the image of someone who I'd been able to help, albeit in the smallest of ways, had been abruptly interrupted by the reality of one I hadn't. A girl sat patiently on Jiron's huge horse as he tightened the saddle on the driveway of the manor, her fingers twisting in the reins.

"Consuela? What are you doing here?"

The girl glanced over and froze at the sight of me, which wasn't altogether surprising. Last time I'd seen the child, she'd been squabbled over by her father and the man he'd been trying to sell her to, dragged off in front of Ren's court to a fate that didn't bear thinking about. My attempts to give her a voice to her own destiny had seemingly made everything worse.

"Jiron bought her yesterday afternoon," Ren told me, offering his guard a lazy grin. "After realising señorita Sanz was going for only seventeen goats-"

"You sold her for sixteen," I snarled, the focus of my ire returning from Martinez to its usual resting place. The fucking prince.

"Sixteen," Ren corrected. "A bargain Jiron could not pass up. He offered eighteen to the father, three to the other man for his inconvenience in the whole affair, and here we are." He cocked his head. "How many girls have you bought now, Jiron?"

The guard didn't look up, sliding his fingers underneath the straps to test their tightness against the horse's flanks. "I believe Consuela is my eleventh purchased bride," he said, oh so fucking casually. I couldn't believe I'd ever thought him a decent man.

Jiron was too competent for me to ever be able to land a blow on him. But by the Blessed Five, I was going to *try*.

I took a step forward, fists clenched, but Elías' hand fell firmly on my shoulder and he was rude enough not to let me shake him off.

"Mat," Ren chastised. "Read the fucking room." Then he cracked an eye at the sky above us. "Figuratively speaking."

Jiron gave me a small smile as he moved from his horse to Viento, and I felt my anger seep away at the expression on Consuela's face. Not angry, not fearful.

Almost...hopeful?

I swallowed. "What did you do?"

"Offered her a serving job at *la Cortina*," Ren said. "As we have with all the others. Even Camila was once in Consuela's position."

Oh.

I rounded on him, which proved to be difficult with El still holding me in place. Ren gave an amused twitch of his lips and shooed his guard away.

"So why the fuc-" I remembered Consuela's age, not that Ren had bothered with such courtesies. "Why didn't you do that *before*? When she had two men fighting over her like she was property?"

"I suppose it was too much to hope that what we did last night would rob you of your incredibly judgmental side, *mi cielo*," Ren mused, and fuck, didn't he know the meaning of *discretion?*

Ademar sniggered at my side.

"Use your head, Mathias," Ren said to me. "If I'd offered to buy her in front of the court, how many more beaten girls would have found themselves thrust in my direction the next time I held citizen appearances? Oh look, gentlemen, all it takes is a sad face and an outstretched hand, and the prince will make you rich!" He fed Viento an apple I hadn't seen him take from the breakfast table, and the horse promptly crunched down on it before turning a baleful look at him as if to remonstrate with him for being so short-sighted. Ren shook his head and pulled a second apple from his pocket. "It always has to be done without my involvement," he added as Viento damn near bit his hand off trying to get to the fruit. "Hence, the second reason we stopped here for the night. Her village is only a few miles south."

I still hadn't figured out the *first* reason for our presence at the Martinez estate, and I just hoped it hadn't actually been Abril. The servant had fluttered around Ren at breakfast, flashing her curves in his direction while doing her level best to spill the jug of freshly-squeezed orange juice over my lap. But the joke was on her, because Renato Aratorre adored his oranges and had guarded that jug like his life depended on it.

Luis made his way to us from the stable, giving Jiron a brusque shake of his head. "Apologies, Your Highness," Jiron said, as he finished checking Viento's tack. "We weren't able to get your borrowed horse's shoe fixed. Martinez and his retinue cleared out the estate's horses last night, and all that's left are carriage beasts."

"So I'll have to continue doubling up with Mat? What a *shame*," Ren said with a laugh, smacking his palm hard against my ass.

I whirled around. We hadn't had the chance to talk about what had happened last night nor work out where we stood, but I had expected him to show a modicum of common sense.

"Hands to yourself, prince," I hissed, and then switched to Mazekhstani. "Are you really that stupid?"

"Relax," he drawled in my language. "My men are discreet."

"Unlike you. Anyone could be watching us from the house!"

Ren's gaze flickered in that direction and his expression soured. "So that's it, then? The second prince of Quareh is your dirty little secret? It's fine to indulge in the darkness of night, but come morning, I'm not allowed near you?"

"You know perfectly well why it has to be that way."

He flicked his hair over his shoulder and climbed up onto Viento, clicking his tongue to move him off before the rest of us could even blink. All except Jiron, of course, who was already astride his own mount, his huge arms protectively around Consuela as he pulled up alongside his prince.

"Mathias may ride with Ad," Ren said in Quarehian without turning around, clearly an order rather than a suggestion, and Ademar shot me a look of exasperated disgust.

"*Fantástico,*" he said sarcastically, but I didn't give a fuck what he thought.

Ren's childish little tantrum was making him blind to the reality of our situation. Did he think last night had meant nothing to me? It had been *marvellous.* The memory of him on his knees at my feet, lips glistening wetly, was making me hard all on its own, and the knowledge that he'd found his release through nothing but the mere *sight* of me was something I was still trying to work through.

But yes, the cold light of day brought with it a different set of rules. How could it not? If Quareh had spies in Mazekhstam, then the north sure as fuck had spies here. It was one thing to *indulge,* as he'd put it, behind closed doors, and another to confirm to the entirety of Riehse Eshan that I was every bit as depraved as the prince had accused me of being. It was bad enough that my brother's men had probably seen me kiss Ren on Sesveko. How could I ever return home and hope to stay in one piece if I had my sins bared so publicly to the continent?

I sighed, and climbed up onto Ademar's bay horse, pleasantly surprised when he allowed me to share far more of the saddle than the prince had done the previous day when his own borrowed horse lost its shoe and he'd claimed Viento and me as his alternative ride, because woe betide anyone who got between Ren and his self-declared royal entitlement to a comfortable seat. And at least the guard wasn't trying to feel me up the whole time.

But that particular arrangement lasted less than ten minutes before Ren called us to a halt, declared that Ademar was getting far too cuddly with foreign princes – I'd glanced at Consuela, but she didn't seem to have noticed the slip – and told his guard loudly that he could help out with that little issue. And then somehow I found myself thrown back astride Viento, practically in Ren's lap with his arms tucked around my waist, without ever having had a say in it.

"That's better," he purred in my ear, and seeing as he didn't seem inclined to let go of me to take the reins, I did it myself.

Having him so close, his warm chin resting on my shoulder, made it impossible to remember why I was mad at him, and my frustration had decidedly eased by the time we passed through the gates of the palace a few hours later, calmed by Jiron's soothing voice as he entreated Consuela to the history of the lands we passed through. He told her of hundred-year-old wines made by the grapes of that vineyard and the legend of the three-eyed crow in that forest, but in true childlike glee, it was the battles she wanted to hear the most about. His tales of skirmishes were clearly embellished, but only so much as to avoid regaling the girl with the true horrors of war.

But as the portcullis slammed down behind us, trapping me in *la Cortina* once more, I knew it was me who was looking at the world through a lie. Because despite what Ren and I had shared last night, despite where it might have led if left uninterrupted, I couldn't forget that I was a prisoner in this place. And Ren was the one holding me here.

He was my captor, my fucking enemy.

But by the Blessed Five, how I wanted to kiss him again.

*

Chapter Fifteen

Ren

Death was a funny thing. One could go months without encountering it, and then suddenly it was haunting you from every which way. Miel. Vitorona. And now, the day after we'd returned to *la Cortina,* something even closer to home.

Starling appeared in the doorway to the dining hall, eyes wide, and Jiron pointed at the man on the floor when it became clear I couldn't speak. The bastard was too stubborn to die, but his chest wasn't moving, and it seemed impossible to believe that after everything, *everything* he'd survived and endured, this would be his end.

"Starling," I finally managed to get out, and she flung a frown in my direction before falling to her knees at his side and placing a hand to his forehead. Froth pooled at his pale lips, his eyes closed as if in sleep and – fuck, the young healer had just shaken her head.

"He's…?"

"Already gone," she confirmed in a soft voice, her mouth twisted into an ugly grimace.

Gone? He couldn't be dead.

It was hard…it was *impossible* to imagine a world without him. And from such a stupid thing!

I mean poisoned food, really? In my fucking court? I had no idea how my meal of paella valenciana, pimientos de padron and albondigas – because okay, it was less of a meal than a Blessed banquet, and it seemed that more than one of the kitchen servants were sweet on Mathias after what he'd done for one of their own as there was even a sorry-looking plate of Mazekhstani stroganoff in there that he'd decidedly steered clear of – had ended up sending a man into convulsions, but there he had been, shaking and frothing and apparently fucking *dying*.

I sighed. "Move his body somewhere that isn't here. I suppose we'll have to have a funeral or something."

"Charming," Starling muttered, but in a low enough voice that I could pretend I hadn't heard her.

"That's cold, asshole."

Yeah, now *he* certainly wasn't being quiet enough to ignore. He never was.

I gave a side glance to Mathias and his judgmental glare. "What would you have me do, cry over the prick? Valentinus has been an inch from death as long as I've known him."

The herald had also never shown me, or any of the people I cared about, a shred of kindness, and I'd never forgiven him for ratting on me and Al when we dared to climb up onto the roof of *la Cortina* that time. The image of twelve-year-old Alta emerging from her father's office, arms wrapped around her waist and a hitch in her breathing from the injuries that lay hidden beneath her dress, was one that had never left me. Moreno had disciplined his daughter many times over the years, just as he'd regularly taken his pound of flesh from me too, but it never got easier to bear those little winces Al would sometimes make when she moved too sharply while we were dining or reading together.

At Jiron's direction, two palace guards entered the room and removed Valentinus' corpse from it. I rather suspected two was overkill, as the frail herald could probably be tucked under one of their arms and leave the other three limbs free, but if they wanted to give the old man his final dignities, I wasn't going to argue.

I had more pressing concerns. Like who the fuck had killed him.

"What dish was he eating at the time?" I asked the room, and they all gave me perplexed shrugs. I hissed out an annoyed breath.

"No one saw him?"

"We had better things to do than watch your herald stuff his face," Mat pointed out, although considering he hadn't been sucking me off under the table I'd been conducting my business at, apparently his definition of *better things* differed to mine.

I looked at Valentinus' apprentice, Clementina, who set her jaw as she held my gaze.

"Apologies, Your Highness," she said, not sounding fucking sorry at all. It seemed she was mourning her master's loss as terribly as I was. "I was transcribing."

Of course she had been. We'd all moved in here eight hours ago as I worked through the shit that had piled up in my absence; taking reports, untangling messes, confirming interim directions, and not giving into the urge to pull Mathias down onto my lap and re-introduce my tongue to his tonsils. There had been people in and out of the dining hall all morning: lords and landowners I'd been meeting with, heads of staff I'd given directions to for the upcoming Solstice, bored courtiers looking for distraction.

Even Isobella had swanned past early in the afternoon, wearing a low-cut cream gown that caught my attention – and that of most of the others in the room at that time – only to flounce away in a sulk when I refused her invitation to *refresh myself with a short break.*

Well, I say *I* refused, but it was funny how a Quarehian prince's voice inexplicably took on a northern accent during that particular encounter, wasn't it?

And there had been dozens of servants slipping through the throngs of people with enviable grace and patience as they took coats, shined boots, and topped up all of the platters laid out over the back table. There were crumbs, stripped chicken bones and sticky rice piled up on every surface, with even the servants unable to keep up with the sheer amount of mess a bunch of rich assholes can make. Despite it being his Dios-damned job, Valentinus had given up introducing newcomers after the fourth or fifth hour, retiring his voice and sour self to the banquet table where I'd occasionally caught glimpses of him picking through the food.

Pretty much the entire court had been in here at some point this afternoon. So what all that came down to is that it could have been anything and anyone who poisoned him.

Exhaustion hit as I thought about all the guests and staff I'd have to question.

"What was the poison?" I asked Starling, hoping she could narrow it down for me. She gave a shrug just as insolent as any of Mathias' own.

"Señorita Ortega, you *will* answer my question or Dios help you, you'll be healing pieces of your own tongue back together."

"*Fuck*, Ren," Mat hissed, startled. Starling glowered at me, but didn't look as cowed as I'd expected. She'd never shown me the respect I received from the others, but it seemed Mathias' presence inspired even greater rebelliousness in her.

"I'm not dealing with *two* of you," I snapped. "Starling. Do your fucking job as my healer and tell me what killed my herald."

The girl seemed to think carefully about it for a long moment, and then perked up.

"Poison," she said brightly, and by Dios, I wanted to hit her. And then Mat too, for that smirk he was wearing was driving my mood into dangerous territories where things ended up unpleasant for everyone except me.

"Luis," I barked. "Take Mathias back to my rooms while I have a word with Estrella."

Mat protested, as I knew he would, everything from threats if I hurt her to demands that he stay. And of course, plenty of insults shot in my direction that made me glad of my foresight in removing everyone but my guards and Clementina from the room when Valentinus had first started convulsing on the floor.

As much as I normally loved winding my northerner up, I didn't have time for his shit now. I gave Luis a meaningful look and he hauled Mathias from the room, clapping a meaty hand over his mouth to silence him. I was pretty sure I saw my guard wince as they passed out of sight, and wondered at the state of his hand when he was finally able to peel it free of my wildcat's teeth.

I turned to Starling, whose resolute glare had turned a little less sure. Good.

"*Ahora*, Starling," I snapped. "A man has just been killed in my court. How the fuck did it happen?"

"I don't know, Your Highness," she said, just as my favourite person in the world strode into the dining hall like he owned it.

"An assassination attempt?" Moreno barked, his eyes scanning the room. He looked pissed, and I was impressed at his acting. I hadn't known the man was capable of such deception. Sure, he plotted against me, but he never *looked* like he wasn't.

"It's sweet you care," I drawled.

He frowned. "Of course I care. You're my prince." The hurt in his voice sounded real.

Just when I thought the man couldn't be any more transparent, he had to go and prove himself *complicated*.

"Might be," I admitted in response to his earlier question. I didn't know if Valentinus had eaten or drunk something intended for me, or whether he'd been the actual target. "No one else present is showing symptoms."

We both turned to Starling, our last hope at a clue. She twisted her thumbs together.

"I don't know," she said again. "The Blessed's gifts work on the living, not the dead. Valentinus had already passed when I arrived, so I couldn't tell you anything about him, except that he wasn't *there* anymore."

"Have Dr. Sánchez run an autopsy," I ordered. "Find out what was in his stomach."

Starling curtsied and damn near ran from the room.

"Clementina. Get me a list of everyone who passed through those doors today. Jiron, start organising them into some sort of order for questioning, starting with the kitchen staff."

"Your Highness," Moreno said smoothly. "I can handle the interrogations for you."

"*Questioning*," I snapped. "The guests were mostly nobles, and this needs to be handled without inciting a fucking rebellion, which is exactly what will happen if you pull out your thumbscrews."

He gave me a dark smile. "I'll ensure they remember their places at your feet, my prince."

Dios help me, was it bad that I was a little tempted? Hearing the priggish bastards scream at the Comandante's hands would probably cheer my evening right up. But torturing an entire court was how royal families lost their crowns, and I rather liked mine.

I lifted a hand to run a finger along the band of metal resting on my head. It was so light I'd forgotten it was there, a necessity to holding court all day.

I didn't know how the previous line of princes had done it, but the Padilla crowns had been monstrously heavy. How could one be fit to rule if they didn't have the brains to engage a metalsmith to design something that could be worn without inflicting cranial damage?

"As delicious as it would be," I said, dragging my eyes back to Moreno only to find him also staring at my crown, with a look of hunger in his gaze, "we need them on our side."

Moreno's lip curled. "Too soft," he said derisively, but it was all bluster. Even he knew that pushing too many people too far was a recipe for disaster.

I glanced down at the parchment under Clementina's hands, and the three dozen names already scrawled on its surface.

"Fine," I said wearily. "Send the first one in. Let's get this over with."

It was going to be a long fucking night.

*

Chapter Sixteen

Mat

I woke to Ren expressing fervent declarations of love and affection...to someone else.

"*Te amo*, Camila," he groaned from where he was seated behind his desk, his eyes freshly painted with kohl and closed in ecstasy. "I missed you so much."

Camila didn't even pause in her ministrations to acknowledge the remark, pulling the brush through Ren's hair with a resigned expression on her face. With how smoothly the bristles slid between the long strands, she'd long since finished working through any knots and was now just indulging her prince in his need for luxurious petting.

I had never before been jealous of Camila and her role in running around after the prince and his frequent wardrobe and hair changes, but I was beginning to be.

Or that brush. I could definitely be that hairbrush right now, getting to run myself through those soft dark locks, his citrus scent creeping up to envelop me in him and-

Blessed save me.

I rolled my neck, stiff from where I'd been curled into the armchair all night. I'd stayed awake for hours, prepared to tear into the prince for having me dragged from his side when someone had attempted to *fucking poison him,* but Ren still hadn't returned by the time the dawn lit the horizon and my eyes had started to close. I wondered how much sleep he'd actually gotten.

"Your pampering woke me," I told him now, relief flooding through me at seeing him whole and undamaged. I crossed over to the bed and perched on the edge of it, irritated at myself for giving into the need to draw closer to him. "Or rather, your excessively loud moans over said pampering did. I don't suppose I could ask you to *not* make it sound like you're having sex over there?"

"I don't suppose you could," Ren responded without opening his eyes. "*Sí,*

that's the spot."

I watched with amusement and somewhat growing envy as Camila, having set the brush aside, massaged her fingers into the prince's scalp. He let out obscene little groans that I was now certain were entirely for my benefit.

"Are you actually planning to do anything today?" I snapped, sounding far more irritable than I'd expected.

Ren finally opened his eyes.

"Why? Would you like to put yourself on the list?"

His gaze dropped to my mouth, and I realised I'd been biting my lip. In annoyance, not like a wanton whore looking to pick up clients, but fuck, could I even tell the difference anymore when it came to *him*? I found myself doing all sorts of shit I never would have normally, whether to catch his attention or simply because he made me *want* to.

"Keep doing that, Mathias, and you may find yourself at the *top* of my to-do list."

There was now a heat in Ren's expression that held a weight greater than his teasing tone suggested, and I realised we'd just crossed from his usual provocative banter into something more private. More real.

My heart raced with the hope that what had happened three nights ago might not have been a one-off thing after all. We'd avoided talking about it since our return to the palace, and while that was *good, damn it,* it had also been painful. Because having him in my arms, his mouth on mine, had been all I could think about since.

Yet Ren's flirtatious teasing towards me had eased since I'd snapped at him about his lack of discretion, and I'd been terrified that I'd ruined it all. And fuck, I wanted that playful side of him back so badly it *hurt*.

Feeling daring, I bit down on my bottom lip again. If it got the prince hot, who was I to argue?

"Camila," Ren said in a low voice, not taking his eyes from me. "We're done here."

If the servant thought the dismissal brusque, she didn't show it, dropping into a slight curtsey and leaving the room without hesitation. Ren kicked back his chair and prowled towards me, the kohl and lust working to darken his eyes so they looked almost black.

Diverting my gaze, I stretched. "Look at the time. We best get you to breakfas-"

I smothered my visible satisfaction when he pounced on me, knocking me onto my back. He snagged my hands as he pinned me to the bed and pressed his mouth against mine, hungry and demanding.

"You're not going anywhere, Nathanael," Ren told me huskily, fingers entangling in mine. "Not until you've worked to dispel the problem you just caused."

The so-called problem pressed into my hip, and I laughed against his mouth before he sank his tongue in, hot and vicious as he deepened our kiss and took what he wanted, as per fucking usual.

My heart lightened as heat flushed through me, dispelling my fear that my pushing him away the other morning had damaged the fragile *newness* of whatever had developed between us that night at the Martinez estate, and that Ren would be as distant with me in here as I needed him to be out there, in public.

His hands pulled away to trail down my neck, my arms, my hips, and he held me at the waist with his contradictory rough tenderness, fingernails digging into my skin.

I took the opportunity to run my hands through his hair just like I had wanted to do, and by the Blessed Five, it was as soft as it had looked, Camila having made it so smooth and perfect, it was almost unreal. And then I made sure to mess it up just as diligently, because I was an asshole at heart and tangles were the least of what Renato Aratorre deserved.

Ren growled into my mouth and slipped his hands around the back of my hips so his palms were firmly planted on my ass.

"More problems," he murmured when we both finally came up for air. "You're really asking for it, aren't you?"

"Maybe I just want to hear those filthy noises from your mouth again as she brushes this out," I said, petting his hair. He liked that, leaning into my touch and closing his eyes.

"Maybe I'll make *you* brush it for me, Mat."

"Finally, a genuine threat," I teased, and his eyes shot open in indignation.

"All my threats to you are *genuine*," the prince snarled, and one of his hands slid under the waistband of my trousers to graze down the crack of my ass.

I gasped under his hold, arousal shooting through me, and he gave a soft snicker.

"For example," purred Ren happily, my reaction seeming to have instantly turned his mood, "when I say that someday soon I'll be having this exquisite ass of yours, you can bet every gold piece in the treasury that I'm right."

And with absolutely no fucking warning whatsoever, his fingers grazed that most sensitive part of me and pressed in.

"Relax, *mi amor*," he whispered, as the surprise made me buck against him.

Rationally, I knew it was no more than the tip of a single finger he had inside me, but by the Blessed I felt full from that alone. The sensation was intense, foreign, and I fought the urge to *fight* as I tried to do as he said.

It wasn't unpleasant. Just…different.

"Good boy," Ren breathed, pressing a kiss to my forehead as I forced myself to relax beneath him. Those words, once so condescending, sent an inexplicable rush of heat through me. "Let me get the oil. I want to see what you can take before I even think of putting anything but my fingers near you."

I flushed at the crudeness of what he was saying, yet it sparked an odd type of affection. I hadn't even thought about what it would take to make…*that* happen, and the idea that he would be so careful, despite the roughness he offered when we kissed, was kind of sweet.

Ren drew his tongue lightly along my jaw, and then nipped at the skin.

I was still nervous as fuck about the whole thing, but if what I was feeling right now was any indication, then maybe it wouldn't be as terrifying as I was letting my imagination advise. I could at least…try it, right?

Fuck, with the way the prince was looking at me now, I definitely could. The challenge in his eyes, the quirk of his lips, the way his hair was mussed behind his ears from what *I'd* done. It was the hottest sight I'd ever seen, and it was difficult to remember all the reasons I'd ever had to say no.

He pulled off me, and I pushed myself up onto my elbows to watch as he grabbed a bottle of oil from his bedside drawers, my heart beating so loudly I worried he could hear it.

Ren flung a wicked grin over his shoulder but made no attempt to return to me on the bed. Instead, he tapped the top of the bedside table like he expected me to come to heel. Arrogant bastard.

I gave him a lazy smile. "I'm fine here."

He growled. "Nat…"

"I've just recalled how fucking irritating you were yesterday afternoon when you had Luis haul me off," I said. "And how you haven't apologised."

"I'm not going to. You were distracting my healer."

"*Ren,*" I snapped, the horror of all the events of yesterday afternoon hitting my sleep-deprived brain at once and temporarily dousing my arousal. I rolled off the bed and stalked closer, jabbing a finger to his silver and green coat. "Someone tried to kill you, and you sent me away? You didn't return for *hours,* and I didn't know if that meant they'd gotten to you after all! Do you have any idea what that felt like, you bastard?"

He blinked at me. "I didn't–"

"Didn't think? Didn't care?" I demanded. "By the Blessed, Ren!"

I ran a hand through my hair in frustration and turned away, but he snaked an arm around my waist, pulling me back against him. His body was warm and his thigh was pressed between mine. "Mathias."

I waited.

And then when he didn't even try to speak, waited some more.

"Fuck, you're annoying," Ren muttered, and then shot me a dazzling, seductive smile as if hoping that would be enough to distract me. And it certainly distracted *some* parts of me, but I wasn't letting this go.

"Still not hearing an apology."

The prince blew out a breath. "Sorry?"

"Are you asking me or telling me?"

He mewled and bent his head forward so it was resting on my chest. "I'm sorry, *mi cielo*," he said into my shirt, clearly unable to say it to my face. "I should have stopped by earlier, or at least sent word. I was busy questioning the staff and nobility all night, and…"

I stiffened, because on those last few words, his voice had changed from sincere to sly.

"…and the thought of you waiting up here for me had me all sorts of hard," he finished, lifting his head. His expression had returned to one of pure arrogance glinted with mischief, and I knew that pitiful apology was all I was going to get from him.

"Well, the joke's on you, Your Highness," I told him, narrowing my eyes. "I was asleep within minutes of getting back here. There was no *waiting*."

He let out a low laugh. "Mathias, when will you realise my guards tell me everything? I know you were pestering Luis about my return until at least dawn."

"*Blyat*," I swore, looking away.

"Indeed."

Ren held up the glass bottle of oil and tapped me on the nose with it. "Now. Are you done sulking?"

"Probably not," I said, and he conceded that with a shrug before grabbing the collar of my shirt and shoving me down over the bedside table. I only just caught myself, my palms slamming hard onto its surface a moment before my face could do the same.

"A little warning," I snapped.

The prince laughed. Heat shot through me at the sound, my cock already straining at my trousers from his rough treatment.

"Very well. Unless you wish to safe word, I'm going to put my fingers in your ass and you're going to like it. Consider yourself warned."

I swallowed, my heart racing even faster. Fuck me, his dirty talk alone could get me hard. And considering Ren was nothing *but* dirty talk, I was a constant mess in his presence.

I glanced over my shoulder.

"Ren," I said, watching him uncork the oil. "Your rings."

He drew his hand back and looked at them. "Hmm?"

"If we're doing this, you need to take them off."

His expression was one of wicked delight. "Do I now? Are you trying to give me orders, *Your Highness*?"

Gah. Even used sardonically, my title on his lips was something else.

He reached around and unbuckled my belt, not looking away from my face. "I know exactly what will fit and what won't, Mat. Stay still so I can prove it to you."

He leaned over me, covering my body with his, and our mouths collided in a hot and desperate kiss. Fuck, were we really doing this? When we parted, my breathing was coming out in harsh, anticipatory gasps and his wasn't much better.

"Mathias," Ren murmured, his voice thick with arousal, and then two heavy thuds on the main doors made me freeze. I glanced up even as the prince buried his face against the back of my neck.

"Ignore it," he whispered, the words practically a moan.

When I straightened, he tried to push me back down. I swatted his hands away.

"Bend the fuck over, Nat, and *ignore it*."

I gave him an unimpressed look. "I can't."

"Why?"

The doors swung open and Jiron and Luis stepped through, their gazes sweeping the room until they fell on the prince by my side, frowns easing.

"Because," I explained patiently, hoping they wouldn't spot my unclasped belt before I could fix it up. "When you don't answer, your guards do *that*."

"Your Highness," Luis said. "You're well?"

"I *was*," Ren complained, screwing up his face, "until you ruined what was shaping up to be an excellent morning. Look, I had his belt off and everything."

I sighed.

"Very good, Your Highness," said Jiron impassively. "The remainder of your interviews with the nobility are set up for this morning, as you directed. They're waiting for you."

Ren blew out a breath. "Fine," he said eventually, stepping away from me and shaking out his messed-up hair. "But if I have to sit through *another* seven hours of questioning without earning a single Blessed clue as to who wants to see me choking on my own vomit, the three of you are going to be suffering right alongside me the whole time."

"Very good, Your Highness," Jiron repeated. "Mathias?"

"Yes, Jiron?"

"Your belt is undone. You might want to fix that."

"Yes, Jiron."

*

Chapter Seventeen

Ren

I was wrong. It hadn't been seven hours, but nine. Nine torturous, agonising hours of having Mat so close I could reach out and touch him, and yet not being able to do that *at fucking all.*

Maybe it was my fault for indulging my people as I met with them, allowing each one to whinge and complain about their lives after I was done questioning their role in the assassination attempt. But I hadn't held citizen appearances in far too long, and it seemed like as good an opportunity as any to solidify my relationships across my province, even if I couldn't do much about the hardships that were plaguing them. Considering said hardships could generally be summed up as *oh, if only I had five times my wealth so I could spend it on fancier whores,* or *I would greatly benefit from owning half of Quareh's fertile land such that my neighbour can no longer gloat about having more than me,* or *dear Renato, please fuck me in that deliciously talented way you did last time because I've found no one else can compare.*

Okay, the last one I would normally have done something about, being a generous fucking prince and all, but Mathias' presence and the memory of him under my hands this morning, quivering and demanding and by Dios, so very vexing, made taking any of those courtiers to bed into a truly unappealing idea.

Which was stupid, because I knew what each of them were capable of, and it would be far easier to seek pleasure in their willing arms than attempting to tame my little wildcat in the mere minutes we could snatch unobserved in this place. Mat could pull away from me at any moment, or we could be caught together, and it would all fall to sand between my fingers.

Because it had taken the ride back home from Martinez's estate to realise he'd been right about needing to keep *us* quiet.

As much as I wasn't used to being someone's shameful secret, and had *slightly* more self-respect than letting him use me like a whore in the night and discarding me in the morning would suggest, it was the only way this could happen. Because it wasn't only dangerous for Mat to publicly advertise his so-called sin. It was just as risky for *me*...only it wasn't the fact that he was a man that was so damning, but that he was a northerner. If I'd been worried about him undermining my reputation over the province with his outspoken defiance, such a disaster could be wreaked even quicker with his affection. A prince of Quareh did not fawn over foreigners without losing his people's trust or their belief that he had their interests at heart. Appearances were everything.

So as much as I wanted to tell my guards to look away while he and I tested the sturdiness of the lounge I'd been draped across during the interviews – comfort was a perk of being an Aratorre, as was being able to order everyone else to stand all fucking day – the grumbles of discontent from my people as they each laid eyes on Mathias at my back was an excellent reminder that anything I directed at him in excess of my usual indiscriminate flirting would be costly for my hold on north Quareh and what I was trying to achieve with it.

And fuck, I hated feeling so *trapped* in my own palace, but it was the truth of it.

Displays of public sentiment witnessed by anyone other than my personal guards could mean nothing good for either of us, and if I hadn't been so Dios-damned delicate about it all, I'd have realised that before Mat had needed to say anything.

Not that I'd be telling him he'd been right. Because not only was he annoyingly obstinate and always scowly and had the self-preservation instincts of a moth – the type that's being burned alive due to drawing too close to a flame, in case that metaphor wasn't sufficiently clear, or maybe I should just ditch the wordplay entirely and describe it as the self-preservation instincts of an unarmed, skinny, not-Mazekhstani prisoner who had somehow managed to irritate most of the lords I'd interviewed today, rapidly improving his ability to piss people off until he could manage it merely by opening his mouth – well. Not only was he all of those things, but to be *right* would be one fucking thing too much.

"Pass me the cherries," I said, leaning back in my chair on the terrace. There was a pleasant evening breeze, and I loosened my coat to better feel it against my skin. We'd been cooped up inside all day with the nobles and it was nice to see the sky again, even if we were still inside the palace's outer walls.

"Well?" Luis said testily, slapping at his neck where I assumed a mosquito had been feasting. "You're closer."

Mathias blew out a breath as he realised the guard had been speaking to him. "And you expect *me* to wait on His Highness?"

"You wear his uniform, you're at his pleasure," Luis said to him, emphasising the last word with innuendo even I would be proud of. The northerner scowled at him, neither of them moving.

"I've just had to sit here and watch someone taste all my food for poison," I said, eyeing the huge mouthful taken out of each dish with distaste. "So someone better get me my fucking cherries, or *neither* of you are going to like how creative I get with my punishment for your disobedience."

Luis nudged Mat with his elbow. "As Jiron is collecting Lady Moreno, I'm in charge here. And I'm delegating this task to you."

"Then I guess I have no choice, do I?" Mat responded, looking up at him all wide-eyed and innocent.

I watched him carefully, knowing he had plenty of *choices* that didn't involve giving in so easily, and wondering what he was up to.

Mathias stepped forward and grabbed a bowl from the table, offering it to me.

"No," Luis snapped. "That's salsa, *imbécil.*"

"Oh. This one?" asked Mat.

"No."

"This one?"

"No. Don't you know what cherries look like?"

"Well, I thought I did, but your yelling suggests not. How about this one?"

"That's the same one."

"So it must be *this* one," Mat declared, satisfaction in his voice as he held it up.

"Oh for fuck's sake," Luis snapped, sweeping down over Mat's shoulder to grab the one bowl he'd had been determinedly avoiding, and thrusting it into my hands. Mat smirked at me, and I swallowed my laugh.

"*Gracias* Mathias," I said, biting into a cherry and pulling the stalk free as I held it between my teeth. "I appreciate your prompt attendance to my needs."

My guard fumed.

"It was a pleasure to assist. I guess that means the prince's next *task* will be yours, Luis," Mathias said good-naturedly, returning to stand by my side.

I dropped my fork and it landed beneath the table. "I'm going to need that back."

Mat and I both looked at Luis expectantly, who sighed.

"Yes, Your Highness."

As soon as the guard's head disappeared under the table, I had my fingers fisted in the buttons of Mat's coat, pulling him down to meet me even as his hand cupped the back of my neck. Our mouths collided, his tongue claiming mine as if he'd been just as desperate for this as I was, and by the Blessed, that was an exhilarating thought. I let myself drown in him, the taste of a winter's day wrapped in spun sugar and even greater poetic bullshit that I couldn't think of right now because everything had become *Nathanael*.

When Luis emerged a few seconds later, his meaty fist clutched around the fork, Mat was once again a foot and a half away from me and looking convincingly bored. I tossed another cherry into my mouth.

"Your Highness!"

I rose and greeted Alta as she stepped out onto the terrace with Jiron. Squinting in the afternoon sun as I kissed her cheeks, she shot Mathias a gracious smile when he bowed to her, and we made our way back to the table. Al immediately attacked the meal's dessert options, ignoring the large spoonfuls that had been taken out of each one.

I pulled the cherry pit from my tongue and dropped it into an empty bowl.

"I missed you, Ren," she said. "*La Cortina* isn't the same without you."

"And I you. Are you well? Your father wasn't too..." I trailed off, and she raised a perfectly sculpted eyebrow.

"Too what?"

"Too *himself?*" I asked, and Mat snorted from where he was still standing by my side. He leaned over my shoulder, retrieving the pit of my first cherry from his mouth and letting it fall into the bowl. Luis blinked, his head snapping between us with suspicion.

"My father is fine," Alta said tightly.

"That wasn't what I asked."

"And what you asked wasn't what you meant." She held my gaze for a moment and then dropped her head in submission, even though I hadn't asked it of her. "He did nothing that you have not already dealt with since your return. Now please, Your Highness, ask what is really on your mind."

I exhaled. Fuck, Alta knew me too well.

"We saw what was left of Vitorona," I said in a low voice, and she caught my gaze with a wide-eyed look of her own. "We know Moreno was there that day. It was when he took you on that trip three weeks ago, wasn't it?"

Altagracia briefly closed her eyes, her delicate hands folding together on the table before her.

"Al," I pressed. "You said you knew something about the village. Before I left, remember?"

She smiled and shook her head. "I was mistaken."

"My lady," Mat said, a growl creeping into his voice. "Hundreds of people are *dead* because of him."

But Alta just frowned. "No. My father did not kill those people, Lord Grachyov, and I suggest you keep such accusations to yourself. They will not do either of you any good." Her gaze was on me now, deliberate and unflinching. "Do not pursue this further, Ren, I beg of you."

"Luis," I said. "Step outside with Mat."

Mathias stirred, but before he could protest about it *again,* Alta waved Luis back.

"There is no need," she said graciously. "There is nothing I need to say to you that I cannot say in front of your men. Ren, I swear to you: whatever foul fate fell upon those villagers, it was not at my father's hand. And it is nothing I can help you with." Her eyes were wide, as clear and honest as they'd ever been.

I sank back into my chair. *Fuck*. Alta's words were a dead end if I'd ever heard one.

Where did that leave us? Two ambushes that had lain in wait for me in a direction I was never supposed to have taken, full of northerners who shouldn't have been there. One dead herald, poisoned by food prepared primarily for me. And a massacre that apparently no one had witnessed.

Nothing made any sense.

We both ate in stilted silence for a while until Mat mused about the benefits of chocolate versus vanilla cream as a dessert dipping sauce, and then Alta was off, talking animatedly about her favourite subject of food. I caught Mathias' eye and gave him a grateful twitch of my lips, the tension easing somewhat from the awkward subject I'd taken it in, and it felt like no time at all before my next guest arrived.

Lord de la Vega cut a portly figure, wider than even Lord Martinez, with jowls too numerous to count and rolls of fat that hung generously from his body. But unlike Martinez, he was a decent man, and one I didn't mind the company of whenever he found himself at my palace.

"Your Highness," he said, dropping into a deep bow that looked pretty fucking painful to rise from considering his bulk, and yet I had to smile when he folded himself over a second time immediately afterwards. "My lady."

"I like this one," Mat breathed to me, quiet enough that the lord wouldn't hear him over his puffing as he straightened.

My northerner seemed amused when de la Vega offered up a third bow in his direction.

"My…lord?" my guest said hesitatingly, glancing at me for confirmation. I nodded, and Mat took that as his cue to return the courtesy.

"My lord," Mat repeated smoothly as he rose from his own bow, the sharp, precise kind practised by his people. "It is a welcome relief to encounter someone with manners."

De la Vega chuckled, a hearty sound that boomed off the low walls of the terrace. Jiron stepped forward and offered his arm to help the man into a seat.

"Manners, dear boy, are certainly a rarity in these parts. And considering how often I find myself in Mazekhstam and Temar, I fear I must speak for the whole of Riehse Eshan when I say that."

Mat frowned, and I could see all the questions and objections that vied for precedence on his tongue.

"You're often in the north?"

"I am. A trader by trade, a lord by title, and a man by nothing more than the clothes on my back."

Whatever the fuck that meant.

"Do you have any news from Stavroyarsk?" Mathias asked eagerly, and I gave a quiet cough.

"Mat. Jiron. Please escort Lady Moreno back to her rooms and then enquire at the surgery as to how Dr. Sánchez's autopsy on Valentinus is progressing."

Mat scowled. "You mean *Starling's* autopsy. Don't pretend that prick does anything you pay him for."

But he left at Jiron's side anyway, shooting a wistful look back at Lord de la Vega, although I doubted the man had been to Stavroyarsk any more recently than he had. While the continent was small when compared to the lands that surrounded us across the oceans, it was still a difficult journey up north, when the ground inclined so suddenly as to impose a permanent winter climate in lands only a few days' journey from my own.

But it was true that the lord found himself up there more often than not, or at least his ships of spice and tobacco did. And that was why I had wanted to meet with him.

Because I had an occupied city to save, and a prince to help me do it. But first, I had to find a way to speak to the northern bastard.

I just hoped Valeri Velichkov was in a listening mood.

*

Chapter Eighteen

Mat

"Would you like to hold his heart?"

I didn't have time to answer before the bloody organ was dropped unceremoniously into my hands.

"Thanks," I said dryly. It was cold, and covered in congealed blood. It was also heavier than I'd expected the heart of such a shrivelled old man to be. "But I was going to say no."

"No one ever answers yes," Starling said, a little glumly.

"I can't imagine why. Do you mind if I just put this…anywhere?"

The healer waved a crimson-soaked hand, not looking up from where her nose was an inch deep inside Valentinus' gaping chest, and I dumped the heart into a spare bowl before wiping my hands clean.

"Any luck figuring out what killed him?"

"Poison," Starling offered, and then yelped out a laugh as I dug an elbow in her ribs.

"I'm not Ren," I pointed out, and she finally looked up, shooting an appraising look my way. Some of her curly brown hair had come loose from its tie, and she blew it from her face with irritation only for it to fall back a moment later.

I reached forward and tucked it behind her ear to stop it trailing through Valentinus' innards.

"Thank fuck you're not," Starling said. "If I had to curtsey from this position, I'd end up with a mouthful of kidney. Hold this."

"Is it another piece of corpse? Because I'd rather not."

"*Cobarde,*" she teased, and shoved a different bowl into my hands before depositing a handful of slimy, stringy gloop into it.

"I'm not a coward," I protested, although this not-coward was desperately trying not to look at whatever it was she was pulling from Valentinus' body. Or smell it. By the Blessed, it stank.

"What can I help you with, Mathias?" Starling murmured as she started to poke through the bowl's contents and squeezed out what I now realised were intestines.

"Mm. Can. Wait."

"Please don't throw up over my autopsy. It's so rare that I get to use actual medical knowledge rather than just my magic, and I won't have you ruin this special moment for me."

A greyish mush emerged from the end of the intestines, and I swallowed. "Special."

"Frustrating," she said, rocking back on her heels and glaring at me as if I'd done something wrong. I glanced down into the bowl in case I'd thrown up without realising, but no, that appetising lump of slime was still just human remains. I tossed it onto the table and gratefully followed the healer over to the basin in the corner of the room.

"What's frustrating?"

"That for a tiny old man, Valentinus seemed to have sampled everything at the banquet yesterday before he kicked it," Starling mused. "I've found traces of what looks like a dozen dishes in his stomach, and with none of them having started through his intestines, the timing could fit to any of them. There's no way to know which meal killed him."

"Which means the prince can't narrow down who prepared it," I said. "Fuck. He was really hoping you'd find something. We spent *hours* today talking to everyone who was there, and got nothing."

She raised an eyebrow. "We?"

"Well," I answered awkwardly. "Ren did. I was just…there."

Starling snorted, tossing me a towel to dry my freshly scrubbed hands. "I bet the nobility loved that."

Grinning, I pulled myself up to sit cross-legged on the other table in the surgery, the one *not* covered in an eviscerated dead body. "It was difficult to work out what irritated them more: my mere presence, or Ren's list of seventy-two questions, carefully constructed to expose inconsistencies, assess loyalties, test alibis…and also conveniently gauge how attractive they find him."

She cocked her head.

"Questions fifty-three and sixty-eight," I said. "And sixty-nine, because *naturally*."

Starling barked out a laugh. Oh, she was as filthy as he was, sometimes. She pulled herself up onto the table beside me, needing to jump to give herself the extra height.

"How is His Pevertedness?"

"I…are you talking about Ren?"

"No, I'm talking about the *other* prince with depraved sexual tastes whom you often hang around with." She paused, giving me an assessing look. "Are you blushing, Mathias?"

I buried my face in my collar. "No. But if I was, could you do something about that?"

"You want me to disable all the blood vessels in your face so no one notices how you turn red whenever anyone even mentions the prince?" Starling asked.

"Yes."

"No," she said. "You really don't. Where's your shadow?"

I offered her a smile, tamping down on my embarrassment. "Jiron's waiting in the courtyard, watching the front *and* back of the surgery."

She whistled. "How'd you manage that?"

"I finally called in his punishment."

"Do I want to know?"

"Probably not," I said. "Seeing as it involved me getting injured again."

Her hand immediately shot to mine, covering my fingers with her own. "Mathias, why didn't you say something?"

"I'm fine. See?" I offered a smile, but I didn't feel it. I was remembering what she'd said about her magic being finite. "Save your gift for someone who needs it. You're too valuable."

"Yeah, so Blessed valuable I can't step foot outside the walls without an escort to protect the Aratorres' property," she muttered, and that gave me my answer about whether we were allowed to curse on ourselves. "Maybe I'll get lucky and this assassin will finish the prince off next time."

I wasn't amused. "That isn't funny."

"It's hilarious," she declared, her expression dark. "If there's no Renato Aratorre in *la Cortina,* there's no need for Estrella Ortega in *la Cortina.*"

"So you'd prefer to be recalled to Máros?" I asked. "They're not going to let you go just because one of their princes is dead, Star."

"The king and his heir have their own healers in the capital," she said stubbornly. "*Male* healers. Maybe I'd be posted to the border or something. Anywhere that isn't trapped within these walls."

"That's even worse! You could be killed!"

"As opposed to the haven of safety here?" Starling gave a pointed look at the dead body on the table.

I squeezed her hand, and the healer let out a long breath. "Sorry."

"Don't be," I said in a low voice. "You're going to get out of here, Star. I promise you."

Her eyes, when they met mine, were filled with a steely ferocity. She nodded. "I'll hold you to that, my lord."

The fake title rested hollowly in my ears. I hated lying to her.

"Starli-"

"I sent you to check on a dead body, Mathias, not get it on with my fucking healer."

Starling abruptly let go of my hands, slipped off the table, and sank into a curtsey before her prince, wincing as the door he'd shoved open slammed into the wall. I didn't bother to move.

"No luck," I said. "Valentinus had made his way through most of the banquet, and Star says it's impossible to tell which mouthful killed him. Can't you have all the food tested?"

"Can't *she*?"

"I deal in human bodies, my prince, not flavours of soup," Starling retorted. "Unless one of your men would like to sample each dish and ingredient at a time so I can try to detect the poison in it before it kills them, one shrimp is going to look exactly the same to me as the next."

Ren looked like he was considering it.

"No," I snapped, shutting that shit down.

"Fine. I'll get it tested. And señorita, I have a headache," Ren added disdainfully, clearly expecting Starling to do something about it.

She threw me a pissed off look as she circled behind him and settled her hands at his temples, red and green sparks flickering from her fingers as her Touch flared.

"Better, *Your Highness*? Or shall I exert myself magicking away your every bitten fingernail and blocked pore?"

Ren's expression darkened.

"*Anyway,*" I said with fake brightness, dropping down from the table before he could order some suitably horrendous punishment on the healer, either for the insolence or the insinuation that his skin was less than perfect. "I expect you'd like to retire to your rooms now, Your Highness, considering you were working late last night?"

Ren's scowl predictably turned into a lascivious smirk. "And *I* expect you'd like to join me."

I made various non-committal sounds, and by the time he realised I was just placating him, we were outside in the courtyard, the surgery door firmly closed behind us. The braziers were lit, lending warm flickering glows of orange light to the shadows that roamed in the corners, and I could smell the oranges of the orchards beyond the walls. Ademar, who had apparently swapped out shifts with Luis in the hour or so I'd been with Starling, bowed alongside Jiron at the prince's appearance.

Ren frowned. "Wait. I-"

"No," I said, stepping in front of the door. "You *can't* go back in there to have the last word."

He pulled a pathetic face that was a cross between a pout and a snarl. "You're a bad influence on that girl, Nat."

"I don't have any influence."

"Tell that to my cock, *mi cielo*."

I elbowed him in the ribs for that, only for Ademar to smack me hard across the face.

"For fuck's sake," I muttered, pressing a hand to my stinging cheek as Ren rounded on his guard.

"What," he asked, his voice in that quiet, deadly tone that gave me shivers every time I heard it, "did I say about hitting him?"

"Your Highness, he struck yo-"

"Shut the fuck up, Ademar," Ren interrupted. "In case it isn't getting through to any of you, I don't want you hurting Mat unless I tell you to. And currently, I am *not telling you to*. Understand?"

Ademar's jaw set but he eventually nodded. Jiron inclined his head mildly, looking his usual unflustered self.

"Mathias, you may declare a fitting punishment for Ad being far too slow on the uptake," Ren declared, striding off towards the opposite wing of the palace, and I'll admit it was momentarily gratifying to watch the way the guard's shoulders tensed at the threat.

"Not this again," I said. "I thought I made my feelings clear on such barbarism?"

I didn't mention the fact that I'd shamelessly used my power over Jiron to score an hour alone in the surgery, and I noticed he didn't either. Although I suspected it would make its way to Ren soon enough; none of them appeared capable of keeping anything from him.

"Are you sure you're a prince?" Ren asked, dropping his voice so it wouldn't carry beyond the four of us as we climbed the circular stairs. "You're far too soft, you daft bastard."

"Are we using you as the benchmark? Not all of us are so cruel."

"Or handsome," he said, cocking his head. "But you're not doing *too* terribly in that area, *mi amor*."

"Or egotistical," I mused. "Or smug. Or capricious. Or-"

"We get it, you adore me," Ren drawled, waving a hand.

I snorted. "I just wanted to make sure I had your best qualities down."

We reached his antechamber and he shoved open the bedchamber doors as dramatically as he had the one in the surgery, clearly not giving a fuck about the state of the palace's walls. I shrugged a farewell to Jiron and Ad, closing the doors with considerably more care to find Ren had already thrown himself on top of his bed in the darkened room, boots kicked off and ankles crossed.

He slapped the blankets next to him without looking at me, and I swallowed, feeling the loss of every inch of distance between us as I moved closer. But when I lay down beside him, staring up at the underside of the bed frame he'd once had me tied to and flogged, the nerves disappeared.

I didn't know who the fuck I was becoming in this strange land of forbidden desires, or what would happen once…*if* I was released. But it was moments like this, just him and me, that made everything else disappear. He was obnoxious, arrogant, coarse and maddening, but he was also *Ren,* with his huge heart and clever mind, and I wouldn't change a Blessed thing about him.

The prince's fingers slipped into mine, and my skin blazed with heat at the touch.

"Tell me about Stavroyarsk," he said softly, and when I turned my head, I found him watching me with those deep brown eyes I could easily drown in. "And this time give me the version where you're Nathanael, not Mathias."

"It was true," I assured him, needing him to know that not everything between us had been a lie. "What I told you, before."

"Even the Astrid zefir?"

I laughed, unable to believe he'd remembered my tales in that much detail. "Yes."

"Perhaps I could have used that to discover who you were," Ren mused, tipping my hand over and tracing circles on my palm with his thumb. "Sent a spy to Mazekhstam's capital to ask around about a boy obsessed with face-shaped zefir. Whatever the fuck that is."

"It's confectionery. Marshmallow and meringue."

"Ah. I thought so."

"Did you," I said flatly.

He shrugged and yawned, amusement flashing in his eyes. "It *is* the north we're talking about. It could have just as easily been fermented donkey shit."

"You just lost your chance to ever get your face on one," I told him with mock severity. "Lady Moreno would like it, I'm sure."

"She does have an appreciation for fine, sweet things. Why do you think she's friends with me?"

"A distinct lack of better choices?" I suggested, and Ren chuckled. His hand slid out of mine and he sat up, shrugging out of his expensive coat and hurling it carelessly to the floor. I watched his movements, memorising every toss of his head, every flick of those long fingers as he pulled his hair free of its binding and lay back down beside me, tugging a blanket from underneath my ass only to lay it back over the both of us.

"Tell me more, Nat," he breathed into the twilit room, his voice a soft murmur.

I fidgeted. "About what?"

"Anything. I just like hearing you talk."

He sounded sleepy and content, and I absolutely adored the way his eyes were half-lidded as they gazed over at me from the other pillow. As I spoke about Princess Astrid and Prince Kolya, and how there was nothing more beautiful on the continent than a fresh snowfall over Stavroyarsk, and a hundred other things I couldn't remember in the morning, his delicate eyelashes fluttered closed.

And it was then, watching Ren fall asleep beside me, his knee pressed against the edge of my thigh and the warmth of his breath on my face, that I realised I'd been wrong about the snowfalls.

*

Chapter Nineteen

Ren

Long shadows stretched out in front of us as walked across the paddocks outside the walls of *la Cortina*, the warm haze of another day settling into a pleasant summer's evening.

Mat's eyes flickered around us and his shoulders were tensed as if he was planning to take off running now that we were back outside of the palace. Jiron watched our northerner like a hawk, ready to grab him at a moment's notice if he tried anything so stupid. Because if Mathias thought he could escape me, he'd never been more wrong in his life. He was *mine*.

Perhaps it was cruel, dangling false freedom in front of him like this, but I hadn't meant it to be. I'd thought he might enjoy the luxury of not having walls pressing in around him, particularly when I recalled the wistful joy in his voice as he'd spoken last night of the lakes up in the north and their endless frozen reaches. I didn't have any snow to give him, and I personally didn't see the appeal of the horrid stuff, but this stretch of land outside *la Cortina* was even more beautiful.

Or maybe it was the palace I was doing a favour by temporarily removing Mathias from it, considering the numerous denizens he'd wound up today with his acerbic, biting remarks. Nothing that could be construed as undermining my authority, as he'd always reluctantly shut up when ordered to do so, but enough to leave nearly every lord that I'd met with about the security of the northern border in a state of fluster. It hadn't been deliberate insults like he'd thrown at Martinez, but rather questions and comments that probed at the heart of Quarehian society in a way that most of my guests had found rather uncomfortable. Perhaps it was the righteousness with which he'd spoken, that arrogant northern judgment that demanded they explain why they referred to their wives so derogatorily, how they could justify arrangements to marry off their daughters without their input or consent, why they felt they had the right to dictate the terms of other men's lives.

It had been illuminating, I'd found, watching these proud nobles attempt to account for their views, some forced to resort to disdain, disparagement and even threats as the northerner systematically worked his way under their skin. It had told me a lot about both their personalities and leadership capability, and after cataloguing their responses, I'd made some adjustments to their responsibilities in Quareh's northern province that would have been disastrous if left unchecked.

I'd also yelled at Mat in front of them to ensure he was seen to be put back in his place, returned the smirks he shot me when no one was looking, and loudly advised that I'd be handling his punishment for such unruliness *privately*.

Unlike the poor servant we'd encountered in the outer courtyard as we passed through on our way out of *la Cortina's* gate. He'd been strung up for a public flogging for speaking ill of my family in a way that I knew all of the staff did at some time or another, but the fucker had been stupid enough to get caught. I didn't know how that was *my* fault.

But of course, Mathias had been disapproving of that too, fixing me with a glare and a series of snide comments about the fragility of princely egos and the hypocrisy of *some people* in ordering floggings as punishments until I'd told the stablemaster to cut the man down just to shut him the fuck up.

I glowered at Mat, only now just registering how the prick had essentially manipulated me into exonerating the servant in front of everyone.

Dios, he really had me by the fucking balls.

"That was your favour for today," I told him, as we approached the training ring a half mile from the palace. "Don't expect any more niceties."

Mathias raised an eyebrow. "I've learned to keep my expectations of you low, Your Highness."

"Asshole," I said on a sigh. "You know, if you were clever enough to keep me in a good mood, you might have been able to carve yourself out a halfway comfortable life here. Instead, you always squander it on pulling shit like that." I waved an arm at the palace behind us as Ademar and Elías shucked their coats off and jumped into the ring, starting to circle each other.

"Shit like what?" Mat asked, pulling a confused face as if he believed himself totally innocent of what he'd just done.

"Like helping Dios-damned strangers who owe you nothing in turn," I said.

"I doubt that man even noticed you."

Mathias' frown deepened. "Why would it matter if he notic-"

He jumped at the harsh clang of metal behind him. El laughed and pressed his advantage over his brother, driving him backwards with a few strikes that Ad blocked just as desperately as he'd swung the first.

"By the Blessed Five," Mat breathed, his eyes wide. "They use their real swords for this?"

"Sometimes," I said, moving to lean on the wooden fence surrounding the training ring. I tried to make the time to come out here when I could, as it was the only chance my guards had to train with all four of them present. "Depends on how worked up they are."

"And thanks to a certain Temarian prince trying to escape on his watch during siesta earlier," Jiron added quietly, "Ademar is feeling plenty worked up. To which Elías is appropriately schooling him in his folly."

"*No*," I warned, as Mat grinned and opened his mouth as if to yell something to Ademar. "No more winding him up today. Not while they have raw steel in their hands."

He promptly shut up, looking properly chastised for once, and fuck me, that contrite expression was so rare that I was tempted to commission a portrait artist to capture it for posterity. Well, posterity and also for shoving it in his face when he was being his usual insolent self.

Despite the siblings being evenly matched in talent, Jiron hadn't been wrong when he'd said that Ademar's current aggravation made him an easy target, and it wasn't long before El called his victory with his sword at his brother's neck. Luis hopped over the fence to challenge the victor before Ad had even muttered his surrender.

"That was terrible," Mat said to Ademar cheerily, apparently having shaken off my order already. "I'm almost embarrassed that you managed to catch me earlier."

My guard just gave him an unimpressed look. Jiron was being generous calling it an escape attempt: Mathias had merely slammed the antechamber door on Ademar's face when we retired for siesta and legged it halfway down the corridor before Ad had caught him. It was clearly more to keep my men on their toes than a serious plan to escape the heavily guarded palace, but Ademar had taken it as a personal insult to his competence.

"My prince," Jiron murmured, and I followed his gaze to find a dozen guards weaving their way through the horse paddocks towards us. It was pretty much all of the palace guard but for those who would have been on duty, and made for a formidable sight.

"That's mildly terrifying," Mat commented in an echo of my thoughts. He put a hand up to shield his eyes from the dying sun as we watched them move closer. "What do you think they want?"

"Moreno occasionally hijacks my men's training sessions," I said distastefully. "He likes to throw his weight around and remind me that his guards are just as...*armed* as mine."

The Comandante would have inserted another word in there, I was sure. Skilled, perhaps. Deadly. But I knew my men, and I also knew they were the four I'd pick every time to have my back, no matter my other choices.

Luis, Ademar and even Jiron had once trained under the Comandante, but they all had something the others didn't, other than the obvious traits of actual loyalty and a sense of fucking humour. A dogged determination to be the best they could be, and to achieve that because they aspired to it, not because they'd be punished for anything less. It was why you would find my men training anytime they weren't working, sleeping or eating, and why the palace guards were regularly caught gambling and whoring.

I turned back to the fight where Luis caught Elías off guard with a fancy flick of his sword I'd never seen him use before, drawing a line of blood across the smaller guard's wrist.

"Shit," Luis said, diving forward only to be stopped by the tip of El's blade as it rested neatly against his heart. "I didn't mean to cut you."

"I didn't mean to let you," Elías said, his eyes sparkling with amusement even as the curve of his lips displayed his irritation at being bested. "Show me how you did it."

They fell in side by side rather than in opposition as Luis demonstrated the move, but I was only half watching, distracted by how Mat's left hand was nestled on the fence against my right, his little finger snaking around mine.

"Sleep had you last night, Nat," I said to him in a low voice, ignoring the fact that I'd fallen asleep first because convenient disregard of inconvenient facts was a prince's prerogative. Besides, when I'd woken up ready to put all my newfound energy to good use, I'd found him sleeping soundly in the bed beside me. "I hope you've realised that tonight, it's *my* turn."

He let out a soft laugh, and there was a defiant bite to it that made me want to pin him down right here, regardless of all the eyes closing in on us.

"You're awfully sure of yourself, Your Highness. Are you supposing I'll let you near me?"

"Oh, you'll let me," I assured him. "And everything else I plan to do to you. I will have you begging before the night is out."

Mathias snickered at my side. "I'll take that bet."

From someone as stubborn as him, maybe that should have been disheartening. I just took it as the shameless plea it was.

I turned as the voices of the palace guards reached us, ensuring I appeared suitably nonchalant as I rested my ass back against the fence. A dozen something men sank into simultaneous bows.

"Your Highness," Moreno drawled from their ranks. "Mind if we join you?"

Of course I fucking mind.

I gave him an easy smile, not about to share anything as valuable as my genuine feelings with the man. "I don't suppose you brought snacks? I've been out here for ten minutes now, and I'm starving."

I was shot a look of disgust that he barely tried to hide.

"Unfortunately not, my prince." His gaze flickered behind me. "Are your men sparring or comparing crochet patterns?"

I fluttered my fingers and heard El and Luis resume their fight, the sound of colliding metal jarring in the crisp evening air. The sun was on its way down but we still had an hour of light left, and I suddenly wished it would hurry up so I could get back to the palace and engage in my favourite hobby of avoiding Moreno.

To my dismay, the Comandante joined us at the fence as his men broke into organised stretches on the grass, the disdain on his face even less masked when he turned it on Mathias. I just hoped my wildcat remembered that as a high-standing noble, Moreno spoke both Mazekhstani and Temarian, and that he didn't attempt to pull what he had on Lord Martinez. Mat had been exceedingly lucky that Martinez considered learning the northern tongues beneath him.

The chatter of the palace guards faded into a hum as I turned to watch my own men continue to spar, my anxiety easing a fraction when neither Mathias nor Moreno bothered to address each other. And then it spiked back up when I spotted the frown on the Comandante's face as he intently tracked Elías' movements across the increasingly muddy ring.

"All right, wrap it up," I said loudly to my guards, when neither showed any signs of getting the upper hand. El had more experience, but his talents had always lain more in bow work rather than the sword, and Luis was excellent at keeping up his guard. "There's plenty of fine gentlemen looking to take a turn."

They both tossed their swords to their left hands and seamlessly continued their fight, only now their movements were a lot less refined. Clumsy strokes met awkward parries, and within moments El had Luis backed up against the far side of the fence. A second more, and Luis swore as his sword was batted from his weaker hand.

"Your men are welcome to the ring," I told Moreno, but he shook his head.

"Victor plays on, isn't that the rule?" He waved a hand and one of his guards climbed the fence to face off against a weary Elías.

Even exhausted, my man held his own against him, disrupting his opponent's flurries and ensuring to keep the sun at his own back. Yet his strength was flagging quickly.

Moreno scoffed as El made a mistake with a block and the palace guard pressed the advantage. "Terrible footwork. He's all over the place! He wouldn't have lasted five minutes under my command."

He slammed his fist down onto the fence and made Mathias, who'd been leaning on it, jump in surprise.

"I won't stand for my prince's security being so compromised, not considering the recent attempt on your life," the Comandante hissed. "A country hack with a sword in his hands does not a royal guard make. I'll find you someone more suitable immediately, Your Highness."

Fuck me, not this again.

"Moreno," I said wearily. "You've raised this objection before. Elías is perfectly capable, despite his unorthodox training."

The man's lip curled back into a sneer. "Unorthodox? I find it difficult to believe he had any training at all." He shot Ademar a dirty look. "Just a brother willing to go to his knees for him."

I tsked. "Leave the disreputable insinuations to me, Comandante. I hired Elías for his own capability, not at Ademar's behest."

Not entirely true, but El had more than proven his worth since he'd joined my retinue, and I didn't want to sour that with the recognition that it had been a favour to Ad at the time.

And then – *fuck* – his opponent got in a lucky hit and swept past Elías' guard. A sword to his neck, and El was yielding, amicably nodding his head at the other man. Because to them, it had just been a game, and what did losing matter when he'd won a hundred times before?

But the way Mat tensed at my side told me he knew just as well as I did that the Comandante would turn it into something more.

"I look forward to correcting that atrocious form of yours," Moreno told Elías as he climbed out of the ring, and my guard's startled gaze shot up to meet his.

"Sir?" El enquired politely.

"He doesn't have the time," I snapped. "I will not release him from his duties for you to play with, Comandante."

Moreno's smile turned nasty. "He'll have plenty of time. For he won't be taking another shift at your side until I'm satisfied he deserves to be there."

Elías swallowed uneasily as he sheathed his sword at his belt, and I didn't blame him. We'd all been regaled by horrific stories from the other three about Moreno's training methods, and while it sounded rough enough for the average soldier, those he took a particular disliking to never lasted long under his attentions. More than one guard-in-training had died from the exhaustion of attempting to meet his demands, or the brutal punishment of failing to do so.

I shook my head. "No. I need him."

"You *need* competent guards. And considering my man just bested yours in less than a minute, he's more than proven himself such. Diego!"

Elías' opponent, still in the ring, lifted his chin.

"You're serving the prince now," Moreno told him, and Mat hissed out an angry breath.

My mind ran through all the ways I could persuade him to change his mind, discarding each possibility just as quickly. Moreno knew how much Elías meant to me, what *all* of my men meant to me, and this was a calculated move that couldn't be undone by my order alone. The Comandante had authority over my security, and while he couldn't exercise it arbitrarily, he'd used this tiny sliver of victory to ram the knife home. It didn't matter that El had been sparring for an exhausting twenty minutes straight, having taken out two of my men already. He'd lost a fight at an inopportune moment, and that had given Moreno the edge he needed.

I just needed to reclaim my own.

"Let's see how this man of yours does, then," I said sharply, wondering if it could be so simple as to have Diego beaten in the same way. But Moreno had clearly plotted this before he arrived here, as his men systematically fell to Diego's sword in such ways as to make it more than fucking obvious they were faking their losses. I seethed silently, all while keeping a pleasant smile on my face.

The Comandante wouldn't win this little game, but I wasn't sure how long it would take me to undo his victory. And even a day under his command could be too long for Elías. If Moreno discovered his secret…

A squabble broke out behind us, and I glanced around with irritation to find three of the palace guards in a punch up, another couple attempting to separate them. One took a hard hit to the jaw that sent him staggering.

"Get your shit together and at least *try* to act like the soldiers you're supposed to be," I snapped. The Comandante gave the men a withering look that had all five of them promptly straightening into bows.

"Apologies, Your Highness."

"Sorry, sire."

I narrowed my eyes, exhausted and just wanting to have this shitshow of a day over with so I could get Mathias into bed. "Fighting only in the ring, you hear me? Anyone else who wishes to lower themselves to petty *brawling* will spend their night chained to a wall down in the fucking cells. Do I make myself clear?"

Moreno's mouth twitched in delight at the threat. "Well? Your prince is speaking to you."

The one who'd been hit spat blood to the ground and then joined the remainder of the palace guard in their chorus of declared obedience. They stood tall, chins high, as if determined to impress me with their stances alone. I caught Jiron's eye as he silently communicated to me his amusement at their efforts.

I turned back to the ring. "Next," I growled. "Give me a show that isn't Diego taking out his so-called opponents without seeming to even land a hit."

"I'd be interested to see the Mazekhstani fight," Moreno offered unexpectedly. His gaze roamed over Mat at my side, and then flickered back to mine. "Seeing as you grant him so many liberties, Ren, I can't expect you'd have a problem with this one."

"Liberties he's *earned* from me," I said sweetly, not caring how it sounded until Mat gave a half-choked cough. And then I cared very much, and wanted to say it again, only way louder and far more suggestively.

"Come," the Comandante said with a feral smile. "Aren't you interested in seeing how the boy holds up to his sire?"

"It's not an inherited title, as you well know," Mathias pointed out. "I'm no more a Commander than your daughter is."

Moreno's lip curled. "I find it difficult to believe that Grachyov wouldn't have taught his son anything of his craft. You will show us."

A shout from Diego's latest sparring victim caught his attention and Moreno pulled away to address the man, giving me time to turn my head close to Mat's.

"Do you have *any* idea how to use a sword?"

"They didn't exactly let their political hostage near many of them," he muttered back, shooting me a grimace that told me exactly how fucked his story would be if Moreno got him into that ring.

And then the Comandante had turned back to us. "Do you fight one handed or two, Grachyov?"

"He's not going anywhere near a blade," I drawled. "I'd rather not give him the opportunity."

"Ren!" Mat protested, annoyed resentment dripping into his voice as he took my cue and fell effortlessly into the role of a war hero's son with something to prove. "Don't you dare take away my chance to show these assholes up. I'm not going to try anything."

"I'll be right here," the Comandante agreed with a sly smile. "I won't let him hurt anyone."

I shook my head. "No."

"Why?"

"Because you want it, that's why," I told Mathias, and he wore such a perfectly pissed off scowl that I had to fight hard to conceal my smile. Deceitful fucker.

I turned to the man at our side. "If it's humiliation in the ring you're looking for, may I suggest an alternative candidate? Someone standing right here, perhaps?"

Moreno's grin grew wider, and he looked me up and down.

I cleared my throat. "Jiron? Moreno's looking for someone to hand his ass to him. You're up next."

—

I'd always hoped that being a despicable, abusive prick would have consumed all of Moreno's energy and left him with few other qualities. Unfortunately, his time spent as a strategic military leader had never dampened his physical ability in the field, and that proved just as true today as it had all the other times I'd watched him fight. His blows were sharp, precise, and well-matched to Jiron's own skill.

But my guard was in his element, his sword flashing to meet the

Comandante's with impossible speed, and the two men fought on without flagging. The sheer competence of their deadly dance was both beautiful and terrifying. Metal clashed with awful shrieks, any of the blows capable of cleaving either of the men in two if they failed to block in time.

Mat inhaled sharply whenever it seemed that Moreno had Jiron dead to rights, but I knew my man. He wouldn't be beaten so easily. And he was giving me the time to think up a plan to recover Elías. Which, Dios damn me, I couldn't. What hadn't I thought of? What was I missing?

Helplessness and frustration threatened to sink me, that dark, ominous threat that always lingered just below the surface.

Think, Ren. Don't let him take El.

Jiron grunted as he barely blocked a blow in time, ducking under a second swipe. As he turned, I saw the blood that was staining the left arm of his white shirt. He grimaced at Moreno and pressed his attack, and they fell upon each other once more in a rapid flurry of strikes.

I heard the palace guards behind me break into excited muttering as they started to make bets on the outcome of the fight, obviously assuming I was too far away to hear them despite the citrus-laden air being so still tonight.

"Twenty-five silver on Jiron-"

"My money's on the Comandante. He trained him, after all-"

"Twenty. Arrogant prick that he is-"

There were darker murmurings mixed in there too, growing bolder as they spurred each other on.

"Personally, I wouldn't give a shit if they finished each other off-"

"The prince wouldn't be happy-"

"He'll be fine. He's got his Mazekhstani whore-"

"You reckon he-"

"Oh, for sure-"

"I'd have that mouth of his warming my cock all night-"

"Gotta be satisfying, sticking it to Mazekhstam so literally-"

Mat hummed in annoyance beside me.

"I'll be right back," he muttered, and then disappeared from my side.

"What the fuck did you just say?" I heard him snap distantly behind me, but my mind was still on the shit the Comandante had just pulled with Elías and Diego.

Think, Ren. You're running out of time! Once Moreno has El, he'll learn everything. Think!

There was more laughter and taunts from the guards behind me, although it was now aimed directly at Mathias instead of about him.

"*Fuck* is about right, boy."

"Reckon the prince will let us all have a go with you when he gets bored?"

"Come, *puta*, I'll show you a good time."

"Your Highness," Ademar muttered to me, his posture stiffening, but I shook my head. Mathias went poking at ants' nests on a daily basis, and he could more than handle the teasing. We'd all hear the verbal lashing he'd be delivering upon them shortly.

"Something *you'd* like to say to me, Diego?" Mat demanded.

"Not say to you, no. But there's certainly a lot I'd like to *do*," I heard Diego drawl, his tone steeped in crude implication. The others laughed and renewed their uninventive descriptions of how they envisioned Mat and I spent our time.

There was a shout, followed by a low, appreciative whistle, and more laughter. A smack of flesh on flesh. And then the unmistakeable sound of my boy's face being beaten in, something I'd heard far too many Dios-damned times.

I closed my eyes.

For fuck's sake, Mat, could you not last a week *without getting into a Blessed fight?*

Did he not realise I had enough problems already? Did he *always* have to add to them?

"You little bitch," Diego hissed, and I quirked an interested eye open as I listened to his grunts mixed in with Mathias' own hisses of pain.

Oh, I take it back. You brilliant, glorious man.

I fought down my smile and forced myself to wait a few further seconds to make sure their fight was well and truly underway before spinning on my heel.

"Get them up!" I spat, taking in Mathias and Diego rolling on the ground, one of the guard's hands wrapped around Mat's slender neck while the other sank punches into his stomach. Then Mat did something clever and got Diego's arm up and twisted behind his back, causing the man to briefly cry out before they were yanked apart, bleeding and spitting.

Elías pulled Mathias to his feet, pinning his arms at his sides even as the northerner tried to continue the fight. A few feet away, two of Diego's friends did the same to him.

"Your Highness?" Moreno and Jiron appeared on either side of me, breathing heavily with raw steel in their hands. And most importantly, no longer trying to kill each other. I tallied up another one I owed to Mat.

"It appears your man is incapable of following a simple order," I said coldly, levelling a glare on Diego.

He had the decency to fall still, his eyes flickering between me and the Comandante.

"My prince," Moreno began, and I held up a hand.

"I appreciate you had my interests at heart, Comandante, but surely you cannot expect me to tolerate disobedience from those who would be my personal guard? I gave strict instruction to everyone here not to engage in brawling, did I not?"

"You did," Ademar supplied helpfully, when no one else seemed inclined to answer.

I raised an eyebrow. "And what do I find my newly christened guard *Diego* doing within minutes of those same orders?"

Moreno set his jaw. "Of course, Your Highness. We will find someone else who is more suitable for-"

"Considering I just watched Diego soundly thrash each of your men within a grand total of ten minutes," I interrupted, "I can't imagine a single one of them will be *suitable*."

The Comandante visibly swallowed as he realised he'd overplayed his hand with that little spectacle.

"Elías," I said. "You'll remain by my side in the absence of a better candidate. Jiron will work with you on your footwork."

"Very good, my prince." El's bland expression showed no indication he held any feelings either way. I glanced down to the man he held in his arms, who looked equally unaffected by his victory over the military leader at my side.

Oh Nat, I could kiss you. Soon.

"Well?" I demanded of the men restraining Diego. "Did I not also explain what would happen if I was disobeyed?"

"I believe you were quite explicit," Ad chimed in, clearly enjoying himself far too much now his brother's fate had been avoided. "Chained to a cell wall for the night, was it not, Your Highness?"

Diego shot a dirty look at him, and then lowered his head.

"I apologise, my prince," he muttered.

"That's awfully kind of you," I said. "Does it look like I give a fuck?"

Diego wet his lips but wisely didn't say anything further.

"He started it," sneered one of the palace guards at his side as he pointed an accusing finger at Mat. "Shouldn't he be punished too?"

Moreno shifted at my side, clearly sensing an opening.

"Your Highness, you did give the order to all present. If you're not prepared to-"

"Did I say otherwise?" I demanded, ignoring him. "Get them both out of my sight before I write the rest of you up for disobedience as well."

Mat's impassive gaze caught mine, and then Elías tugged at his arm and hauled him away.

*

Chapter Twenty

Mat

I wasn't asleep, not exactly. How could one sleep standing up, wet slime dripping down their back from the wall they were held against, and arms aching from being chained above their head for the last several hours? Add in the continuous angry mutterings of Diego from the cell next to mine and you had several decent reasons why sleep wasn't happening for me tonight.

But I *was* in a state of unawareness, a kind of half-doze where both the pain and Diego's whingeing were thankfully muted, when I heard the noise.

In that dull dead-of-night haze, I assumed it was just Luis, who had stayed with us since we'd first been strung up down here by some very pissed off prison guards. Even if he'd remained standing near the corridor steps where I couldn't see him from my position against the wall, I appreciated his presence. Ren had ordered the cell guards flogged after what happened to me last time I was kept in here, and I suspected from their hateful expressions and more than one rough shove as they'd forced my wrists into the grimy manacles hanging from the cell wall that they blamed me for that.

But considering that when he'd arrived down here on our heels, Luis had gleefully ordered me into this particular cell *"on His Highness' orders"* – and it was not lost on me that the pleasant surroundings I now found myself in were those of the same fucking cell I'd spent my first two weeks in Quareh occupying – I wasn't going to be thanking the prince for sending him. Ren's perverse sense of humour often left a lot to be desired, and being locked in the same dank space as I'd almost died in before, only this time with decidedly less freedom, was not nearly as amusing to me as he clearly found it.

I frowned at the shadow that I could make out just beyond the bars of the cell as it split into two, its larger self moving to the left and taking on Luis' hulking silhouette even as the smaller one pushed open my cell door and slipped inside.

"You right, Mathias, Diego?" Luis asked loudly, the boom of his voice covering up any squeal of hinges.

"I'd be more *right* if that bitch healer had fixed up my Dios-damned wrists like I told her to," Diego snapped.

Unable to see him, I instead glared at the wall separating us. Starling had been by earlier to heal the injuries from our fight, but she'd informed Diego in no uncertain terms that the prince's orders hadn't extended to protecting his delicate little wrists from the chafing of the manacles that bound us. She'd also, when it was my turn, quietly offered to do just that, but I hadn't been about to let her incur Ren's wrath.

Luis huffed out a non-answer and passed by my cell again, returning to his unseen spot near the stairs. But I was busy watching the Ren-shaped darkness as it prowled closer and formed into a broad grin and a cascade of dark hair falling over one shoulder.

His lips met mine and I sank into the taste of him, that summery scent of citrus that felt so out of place down here among the damp filth of rats and mould.

"I've missed you," Ren breathed, dragging his mouth up to my ear. "I told you that you were mine tonight, and then you went and got yourself locked up. If I were less irresistible, I might think you were avoiding me."

I shrugged out of habit, and the chains binding my hands rattled with the movement. Our eyes both flickered upwards at the noise, and I froze.

"I find it interesting," Ren mused quietly, "that Diego hadn't joined in with the others' taunts until you invited him to do so. And yet *he* was the one whose face met your fist?"

"Oh no," I whispered back. "I must have misheard."

"Conveniently for me and Elías."

I grinned into the darkness, matching his own mischievous smile. I liked El: the smooth-shaven man was far gentler in temperament than his brother, and while he didn't let me get away with shit any more than any of the others did, he'd never made it personal. It has been the least I could do for him. "I have no idea what you're talking about."

"You're a clever fool, Mat."

I pulled a face. "Not according to your palace guards."

Ren stilled against me. "I heard them."

"Did you?"

"They called you my whore," Ren murmured, his lips tracing the shell of my ear and sending shivers through me. "Don't listen to them. We both know the truth."

"That I'm not?" I gritted out, knowing that Ren never spoke plainly. I needed him to say it.

His hand pressed over my mouth to stifle the gasp that he drew from me as he bit down on where my neck met my shoulder. "That I'm *yours*, Nathanael."

His other hand deftly untied my trousers and freed my cock, already hard from both his touch and his words.

"*Mi amor*. Let me show you?"

I glanced over his shoulder, but Luis was nowhere to be seen. This was crazy and foolish and probably highly unhygienic considering where we were, yet my pulse was pounding and I wanted him as badly as I had that night at the Martinez estate, if not more. I didn't know how the prince was here or what he'd done to distract the cell guards to get past them, but if this was the *why*, I only had one answer for him.

Damn this impossible man and the way he set my heart alight and my soul demanding.

I nodded against his hand.

Ren's fingers delicately fondled my length, fingertips dancing over the heated skin and down to my balls, but by the Blessed, this was neither the time nor the place to be *gentle*. I wanted to touch him, to grab him, to force him to give me *more*.

Unable to speak, I tossed my head as I tried to free my mouth or at least catch his eye, but Ren held firmly onto my face, too focused on delivering frustratingly tender sensations to my cock to look up.

I nipped my teeth at the skin of his palm, unable to bite him properly, but finally – *finally* – getting his attention.

He pulled his hand free and cocked his head in a silent question.

"Aren't you going to let me out of these?" I hissed, lifting my chin towards the chains that still bound me to the wall.

Ren snickered. His eyes were bright and full of mischief. "Hah. *No.*"

He wrapped his hand more securely around me and started to work me over, the skilful swipes of his thumb over the head driving all rational thought from my mind. Distantly, I heard myself groan.

"What the fuck are you doing in there?"

"Shut up, Diego," I snarled back, annoyed at the man's irritating voice ruining this blissful moment.

He let out a low chuckle, nasty and dark. "You really are gagging for it, aren't you, Lord Grachyov? The men were right. What a desperate fucking whore you are, unable to take even one night without your ass full."

But his crude words scattered harmlessly around me, drowned out by the sensation of Ren's rough kisses along my jaw, his hand still adeptly sliding up and down my cock and bringing it to attention with what it needed more surely than if it had been my own touch. Fuck, this man knew me better than I knew myself, and *just like that, more, more-*

"Shush, Mat," the prince whispered, smiling against my mouth, and I could hear the faint laughter in his voice. "You're going to get us caught."

And how the fuck did he expect me to stay quiet when he was doing shit like *that*?

Ren tugged at the hem of my shirt from where it trailed around my hips and swiped it across the tip of my leaking cock, the gentle caress making me shiver. Then he gathered the folds of fabric as he carefully lifted it up over my chest, hooking his thumbs under the shirt's collar to form a thick strip of material that he'd forced between my teeth before I realised his intention.

The shirt was partly wet from the mess he'd already made below, yet that gave me no relief from how the rough fabric chafed against the seam of my lips as he pressed it in further.

But then Ren dropped to his knees on the putrid floor, gave me a filthy look through the gloom, and I was suddenly glad of the makeshift gag stealing my moans as his tongue flicked out to lick beads of precum from the sensitive crown of my cock before taking me deeper in that warm, wicked mouth of his. I blinked down at the mass of dark hair below me, turned on like never before and so achingly hard for this man.

Fuck, the sight of him like that, on his knees and eager to please? Haughty, arrogant Ren, dirtying himself in the muck for *me?*

My chains rattled as his tongue licked shameless lines of pleasure down me. Ren's hands were pressed to my thighs in an effort to hold me still, although with what he was doing to me, that was like trying to stop the snow from falling in the winter.

I'd never been brought to the edge so quickly, so cleverly, and for it to be a man's mouth that was doing this to me made my head swim. My breathing through the gag was ragged, air seeming inconsequential in comparison to the pleasure his hot tongue was ruthlessly pulling out of me.

I ached to touch him, but my wrists were held firmly by the manacles far above my head. All I could do was groan as he dipped his head further, taking me right to the back of his throat without any hesitation or choking, and *yes, that was it, like that, so close, so close-*

The prince pulled back and stood up, tilting his head to watch me. His eyes were sparkling with elation, his lips red and swollen. It was an obscene, filthy image, and I was terrified at its intensity; terrified at how much it made my heart race and my groin throb with heat.

And then he took a step backwards, away from me.

I spat out the mouthful of my shirt. "What are you doing?"

"Payback for you interrupting us yesterday," Ren said quietly as he leaned in, and I could see the white flash of teeth in the darkness that told me the prick was smirking. *Me* interrupting us? It had been his fucking guards, and he knew it. "I told you I wasn't going to let you come tonight."

I stared at him. "No, you didn't!"

Ren shrugged, resting his cheek against mine so he could whisper his response in my ear. "Maybe it was when you were busy *not being at my side*, Mat, because you were having your ass dragged off here for disobeying my orders."

He ran a teasing fingernail up my far-too-ready cock. The layer of saliva on it made it extra sensitive to the night air.

"*Svoloch*," I hissed, shuddering, and Ren pressed his lips to mine. I tasted myself on his tongue as he forced it inside my mouth, hungry and unstoppable, and I met his eagerness with my own. The prince swallowed my moans as I did his, the vibrations echoing through us where we were joined.

"The image of you like this, Mat," Ren whispered when he eventually pulled away from the kiss, his pupils fully dilated as he raked his hungry gaze down me. "I'm not sure I'll make it all the way back to my bedchamber. Maybe I'll stop in a dark corner somewhere and jerk off to the thought of you all chained up and aching for me, yet unable to do a damn thing about it."

He moved away, depriving me of both his warmth and touch. I made a desperate, instinctual noise, and he smirked, his eyes flicking up to where my wrists were restrained as if to remind me of how helpless I was to stop him leaving.

"I want you," I breathed desperately, before I could remember what a terrible fucking idea it was to show weakness in front of Renato Aratorre. All I knew was that the thought of my cock standing hard and desperate without even being able to touch myself to bring it relief, made my head spin and my mouth utter words I never thought I would be brought low enough to say.

Ren's lips pressed together as if he was fighting a laugh.

"What was that, Mathias? I didn't quite catch it."

I repeated the plea through gritted teeth as my cock jerked against my stomach, simultaneously rebelling against and craving the humiliating submission he was drawing from me. But Ren just gave a mock frown, shaking his head as his eyes danced with amusement.

"Sorry, I'm still not getting it," he breathed. "Perhaps we can speak in the morning?"

He turned away, and I let out a whimper. A fucking whimper, loud enough for Diego to hear judging from the lascivious chuckle that erupted from my left.

My mind scratched at the remnants of my pride, pleading for me to hold firm against the prince's cruelty, but my body was louder. I was *done*. I'd say, do, *be* whatever he wanted, as long as he didn't leave me like this, aching and craving his touch so badly that it hurt.

"*Please*, Ren," I panted quietly. The bastard would finish what he'd started.

He paused, and looked back at me.

"I lied about the not coming thing," the prince said thoughtfully. "But I *did* say I'd have you begging before sunrise, did I not?"

Oh, fuck.

"And seeing as you do it so beautifully…"

He knelt and took me into his mouth again, and I forgot that there was nothing to keep me quiet as the sheer pleasure of that silver tongue took possession of me once more.

"Oh, don't fucking stop on my account," Diego said in disgust, yet slightly breathlessly, as if he'd very much prefer that I didn't stop. "I don't want to have to listen to you getting off as you imagine bending over for the prince's cock."

The prince in question lifted an amused eyebrow at that remark.

I closed my eyes and tried to ignore Diego's taunts as Ren's skilled mouth worked to bring me to ruin, finding that task infinitely easier when he moved his hands from my legs to my balls, caressing and tugging in a way that spiralled bliss through me.

And then slicked-up fingers danced further backwards, circling my hole. Where the fuck had the oil come from? I was clearly out of touch with any sense of time or logic, because Ren was taking me apart piece by piece with every touch and flick of his tongue.

I heaved out a harsh, desperate breath. "More."

The prince pulled his mouth off me, glanced up, and mouthed *are you sure?*

That stupid, warm feeling spread through me again. The one that wasn't lust but *affection*, and which I tried to bite down on whenever I felt it get its hooks in me. We were messing around, not falling in Blessed love, but neither my head nor my cock had received that message because both were feeling exceedingly happy about this.

I nodded at him, lost to the euphoria. We were in the foulest depths of the palace, and there were better places than the damn prison cells to experience so many of my firsts, but I didn't care. As long as they were with *Ren*, I didn't fucking care.

I felt daring and wild and so unlike Nathanael Velichkov at this moment that it was unreal.

But I didn't have to be him, not here. Here I could be Mathias, not a northern prince but just a man caught up in circumstances where what Ren was about to do to me was not only a possibility, but a desperate and growing need I could never admit to anyone else. A lie, a fantasy, and a life that wasn't mine.

Ren rose to his feet, kissing my neck but keeping his hands where they were. He exhaled as he pressed a slick finger inside me, pushing through the first ring of my body. I tensed at the initial burn, the foreign feeling of intrusion that my muscles reflexively tried to expel, but the prince didn't let up as he patiently eased his way inside.

And *fuck me,* when the pain gave way to something so unexpectedly pleasurable that I nearly howled?

One knuckle, then two, and the whispered praise that dripped from Ren's mouth as he told me how good I felt stretched around him before he dropped back down to take me into his mouth for a third time was something I was sure would stay with me for the rest of my Blessed life.

The dual sensations of pleasure tugged me in two directions, overwhelming in their intensity. Fuck, this was *exquisite.*

His finger thrust against something inside me that stole all thoughts from my head, pure ecstasy slamming through my body. He did it again and again, somehow hitting that same spot each time, and the overwhelming pleasure was almost too much.

Heat crested in my head and groin, and I bit down on my lip as I came harder than I ever had in my life, clenching around Ren's fingers. Riding the high, I tasted blood as I returned to myself.

"So that's what does it for you," Diego muttered, and I blinked, wondering what the fuck the guard was on about and whether he'd been talking that entire time.

My breathing started to slow as Ren slowly lapped up my seed from my satiated cock, eyes fixed on mine and a pleased smirk twisted across his lips. A lock of hair had fallen over the prince's face and I wanted more than anything to be able to tuck it behind his ear.

"Wait," Diego suddenly snapped, sounding irritated. "Aren't you shackled? I am. Why am I shackled and you're not-"

"Yes, I'm fucking shackled!" I shook the manacles for emphasis, the chains rattling against the metal ring in the wall.

"Then how did you..."

I looked down at the second prince of Quareh, still on his knees as he busied himself with tucking me away.

"Mind your own business, Diego," I drawled, too content to give a fuck about what he might think of me.

Ren stood, licked the blood from my lip, and disappeared back into the darkness with a broad, self-satisfied smile.

*

Chapter Twenty-One

Ren

A tired and scowling Mathias had been brought to my rooms by Luis this morning when his and Diego's punishment had been deemed to have run its course, and as much as his dishevelled, slightly bloodied look was doing it for me, I couldn't begrudge him when he headed straight for the bathing room. I *could* begrudge my lack of invitation, however, and had to satisfy myself with my imagination as I sighed my way through reading dozens of scout reports that suggested I was no closer to saving my people than the day we'd captured Mat.

We had always believed Mazekhstam's taking of Algejón to have been the final desperate act of its dying king, who wished to realise his dream of expansion without worrying about the consequences of such aggression. Powerful people who know their days are numbered will often do reckless things they would not have otherwise considered in an effort to either wreak havoc or secure their legacy on the continent they are leaving behind, and his knowledge of his failing health had made King Oleg Panarin a formidable foe. But with the monarch now comatose despite the best efforts of his healers, it was Oleg's daughter left with the clean-up. Astrid Panarina, Regent of Mazekhstam, had been the unknown equation in all of this.

As a new ruler, would it be better for her to continue to hold the occupied city and show her strength rivalled her father's, or cede it back to Quareh to indicate her reign would be a peaceful one? What would the Mazekhstani people view more favourably?

We now had our answer.

Famine and disease reported as widespread across the city without sign of relief, one coded slip of parchment proclaimed in angry capital letters.

Missing trader found executed in Algejón following allegations of spycraft. Maz. have introduced stricter entry protocols.

Twenty-six Quarehian bodies strung up outside the south gates, another report read in hastily scrawled handwriting. *Lord and Lady Jiménez confirmed among the deceased.*

Fuck. I still remembered Imelda Jiménez's fifteenth birthday party being held at *la Cortina* last year, just before her marriage. I *particularly* remembered walking in on her and Camila kissing in the music room. My servant hadn't been able to look me in the eye for weeks.

"Ren?"

Mat was at my back, a hand on my shoulder as he murmured my name. The doors to my chambers were wide open as I was working, not resting, but for the moment, we were alone.

I heaved out a breath. "*Buenos días,* Nathanael."

"Is it?" he asked, tugging the parchment from my hand. He wouldn't be able to decipher the message so I let him take it, even if he was being a nosy bastard. "What's the bad news?"

I forced a smile. "Nothing. Just the same boring shit as usual."

Mathias clearly wasn't buying it.

"Right," he said. "Which is why you're gripping the desk so hard you're leaving grooves in the wood."

I glanced down at my left hand and unclenched it, scowling at the crescent moon marks made by my fingernails.

"Oh *that* bad news," I said airily. "My favourite riding crop broke last month and I'm having trouble finding a replacement."

His eyebrows creased into a confused frown. "I'm sure the stablemaster would have plenty spare, would he not? Do any of your horses even require a crop?"

"I didn't say I needed it for a *horse*, Mathias."

His mouth snapped shut and he glared at me, pink flushing through his cheeks. "I thought you were actually upset, you asshole."

"Nope. I just wanted your delicious self to make its way over here," I said, winking at him as I took back the missive.

"Oh. You are."

"I'm what?"

"Upset."

I blew out an annoyed breath. "Am I incapable of distracting you anymore? Do I need to make my comments even more inappropriate?"

Mathias settled himself on my desk, carelessly seating his ass on the scraps of loose parchment that littered its surface. He was wearing a fresh shirt, and I wondered if it had been El's way of saying thanks for what he'd done.

"I'm not sure you can be more inappropriate."

"That's where you're hopelessly wrong," I told him. "How about if I-"

"*Ren,*" Mat said in a low voice, ducking his chin to catch my eye. "Tell me what's bothering you."

"Tell *me* something first," I asked. "Astrid. What's she like?"

He gave a happy, fond smile. "Amazing."

Real fucking helpful.

"Clever," he added wistfully. "Kind."

Yeah, so kind that she just executed a sixteen-year-old girl along with twenty-five of my other citizens, I thought. But he didn't need to hear that, not when he thought the entire continent revolved around that woman.

"Would you say she was ever…reckless? Impulsive?"

Mat shook his head. "Not at all. Astrid is the most patient and considered person I've ever met. She does nothing without six reasons behind it."

"I was afraid you'd say that. More afraid you'd say something preposterous like 'amazing', though. Oh. Wait."

He scowled. "She *is* amazing."

"I heard you the first time, Nat. I do hope you extol my virtues in my absence just as vigorously."

"Not when you put such ridiculous innuendo on words like *vigorously,*" he said with a sigh, and I chose to take that as a *hell fucking yes, I do.*

I ran a hand up his leg and settled it on his knee, reassured by his closeness, his warmth, the giddy high of being able to touch him. It helped to ease the swirling pit of messy dread gathering in my stomach.

"Over two dozen of my people were just killed and displayed outside

Algejón."

Mathias hissed in a breath, tensing under my touch. "Shit."

"Yeah."

We sat quietly for a moment, taking that in. Then he frowned and shook his head. "But you can't believe *Astrid* had anything to do with that?"

I stayed silent. I didn't want to argue with him – for once – but the execution of so many foreigners, including nobles, was not something done lightly, not when it could…perhaps *would,* lead to war. If it had been the actions of a renegade lord or soldier, my father would have already been showered in contrition from Mazekhstam's regent. The fact that the bodies had been left facing Quareh was a threat so unsubtle it hardly needed to be acknowledged.

"What about Commander Grachyov?" Mat asked in a quiet voice, his blue-grey eyes flickering with wariness as he voiced the accusation.

"I'm amazed it took you so long to ask. Your so-called father's deadline for responding to your ransom was two days ago."

His expression turned to surprise. Naww, what was that saying about time flying when you were having fun?

"And…"

I cocked my head. "And?"

"You know perfectly well what I'm asking."

"And yet you're *not* asking."

Considering Mathias still had all of his limbs intact, I thought the answer fairly obvious, but I wasn't above teasing him. Grachyov's man – not his son this time, unfortunately – had arrived at *la Cortina* with only a few hours to spare on the king's deadline, and had been sent off again the same night with our response. The best that could be said was that negotiations were *progressing,* but based on what I now knew about Nathanael's identity, it worried me that Mazekhstam wasn't trying harder to get him back. Clearly Grachyov was a smoother player than we'd given him credit for, as he seemed determined to get the best deal for his people even if it meant leaving Mat in Quarehian hands a little while longer.

"I'm surprised you don't get punched in the face more often," Mathias said to me sourly, looking very much like he wished to remedy that.

I stretched. "A perk of being a prince. An *actual* one," I added, just to rile him, and he knocked a pile of papers off my desk with a movement so casual that if it were anyone else, I might have thought it an accident.

I levelled a look at him. "Now you're just being a brat."

Movement caught my eye and I looked over to find Jiron rising from a bow at the doorway.

"Your Highness," he murmured as he crossed the room towards us and glanced down at the scraps of parchment strewn at his feet. "Would you like your morning report?"

"A moment," I said. I returned my gaze to my little wildcat, who would soon be discovering that my going down on him last night did not at all mean I'd tolerate his impertinence today. "Nathanael Velichkov is about to find himself on his hands and knees as he works to fix the mess he just made."

Jiron made a choking noise, yet Mat just gave me a lazy, insolent smile that made my blood heat. I held his stare, refusing to blink first, and tightened my grip on his knee.

My guard moved in the corner of my eye but I didn't spare him a glance, too intent on dominating the beautiful, proud fucker perched languidly on my desk.

I lowered my voice. "*Pick. Them. Up.* Or I'll make you-"

Mat held up a hand to interrupt me.

I stared at him, unable to believe his Blessed nerve. By Dios, I'd have him collecting the papers with his fucking *teeth*, and he'd be lucky if I didn't-

He turned his head and his face split into a broad smile.

"*Thank you*, Jiron," Mathias said with exaggerated enthusiasm, reaching out to take the carefully gathered pile of parchment my guard was holding out. "Your thoughtful anticipation of the prince's needs is quite admirable. Just *imagine* if he'd had to clean these up himself!"

Jiron gave him a distracted nod, and then glanced at me hopefully. "You were saying something about-"

"You've lost the privilege of getting to watch," I drawled, amused at his eagerness. "Report."

Jiron squared his shoulders and delivered it with his usual professionalism as I kept hold of my northerner, ready to teach him his lesson as soon as the guard left.

But Mathias wasn't stupid. He made sure to pull free of my grasp before Jiron was done, slipping from the desk despite my efforts to hold him still, and wandering over to the bookcase. I tried to focus on the names of the arrivals and departures from the palace, I really did, but even Jiron's sexy voice couldn't make that shit interesting, especially not when Mat leaned down to pull a book from a lower shelf and I was entreated to the mouth-watering sight of how his borrowed trousers stretched around that perfect ass.

"Your Highness?"

"Mmm," I murmured, tilting my head to get a better view. "I *know*."

Jiron let out a low laugh and reluctantly, I dragged my eyes back to his.

"You mentioned something about...Gerald?"

"Herald, my prince. The palace requires a new herald."

I waved a hand. "If Valentinus is going to let a little thing like death stop him from doing his job, then he's not as tough as I always gave him credit for."

"Perhaps death wouldn't," Mat commented, heading over to his usual armchair. I'd missed him in it last night. I'd missed him in my bed more, and never mind that he'd only ever spent one night there, because the silk sheets suited his ivory skin and ash-brown hair far too much. "But I expect being in six different pieces in Starling's surgery might have some impact."

"Inconvenient of him," I said. "Jiron, you have a list of candidates for me?"

"I do, Your Highness. There are three men waiting for your assessment in the throne room."

"I'll meet with them befor-"

"Seriously?" Mat asked, that scornful tone of his instantly raising my defences.

I set my jaw and leant back in my chair. "I'll be taking citizen appearances later this morning, Mat. Tell me you aren't going to interrupt me like that in public, *again*, or Dios help me, I will have you gagged for the duration of the session."

Mathias rolled his eyes, clearly not believing I was serious. That was his mistake.

"It's funny you think I'm joking."

"Jiron doesn't count as *in public*," he said dismissively.

"No, but the candidates for the role of herald will. So say what you have to say about them before we leave this room," I ordered.

Mat raised an eyebrow, unfazed. "What about Valentinus' apprentice? She knows the job, and it seemed to me like she was always doing twice as much work as him. Why can't Clementina be your herald?"

I exchanged a despairing glance with Jiron.

Fuck, Mathias was always so…*urgh*, Mathias-like.

"She…" I trailed off, and when he clearly didn't get the issue, I said it again. "*She*, Mat!"

He gave me a disgusted look and then lifted the book in front of his face as if to save himself from having to look at me.

"I'm not being cruel," I protested, spurred by the irrational need to justify myself to him. I didn't like how ending up on the wrong side of his moral compass made me feel, not when he could do *self-righteously judgmental* like no one else. "I'm being practical. Clementina is extremely capable, and I have no doubt she could handle the responsibilities."

Mat lowered the book so I could see how his eyebrows were creased into a frown. "*But?*"

"But, as a female, no one will listen to her," I explained. "And that's one thing for the announcements, because they can either accept they've been introduced to court or they can fuck off, but *la Cortina's* herald is also responsible for ensuring my decrees are implemented. And how do you think a *male* lord is going to react when a woman tells him he has to increase his taxes to the crown, or serve in the army, or forfeit a portion of his land?"

"And whose fault is that, Quarehian?"

I sighed and sent a quick prayer to Dios to save me from pesky northerners who were idiotic enough to believe He would condemn them merely for who they took to bed, and yet complained about following *centuries* of tradition and laws. And then I further prayed that there was only one such northerner in Riehse Eshan, because I wasn't sure I could survive a second.

"I'll consider it," I conceded, trying to ignore the way my heart soared at the soft smile he gave me in return. Why did I constantly feel the need to please him? Why did I question every decision I made on the basis of whether Mathias would approve of it?

Fuck me, I was a *prince*.

But in his company, that didn't mean shit. He'd never treated me as a royal, and he'd certainly never demanded the same, even after I discovered his true identity. For a deceitful little wretch, he was remarkably *genuine* in his interactions. If he liked you, respected you, you got his smiles and good humour. If you were a wife-beating prick like Martinez, you saw Mathias' darker side.

And if you were me…well. I suppose that depended on the day.

*

Chapter Twenty-Two

Mat

"I'm going to lick you, and I'm going to taste you, and you can be damn sure I'm going to enjoy every delicious inch of you," Ren promised, and I ran a hand down my face.

"*Really?*"

"Oh, you can count on it, Nat," he purred, his eyes lit up with gleeful anticipation. "I've been waiting a long time for this."

"Two hours," I reminded him. "You've only been waiting two hours. And do you have to make it sound so filthy?"

He glanced up and winked at me, and then returned to the current object of his affections: the glistening dessert perched on the desk before him. He'd had *cravings* earlier this morning, sending an order down to the kitchen for them to bake him orange and almond flan, and now it quivered under Ren's eager gaze as if his salacious words were having as much of an impact on the food as they did me.

"Shouldn't that have been tasted first?" I asked, frowning at the unblemished smoothness of the flan, all prettied up on the plate for its prince.

"I had Luis watch the staff make it from scratch. I'm not eating flan that has already had a mouthful taken from it," he said scornfully. "No one gets to defile my dessert but me. This baby's virginity is all *mine.*"

I sucked in a sudden breath, my hands rushing to my head. As the prince's fork descended towards the pristine surface, I cried out to stop him.

"Ren, don't! It'll kill you!"

He froze, staring at me. "Luis!"

The guard came rushing into the room just as I managed to straighten in my armchair. Rubbing at my temples, I hobbled over to where Ren was seated at his desk. He'd been working all morning while I lounged in my usual armchair, reading.

Now, his eyes were wide and fearful, mirroring my own expression.

"Luis, when I told you to watch the kitchen staff carefully," Ren hissed, "I didn't mean for the fucking recipe. I was hoping you might have noticed someone poisoning my Blessed food!"

"Your Highness, I didn't see-"

"Luckily, Mathias did all the Seeing for you." Ren threw down his fork in disgust, eyeing the flan suspiciously. "Get me the names of everyone who-"

He stared in open-mouthed disbelief as I grabbed the fork, sank it into the soft dessert, and swallowed down the resulting mouthful.

"Huh," I said, licking the back of the fork for good measure. "That *is* delicious."

"I am going to murder you," promised Ren with absolute sincerity in his brown eyes, which were now fixed on me in deadly threat. "Luis, hold him still while I cut out his lying northern tongue."

I was laughing too hard to avoid the guard grabbing my arm, but I did have the presence of mind to bring the plate with me.

"One more step, Ren, and the rest of your precious orange flan ends up on the floor," I teased, tilting the plate dangerously. "Feel like waiting another two hours for the next batch?"

The prince stilled, raising his ring-adorned hands in what seemed to be surrender, but if it was, he wasn't very good at it. His hands were barely lifted above his hips, and he waved them carelessly. *"Ten compasión, por favor?"*

I snorted. If Ren thought I would show him an ounce of the mercy he'd just requested after what he'd done to me last night, he'd clearly underestimated how much I wished to repay his cruelty. Making me *beg*, for fuck's sake?

"Sorry, I'm still not getting it," I mocked, echoing his words from the cells. *"Perhaps we can speak in the morning?"*

Ren's eyes flashed with amusement as he realised my intentions for revenge.

"Luis, I'm afraid I'm going to have to deal with Mathias on my own," the prince said with feigned sadness, shaking his head at me. "You may leave. But keep the doors open."

I frowned at him as Luis released my arm and obliged his prince.

"Doors open? Do you want your guards to hear your cries of anguish as I finish off your dessert in front of you?"

"No," Ren said, taking a step closer towards me. I tilted the plate further in warning. "But I do want them to hear *yours* as you get what's coming to you, *mi cielo*."

He moved even closer, and I shrugged. He'd had his chance.

I tipped the plate vertically, and we both watched – me in delight, him in horror – as the flan slid off and splattered onto the floorboards between two of the huge rugs that covered the bedchamber floor. I wasn't a complete asshole; I knew it wouldn't be Ren cleaning it up, but his servants.

"A terrible shame," I commented lightly, tossing the empty plate back onto his desk as I grinned down at the mess. "But I suppose it was *defiled*."

"No more than you will be, my insolent Temarian," Ren purred, and I looked up in alarm to find him at my side, reaching for me. I raised my hands to defend myself, but it was too late. He kicked out at the back of my knees and sent me to the floor.

"This was *my* revenge," I protested, and he just laughed, dropping his weight down onto me.

"Now it's mine."

I tried to glance towards the doors to check if anyone was watching, but he was pressing down against the back of my neck to hold me in place. "Ren, we can't-"

"I don't like that word," the prince breathed.

"We?"

"*'Can't'*, you asshole." He forced my head down further. "I simply *adore* the word 'we'."

I struggled against his grip as I finally realised what he intended.

"Don't you dare!"

Ren chuckled. "Just remember you started this."

I opened my mouth to retort, and that was when he managed to push me down the final few inches to the floor such that I got a faceful of squished flan instead.

"Hill velishus," I mumbled, and he let go.

"What was that?"

"Still delicious," I repeated, and pounced on him, rubbing my cheek against his to make sure he got just as messy. The prince gave a surprised bark of laughter and then licked at my chin, his eyes sparking with amusement.

Ren was never more lively, more sharp, than when he was in conflict. Tested and challenged, it was the resistance that woke something in him and made him fight harder. Perhaps it was the dullness of having so many people bow and simper to him all day, or maybe it was just his contrary personality, but I loved how he thrived on the struggle, whether it was merely our bickering or a bigger challenge.

"Hmm. It tastes even *better* like this," he commented, rocking back onto his hands. "Perhaps I'll eat all of my food off you, Nathanael."

I wiped my mouth with the back of my hand. "That seems impractical."

"With clothes on, I imagine it would be."

I choked, tried to turn it into a cough, and Ren rolled to his feet as he laughed some more.

"Your Highness?"

I turned my face away and scrubbed hastily at it with the sleeve of my shirt, scrambling upright. Ren didn't bother to even attempt to clean himself up, waving a careless hand at a curtseying Clementina to usher her in from the doorway. She politely averted her eyes from the mess on his face.

"You asked to see me, sire?"

"I did. Four days ago, I issued a decree regarding Lord de Leon. What was it? You may summarise."

"For him to calculate, on a basis per annum, the reasonable cost of maintaining the path through his northern pastures, plus the anticipated expenditure of an additional cattle gate where his lands meet those of Lord González," Clementina replied immediately, clearly not needing to *summarise* at all. "There were also two decrees reasonably ancillary to Lord de Leon, which was the order for all northern province nobles to add 2.75 percent to their taxation dues this quarter for contributions to Quareh's military efforts, and for a watching brief to be held over any northern movements that came to his attention."

I smirked at Ren. "She pass your test?"

Clementina's eyes flickered to mine, and she swallowed, something like distaste crossing her features. I stilled. The woman had never shown me hostility before, but clearly I'd done something to irritate her. Perhaps she didn't want the promotion after all, and I'd once again fucked up while trying to help someone.

"You're my new herald," Ren said without preamble, and at those words Clementina's face lit up with wonderous exhilaration, ruining my theory.

"Your Highness! I would be honoured! But I…"

"Will find it difficult," he acknowledged. "I know. I will appoint a male…assistant," the prince added, glancing at me, "to give effect to my orders where you may encounter resistance, at least initially. It's an unfortunate necessity, Mathias," he said, as I opened my mouth. "Patience."

Clementina curtsied again, tossing her braided hair over one shoulder. "I won't let you down, my prince." Her voice sounded almost breathless, her grin infectious in its veracity.

"Please do. In fact, please mess this up terribly and irrevocably," Ren said to her, waving a hand at me without looking in my direction. "Otherwise, this one will be absolutely insufferable."

I prepared to give the prince a hard smack across the face, consequences to the royal's reputation and my own bodily health be damned, but Ren's next words saved him from a broken nose.

"So I'm anticipating at least two solid days of irritating Mazekhstani smugness, because I know you'll handle it beautifully, señorita."

But Clementina didn't look happy when she glanced at me. "My lord," she said woodenly, and then Ren dismissed her.

"What the fuck did you do to that girl?" he asked incredulously once she was out of earshot.

"I have no idea," I said.

"Hmm. Maybe she's sick of your continuous scowl, Mat."

I hadn't been scowling. "Or maybe she's pissed at *you*, and is just projecting it onto me because people who criticise you have an unfortunate habit of having their backs laid open."

"And why should Clementina be upset with me?"

"Oh, you know," I said. "Same reason as any Quarehian woman would be upset with an Aratorre. A fostered culture of subjugation, misogyny and sexism springs to mind."

Ren groaned, and wandered into the bathing room. "Your judginess is too loud for this time of the day."

I followed him. *Where I go, you go* had just become a very convenient rule for me.

"Why the fuck does your country apprentice girls if they're never appointed to the trade?"

Ren ran water into the basin and didn't answer.

"What was the point of having Clementina learn from Valentinus if she was never going to take his place?" I pressed. "Why would you replace him with a man who doesn't have a clue? Did you *ever* intend for her to become herald, or is this whole apprentice nonsense just a tidy way to keep women looking busy and further in the shadows of men?"

The prince sighed, slumped forward, and dunked his entire head into the now-full basin.

I yanked him back out by his hair.

"For that matter, why have Sánchez on your staff when he does shit all and it's Starling who heals everyone?" I demanded, as water streamed down his face and neck. "She's a better doctor than he will ever be, and you know it. Why keep her under his heel?"

Ren promptly submerged himself again, filling his ears with water to escape the questions.

I gave him a good half a minute to indulge his overly dramatic self before I dropped my hand to the back of his head. I held him down for another few seconds as he thrashed under my grip.

"Fuck," he spluttered, when I finally let him up. "I should have realised that *you* would have no compunctions about drowning the second prince of Quareh."

"None at all," I agreed cheerily.

"Very well." Ren reached for a towel to dry his face. "As long as you know I'll be returning that favour one day, you prick."

I made a mental note to start putting the chair back under the bathing room door's handle whenever I took a bath. "About Starling-"

"What do you expect me to do? Dismiss Dr. Sánchez?"

"Yes."

"No."

"Ren."

The prince looked at the ceiling. "Nuh-uh, Nathanael. You can't puppy-dog-eyes me into this one."

"He's utterly useless," I protested. "Starling does all his work for him!"

"Sánchez was sent by my father to *la Cortina* at the same time as he exiled me and Moreno here," Ren said quietly, dragging his gaze back down to mine.

It wasn't a sign of favour to be sent from the king's side, so that meant…

"He's Iván's spy?" I guessed. Ren inclined his head. "Which you're not upset about, so…" I frowned as I worked it out. "You have an arrangement with him."

"I love watching you think, Mat," Ren murmured, kissing my forehead. "Yes. I don't bother him in his position, and in turn, he reports certain *issues* in my favour to the king. It's delicate of course, with Moreno able to correct anything too obviously false, but Sánchez speaks as to matters beyond the Comandante's reach."

"Such as?"

"Such as my mental state," he said, his tone turning momentarily bitter.

Oh.

"But where does that leave Star?" I asked, frustrated.

"The doctor's laxness in his role has allowed Estrella to forge somewhat of a reputation for herself within the palace." Ren flashed me a smile. "A rarity for a female. It's not the worst situation on the continent."

"Just shy of."

The prince groaned again. "*No,* Mat. Let's keep it to one revolutionary act a day, shall we? I'm already going to have my hands full with all the problems you've caused me with Clementina's appointment."

I considered that, tilting my head to take him in. Ren blinked at me, bemused, wet tendrils of dark hair framing his handsome face.

"And yet you still agreed to do it," I said quietly.

Ren fidgeted with the towel in his hand and then started to dry himself. "Don't go thinking you've tamed me to your northern nonsense," he muttered into its folds. "I just want to get you into bed, that's all."

But when he finally pulled the towel away, he wouldn't meet my eye.

*

Chapter Twenty-Three

Ren

I was pretty sure I'd read the same page three times, but it was difficult to care about my lack of productivity when its cause was looking so Blessed irresistible in his armchair, boots kicked off and legs folded up beneath him. Mat's brow was crinkled in concentration as he stared at his book, and he was chewing absently on a thumbnail. I wanted to chide him for the terrible habit, but the companionable silence that had grown between us in these last couple of hours was nice, damn it, and I could only imagine the scathing retort that would be sent my way if I ruined it with an admonishment.

So I returned to my piles of letters, lists and missives, sneaking another look at him a few seconds later because really, how could I not? Mathias was fucking addictive, and I didn't know what it was about him that made me just want to breathe him in like air, just that I *did*. His northern accent that clipped words when they should have rolled. His messy, short hair, and the pale skin that coloured so prettily at my teasing. His long limbs, his delicate wrists, his defined cheekbones. All of it added up to one sexy as fuck image, but Nathanael Velichkov was more than his looks. He was a presence, a sheer force of will that demanded your attention, and if I hadn't heard him bitching and moaning about his capture so often, I might have imagined he'd been deliberately sent here by Mazekhstam to utterly ruin me.

Because I was wrecked, a ship cast apart by the same brutal waves that I was praying would carry me safely to an unseen shore. Mathias had been in my life for such a short time, yet his impact on it was unfathomable and quite frankly, terrifying. How could one man, a northerner no less, turn me so completely upside down and inside out? I mean fuck, he believed homosexuality was a *sin*. Why was I listening to him about *anything*?

I should have sent him back to the cells as soon as Starling finished healing him, all those weeks ago. I'd been a fool to let him in, to feed my obsession, and now I was hooked more surely than a fish on a line. And apparently just as dumb, because we were alone here, and I wasn't doing anything to take advantage of it. With how beautifully he'd responded last night, I knew Mat would let me take things further between us, if I played it right. With just the right amount of pressure inflicted with my words and my hands, I could have him naked and stretched around my cock within minutes.

So why, for the love of Dios, *wasn't I doing that?*

Because I was terrified, damn it. If I pushed too far or too fast, I could scare him off, and I wasn't sure I could survive losing him. Mathias wasn't a horse to be broken in; he was an adorable little kitten – with admittedly sharp claws and teeth – who had to be coaxed closer one tiny step at a time.

I dragged my gaze from the man with reluctance, only to let it flicker back to him a second later as he gave a sudden inhale, frowning in confusion at his book.

"If it's page 35 that you're trying to figure out," I said, having recognised the cover, "then yes, it's anatomically impossible. But I'm happy to try a fourth time if you don't believe me."

Mat scowled at the book as if it had personally offended him.

"What are we doing?" he asked.

"I'm working out how much money can be spent on the Solstice celebrations without appearing overly ostentatious and frivolous and losing my people's trust, or appearing overly frugal and broke and losing my people's trust," I told him. "And you're reading porn."

"No, I meant...I'm not...I didn't know that was what the book was going to be about," he stammered, tossing it away from him like he seriously thought I was going to be judgmental about his reading habits when he'd found the thing on *my* fucking bookshelf.

I blew out an amused breath. "Of course," I said reasonably. "I can see how a novel entitled *The Duke and his Virgin Harem: Tales from the Pleasure Palace* could have been misleading about its genre."

"Ren. I meant what are *we* doing? Us, this thing, last night?"

"I don't know," I offered carefully, not meeting his eye. It seemed his thoughts had been running in a similar direction to mine. "Did you enjoy last night?"

I watched his throat move as he swallowed. "I-"

A WHISPER AND A BREATH

"Your Highness."

Oh, I was going to have those words *banned* if it meant I could avoid just one more inconvenient interruption.

"What?" I snapped, glancing up at the doors and spotting my room servant as she closed them behind her. Camila kept her head down when she rose from her curtsey; she'd experienced my moods before, and the girl was no fool.

"You're due to take citizen appearances shortly, my prince," she murmured, and I sighed, rising from my chair and holding out my arms so she could unlace my sleeves.

Mathias pretended to bury his nose in the book again, but it seemed his concentration skills were as good as mine had been earlier, and I caught him shamelessly eyefucking me as Camila pulled off my clothes and swapped them for something more appropriate for presenting at court. I grinned at him over her shoulder, and he gave me a shy smile back before promptly replacing it with the usual glare, as if disconcerted to find his mouth had moved in an upwards direction for once.

Camila was painstakingly ignoring him so I did the decent thing and gave him enough attention for the both of us, enjoying watching him watching me. At least, until his eyes slid downwards, and he scoffed.

"Careful," I warned. "There's a conveniently open window just there for people who mock their prince."

Mat's head turned in its direction. "So there is," he noted. "But if you have such a fondness for defenestration, may I recommend the first thing you throw out of the window is those boots?"

"Just because you northerners have the dress sense of a…well, a skinned bear," I said, giving the huge fur coat that hung off the back of his chair a nasty glare. He'd held onto it all the way back from Sesveko, and while it was too hot for him to wear this far south, I hadn't yet been successful in convincing him to dispose of it. I wasn't sure if it was because he was stubbornly clinging onto a sliver of his home, or just to piss me off, but I was nine-tenths sure it was the latter.

"Ren. Those boots go all the way up to your fucking knees. You look like a show pony."

I glanced down at them, at the polished blue leather and the delicate buckles that adorned their length, and sighed. Gesturing for Camila to step back, I obediently tugged the boots off and handed them to her with a reluctantly muttered command to swap them out for the cream shoes I'd purchased last spring.

"I'm just saving you from court-wide ridicule, Your Highness," Mathias drawled, and I gave him a forlorn nod.

"You're right. They were ridiculous." As his self-satisfied smirk grew, I moved to sit on the edge of the bed so I could let Camila dress me in the replacement boots. "Far too short, for one thing." I flopped down onto the blankets and lazily lifted a leg, rewarded by the sound of Mat muttering something uncomplimentary in Mazekhstani as he caught sight of what the servant held.

"For fuck's sake."

"You really should have learned by now, Mathias," I told him, when Camila had finished lacing up the mid-thigh cream boots. They took a few minutes to put on but they looked fucking gorgeous, all soft suede and laces. Most importantly, they were a good five inches higher than the blue ones.

"I really should," Mat agreed readily. His voice was amused, and something playful flickered in his eyes that made it suddenly hard for me to breathe. We stared at each other.

And then Camila moved towards the mess we'd made on the floorboards with the orange and almond flan – Dios preserve its sacred soul, for it was cruelly taken from this life too soon – and pulled a cloth from within the folds of her dress to clean it up. Mat hurriedly uncurled his legs and jumped up from his chair, tugging the cloth from her grip before she could bend down and making to do it himself.

Yet I couldn't even enjoy the sight of a Temarian prince on his hands and knees as he scrubbed my bedchamber floor, because the disdainful look Camila was giving him at her feet chilled my blood.

And when my northerner straightened and flashed her a tentative smile as if seeking confirmation on how well he'd performed the mundane task, her mouth just tightened into a sneer. An expression I'd never seen on the servant's face other than when we first met, in the shadow of her father and brothers as they beat her for running away from the husband to whom she'd been sold.

Mat's expression fell, and he glanced back down at the spotless floor with a frown, as if wondering what he'd done wrong. It was fucking heartbreaking.

I grabbed the girl by the chin, forcibly walking her backwards until I had her pressed flat against the wardrobe door.

"Camila," I said sweetly, making sure that my expression was the exact opposite of *sweet*. Her eyes flared with apprehension. "I thought you were over this."

"Ren," Mathias protested. "Let go of her."

I ignored him. I wasn't hurting her; I just wanted to make sure the servant couldn't look away from me, like she was currently attempting to do. I forced her head up, and her eyes shot to mine.

"Speak. What it is about him that you still seem to find so incredibly distasteful?"

"Nothing, Your Highn-"

"Don't you fucking lie to me."

Camila swallowed. I could feel the movement under my fingers, the delicate swell of her throat as it bobbed.

"Lady Jiménez didn't deserve that," she whispered, and I closed my eyes, letting go and shooing her from the room with a flick of my hand.

"Come," I muttered to Mathias. Fuck, this was going to be painful. "I must attend on these appearances before my court."

"Who's Lady Jiménez?" he asked, still holding the flan-soaked rag.

"A name I expect you may hear more than once today," I said softly, cursing the rapid gossip of servants and courtiers alike. I leaned sideways and caught Jiron's eye through the open doorway, giving him a look. He frowned, nodded, and disappeared from sight. "Mat, this isn't going to be pleasant for you."

"I don't understand."

"Algejón. It seems news of the tragedy has already made its way through *la*

Cortina."

Mathias stilled. "Oh."

It wasn't fair that my people would blame him for a crime committed by someone else, a someone who shared nothing but the colour of their skin...and perhaps, if my suspicions were right about its perpetrator, a box of oddly shaped confectionery. But fair had fuck all to do with life.

"Roll up your shirtsleeves," I ordered, and he looked at me oddly before doing so. And damn it, I almost wished he hadn't chosen *that* moment to be obedient, that instead he'd been his usual obnoxious self about the whole thing. Because when Jiron stepped into the room holding a set of iron shackles, the confused hurt in Mat's expression felt like a physical blow.

He hissed out an angry breath. "*That's* your solution? To parade me around as your Blessed prisoner?"

"I'm not the one making you into our enemy," I reminded him, swallowing around the lump in my throat. "Your skin and your accent do that for you. I'm merely giving my people reassurance as to Quareh's response to a threat, on a day where anti-Mazekhstani sentiment is going to be at an all-time high. Nat, you saw how Clementina and Camila treated you. How the fuck do you think it's going to go over with those who are less civil? If they see you walking around free?"

"I've never been *free*," he growled, and I tried not to think about the two-year-old version of the man before me, the child who was taken from his home and his family for *fucking politics* and forced to live the ostracising life of a foreign hostage.

I swiped the dirty cloth from Mathias' hand and let it fall, expecting he'd need to be held down by Jiron to make this work. But Mat just lifted his chin, giving me such a disappointed look as he raised his wrists to allow my guard to lock the manacles around them that I felt nauseous.

"Sorry, little one," Jiron murmured, and I couldn't blame him for that, even if he was speaking out of turn.

But the illusion we could deliver to my people with this farce was worth a few hours of discomfort for Mathias. And it wasn't like he *wasn't* a prisoner here; all I was doing was reminding the palace's inhabitants of that fact. The perception of control over Mazekhstam, however symbolic, would help settle their fears and their anger over Algejón's massacre.

It wouldn't solve everything. Nothing could, and Astrid Panarina would pay for what she'd done, but some display of strength was required to avoid mass panic among the nobles currently gathered in *la Cortina*. Why should the north be feared when we had one of their own in chains right here? Look how weak they are; watch how we can control them and beat them down; can you not see that they are only human, after all?

"My prince," Jiron offered, his voice low and apologetic. "Could you not just leave him in your rooms?"

I set my jaw. "No."

"That would be worse," Mathias said softly. "To look as though he's hiding me, *favouring* me. If they didn't know I was here, or that the prince normally keeps me at his side…"

"But they do," I finished, and as shitty as the situation was, to know that Mat understood what I was doing even if he was pissed off about it, warmed something inside me. "Stay close to him today, Jiron. I wouldn't put it past some of the courtiers or lords to attempt to inflict *justice* with their own hands."

*

Chapter Twenty-Four

Mat

"Are your wrists still okay?"

"Yes," I said, for the fifth time in as many minutes. "And you're not going to earn my forgiveness by *fussing*, Ren."

But it was cute that he kept asking, and made it hard to stay mad at him. Besides, my ire was more than used up on the rest of *la Cortina's* inhabitants, who were alternating between flinging muttered slurs and threats in my direction, and giving me the same silent yet hateful glares I'd received from Clementina and Camila earlier. One man even went so far as to spit at me, for which Ren promptly ordered him flogged for attempting to assault a prince of Quareh despite my protests and the fact that Ren had been six feet away at the time.

"Fine," the prince muttered now from the corner of his mouth as we walked through the palace's twisty corridors amid hostile glowers shot pointedly in my direction. "I'll let you suffer."

But it was only a few seconds later that I heard his soft murmur in my ear again. "If the chafing breaks the skin, let me know and I'll get Starling to fix it."

I blew out an amused breath at the offer. "I expect that would defeat the point of this little charade, Your Highness."

"Mat," he hissed. "I don't want you hurt."

I threw him a disbelieving look as we passed another cluster of whispering courtiers, and the prince let out a low, wicked laugh that sent shivers through me.

"So I do," he admitted when we were alone again. "But you know I only want you hurting for me, right? Not the rest of these fuckers."

But it was *these fuckers* whom he had me in chains for, thick iron links trailing between the manacles around my wrists. The length of chain was impractically long: these were showy restraints, designed for discomfort and humiliation rather than restriction.

I sighed.

"Are they too heavy?"

"Yes," I said. "Stop fretting."

"Your Highness."

Ren drew to a reluctant halt at the greeting, and Jiron's hand fell heavily on my shoulder as I tried to keep walking in the vain hope I'd be allowed to avoid the whole ordeal.

The prince murmured the titles of the women gathered at the window seat as they curtsied for him, but their eyes quickly flickered to me.

"A dreadful shame," one muttered, while another fluttered her hand over her heart.

"Those *poor* people."

"The Mazekhstani are utter heathens, I've always said."

"Imelda deserved better."

"And who will be next?"

"A true tragedy," Ren agreed politely. "But you have nothing to fear, my ladies. It will be taken care of."

"But they're so *wild!*"

"Is it dangerous?" one of the women asked of me, her belly round with child.

"Of course not," said the prince. "Lord Grachyov, come here."

I swallowed down a retort that would have told him where he could shove it, and stepped forward. Ren lay a possessive hand on my shoulder.

"See? Soon we will bring the north to heel in much the same way, and we won't ever have to endure such suffering at its hands again."

But it seemed the noblewomen were less concerned about their friend's fate than they were about giggling behind their hands.

"So pale."

"Those *eyes*."

A WHISPER AND A BREATH

"Can it even talk?"

I gave the woman behind those words an exasperated look. She and I had had an entire fucking conversation two days ago when the prince had been questioning half the palace.

"Not a word," said Ren cheerily, who had been part of that very same discussion. "Just lots of vague growls."

The noblewoman reached her hand up, hovering it a hair's breadth from my cheek. Out of the corner of my eye I saw Jiron tense up, but he didn't try to stop her, and probably wouldn't until she posed an actual threat. He'd be in trouble if he touched a noble without provocation, although I wondered whether his gender gave him any advantage in that regard.

As the woman's fingers brushed my skin, I turned my head and snapped my teeth at her fingers, causing her to pull back with a sharp yelp. She clutched her hand to her chest as if I'd actually bitten it, and the others crowded around her, fussing loudly.

"My ladies," said Ren in dismissal and ushered us along the corridor, letting out a loud cackle once we'd turned a few corners.

"Nat, you're truly something. Is it bad that I'm enjoying this just a *little* bit?"

"Yes," I said. "It's fucking humiliating."

"They're not seeing *you*, just a nameless barbarian," he pointed out, waving a careless hand. "Their fickle minds will forget all about it tomorrow. How are your wrists?"

"You weren't this concerned about them last night in the cells. They hurt a lot more then."

Ren gave me that wicked grin again. "I told you. That was for me, *mi sol*."

My sun. I was really earning quite the collection of names from him. I'd accuse the prince of forgetting what he liked to call me, only he used them all with such frequency that it was clear he just enjoyed mixing them up, like how he switched between Mathias and Nathanael at a moment's whim. And while that should have been weird, as if I was losing my identity to the real Mathias, it felt strangely right. I was pieces of a whole here, not one thing but dozens. A prisoner. A northerner in a palace – a *country* – of southerners. A secret Temarian prince. A…whatever I was to Ren.

And right now, the same show pony I'd accused him of being earlier, paraded around by its Blessed master in front of yet more endless groups of people. Servants, nobles, courtiers…it felt like the entirety of *la Cortina's* occupants were conveniently strewn along our route to the throne room to glare and curse at me, and while few dared to interrupt the prince's purposeful stride to greet him, few was more than fucking enough.

"Mat," Ren said quietly as I snarled at a couple walking arm in arm down a flight of stairs towards us, whose venomous glances in my direction indicated that they were feeling just as unfavourably about my people as the rest of the Blessed palace. "As impressed as I am with your efforts to get into character, so to speak, the point of this little exercise is to make it look like you're under control, not a wild beast ready to bite."

"Maybe I do bite," I snapped, my words drawing a delighted laugh from him.

"That's my job, Mat, remember? Or do you need another reminder?"

I flushed, suddenly remembering our company and glancing around at Jiron, who stared back at us impassively. Luis wasn't quite as restrained, biting his lip in amusement and glancing studiously at one of the naked lovers statues adorning the corridors. And, oh fuck, it happened to be something inordinately similar to how Ren had pinned me down that night at the Martinez estate, his body above mine, my wrists held and-

"Is that a yes?"

I fixed him with a stare. "It's a *get-a-fucking-move-on,* Your Highness. You're going to be late."

Ren shrugged. "Let them wait for their prince. Teasing you is much more fun." His eyes glittered with humour and dark promise, and after all the shit he was putting me through, I was half tempted to drag him into some shadowy alcove and take out my frustrations on that fucking mouth of his. Maybe I'd ever so accidentally get the chains wrapped around his delicate neck, and then he'd see just how irritating they really were.

"That," the prince said, pointing at my face. "Whatever that is, I *want* it."

"What?"

"Whatever you're thinking of right now that's putting such heat in your gaze, Mathias."

I laughed. "You really don't."

"Try me," he purred, and just as I was about to take him up on that offer and teach him to be careful what he wished for, a figure appeared at the end of the corridor and reminded me that we were never truly alone in this place.

I recognised Isobella as she moved closer and offered Ren a smile that came across as shy, but even the short amount of time I'd known her told me that was calculated. And I admired her for knowing what she wanted and going after it, especially in a country that would beat down any female for trying, but did it really have to be *my* man?

Fuck, fuck, fuck. What was *that*, Nathanael?

Possessive, clingy thoughts were not welcome under any circumstances, least of all these. A person couldn't be owned, and the hedonistic prince at my side demonstrated that truer than anyone. Ren was free with his affections, and trying to stake a claim on him would be like attempting to hold back the ocean with your fingers.

He beamed at the woman as she approached. "My lady."

Isobella's curly hair lay loose around her bare shoulders, and I couldn't help but notice the way she leaned forward slightly as she sank into her curtsey so that her breasts damn near spilled from her dress. Or maybe it was so she could conveniently stumble into Ren's arms as she straightened.

Subtle.

"My prince," murmured Isobella, clutching at Ren's arm. He didn't seem all that inclined to let go of her, and for fuck's sake, did his mouth *have* to be that close to hers? "You're always so good to me."

I sighed and stared out of the window above her head, but even the cloudless azure sky wasn't enough to distract me from her next words.

"But maybe you could be bad to me too? Tonight, perhaps?" Her voice was dripping in simpering seduction, and I wondered if Ren would object if I really did throw myself from a window. This one was only on the first floor rather than the fifth storey of Ren's bedchambers, but it was wide enough that even Jiron could fit through its frame if he wished.

Which I expect he did, having to listen to such shit every day without even the luxury of being able to roll his eyes.

"Not tonight, Issy," Ren whispered, and stupidly strong relief shot through me. And then he ruined it by fucking kissing her. By Quarehian standards, it probably could have been called a polite goodbye kind of kiss, but it was still the type that had tongue, and now I was envisioning a different use for the window, namely one where I threw the both of them out of it and Jiron fell to his knees before me in gratitude.

And then I remembered that he'd had to put up with mine and Ren's nonsense too, and expected the guard would probably rather be done with the lot of us.

Isobella sniffed loudly when the prince finally drew them apart. "Do you not want me anymore? Am I no longer beautiful?"

I narrowed my eyes at the shameless manipulation.

"Of course you are," Ren cooed. "And you always will be, Issy." He gave her a soft smile that felt far too intimate, and I decided that I would have preferred her to join in with the others in hating me for nothing more than my race, rather than...*this*. "You light up every room you walk into."

She let out a delicate exhale. "Then why will you not take me to your bed, my prince?"

"Alas, señorita, I am...fulfilling a period of abstinence."

I choked, and Ren shot me an amused look.

"Abstinence?" Isobella spluttered. "By Dios, *why?*"

"I am to be married soon," Ren reminded her. And me. "I would offer my wife certain dignities."

Isobella offered a theatrical sigh and swept away, glancing back over her shoulder several times as if hoping Ren would be following her. He wasn't.

Instead, the prince leaned against the wall and languidly looked me up and down, clearly ready to pick up where we'd left off. "Jiron, Luis. Stand at either end of the corridor and stop anyone else from interrupting us. Mat and I-"

"Married," I said quietly. "Somehow, I always forget that." I walked away, needing to put distance between us and the reminder that Ren was promised to Alta, and anything between me and him could only be temporary at best.

Only I found that Luis' hand had snagged the chain between my wrists, and

I was jerked back into place. I swore at him, kicking at his shin in the hope it might make him let go.

It did not.

"I'm sorry," Ren said from behind me. "Were you trying to make as dramatic an exit as Issy? Because she has the shoulders and the dress to pull it off, while you just look…sulky."

I scowled.

"Maybe you could let us know your intentions in advance next time you'd like to leave in an indignant huff," he suggested to me. "That way, I might let you move more than a foot away from me. Or not."

The prince took the chain from Luis, giving it a condescending tug while clicking his tongue. I raised a disbelieving eyebrow.

"I'm not a fucking horse, Ren."

He looked like he was trying not to laugh. "Mmm."

But the asshole didn't let go, stepping past and yanking me along with him.

I sighed as I was forced to follow, Jiron and Luis trailing at our heels. "I rather think you've made your point with all this by now."

"Oh, I don't know," Ren said lazily as we approached the side doors to the palace's throne room. "Making you gag on my cock in front of the whole court would send a *very* potent message about Quareh's strength against the north."

I made a rude gesture at him, a movement made infinitely more difficult by the iron that weighed down my wrists, but I managed.

I was just thankful Ren had said it in Mazekhstani, such that the others wouldn't have understood the idle threat. The man could be so fucking crude sometimes, and his unaffected tone said it could have been a serious suggestion just as easily as it was a joke.

"These are far too heavy," Ren complained loudly in his own language, dropping the chain as we passed into the throne room. "Carry your own damn shackles, Mathias." He snatched his crown off the cushion held out by a servant and stalked up the stairs of the dais to the throne, tossing out rapid-fire instructions to Clementina regarding her new duties. I was pleased to note she bore a navy and gold sash like the one Valentinus used to wear, presumably to designate their status as palace heralds, even if her hands were shaking as she adjusted it over her shoulder.

I let my eyes wander, trailing across the decorative floor and up the ornate pillars, across to the darkened balcony where a palace guard stood with a bow in his hands and watched everything happening below. Braziers burned along each wall of the throne room, and there was a cluster of low lounges and tables at the back of the hall below the large stained-glass windows.

A muffled buzz of noise sounded from beyond the main doors, which I suspected were the citizens looking to meet with their prince today, and I swallowed, knowing I'd be facing even more hostility from Ren's people once they opened.

"No, not there, Lord Grachyov," I heard the prince say. "Stand closer to Jiron."

I dragged my feet from the relative safety of the wall and towards the base of the dais steps where the huge guard stood. Front and centre; just the place to exhibit the northern pet.

"Closer."

That was reassuring, actually. Despite what he'd done to me at Sesveko, despite knowing he'd tear me apart without hesitation if his master ever commanded it, there was something about Jiron that was inherently calming. He was so unflappable and competent that he gave off the impression of near indestructibility, and there were worse things to be standing beside when it came time to face a mob of pissed off Quarehians.

Not that I'd be admitting that. "And why?"

"Impact, Mat, impact!" Ren declared with enthusiasm from up on his throne behind us. "He makes you look absolutely tiny. Adorably so, if I'm being honest, so maybe you should be a little bit growly after all. Think...two-week-old kitten, fierce but terribly pathetic. That's what you should aim for."

"This is exhausting," I told Jiron.

The giant raised an eyebrow as he looked down at me at his side. "You think *this* is bad? When he was twelve years old, he decided that-"

"Anyone caught muttering in my presence shall be immediately executed,"

Ren said loudly.

Jiron clamped his mouth shut, which I thought was a shame. I'd have liked to hear tales about Ren's childhood, even if he had likely been as much of an irritating tyrant as he was now.

"Now, Your Highness?" one of the guards asked from the far end of the hall, his hand resting on the main doors.

"A moment. Clementina, ready?"

"Ready, my prince."

Ren switched from Quarehian to Mazekhstani. "Mathias, wrists?"

I tried not to smile. *"Khorosho."* Fine.

"Very well. Guards, let them in."

*

A WHISPER AND A BREATH

Chapter Twenty-Five

Ren

Mathias rubbed his wrists absently as Jiron unshackled them, wandering over to the tall windows at the back of the hall where the sunlight filtered through the coloured glass. Dios, he was resilient. I'd pushed him hard today, wondering what he could handle, and it turned out to be everything my people had thrown at him.

It wasn't that I'd wanted to break him; I'd just intended to test his limits, to see what would be too much so I could manage it in the future. Quareh's hatred of the north wasn't going away anytime soon, regardless of what I might have said about short memories, and the recent Mazekhstani violence would make Mat's position here even more unpleasant for him.

And if I was being really honest with myself, which I wasn't a fan of doing because it gave me a headache, I had been looking for an excuse to stop the whole thing. A wince, tears, a bowed head; if Mat had shown me that he was *done,* then so was I. I'd have called an end to the citizen appearances, taken him back to my room, and let him run as many baths as he wanted in a row without bitching about it once.

But because *mi gato montés* was stronger than I could have ever been in his borrowed boots, he'd *endured.* He'd kept his head high throughout it all, bearing the quiet mutterings and the overt comments with unflinching determination, and while he hadn't looked happy about being simultaneously accused of mass murder and threatened with the same level of violence by overzealous citizens, he hadn't shown them his fear, either. And even now, after I'd shooed everyone else out at the end of what had proven to be an exceedingly tiring day, the first thing he'd spoken in our newfound privacy had been condolences.

"The Jiménezes and the others were obviously well-loved here," Mat murmured, and I just blinked at him and the ridiculousness of him making such a statement after everything I'd just put him through by *parading* him – Mat's word, but it was really the only applicable one – in front of my people as a symbol of our supposed superiority. Supposed, because *fuck*: if the

Mazekhstani were half as good people as Mathias was, maybe they *should* be ruling over Quareh after all.

And then I remembered their senseless massacre of over two dozen innocents, and dispelled that treasonous idea as quickly as it had arrived.

"You're allowed to be mad," I told him, but he shook his head.

"How can I? They're all just grieving. What happened was horrific."

I blew out a breath. "Stop being so fucking forgiving, *mi sol.* It's irritating. Did you not hear Lord González calling for your head?"

"His nephew was one of those killed," Mat pointed out, because of course he'd kept up with everything that had been said while I'd been diverting death threats, avoiding calls for war, talking the lords down from a counterattack and keeping an eye on my lover. There hadn't been much business brought before me today that hadn't related to the north, and I expected that my father and brother were probably dealing with the same shit in the capital.

"You may leave us," I told my guards, and even Luis had been with me for long enough to know that there was no *may* about it, even if his frown told me that he was remembering what had happened last time he'd been ordered to leave me and Mat alone in here.

I hoped there would be less blood this time. I really liked these boots.

The door clicked shut behind the two of them, giving Mat the time and space to yell at me, if he wished. We'd have to restore the act when we left the hall, drape him back in chains and return to the pretence of being enemies, but after hours of being subjected to racial slurs and the anger of a palace with nothing else within reach to blame, he deserved a moment to himself to recover.

I threw my legs over one of the throne's arms and draped my shoulders over the other, lazing across the ancient symbol of Quarehian royalty and power both because I was done with the day, and because I fucking felt like it.

I closed my eyes.

"If I ordered you to service me," I drawled, teasing, "would you listen?"

"What do you think?" Mathias asked, and I tried to hide my surprise at the sound of his voice coming from far closer than I'd expected.

"You do know that no one is allowed to fully ascend those dais stairs but me and my father, right?"

"That makes no sense," he shot back. "Unless *you or your father* regularly take a feather duster to all that ornamentation, there's been a servant or two up here more than once."

I cracked an eye and stared up at the throne's intricately carved back that was admittedly and suspiciously free of dust.

"Well," I said, trying to recover. "Certainly not heathens like yourself. Quarehian law says you're not even permitted up the first step."

Mat's hand dropped to my thigh, stroking the cream suede of my left boot. Then his delicate fingers followed the neat laces all the way down, and he traced gentle circles around my ankle.

"So you *do* like them," I accused him, delighted.

"I like how you look in them," he admitted softly, and the filthy expression on his face as he raked his gaze over the rest of me made my cock thicken. He swapped hands and I felt his scorching touch trail back up my leg, continuing along my hip, my arm, my neck.

I shivered. He circled around behind my head, settling his hands on my shoulders.

"I also," Mathias murmured, dropping down to a crouch to whisper directly in my ear, "like how *I* look in *this*."

And then without warning, the bastard snatched my fucking crown.

"*¡Por Dios!*"

I twisted on the throne and clawed at him, but he stepped neatly out of reach and my fingers closed on only air. Laughing, Mat took the steps two at a time, and the devilish smirk when he spun around at the bottom of the dais made my heart soar. He was smiling so much more lately, despite everything that had happened to him, and getting to hear his laughter on a daily basis was quickly becoming addictive. It was why I couldn't help but tease him, hoping to draw that joy out more often, and every time he smiled at *me*, it felt like a victory.

"You better bring that back," I warned, climbing from my seat and following him down. He continued to retreat, keeping distance between us. "If I have to retrieve it from you myself, Mathias, you won't like how it goes."

"I think I'll like it just fine," he declared, giving me a wicked, smouldering look, and then perched the crown atop his own head.

"Mmm," I said intelligently. Fuck me, the sight of *it* and *him* together made my cock immediately jump to attention, stealing all other thoughts from my head. The band of bronzed metal, styled in elegant Quarehian curves, was nested in ash brown hair that was far too pale and short to belong to any southerner. While it should have looked wrong, I had the sudden urge to tell him to never take it off.

"What do you think? Could I pull off being a snobbish, obnoxious Quarehian prince?" Mat tossed his head in a way that reminded me of Viento, and gave me a look of mock contemptuousness.

I snorted. "You certainly have those qualities down, *mi amor*. What would they all say, do you imagine, if you were to appear among my people wearing *that?*"

We grinned at each other, envisioning the absolute uproar that would result.

"I expect Ademar's head might explode," Mat mused. "For that reason alone, it would be worth it."

I took another step forward. He took one back.

"I don't know where you think you're going," I told him, amused. "The doors are guarded, and you're not getting away with stealing my crown, *ladrón*."

This time, when I moved, he didn't.

Mat bit his lip in that provocative way of his, watching me draw closer. "Then if I'm to be accused of being a thief, know that I intend to steal something else from you, prince."

His words didn't register until I'd taken the final step to close the distance between us, and then his lips were on mine, his body pressing close and his hands hungrily raking down my arms and back. I sank into the kiss, my mind happily falling into that familiar mantra of *mine, mine, mine* as I clutched him to me.

Mathias' hands searched lower, stroking through my trousers, and I groaned against him.

"I'm going to have to stop you right there, Nathanael," I murmured, and he froze, letting go. His storm-coloured eyes snapped uncertainly to mine.

"You don't want...?"

"Oh, I *want*," I assured him, giving him a heated look to leave no doubt that I spoke true. "But did I give you permission to touch me?"

He cocked his head, confused. Bless him. He was adorable.

"Will...will you let me touch you?" he asked slowly, and that request, so innocently filthy, made my cock throb.

"I will," I said, and as he reached for me again, I slapped his hand away. "When you earn it."

Mat's mouth twisted in irritation.

"*Ren.*"

"Prince Ren," I corrected, leaning in to kiss him, and the bastard had the audacity to laugh at the same moment so our mouths collided in sloppy, wet awkwardness. I didn't care, deepening our kiss and feeling him melt against me. He ran his hands through my hair, and that I permitted, because it felt so fucking good I didn't have the willpower to refuse even for the sake of the game I was playing with him.

I moved my lips to his cheek, his jaw, his neck, kissing and licking every inch of his skin. Mathias moaned, pressing a leg between mine and rubbing his hips against me, and the friction against my cock pulled a sharp exhale from my lips.

His words were a gentle, affected murmur. "If this is some kind of power trip to get me to use your title..."

"I don't care what you call me," I growled, grabbing his hands where they were still nestled in my hair, because he'd been half right in his words. This was power, or control at the least, and it was largely what got me off. "I care what you can give me."

I pulled his wrists down and held them behind his back, my heart pounding as I waited to see how he'd react. He'd seemed to enjoy me pinning him down before, but that had been an almost natural position while we were tangled on the bed. This was different, or at least it felt as such, a precarious knife edge on which we rested. Would he give me this, or had I pushed too far?

Mat's gaze searched mine intently, and a lump grew in my throat at his silence.

Fuck, I'd take whatever this beautiful man deigned to grant me, no matter how vanilla. Why had I risked that? *Of course* Mathias wasn't going to be into this, into even the most tame of the fucked up things I liked.

I'd ruined everything by pushing for something that wasn't fair to ask, and now he'd pull away, that shutter coming down over those grey-blue eyes of his I loved so much-

And then Mat's chin dipped in a nod, his mouth twitching into a soft smile, and his wrists pulled gently against my hold…but not to bring them back to his sides.

Barely daring to breathe, I let go, and he obediently kept his arms behind his back. I turned him around, my cock straining against the fabric of my trousers as I saw his hands clutched together, palms crossed.

"You're fucking perfect," I whispered into his ear, trailing my hands down his arms and drawing a shuddering breath from us both. I gently kissed the back of his neck. "Walk towards the wall."

I moved with him, unable to stop touching this unbelievably sexy man before me, turned on in a way I'd never felt before. I felt ready to blow just from *looking* at him, and he still had all his Blessed clothes on. And my damned crown.

I heaved out a breath, reaching down to pinch myself and pull back from the edge. There was plenty I wanted to do to him before we had to leave this hall, and I would not let myself ruin that. I vowed that I wouldn't come until he had…at least twice.

And when Mat obligingly came to a stop facing the wall, and I put a hand to the back of his neck to press his forehead to it? When his hands twitched, but didn't move from behind his back? When he growled out breathless curses as I unclasped his belt and freed his length from his trousers, and he shivered under my touch?

I upped the count to three.

*

Chapter Twenty-Six

Mat

On a scale of one to ten for indecent acts that I should never, *ever* have allowed to happen, this was a Blessed eleven.

If we were in Mazekhstam or Temar, Ren's hand on my cock would be enough to get us both arrested and sentenced to correctional punishment in the form of a brutal flogging. Hell, our kissing alone might have sealed our fates, and yet it was becoming harder and harder to remind myself of that each time I sought out his mouth. That clever tongue of his that had talked his people down from the various proposals of vengeance they'd brought to him today was as talented without words as it was with them.

Kissing Ren brought happiness and delight and exhilaration, flavoured with citrus and danger, and I was obsessed. Even reminding myself of his impending marriage to Altagracia couldn't dampen my infatuation for long, as hard as I'd tried.

But if our sin were not enough, we were also messing around with…whatever this was that had me keeping my hands behind my back from nothing more than the desire to please him, submitting to his will in a way I'd sworn I would never do. What the fuck was wrong with me? All I had to do was let go, and yet the thought of the prince's disappointment if I did so kept my fingers clasped so tightly, they had started to ache.

When he'd first grabbed my wrists, pressing on sore skin made tender by the heavy manacles *he'd* put there, I'd been tempted to shake him off. But his expression had stopped me; a vulnerable, almost pleading look that told me the arrogant, coarse prince was close to shattering into a thousand painful shards. And while that alone wouldn't have bought my agreement, there was something undeniably appealing about how he was holding me that pulled heavy breaths from us both. His touch wasn't painful like the shackles had been, or if it was, it didn't *hurt*. His fingers felt warm around my wrists, confident and secure, and was it that which made my entire body burn for him?

A WHISPER AND A BREATH

Or was it his words? The gentle praise, mixed with obscene threats and orders I shouldn't have obeyed yet inexplicably did, was making me light-headed with elation and arousal. He was turning me inside out with what I wanted and what I *thought* I wanted, and how could one even think with the prince's hands on them like that, stroking and tugging while he murmured wicked suggestions into my ear?

Ren yanked me abruptly backwards, my back colliding with his chest and trapping my hands between us. He grabbed my chin and slipped his thumb between my parted lips, swiping it across my tongue. I tasted myself on him, and flushed.

"Good boy," he murmured, and that made my face heat up even more. Because who *liked* being called that?

Me. I definitely liked it. Oh, I was so screwed.

How could this man undo every inch of propriety and dignity I'd ever gained, and not only have me groan in his arms but take his thumb deeper into my mouth, and suck on it like it was the only thing capable of giving me air?

"Fuck, *Nat,*" Ren hissed, and I felt his chin drop down onto my shoulder, the movement heavy and uncontrolled.

And realising that my hands were far from helpless even tucked up where they were, I stroked against him just like he'd stopped me from doing earlier, revelling in the power of making him lose his composure. The prince's breathing harshened as I pressed more firmly against the hardness I found beneath my fingers, and he wheezed out shallow gasps.

"You," he panted, "are going to stop that right now."

I thought about it, decided he wasn't actually telling me to stop, and continued, running my tongue up the pad of his thumb and shamelessly squeezing his clothed cock between my fingers. The prince choked and buried his face into my shoulder, and I grinned around his hand.

Murmuring something about *Dios-damned northerners never doing what they're told,* Ren unexpectedly pulled back out of reach, slipping his thumb from my mouth and smearing it down my cheek to dry it. Then I found myself spun around.

He was on his knees before me just like he had been last night, and by the

Blessed, it was just as intoxicating a sight in the daytime.

His gaze fixed on something above my head, and I realised he was staring at his crown. The circlet was so light I could barely feel it on my head, and while I'd only swiped it in the hope of pissing him off, I couldn't deny that his actual reaction had been far more intoxicating. Ren looked at me as if mesmerised, his eyes half lidded and his throat bobbing as he swallowed.

"Keep your hands behind your back," he commanded, his voice thick with dominance and desire, and again, while I should have told him where he could stick his princely orders, I did what no Temarian royal should ever do for an Aratorre, and obeyed him.

Ren's tongue swirled leisurely down my length and I closed my eyes, letting the back of my head rest against the wall as I revelled in the feel of his hot mouth wrapped around me. It was both the same and different to last night; I wasn't actually restrained, but a traitorous part of me whispered that it hadn't been all that terrible, tied up and at his mercy, and it had sure been easier when I didn't have to resist the temptation to touch him…

"You're being so good for me, Your Highness," Ren murmured, as if realising how hard I was trying to keep my hands in place, and oh fuck, him calling me by my title while on his knees for me was every-fucking-thing.

I growled out an incoherent noise as he took me back between his lips-

-and then yelped as his teeth grazed my cock, my eyes shooting open to find Moreno hauling an indignant Ren to his feet. I choked and brought my hands around to cover myself, tucking everything back into my trousers even as Ren levelled a glare on the man holding him tightly by the bicep.

"*Your Highness?*" the Comandante snarled, and at first I thought it was a pointed address to his prince before I realised he was repeating Ren's words.

Fuck.

Had we really been so caught up in each other as to not to notice him enter? What else had he seen? What else had he *heard?* My real name?

Moreno's eyes narrowed on me, and he used his free hand to swipe at my head. I flinched, but his target was the crown still resting in my hair, and he snatched it off with a vicious growl. "And what the fuck is this?"

Ren wiped his mouth with the back of his free hand. "It's called role play," he drawled scathingly, ripping the crown out of the man's grip and placing it back onto his own head. "Lighten up."

"Aww," I said, marvelling at how fast his mind worked. "Does this mean I don't get to be Quarehian royalty anymore?"

Ren laughed good-naturedly, but it sounded slightly forced. "See? He was into it."

"A prince of Quareh kneels to no one but his king," the Comandante spat, his expression ugly as he glared at him. "I hardly thought that needed to be said."

Ren gave a lazy smile. "And *I* would have thought it difficult to suck someone off without kneeling, but if you have a suggestion for how to achieve that, then feel free to demonstrate," he offered, reaching for his own belt. Moreno let go of him as if burned.

"You're a fucking Aratorre. Take your pleasure from your whore without debasing yourself."

That word again. Perhaps it was no surprise where his men had gotten the idea.

"He's a selfish lover, it seems. It would explain a lot," Ren said to me, and I nodded seriously.

The Comandante's lip curled as he glanced between us both.

"Play with your toys properly, Ren," he hissed. "Or I'll have the Mazekhstani removed from your care."

"Try that," Ren said dangerously, his eyes flashing. "And when the dust settles, we'll see what's left standing."

Moreno seemed taken aback by the vehemence in his tone. He stood up straighter, his hands curling into fists, and for a moment I feared he would hit his prince.

And then I kind of hoped he would, because Ren could take a hit if it came with the reward of having the man punished for striking a royal. Or rather, striking him without the king's approval, and I hated that that was a qualifier.

But Moreno's fingers unclenched, and he said nothing.

"Comandante," the prince prompted, wandering back into the middle of the hall and giving me the chance to fix up my clothing when Moreno's eyes turned to follow him. "As I know Jiron and Luis would not have allowed you to sneak in here, what was so urgent that you had to bully the poor palace guards on the main doors into letting you interrupt me?"

"Your new... *herald*. I just witnessed her attempting to order more guards to the palace gates to monitor new arrivals."

"Well, that was my decree, considering everything that's happened. Do you have concerns about Clementina's performance?"

"I have concerns about what's between her legs," Moreno said disdainfully. "I know a few scullery maids, if you'd like to promote them too? Appoint them to your father's Council, perhaps?"

I stiffened, shooting him a glare that unfortunately he missed entirely, too focused on the prince.

"Dios, Ren, what were you thinking? The palace is in chaos!"

"That seems like an exaggeration," Ren said mildly, examining his fingernails.

"Undo your mess before I'm forced to remove the girl myself."

"Watch who you're speaking to," the prince retorted, his voice quiet. "This isn't a military matter, Comandante. You have no authority to undermine my orders, and any attempt to do so will be met with appropriate punishment."

Moreno narrowed his eyes. "The king will hear of this. And then we'll see whose *shoulders* the punishment falls upon, my prince."

Subtle, asshole. Real subtle. If I didn't already know their secret, I'd have had some serious suspicions.

He inclined his head to Ren in the laziest bow I'd ever seen, and then his eyes flickered to me.

"You. This is your doing, isn't it? You northerners and your obsession with gifting women the illusion of power. What did you *do*?"

"Don't give Lord Grachyov so much credit," Ren drawled before I could speak. "He's nothing more than a pretty face and a hole to fuck. If you have a problem with my orders, Moreno, I expect you to shut up and deal with it, not start harassing my prisoner about matters he doesn't have the faintest clue about."

The insulting misdirection worked; the Comandante's expression immediately turned from accusatory to dismissive, the revolted contempt in the man's sneer far too evident as he directed it at me. I swallowed down the scathing retort I wanted to deliver and instead offered a vacuous smile. What was one more role to play?

"Your Highness," Moreno said, not bothering to bow again, and slithered back through the main doors like the snake he was. The moment they closed, Ren was turning me towards him, gathering my hands up between his own and kissing them.

"*Lo siento*, Nat," he whispered in apology, his brown eyes wide and horrified. "I didn't mean what I said. If Moreno knew you were influencing my decisions, he'd have no trouble convincing my father to hand you over to him."

My prince was breathing heavily, almost panting, and I freed a hand to rest it against his cheek. He closed his eyes and leaned into my touch.

"I get it, Ren," I said. I did. "Talk shit about me all you want."

He gave a hesitant smile, as if unable to quite believe I would forgive him. And I couldn't deny that it had hurt to hear him speak of me so derisively, but after weeks of putting my foot in it, I was beginning to understand that Ren's private and public personas were nothing alike, and he had to present a different image to people like Moreno in order to be effective elsewhere.

"I can't-"

"Appearances are everything, right?" I prompted. "One day I'll probably have to do the same to you."

I tried to ignore the brief flash of pain that crossed Ren's face at that. It was another reminder to us both that what we were doing could only ever be temporary. Its life was limited to my stay here, and the more we indulged, the more work we'd both have to do to rid ourselves of its chains later. Lies and jokes and dismissive comments about the other in the aim of persuading our respective peoples that it hadn't been what we truly wanted it to be – Ren, that there had been no affection behind the physicality of our interactions, and me, that there had been no interactions at fucking all.

But to be smart about it, to *stop* being with him, was beyond unthinkable. I needed him and his bright smile and quick wit, the familiar spicy scent of his skin and the feeling of his mouth on mine…it was everything good in my life right now, and how could I give that up? If that made me weak, so be it. I'd take every damn second of *us* that I could get.

"I should have been more careful," Ren muttered. "To let Moreno get that close…we can't do that anywhere but my chambers from now on."

"It wasn't your fault. I initiated it," I reminded him, and the prince grinned, some of that playful spark returning to his expression.

"I loved that you did, Mat."

I sighed. "And yet now Moreno knows about us."

"I'm just thankful he didn't find us on the throne," Ren said with a low laugh.

I grinned at him. "One day?"

"Fuck yes."

"I'll hold you to that."

"Indeed," he promised. "Still. I am sorry for what I said."

"That tongue of yours can make it up to me tonight."

His eyes twinkled at the suggestion. "It sure can."

"Good," I said firmly. "Because you're going to use it to say at least six nice things about me."

Ren screwed up his face. "I can manage five, *mi sol,* at most."

I pretended to think about it.

"Five," he clarified, "and I'll continue what I started a few moments ago."

I shrugged.

"Alright," I conceded. "Six compliments and you going down on me, it is."

The prince barked out a surprised laugh. "How could I refuse such an offer?"

Then he paused. "And the…rest of it?" he asked quietly, suddenly looking vulnerable again. It was unlike Ren to dance around his words, when the asshole usually took great pleasure in being as vulgar and descriptive as possible.

I grabbed his wrists as he had mine, and laid a kiss on each of them. "I liked it," I muttered into his skin, not quite able to look at him as I voiced the admission. I expected to have hesitated, to have felt torn about letting him have so much control, but the words slipped out without thought. "I'd be okay with seeing where that goes, if that was still an option."

"Hell fucking yes, it's still an option." Ren's breath warmed my neck, and he murmured his next words into my ear. "I want you standing like that, hands behind your back for me again, as soon as we're alone in my room tonight. Only this time, Nat, I want you naked."

I stifled the heady groan that his demand threatened to call forth, because *fuck,* we had literally just agreed that we couldn't do anything in public, and there he was, making me want to crawl all over him again. He was fucking intoxicating.

"I suppose that depends on your behaviour for the rest of the day," I told him, when I'd remembered how to breathe again. "If you're good, I'll *consider* it."

Ren pulled back to look intently at my face. "And the definition of 'good' is…"

"My definition, *sí*."

He blew out an exasperated breath. "No hurting anyone?"

"No hurting anyone. No ordering floggings or other corporal punishment."

"You're incredibly boring."

I gave him a cruel smirk. "And no flirting with those same anyones, either."

The prince stared at me in horror. "You've *got* to be joking."

"You know, my shoulders are really sore," I commented, shaking them out. "I'm probably not going to be able to hold them in one position for long."

"Fine," Ren snarled. "I'll flirt *less*. Happy?"

"We'll see," I said.

*

Chapter Twenty-Seven

Ren

We did see. And even though I couldn't help the fucking flirting – that shit was like breathing: did he expect me to stop doing that too? – I refrained from ordering a single flogging, even for the crimes brought before me that evening which clearly deserved it. It forced me to get quite creative with my punishments.

But it was worth it to see the small nod Mathias gave me after each one, an approving smile playing about those gorgeous lips that I longed to take between my teeth and bite down on until I drew more of those delightfully surprised yelps from him.

And once Mat had forgiven me for the flirtatious comments that had totally accidentally slipped out to one or two…or maybe three of the serving staff over dinner, an apology which involved far too much ego-stroking on my part – and other types of stroking too – it turned out my northerner was as good as his word, obediently falling into position for me. It was exhilarating, controlling him with just a command, watching him struggle to keep his hands in place as I explored him with my own hands and mouth.

And I got to enjoy a whole three and a half minutes of that delicious compliance before Mathias reverted to his usual fidgety and defiant self. But half the fun was in hauling his disobedient ass back into place, and the wide-eyed, breathless looks he gave me said he was enjoying the manhandling just as much as I was.

We lay in bed afterwards, him stubbornly reclothed because he didn't know the meaning of *relaxed*, and I watched him fall asleep next to me. With the taste of his spend on my lips and his fingers entwined in mine, I felt as though I was flying.

And with that, we fell into somewhat of a rhythm over the next two weeks, maintaining our pretence of being enemies whilst out in the palace and then taking out our frustrations of the day on each other when we retired for the night. Mathias still couldn't be good for me for long, despite my repeated corrections, although I adored that he hadn't lost an inch of his contrariness.

I hadn't fucked him. I still hadn't even let him touch me, and that was deliberate, even as it was agonising. I had a plan for my little wildcat, and the current stage involved lavishing him with pleasure with absolutely no obligations in turn. I wasn't going to give him a single reason to feel awkward or uncomfortable, not while I was getting him used to what we were doing. Not that Mat hadn't *tried* to reciprocate, and that made me feel all warm and squishy inside – as well as a little smug that I could have a so-called straight northern royal so desperate to get his hands down my trousers – but that was something else that got his fingers smacked and ordered away.

Unfortunately, things weren't nearly as fun between us during the day. *La Cortina's* anger at Mazekhstam was only just now starting to fade after a fortnight, and while none of them seemed inclined to sign up to our army and *do something* about it, Mat's visible presence in the palace still made him an easy target. I couldn't afford to chide them for their cruel words and taunts each and every time, but by Dios, I'd never realised how fucking bloodthirsty my people were. It was even making Elías and Jiron twitchy, and they were two of the most composed people I'd ever met.

With no choice but to ride out the wave, I'd gotten the same metalsmith who did my crowns to design a set of manacles for Mat that were significantly lighter than the real thing. Oh, they still held my little northerner in place, but it saved him the crooked back and chafed wrists from having to heft the heavy iron around all the time. Mathias had looked at me curiously when I'd introduced them on the fourth day, and I'd had to do some very hasty complaining about not wanting to put up with Starling's bitching about having to constantly heal his wrists to avoid accusations that I was being – Dios forbid – *nice*.

I would have been worried about someone in the palace noticing the switch, but Mat's acting was excellent, and no one had yet suspected that the restraints weren't the painful, heavy chains he pretended to heave around. And frequently whinged about, because apparently surrendering his body to me every night did not make the man any less of a petulant bastard during the day.

Even if I did catch him occasionally pulling a face at me behind the back of whatever lord or landowner I was entertaining at the time.

"Indeed," I said now, smothering a smile as Mat gleefully mimed throttling the younger Lord Lago with the chain linking his shackles. "That sounds like a *terrible* ordeal."

Mathias rolled his eyes, and then as the lord shifted in his seat, bringing him back into his eyeline, gave a long-suffering sigh accompanied by a forlorn expression.

Lago coughed. "He doesn't...he doesn't have to be here."

"I'm afraid he does," I said. "If I let him out of my sight, I fear what may happen. These northerners are awfully fragile, you know." I clicked my tongue and waved an idle hand, my rings reflecting the flames of the candles between us. "This one almost died when he first arrived at *la Cortina*, for absolutely no reason at all."

"Oh," Lago said. "He sounds high maintenance."

At least the nobility had stopped calling Mathias *it* all the time.

"You have no idea," I agreed, and Mat glared at me from over the lord's head. "Other than your...hangnail, Lago, are you otherwise well?"

"Well enough, but it's a stressful time. I expect we could both do with some way to…" He trailed off meaningfully, raising an eyebrow.

I eyed him and the way he was lazing in his chair, one arm thrown casually over the back of it. Terrible posture to be displaying in front of a prince, but *perfect* for this prince, and Lago knew it. His shirt was just pulling up at his hips, showing off his toned stomach, and was loose enough at his neck that I could see the collarbones I'd licked more than once.

I tried not to sigh. Turning down sex was *hard*.

It wasn't like I'd made a promise of monogamy to Mat, but he didn't have to say it for me to know that if I messed around with anyone else, I'd lose any chance with him. It was pretty fucking clear from the way his mouth was currently set in a hard line as he glanced between me and the young lord, and how he'd acted when I'd kissed Isobella, even though that had been downright platonic.

Fuck. Would that...I mean, I was planning to keep Mathias. Forever. Would the price of making him mine mean I lost the chance to play with anyone else *ever again*?

"High maintenance indeed," I muttered with a scowl, and Lago frowned.

"Your Highness?"

"For a reason involving orange and almond flan, a rainy night at the foot of a cliff, and an almost obsessive adoration for baths," I said, "I must immediately depart this conversation."

I leapt from my own chair, ignored the deep furrows of confusion carved into Lago's face, and swept from the room. Mat, El and Ademar were quick on my heels.

I snuck a glance back at Mathias as we ascended the stairs back to my rooms. He snorted.

"Do you want a commendation for doing the decent thing and not fucking up his marriage further?"

"No," I said, although I did. "I thought you might want to know that I received a letter from Velichkov."

I pulled it from my coat and waved it at him. Mat charged up the steps and snatched it from my hand before I could think of a price to exact from him for it.

His grey-blue eyes scanned the parchment with fervour, and I knew he was reading the rambling voyage account of a sailor who had recently docked in eastern Quareh. "I don't..."

"It's encoded. Even your brother isn't that stupid." It was my turn to snort. "He knows I've not publicly announced your true identity yet, and he's got to expect that any letters will first go through hands that aren't mine." I hadn't known until I received the missive earlier today whether de la Vega had come through for me, but sure enough, the bastard hadn't let me down. His ships had gotten my letter to Valeri Velichkov, and here was the proof.

"Tell me what it says!"

I smirked. "Hmm. What's it worth to you?"

Mat narrowed his eyes. "Ren..."

"I'm just saying it took me ten minutes to decode all that sentimental nonsense, so you owe me at least the same amount of time describing how handsome you think I am–"

"Renato Aratorre," he growled, suddenly in my face as we reached the top of the stairs. "Tell me."

The dominance in his tone was astounding. My little wildcat might get heat in his eyes when I pinned him down, but he also didn't take shit from anyone, least of all me. I loved that about him.

"It starts with a detailed threat to cut off certain parts of my body and feed them to me," I said airily, rolling my eyes at Jiron. I'd actually been quite impressed by the Temarian prince's imaginative description as to *how* he would make that happen, although I wouldn't be admitting it. "It seems your precious Val doesn't forgive as easily as you do. Naturally, that takes up half of the letter."

"Naturally," Mathias agreed. "The other half?"

"A begrudging agreement to inflict political pressure on Mazekhstam to cede control of Algejón in exchange for your release."

Mat's breath caught. "He's going to help you get your city back?"

"Indeed."

He made a happy noise, and didn't even bother to plaster on his usual scowl as we passed a throuple half hidden behind one of the salacious statues who were clearly trying to test the physical possibility of the stone lovers' pose. It…valued flexibility, is all I will say.

"The next part intrigues me," I said, once we were out of earshot. "Your brother asks after you, and then talks of attempting to undo a half century promise. I suppose he thinks he's being awfully clever, but neither you nor I earn any prizes for working out what *that's* referring to."

Mat's horrified yet hopeful gaze met mine.

"Do you think he could do it?" he breathed. "End the northern treaty's hostage exchange?"

"I think if anyone is stubborn enough to try, it would be a Velichkov," I said, amused. "There's also a postscript addressed to you."

"Oh?" he asked curiously, falling for it with that little wide-eyed innocent look I adored so much.

"Yeah." I pointed to an innocuous line about the price of salted meat in Onn.

"P.S. let me know if that Quarehian prince of yours is available for sharing, as he's the hottest thing I've ever seen in my fucking life."

"Hilarious," Mathias deadpanned, and then his expression softened. "Can I keep this?"

"No," I said. "If Moreno finds a sailor's diary in the possession of a Mazekhstani prisoner, it's going to look suspicious as fuck."

"You won't let him get close enough to me to find it," he pressed, and aww, that statement and the certainty in which it was expressed made my heart melt a little.

I offered a resigned sigh, letting him know I was giving in. And then as he relaxed, I plucked the parchment from his hands and threw it into the flames of one of the lit braziers lining the hallway.

Mat made an indignant, dismayed sound, and leapt forward to save it. I caught his arm before he could stick his hand in the fucking fire, and his momentum caused him to swing around into me. He all but fell against my chest, the metal around his wrists clinking against the buttons of my coat.

"Don't be a sentimental fool," I murmured, but as his expression turned sly, I sucked in a breath. "And don't be a conniving little wench either, Nathanael. I'm not leaving you alone with a message such as that so you can decrypt the code."

He pouted. "It's clearly not an Aratorre secret if you taught it to Val."

"I *made* it for him," I corrected. "A nice and simple substitution cipher that even brutish thugs like Valeri can get their heads around. Cracking it will not let you read the rest of my letters, *mi amor*."

"Then what's the harm in teaching it to me as well?"

I laughed and shoved him down the corridor ahead of me.

It was an excellent question, yet not one I was inclined to answer. Not when Velichkov had spent two precious paragraphs of his message in assurance that he was praying daily for the deliverance of his brother's immortal, yet sinful, soul.

Mat didn't need to know that shit.

*

Chapter Twenty-Eight

Mat

Ren was a fucking tease. Over these last weeks, he'd gotten me off in all sorts of ways – his hands, his mouth, that unexpectedly mind-shattering sensation of his fingers inside me – but whenever I tried to return the favours, I found my hands knocked away or restrained by his fingers around my wrists.

That wasn't to say Ren didn't come. He took great pleasure in making me watch as he took himself in hand, but he didn't let me do it. Not even once.

And I might have thought it a unique quirk of the prince's had I not seen Lord Lago on his knees before him that time, clearly allowed to do more than fucking touch. What was so special about *him*, when as soon as I tried to do anything more than kiss Ren, I found myself in any number of positions similar to this one, straddled face first down on the bed with one of his hands holding both of mine together at the small of my back and the other clearly getting himself off judging by the pleased, obscene noises the prince was making above me?

I spat out a mouthful of blankets. "Let me up."

"No."

"I want to help."

"You are helping." Ren's voice was both amused and breathless.

"I want to touch you."

"Am I supposed to care what you want?"

I paused. "Yes?"

A snort. "That's adorable. Clothes."

Ren released my wrists and I scrambled to pull off my shirt and mostly undone trousers from my prone position on the bed. Which was Blessed difficult with a prince straddling my hips, but I'd long since learned that pointing out such impracticalities merely netted me a hard cuff around the head and a comment about how I would *manage*.

"You're gorgeous," Ren whispered, shifting backwards to sit on my knees. The prince trailed a fingernail down my bare back from neck to ass, making me shiver, and I heard a cork being unstoppered seconds before I felt oil drizzling between my cheeks. I tried not to clench in anticipation of the fingers that I knew were coming – fuck, it always felt amazing, but I never got used to the shock of that first push, especially if Ren was in one of his crueller moods and not inclined to be gentle – but to my surprise, he ignored my hole and instead smeared the oil lower. There was a rustle of fabric and then the prince was thrusting between my slicked-up thighs, pressing tender kisses to my shoulder blades.

"Dios, you feel so good," he hissed, increasing his pace, and as I wasn't objecting to being rudely thrown down onto the bed and used to get him off, I merely smiled contentedly into the blankets as I savoured the sensation of Ren rutting against me.

"I expect I'd feel even better five inches higher," I pointed out after a moment, but the prince just laughed.

"So fucking greedy," he said with a breathless chuckle, as he always did when I felt brave enough to suggest taking things further. For a man who crowed about fucking me in the ass far too often, he never seemed inclined to actually want to do so. Again, what had happened that night with Lago told me that it wasn't a Ren thing, it was a *me* thing, yet no amount of pestering would get the prince to open up about why he wouldn't do it.

"I'm ready," I whispered to him, and I was. As terrifying as the prospect of allowing him in had once been, it now gave me a thrill each time I let myself imagine it. I wanted to be even closer than we were now, to hold him and *feel* him, and I may or may not have been looking a little more intently at the raunchy statues that adorned the palace's corridors for ideas.

"That's nice for you," the prince said, not slowing his pace between my thighs even for a moment.

"*Ren*. We can do this. I'm ready."

"I'm not." He gave a long-suffering sigh that he ruined with a snicker. "I hope you're not trying to pressure me into something so *personal,* so *intimate-*"

"Asshole."

I felt his weight lift off me and then I was being rolled over, his unbound hair tickling my bare chest as he leaned forward and tenderly teased one of my nipples with his tongue. And then the bastard bit down without even a graze of his teeth to warn me.

"Ah! *Blyat!*"

"You're always so surprised when I hurt you," Ren murmured, his voice thick with arousal. He pressed soothing kisses to the tender nub of flesh, offering sweet reassurances as he always did immediately after inflicting pain. "I tell you that I will, that I enjoy doing it to you, and yet you still startle and scream for me, *mi sol*." His grin turned wicked. "I love it."

I threw my head back against the pillow as his kisses turned to insistent licks that made the sensitive, hurt skin tingle so fucking deliciously. "I'm glad my suffering entertains you." My words were little more than heaving gasps.

"Immensely," he assured me. "Want me to go easier on this one?" His mouth moved to my other nipple, and he kissed it gently.

"Yes, please," I begged.

"Too bad."

"Ow!"

Ren laughed against my chest before he returned to the bitten skin to soothe the hurt away with his tongue.

Bastard. I shouldn't still be falling for his tricks, but I was, and I couldn't entirely hate it. Getting his hands on me on a nightly basis, because he was the horniest fucker I'd ever met, all seemed to put him in a fantastic mood. No two nights were ever the same with him, his creativity boundless even if he was still keeping certain things between us off limit for whatever reason, and I watched, curious and turned on, as he shuffled forward on his knees to straddle my hips before taking both of our cocks in his fist and stroking them together.

The prince's movements were smooth, practised, and I gasped as he started to tug more urgently, lost to the sensation of both his hand and the velvet smoothness of his cock sliding against mine. The sight was mesmerising.

My hands came to rest at his slender waist.

A WHISPER AND A BREATH

"Nathanael," Ren warned, slowing his pace, and I obediently tucked my hands under my head, albeit with a frustrated whine because I wasn't above letting him know how irritating he was, even when naked. Perhaps especially so.

"Why do you never let me touch you?"

"Because," he said, answering me for once. "Because it drives you insane. Because I like you at my mercy. And because I enjoy watching you obey me."

I heaved in a breath at each admission, watching his gaze darken with lust. "In *that* case, Your Highness…"

I drew my hands back to run them down his legs, relishing the feeling of the prince's taut muscles beneath my fingers.

Ren tsked in mock admonishment. "Keep doing that and I'll tie you to the fucking bed, Mathias."

I squeezed his knees where they rested on either side of my hips, and then traced my fingers back up the inside of his thighs, the back of my hand knocking against his as he continued to jerk us off together. Ren shuddered under my touch, and fully growled when I travelled further to graze my fingertips against his balls.

"Brat. Did you not hear me?"

"I heard you," I murmured, my eyes fluttering closed of their own accord as he built up the pace between us both once more. "Maybe I'll even let you."

Ren let out an interested little groan.

"Oh Nat, sometimes I think you can't possibly have any other surprises left in you. And then you go and say things like that." He huffed out a harsh breath, almost sounding winded, and dragged the nails of his free hand down my chest.

I gasped under the pain delivered by one of his hands and the pleasure by the other, heat and pure fucking *need* rapidly building within me. I didn't have the words to reply to him. All coherent thoughts had been driven from my head, and the world had narrowed to the feel of his body against mine, hot and desperate and so damn right I wanted to scream.

Strong fingers gripped my chin and I opened my eyes to find the prince staring intently at me, his face clouded with pleasure as he jerked us both faster. "I assure you I intend to find out just how much you meant that," Ren promised with a hiss, his expression feverishly wild, "but right now, I couldn't stop myself if I tried. I want you so much it hurts."

His words took me over the edge and I cried out his name as I shattered into pieces, hearing my own echoed around me as he followed me over the edge.

Ren tensed, his back arching, and for a moment there was nothing but timeless, blissful ecstasy. Warmth splashed across my stomach in invigorated evidence of our shared moment, and his lips curved in satisfaction as he stared down at me.

And then we heaved in simultaneous breaths.

"Oh, *mi cielo*, you are so Blessed perfect," Ren whispered, and I loved this moment, this softness that always showed in the seconds after the prince found his release. His gaze was unguarded, his expression content, and he swayed above me as if drunk.

I lifted my head and found Ren's mouth with my own, tasting his gentle moans as he came down from his high and running my hands through his loose hair in the way I'd discovered he adored.

The prince gave a happy sigh and collapsed bonelessly on top of me, letting me wrap him up in my arms and hold him close. We stayed like that for a moment, sharing breaths and nuzzling against each other, and then Ren uncurled his legs and rolled over to lie beside me.

He lifted a hand to smear the mess we'd made from my stomach up to my chest, lazily tracing patterns in the mixed cum with his index finger. Just as I was about to point out that he was equally filthy from where he'd lain on me, I realised the swirls and circles had taken on edges and a deliberate design.

Letters.

I watched, contented and amused, as he finished writing his name in our shared seed.

"There," Ren declared, giving me an indulgent grin. "You're officially mine, Nathanael Velichkov. Says so right here." He underlined the words.

"'Property of Renato Aratorre'," I read. "Awfully presumptuous of you, Quarehian."

"Not at all. You are." He kissed me, and then sighed against my mouth. "We need to get to breakfast."

"Bath first, I think," I said with a laugh.

"I don't know. I quite like the idea of having you wear my name all day."

I was wearing a lot fucking more than just his name. I could already feel the cum hardening on me as it dried. "Bath first," I repeated firmly.

After a bath – which of course was peaceful and uninterrupted, and didn't at all involve an impossibly horny prince offering to wash me clean and ultimately ending up in a second round of wet and soapy sex – I wandered out into the antechamber while Camila dressed and prepared Ren for the day.

"Morning, Mathias," Jiron murmured in greeting, and his friendly, neutral smile gave me hope that he hadn't heard anything…*untoward* coming from behind the doors he was guarding this morning.

And then the sly smirk worn by the man standing next to him undid that optimism immediately.

"Something to say, Ademar?" I snapped, and he shook his head slowly, not bothering to wipe an ounce of the smugness off his face.

"I believe you've said it all," he offered. "Or screamed it. What does *da, bystreye!* mean, anyway?"

"Yes, faster!" Ren helpfully supplied from behind me where Camila was painting his eyes with kohl. Flushing, I pulled the door shut and slammed it between us.

"Quite clearly, it means *mind your own fucking business,*" I told the guard through gritted teeth. I hadn't realised I'd been loud enough for him to have made out my words. By the Blessed, this was *humiliating*.

"Right," Ademar said, but if anything, his grin became even wider. "And *ya blizko!?*"

I was not telling him *that*. Had he really heard me yell out how close I'd been?

"That's capable of a few interpretations," I responded sweetly. "It doesn't have a direct translation, but most northern scholars would agree that the closest Quarehian equivalent is *go fuck yourself, Ademar, because clearly no one else wants to.*"

Ad grabbed at me, irritated, but I'd been fully expecting it and danced out of his reach.

"Growing slow in your old age?" I teased, watching his gaze darken with fury. "If you keep letting me get away like that, people are going to think you're as terrible at your job as you really are."

He let out a low growl, flicking his hair from his face. "Come here, you little shit!"

I dove around the back of Jiron, using his muscular bulk as a shield as Ad chased me around and hissed out threats when I managed to evade him.

"Do you believe I will protect you, little one?" Jiron asked, sounding amused as he looked down at me.

"Well," I said carefully, continuing to circle his massive form to keep him between me and the other guard. "You won't gang up with me against Ren...but Ademar? Surely *he's* fair game?"

There was silence for a moment, and then Jiron shifted, a sudden explosion of movement like a snake striking at its prey. He wrapped a massive arm around Ad's neck and hooked the smaller man into a headlock. Ademar grunted in surprise but I had to give him credit for recovering quickly, because he drove a vicious fist into Jiron's side as he swung him around. Jiron yanked him backwards across the antechamber, attempting to pull him off balance even as Ademar kicked out at his knees.

I barked a laugh.

"Cute," said a voice in my ear. "But do you think I'm going to let you get away with setting my brother up like that?"

I turned around slowly, greeted by Elías' unimpressed expression and folded arms.

"El-"

The breath was knocked out of my lungs as he bodily lifted me and threw me over his shoulder. I smacked at his back, but it was entirely ineffective. Ren's guards were made of pure muscle.

"Jiron!" Elías said loudly, striding over to where him and Ad were still struggling. "Release him, or your *little one* gets it."

"Let go of me," I ordered, tugging at his dark blue coat, but he just wrapped an arm more securely around my legs to hold them still.

I couldn't see what was happening from my inverted position at El's back, but I felt the reverberating thud as something heavy hit the ground. Jiron chuckled, but it sounded breathless.

"That's a dangerous game you seem to be playing with me, Ademar."

"Luis!" I yelled, spotting him as he peeked out of the guards' bedroom. He wore an irritated expression and nothing else, clearly woken by our noise. "You remember those lemon biscuits you managed to sequester away last week that were gone the next day? Elías was the one who ate them!"

Actually it had been me and Ren in our endless quest to wind Luis up, but this narrative suited me perfectly. Luis narrowed his eyes and charged at El without hesitation, his huge arms coming around to encompass the smaller man's frame.

I realised my mistake at pretty much the same time as the naked guard collided with not just Elías, but me on his shoulder, and the three of us fell into a heap on the ground. My face was pressed uncomfortably into Luis' armpit, and I only escaped the indignity when he reached out to grab hold of Elías' braided hair.

Luis growled out death threats as El kicked him, and somehow I managed to wriggle free of their fight, crawling backwards to the wall where I could watch all four guards grappling and laughing. Ad rolled Jiron into the low table between the lounges and it abruptly disintegrated, while El managed to slither out from underneath Luis and pin his face to the floor.

"Mathias. What utter fucking chaos have you caused *this* time?"

The guards all froze, hastily disentangling from each other and clambering to their feet to offer messy bows to their prince. Ademar stumbled, having sunk into his bow before he was properly upright, and Jiron caught him by the shoulders before he could fall.

"You assume it's my fault?" I asked Ren with amusement, and he simply raised an eyebrow as he looked down at me on the floor.

"Undoubtedly." He glanced at his men. "Am I wrong?"

A synchronised chorus of "no, Your Highness," made me snort.

"Traitors, the lot of you," I said in dismay, clambering to my feet. "So if we're stabbing people in the back this morning, Luis, you should know that it was actually Ren who plotted to steal your biscuits."

Ren's eyes sparkled. "You'll find it was Nat who did the actual taking."

"While you distracted him," I countered, entertained by how Luis' head was tracking between us both. "Besides, you ate more of them."

"Did not."

"I'm sorry, is six not more than two? Perhaps maths works differently south of the border?"

"Stealing is a sin, Mathias," Ren said piously. "I expect you'll be joining me in my morning prayers to ask His forgiveness for the *seven* stolen lemon biscuits you consumed."

"I can't tell which of them is lying," Ademar muttered to Elías, eyeing me and Ren suspiciously.

"Both of them," said Luis. "There were only three."

—

It was a good day, by which I meant that Ren dined with Altagracia and not one of the myriad of men who always wanted something from him, as I'd found that who he took breakfast with generally set his mood for the next few hours.

And when Alta convinced Ren to not only let me sit and eat with them instead of stealing food from the table, but also to discard the fucking shackles for the day, I could have kissed her.

"The palace has settled," Alta cooed, beaming at Ren in a way that said she knew she'd won him over...or she better have, if he knew what was good for him. "The gossip has turned to other matters, and there are barely any comments about Mazekhstam. I haven't heard a single threat or slur made against Lord Grachyov in over two days."

Neither had I, I realised. It had become so commonplace to be hated everywhere I trod in the palace that I'd started to block it out, but the last couple of days had been relatively painless. Lord de la Vega had started bowing to me again, and even the rest of them were favouring their usual tactic of ignoring me over expressing outright hatred.

Ren gave a sad smile. "I expect you're right," he said quietly, gazing out over the low walls of the terrace and to the orchards beyond.

"So we can finally ditch the manacles?" I pressed, and his lips quirked into a sly grin.

"Say please, *mi sol*."

I blew out an irritated breath and kicked back my chair, stalking over to Jiron and holding my wrists out.

He obediently unlocked the shackles and took them from me, which I knew meant he'd received one of Ren's *looks* of permission. As sweet as the guard could be at times, I'd long learned that he'd never take my side over that of the prince, and occasional sympathetic glances were all I'd get from him that weren't strictly in line with his orders.

I bowed low to Alta, whose gaze danced with satisfaction.

"I would like to visit Starling," I said. "I'll meet you at the chapel in half an hour, Your Highness?"

"Oh, will you? All this newfound freedom seems to be going to your head, Mat."

I eyed him as he lazed back in his chair, face turned to the sun. "It's funny you should talk about heads. Mine is aching, and I expect that I'll be forced to complain about it *all day* unless it's seen to by a healer."

Ren cackled at the threat and waved me away.

Jiron, who accompanied me down to the courtyard, surprised me by offering to stay outside again. "Prince's orders," he said, confirming my earlier thoughts. "And a privilege that will be revoked if you try *anything*, Mathias."

"What would I possibly try?" I asked innocently, blinking up at him. He snorted, and ruffled my hair.

"I am beginning to know you too well to be fooled by you, little one," he said. "Go. Be with your friend."

I knocked on the door of the surgery and heard Starling's voice call for me to enter. Wondering why she hadn't greeted me at it as usual, I opened it cautiously to find her running her hands over the leg of a groaning man lying on one of her tables, red and green sparks flying from her fingers. He wore the blue coat and grey trousers of a guard, a single gold line at his collar marking him as an ordinary palace guard as opposed to those personally belonging to Ren or his father.

The healer acknowledged me with a nod, and then returned her attentions to her injured patient. I stood quietly in the corner until they were done.

"Broke his legs jumping off the fucking walls," Starling muttered darkly, once she'd shooed the man out a few minutes later. "And not by accident, or because he was being chased, or anything *reasonable* like that. No. He just wanted to see what it *felt like. Cabrón,*" she swore, shooting a vicious look at the closed door.

I swallowed.

"Speaking of seeing," I said. "I apparently have the Sight?" It came out like a question.

Starling raised an eyebrow and gathered her frizzy hair in her fists, tying it back with a scrap of string. "Ah. Welcome to the world of unrealistic expectations, constant demands, and petty jealousy. Being Blessed sucks."

"You don't seem that surprised. It scared the hell out of me."

She grinned and poked a finger at the spot between my eyes. "Always knew you were special, my lord."

I snorted. "Bullshit."

"But I wish you'd Seen what a mistake falling into bed with the prince would be," she added, her voice tight. "Then maybe you wouldn't have been such an idiot to do so."

I choked. "Who says I've-"

"My gift allows me insight into a person's body whenever I touch them," Starling said softly, taking my hand in hers. "Any injuries, illnesses…the soreness of certain muscles and multiple bite marks, perhaps?"

I stared at her.

"That's fucking invasive," I spat, wrenching my hand away. "Don't do that again."

"I can't turn it off, Mathias, any more than you can stop yourself Seeing things."

"Then don't *comment on it,* Starling. *Bliiiin!*"

She cocked her head. "What does that mean?"

Her eager question stole my anger and turned it into a surprised laugh. "Uh, pancake."

She blinked at me. *"Pancake?"*

"Technically speaking, yes. But we use it to swear. Nicely."

She grinned. "I like it. *Blin.* I'm going to use that from now on. You'll have to teach me more Mazkehstani, my lord."

The honorific made me bite my tongue. I wanted so badly to tell her who I was, but the secret had already made its way to five too many of *la Cortina's* inhabitants. If the threats delivered by the real Mathias Grachyov were true, my identity was a dangerous secret that could result in the deaths of my best friends back home if Quareh learned of it. I couldn't afford to be careless.

So I told her something else. Something even Ren didn't know.

"There's one thing I've been Seeing over and over again," I said quietly. "A vision, about here in the palace. Up on the terrace, actually."

Starling watched me carefully, not interrupting.

"It's Ren. He…" I swallowed. "He stabs me. And fuck, Starling, I feel it. Every time. My blood just pouring out of me, too quick to stop, and all I can see are those three stupid fucking flags at half mast and then I'm falling over the edge and…"

I inhaled. "I die. So that's fantastic."

I wondered why I was telling her and not the prince, but really, what could I say to him?

Hey asshole, I Saw you kill me. I'd really prefer it if you didn't, thanks.

Either he would, or he wouldn't. When would there ever be a situation where he would have stabbed me but for me asking him real nicely upfront not to? Sometimes this Sight thing was an absolute bitch of a curse. Who needed to know what their insides would look like splashed on their boots?

And I certainly hadn't needed to feel it the three dozen or so times the vision had hit me over the years.

Starling stirred at my side, restless and horrified. "Oh, shit. Do you See anything else about that moment?"

"Not much. Ren has blood on his face."

"Do you know-"

"Why he kills me?" I gave a short laugh that sounded bitter even to my own ears. "Not a fucking clue, Star."

Her lips pressed into a thin line. "Aratorres don't need a *why* to be cruel, Mathias. I was going to ask *when*."

"That's not fair. Ren can be..." I shrugged, swallowing down memories of him being all over me this morning. "Nice."

"Oh, he can be delightful!" Starling agreed readily, an unexpected wistfulness lighting up her face. "So charming, so *clever*. And when he smiles at you, as if you're the only one he truly sees out of everyone who fawns over him on a daily basis?" She gave a happy hum. "It's really something, isn't it?"

I shifted uncomfortably, biting down on the irrational jealousy her words invoked in me. "There's more to him than that."

Her expression softened. "There is. It must be so hard for him, being who he is. Having the weight of the country on his shoulders and bearing all those expectations from his father when he's so young."

"Not just expectations," I growled, and Starling nodded sympathetically at the reminder of what Ren regularly suffered at the king and Moreno's hands.

"And once you get to know him, you realise there's so much more to the prince than his flirting and his jokes. There's such a huge heart behind that hot as fuck exterior, isn't there?"

"Exactly!" I said, pleased that she got it. "He actually cares. No one-"

"*No one else understands him, but he's so compassionate and thoughtful,*" Starling finished for me, but now her voice was cold, mocking. All traces of admiration had disappeared from her face. "Like the true fucking psychopath he is."

The blood drained from my face. "Starling..."

"How the fuck do you think he gets so many people into his bed?" she demanded, sending me cold. "Not all of them are shallow enough to be caught by his looks alone. It's his *hook*, Mathias, and it seems you've fallen straight for it."

"No," I said. "*Don't.*"

"Ren is only nice when it suits him to be," hissed Starling. "The carefree, amused prince, bestowing favours on those who can further his own needs." She gave me a significant look. "You and I have both seen his darker side. Or have you forgotten all the things he's done to you? Or why you're here *at all?*"

Starling didn't wait for my answer, perhaps suspecting I couldn't give one.

"I don't need to tell you what his father is capable of. This entire fucked up country is proof enough of that. And his brother beat a boy to death with his own hands when he was only thirteen, did you know that?"

I exhaled sharply. "They're not Ren."

The healer shot me a dark look. "Ask your precious prince about what Horacio did. Watch him jump to defend him. And then remember that the next time an Aratorre strips your back open or damn near strangles you to death. Or worse, Mathias." Her eyes narrowed, and I knew we were both thinking of what my Sight had shown me. "*Or fucking worse.*"

*

Chapter Twenty-Nine

Ren

"He's good for you," Alta murmured, her head on my shoulder as we stood together at the edge of the terrace, watching Moreno putting his men through their drills at the foot of the palace walls.

"*¿Qué?*"

"Mathias," she said. "You seem more relaxed lately."

"Al, I have a murdered village, an unapprehended assassin, and a bloodthirsty neighbour to contend with," I reminded her with some exasperation. And then there were the things I couldn't tell her about: Mat's real identity, his brother messing around with Riehse Eshan's delicate peace in an effort to end the hostage exchange when he *should* be trying to get me my stolen city back, the suspicious way Moreno had been eying me these last few weeks since he'd caught me and Mathias playing in the throne room. "How can I possibly be *relaxed*?"

"I was talking to my Ren, not Quareh's prince." She lifted her head and gave me a meaningful look from under dark eyelashes. "You'll always have death and politics in your life, but right now, I'm glad you also have him."

"*Y a ti,*" I added. *And you.* For it was Alta's friendship that had held me together this last decade, since we were thrown together by mine and Moreno's joint exile and found solace in our shared circumstances. Both our mothers had died young, and our parental influence consisted of little more than learning how best to avoid or endure our fathers' cruelty.

Even if Altagracia didn't know the full extent of what the king and the Comandante had done to me over the years, I could never have made it between their brutal beatings without her. Al's quick smile and unwavering encouragement, her abject refusal to swear, her streaks of quiet defiance against the role she was expected to play as a Quarehian woman, her private yet vocal anger at the world for what it had thrown at us…I loved her so fucking much, and wished I could give her more than an unwanted fate as my wife.

I'd take care of her when it happened, of course. Yet neither of us would be happy in the role of spouse, not when royal marriage came with the automatic expectation to produce heirs. Not all those who identified as asexual were averse to sex, but Alta had damn near shuddered whenever we'd broached the subject in the past, and I hated that one day it would no longer be just an unpleasant thought for her, but a reality. I vowed I'd be as gentle as possible, ask for none of the shit that I'd normally crave between the sheets, but really, what did that matter when I would still be forcing a woman to lie with me when she didn't want to?

I breathed in her perfume and pressed a chaste kiss to her forehead. "In that case, *mi querida,* let us hold onto this 'right now' you speak of."

"If anyone could sweet talk time into doing something as crazing as stopping, it would be you," she noted fondly, wrapping my left arm around her shoulder and idly rubbing her thumb over the leather cuff at my wrist as she always did. "You'd flirt your ass off and she'd agree in a heartbeat."

"Time is a she?"

"Can you prove otherwise?"

"I can't say that I can," I conceded. Alta gave a laugh, her voice high-pitched and delighted, and then sobered.

"What will you do when you're forced to return Lord Grachyov to his family?"

It was my turn to chuckle, a soft snicker against her ear. "That's not going to happen."

"I don't understand. Aren't you negotiating his release in exchange for Algejón to be handed back over to Quareh?"

"That's what he thinks," I said. "And your father, and mine. They're all confoundingly, terribly *wrong.* Mathias isn't going anywhere."

Alta's sigh was a touch resigned. "And I don't suppose you have a plan for how you will pull off this miracle, when there will be two countries expecting you to honour any bargain struck?"

Three. There was no doubt that Temar would also be watching very fucking closely.

"Is that what you suppose?" I shrugged. "You'd probably be right."

"*Renato.*"

"*Altagracia,*" I said, mimicking her tone and gently squeezing her shoulders before I released her. "You worry about avoiding your father for the day, and I'll worry about keeping my little wildcat where he's supposed to be." I shot her a wink. "Which for your sake I'll say is *by my side,* although we both know what I really mean is-"

"Walking all over you."

"-pinned beneath me," I finished, entirely dissatisfied as I eyed her and the amused expression she was wearing. I waved a hand. "Go on. Say whatever it is you're thinking."

"He's quite the actor," Alta mused, brushing down the sleeves of her dress. "I had thought those chains you had him wearing were heavy, but last week I realised how soft you are on him."

It wasn't an admonishment, not from her. And I didn't bother trying to deny it – Al had always been incredibly observant, and if Mat's pretence hadn't fooled her, mine certainly wouldn't. I hadn't even told her that the northerner had finally given into my attempts to get him into bed: she'd taken one look at us when we arrived back in *la Cortina* and ambushed me in the next private moment we had together to *tell her everything.* Not the 'gory details', as she'd put it so primly, but all the soppy stuff about feelings and shit.

"Hmm," I said noncommittally, but I was still turning her words over in my head as I wandered down to the chapel ten minutes later, surprised to find Mat already waiting outside. Usually I had to drag him away from Starling's surgery after he'd finished testing my patience by staying twice as long as I'd allowed.

Jiron, whose crossed arms gave me an excellent view of his thick biceps straining at the seams of his shirt, shot me a look that said something was wrong but he didn't know what. We both cast our eyes down to his feet, where Mathias was sitting silently against the wall, feet planted on the floor and his forearms resting on his knees.

"Everything okay?" I said carefully, noting the scowl etched across his face.

"Fine." His voice was dull and listless, and held nothing of the joyful playfulness I'd relished hearing in it this morning.

"Very convincing."

His eyes flickered to mine for the first time since I'd arrived, and he swallowed. "Your brother."

I raised an eyebrow. "Yes?"

"Did he..." Mat sighed, clearly reluctant to ask whatever burning question had put him in his mood. "Is it true that when he was younger, he-"

"*No,*" I snarled, knowing what he was about to ask and not allowing those words to leave his mouth. Horacio had been through *enough*. "Who the fuck has been speaking of that to you? If Starling-"

"I heard about it back in Mazekhstam when it happened a decade ago," Mathias said. "You think a child prince who smashes in the skull of a stableboy with his bare hands – *for no reason* – goes unnoticed?"

I grabbed his collar and yanked him to his feet, jabbing a finger to his chest. "Don't believe the spiteful gossip of courts," I hissed at him, unable to believe that out of all the people he fought to protect on a daily basis, Mat would dare to condemn one of the best, most genuine people I knew, without ever having fucking met him. "They weren't there, and neither were you. You have no idea what happened."

"So it's not true?"

I felt sick. "I don't want to talk about it."

"Ren. I'm just asking."

"Horacio is a good man," I said stubbornly, ignoring the twitch of irritation that passed over Mathias' face as I ignored his question.

But what could I say? It *was* true. Every sordid detail they whispered about that day, except for the 'no reason' part, because of course he'd had a fucking *reason* for murdering an innocent child in front of half the palace, for continuing to hit him over and over as the boy's pleas turned to whimpers and then silence, blood smeared across my older brother's fists and the cobblestones beneath them. And a lifetime of geniality and decency, a kindness inherent to him that I would *never* possess, couldn't ever make up for that one gruesome moment that had darkened Horacio Aratorre's name across the entire fucking continent.

I heaved in a breath, pushing down the bad memories this conversation was invoking. "I assure you, he'll make an excellent king."

Once that prick who calls himself our father finally gets what's coming to him.

Mat got that look in his eye then, that grim and accusatory one that promised he was about to be a massive pain in my ass. "Oh? Will your brother revoke Quareh's ownership laws over women and girls, then? Ensure their equality in business dealings? Give them the respect they-"

"For fuck's sake, Nat, you always expect the impossible. And then have the audacity to be disappointed when it doesn't happen."

"I thought you agreed with me on this?" he hissed. "Don't tell me you actually approve of such barbarism!"

I passed a hand over my eyes. "Of course I don't approve! Like I don't *approve* of having to tax the poorest of my people, or order executions for wrongdoing, or send men to their deaths at our borders. But there's certain things in this world that are unavoidable, Mathias, if you want to run a country anywhere but into the fucking ground! If my brother changes the gender laws, do you know what would *happen*?"

He shrugged. "Restoration of some common decency?"

Oh, for…he was so idealistic sometimes, it was unbelievable. Had he not seen how much work it had taken over these last few weeks just to get the palace to accept a single woman in a position of moderate power? I'd had to decline petitions, wrangle compliance, defuse threats and send Jiron to talk sense into some of the more stubborn holdouts – and by *talk,* I meant that it was his knuckles engaging in the discourse – and Clementina had *still* found herself in Starling's care more than once, as some man or another decided to take it upon himself to remind her of her place. I was lucky the herald was showing herself to be every bit as stubborn as Mat at proving them wrong, because not only had she returned to work as soon as Starling had removed the latest blood or bruises she'd *accidentally* found herself coated in, but she'd done so with remarkable grace and efficiency. Her critics had found it difficult to find anything in her work to complain about, which had made my decision in promoting her far easier to justify, but there was still only a certain number of times I could repeat *"because I fucking said so"* before I wanted to hit something.

"Mat," I said instead. "What's wrong?" I doubted it was decade-old killings, or injustices that would still be there tomorrow, that had pulled him down into such a sombre mood. What had that fucking healer done to him that left him looking so exhausted?

He just sighed, and then shot me a fake smile that I saw straight through. "It's nothing. Go and pray, Your Highness."

Knowing I wouldn't get anything out of him while he was like this, I pushed open the chapel door, and then paused. "Would you…would you like to join me?"

It wasn't an invitation I normally extended to anyone. What passed between a man and his god was sacred, and it was in this holy place, the palace's royal chapel with its incense-covered altar and its stained-glass windows, that I always felt closer to Dios than anywhere else on the continent. It brought me peace, serenity, a snatched moment of the day that was His, and His alone.

I fucking hated it when my father was around, because not only did he ruin that for me, but he allowed Moreno access to the chapel too. And if anyone was capable of corrupting this beautiful little room with the blackness that rested inside his soul, it was that snake.

I held out my hand to Mathias, wanting to gift him the same sense of calmness that Dios gave me, but he shook his head.

"I lost my faith a long time ago," he said quietly, and then shot a glare at the altar as if it was to blame for all of his troubles. That stabbed a deep pity and sadness into my heart. How could one be without his god? Did he not feel…alone?

I averted my eyes and sank down to my knees on the delicate cushion set before the altar, sending up a prayer for Mat before I'd even closed my eyes.

Dios, bring his smile back. Please.

*

Chapter Thirty

Mat

"Go ahead. Enjoy your siesta," Ren murmured to me and Ademar as we approached his rooms after lunch. "Jiron needs to speak to me alone."

I didn't bother glancing at the guard's face to confirm it. Jiron and Ren seemed to have an almost telepathic link, and I'd have wondered at one of them having the mind-reading gift of the Hearken, had I not known that branch of the Blessed had died out a long time ago. No, it was nothing more than their deep friendship that allowed them to communicate without words, and it struck an unwelcome thread of jealousy within me as Ademar and I passed through the door into the antechamber and Jiron pulled it closed behind us, remaining in the corridor with his prince.

"What do you reckon that's about?" I asked and Ad snorted, taking off towards the bedroom he shared with the other guards on the opposite side of the antechamber as he stripped off his shirt, obviously planning to get as much rest as he could before he was called back onto duty.

"Just because His Highness is fucking you doesn't mean he has to share everything with you," he called out, not bothering to wait for an answer as he shoved open the door and disappeared from view.

I scowled at the empty doorway. "Prick."

"That he is," Luis agreed from one of the lounges where he was busy stuffing his face with some type of pastry, thankfully now clothed. He made as if to lift his ankle onto the low table that was normally there, seemed to remember it had been shattered into splinters as a result of Ad and Jiron's wrestling earlier, and glowered at the now empty space. "As are we all."

"Can't argue with that."

I kicked a short stool over to him and he shot me a grin as he hooked his foot around it to pull it into place.

"Hey, you got the chains removed. Good for you."

He sounded genuinely pleased for me, so I bit down on the usual sarcastic retort I'd normally have delivered about his observational skills, and offered a small shrug instead.

"Lady Moreno's doing."

Luis gave a hum of approval and kicked up his feet, lazing back as he ate. I tried to ignore the flakes of pastry dusting the cushions, but he must have noticed my annoyed glance, because his grin became wider and his chewing more careless.

I shook my head, diverting my eyes from the mess. "I'm going to get some sleep."

I had my jacket half off by the time I reached the doorway of the guards' room, looking forward to changing into Jiron's oversized shirt and napping the heat of the day away in his bed, but I stopped short at the sight of Ademar and Elías. The siblings were at the back of the room, their clothes discarded, and while they hadn't noticed me, I could certainly see *them*. My cheeks flushed.

Oh. That was...

How had I not realised before?

I pulled back, not wanting them to catch me looking, and promptly smacked into someone. A someone that smelled of saffron and citrus.

"Careful," Ren chuckled, laying his hands on my shoulders to steady us both. He nodded behind me. "Jiron's bed is that way, in case a northerner's sense of direction is as atrocious as they say."

I'd never heard that aspersion in my life, and I was guessing he hadn't either. Stirring asshole.

"Or you can enjoy the siesta in my bed, instead," the prince suggested, perking up at the thought.

"Elías...privacy," I said shortly, and jerked a thumb over my shoulder.

The suggestion that anything should be private of course had Ren immediately ducking around me to take a look.

"Oh," he said quietly as he spotted his guards. "Fuck. I forgot that you..."

He gave me a resigned shrug, and I frowned, tugging him into his own bedchamber and shutting the doors so we could speak without being overheard.

"How long have you known?" I asked, my mind whirring with the implications of what I'd seen.

"Since I hired El," Ren said. He wandered over to the side table and began cutting up an orange, licking the juice from his fingers. "Ademar came to me and asked that I take his brother on in my personal guard due to his extenuating circumstances. But he's more than earned his place."

"Brother?"

"Yes," Ren said firmly. "Elías may have been born with a vagina, but he's a man." The prince's seriousness evaporated with his wink. "He just has different toppings on his dessert, Mathias."

Oh, I was an idiot. When the rest of us had ended up with itchy stubble when travelling to and from Sesveko, how had I never questioned how El remained smooth-shaven the whole time? I'd just been so caught up in everything – what had almost happened to Val, what we'd seen in the ashes in Vitorona…

Now that I thought about it, I realised Elías had always been careful to get changed with his back to me. Not that I'd been *looking* of course, not wanting any of the guards to get the wrong impression of me, but today was the first time I'd seen him unclothed from the front. The sight of his breasts and lack of cock as he and Ademar climbed into their respective beds to rest for the siesta was making me realise that El – and Ren – were far more complex people than I'd realised.

"You knew he had a woman's body and still hired him? *You?*"

Ren shot me an irritated glare. "I knew he was a capable soldier," he corrected. "Ad spoke highly of his skills, and well…you've seen them for yourself. Did I not prove to you with Clementina that I am willing to make decisions based on more than sex?"

"You've also bitched and moaned about it for the past two weeks."

Ren muttered something to his orange before biting into one of the chunks he'd carved out. It sounded suspiciously like *"that's rich"*.

I waited impatiently for him to finish eating.

"Clementina has proved her aptitude already, but her appointment will always be politically charged," the prince said after he'd chewed and swallowed frustratingly slowly, and I watched his tongue dart out to lick his lips clean. Fuck, that tongue of his was the most delightful, wicked thing I'd ever encountered, the source of so much of my simultaneous irritation and pleasure. "No one but me and my men know about El. His voice is low enough, his breasts small enough, his muscles fucking big enough, that no one would think to question the gender of one of the prince's own guards. It's just a shame he has to keep that gorgeous body of his covered all the time."

"Wait, have you-"

"Sadly not," Ren huffed with a dramatic sigh that made me roll my eyes. "Which is also a shame. For *him*."

"You're impossible sometimes."

"Only sometimes? I'll have to try harder." He grinned and bit down into another piece of fruit. "Although I was being semi-serious. Elías' position means he's unable to lie with anyone without them having the ability to unravel his entire life from underneath him." He glanced in the direction of the doors.

I followed his gaze. "How did he get through military training without anyone realising?"

"He didn't," Ren told me. "Ademar made his request to me the day his brother was accepted into Quareh's service under a falsified application. He said Elías was determined to become a soldier despite his best efforts to dissuade him, and he feared what would happen once he was found out."

"That's why Moreno hates El," I said, feeling far too slow on the uptake. "Because he was promoted straight to your retinue without the Comandante ever being able to get his filthy hands on him in training?"

Ren clicked his tongue in confirmation. "Or he's just a cranky *cabrón* with a stick so far up his ass he's lost sight of it," he said lightly. "However will we know which?"

It was then that I remembered the comments the prince and his men had made on the way back from Sesveko. "And how does Martinez fit into all this?"

"Hmm," Ren muttered, his expression half admiring and half reproving. "You've been listening again, I see. For a dull barbarian speaking a foreign language, you can be remarkably perceptive sometimes."

I snorted out a laugh. "Clearly not perceptive enough, if I missed Elías this whole time."

"Don't be so hard on yourself. It's a secret we've worked hard to keep. As for…before El's transition, he caught a young Lord Martinez forcing himself onto a village woman."

My humour abruptly disappeared.

"Elías beat him half to death, an executable offence for a peasant. Ademar helped him escape arrest," Ren continued. "You can see why we don't want Martinez to recognise El, even if the lord wouldn't be expecting a man."

"I can't imagine Elías being so…"

"Reckless? Impulsive? Mat-like?" The prince grinned. "He was probably inwardly cheering that night you decided to follow in his footsteps and smack Martinez around. But no, being a soldier has given him the self-discipline he needed to *not* end up dead for attacking every rapist and misogynist he sees."

He leaned against the wall and folded his arms. "A skill I would prefer you to perfect sooner rather than later."

I ignored that, promptly changing the subject. "And is everything okay with Jiron?"

"He wanted to talk about Luis reaching the end of his six-month probation period. And the resulting increase in pay."

"Did you agree to it?"

The prince gave me a dry look. "Considering he's had to put up with your annoying ass, I'd say he's definitely earned it. Hell, probably twice over."

"Well, while we're on the topic of doubling your guards' wages," I said meaningfully, tugging at the collar of my own navy coat where the prince's two gold bands were stitched along it.

Ren laughed. "Double of nothing is still nothing, Mat. I'm fairly sure you've injured me – or at least tried to – twice as many times as you've saved me, so your record needs some improvement. Besides, what would you do with

Quarehian money?"

"Then pay me in something else."

"Oh, I plan to," he purred, kicking off from the wall and dragging me down onto the bed with him. He tugged up my shirt and pressed ticklish kisses to my stomach until I laughed and shoved him off me, and we lay comfortably side by side for a long moment, catching our breath. While I couldn't forget what he'd said – or hadn't said – about Horacio, and Starling's warning was still playing through my head, that all now felt far enough away for me to do a good job at ignoring it. Ren was…Ren was Ren, his presence beside me comforting and not the unsettling itch it had once been.

"Your guards are good," I said, shifting onto my side to face him and idly walking my fingers up his arm. "Seeing them in action on the return from Sesveko was…well. Terrifying, quite frankly. You're lucky to have them."

"They're the best," Ren agreed. "And Moreno knows that. It's why I'm having difficulty believing he was behind those ambushes at the canyon; I expect he'd have sent twice as many men if that were the case."

"Who else could it have been? Blaming your death on the north would suit his purposes nicely."

"It would, and that's why it otherwise fits. He knows I'm nosy, and it wouldn't have been too outlandish a guess on his part to expect I would return via Vitorona to find out what he's been covering up. He also has a vast network of spies that could have reported on our route back home."

I paused. "Spies that reach all the way to Stavroyarsk?"

"And Delzerce," the prince said, flashing me a broad, teasing grin and catching my fingers so he could kiss them. "The man may be a fuckwit, but he's not entirely terrible at his job. He keeps informed of most major happenings in the northern capitals."

"Not about who I am, apparently."

Ren shrugged beside me. "If he had reason to go looking, I'm sure he'd figure it out quickly. Which makes me suspect that Mazekhstam is keeping both your absence and Mathias Grachyov's presence quiet so as to not rouse suspicion that your kidnapping is anything but what Quareh believes it to be. They'll know we have eyes on them."

"How deep in Astrid's castle are the spies?"

"Wouldn't you like to know?" Ren nudged my elbow with his own, and I scowled.

"I need to understand what we're dealing with," I told him.

"*No*, you're fishing for state secrets so when you finally get out of here, you can warn your regent," said the prince, stretching. "Hah. Don't think I didn't notice that flicker of annoyance that just crossed your face, Nat."

He kicked my leg, clearly enjoying himself far too much. "Do you think I'm going to let you return to the north and out all of our spies?"

"You-"

"Do you think," Ren murmured, rolling over to press his chest against my arm, "that I'm going to let you return to the north *at all?*"

I glanced at him. "You really don't think Commander Grachyov is going to concede Algejón?"

He snorted, as if I was missing the point entirely.

"I don't know. But even if he was on his knees in surrender before me right now, I still wouldn't be releasing you to him."

He nipped at my ear and I gave him a disbelieving look. "So you'd leave your people under occupation?"

"No," the prince said. "I'd get the city. He just wouldn't get you."

"Ren." I let out an exasperated sigh that he stole from me with a kiss.

"Don't *Ren* me. You're not going anywhere."

"Why? What's the point of all this if you're not actually going to hold up any deal they're prepared to make?"

"Naww, do you still think I have honour, after everything you've seen me do? That's cute."

I tugged on his hair where it lay draped over my shoulder. "Is this about Val?" I watched the prince carefully, and then buried my face into the blankets when his lips pressed together in a thin line. "Fuck, it is. You're using me to protect yourself from him."

"Somewhat," Ren admitted. "While his temper cools from Sesveko, I'd prefer to be assured that he won't send a horde of angry wolves or whatever down on me while I have you at my side."

My mouth curled into a cruel smile. "You'd deserve it."

"Undoubtedly," he agreed, far too cheery at the prospect. "Considering all the depraved things he presumably believes I'm inflicting on you as we speak."

I tried not to think of all the depraved things he *had* inflicted on me. "Maybe if you hadn't had your hands all over me that night, asshole, Valeri wouldn't have cause to believe it."

"Maybe," Ren said, conceding the point, and then making a better one of his own. "But then I also wouldn't have gotten to have my hands all over you."

"And now I'm going to have some awkward explaining to do when I get back, thanks to that," I pointed out. And the kiss; my brother might not have seen it, but his guards would have told him what I'd done on the island before I cut the rope to win them their freedom.

Ren's fingers closed tightly around my wrist, as if worried I planned to ride home right that second. "I told you, *mi sol*. You're not going anywhere."

"I'm–"

"Mine," he growled, his eyes dark and his expression scarily possessive. "You're *mine*. No matter what happens with Grachyov *or* your brother."

I stilled at the words, unable to breathe. The first time I'd thought it a joke, but was he really saying what I thought he was? That he had no intention of letting me go even if Mazekhstam *did* come through on the deal?

That was ridiculous. There was no way he could get away with such a thing. The thousands of Quarehians trapped in Algejón were relying on my release for their own freedom: innocent people who didn't deserve to get caught in the lethal political games of Riehse Eshan.

But the way Ren was eyeing me said he didn't fucking care.

"You can't just…*keep* me," I finally choked out, the accusation ragged and breathless.

Ren's other hand wrapped around my throat. He didn't squeeze; just held me down as he rolled on top of me and pressed his body to mine.

"I can, and I will," he murmured, a hungry look on his face. "Why do you think I wanted your brother for a hostage? Him, I'd be happy to get rid of. But you're going to make me break promises, renege on deals, and generally fuck people over to ensure I keep you at my side, Mathias."

Ren frequently accused me of having an answer to everything; that I was incapable of keeping my mouth shut.

But at that moment, I couldn't have uttered a single word to save my life.

*

A WHISPER AND A BREATH

Chapter Thirty-One

Ren

"I know," I murmured to Viento, casting a look at the empty adjacent stall. "I miss her too."

The horse nickered and nudged his nose against my palm. I stroked his muzzle and blinked at the fresh cutting of honeysuckle I'd just noticed draped over the stall's door.

I'd ordered the space be kept empty in memory of Miel and placed the first set of flowers there myself, but they would have died weeks ago.

"*Gracias*, Galo," I said to the stablemaster as he came into sight hefting a saddle, and he sank into an easy bow despite the considerable weight he was carrying. He brought the strong smell of leather with him, and the weathered, tanned lines of his face gave the appearance of the same.

The man offered an embarrassed shrug as he straightened and followed my gaze down to the honeysuckle, as if loath to be caught out at something so sentimental.

"She was a good lass, Miel. Never gave anyone trouble, unlike that wild little thing." He nodded behind me and I smirked, amused, as the gesture accidentally encapsulated not just Viento but also Mat on the horse's other side. "Besides, I find myself with more time on my hands these days, Your Highness." Galo shot a meaningful look to the stable door where his nine tailed whip hung from a large nail.

"I wouldn't know anything about that," I said innocently, and the man pursed his lips.

"Are you well, my prince?"

Oh, that was fantastic. My people thought me ill because I'd eased up on the floggings.

"Maybe everyone is just behaving themselves recently," I suggested, and Mathias gave a soft snort that was promptly echoed by Viento.

"Doubt it," Galo said, nudging open a stall door with his knee and throwing the saddle over the back of a piebald. "Most men here have the devil in them. Only the kiss of the lash is capable of freeing them from their sin."

I gave Mat a look at that to show it wasn't just *me* that favoured the whip as a punishment. It was ingrained in centuries of law and tradition, and I'd received more than one odd look over the last few weeks when I'd eschewed a flogging in favour of a different penalty. Although, after witnessing a man fall to his knees and beg me for the whip over having to act as servant for a month to the family he'd stolen from, I'd warmed to the idea of the alternatives much more quickly. If my people were becoming blasé about enduring such pain on the promise that Starling would simply heal them afterwards, it clearly wasn't working as intended, and the man had looked *much* sorrier two weeks into his temporary servitude than he had after his first flogging last year. Maybe Mathias was onto something.

The bastard smirked at me as if he knew my thoughts were veering dangerously close to complimentary.

"Speaking of lashes," I said casually, "Lord Grachyov here suggested I ask you for a new riding crop. Something flexible, Galo."

"Oh?"

"No," Mat said through gritted teeth, colour rapidly spreading across his pale cheeks. "He's joking."

I tsked. "I most assuredly am not."

The stablemaster shrugged as he tightened the girth on the saddle. "I have a few, Your Highness. You're welcome to take a look."

"Mathias can choose." I offered my northerner a wicked smile. "After all, he's the one *asking for it.*"

He muttered something rude in Mazekhstani, and I promptly covered Viento's velvety ears. "*Mat,*" I rebuked. "He's only five. Are you *trying* to be inappropriate?"

Viento huffed and knocked his head against my chest.

"Reminds me. Lord Hierro was in here this morning," Galo told me, spitting out a mouthful of phlegm onto the dusty floor. "Said you hadn't scheduled any piano lessons with him in a while, my prince."

Mathias glanced at me, curious. "I didn't know you played."

"I play," I murmured, watching my northerner with a sly smile and knowing my answer would rile him. "Just not the piano."

Predictably, I received a scowl in reply. "Oh, for fuck's sake."

Galo led the piebald out of the stable to whomever had commissioned the horse for riding, and I turned back to Mathias. We hadn't spoken properly since I'd…gotten a little intense the other day and voiced the thoughts that should never have been spoken aloud. I didn't have a problem with telling him that he was mine when he clearly fucking was, but he'd gone all quiet and pensive since then and I feared that I'd spooked him with the rest of it.

Shit. I didn't know how to broach the subject, and yet nerves were something I didn't do. I was a master at navigating uncomfortable conversations; doubly talented at making *others* uncomfortable, but I'd never before found myself in a situation where it was my own tongue feeling impossibly large in my mouth as I tried to form the words to ask him where we stood.

Mat bit his lip as he watched me watching him, and the unconsciously provocative act made my cock twitch.

Maybe that was the answer. I needed a distraction so I could talk without my head getting in the way, and he needed…well, he needed to not be able to hit me if he didn't like what I was saying.

"You," I said in a low voice, heat curling through me at the way his eyes widened at my tone. "Take two steps to your right."

Mathias glanced at the spot I'd directed him to, but of course he didn't move an inch.

"Why-"

I shoved at him, forcing him to move, and his boots stumbled in the straw.

"You're so fucking stubborn," I murmured, pressing a kiss to his mouth now that we were out of sight of the main stable doors where my guards waited. I knew they'd be on extra high alert as a result, but I also knew they were clever enough not to interrupt. "Are you going to resist this, too?"

I tugged at the ribbon that held back my hair, feeling it cascade down around my shoulders as the silk fluttered through my fingers. Snagging Mat's hands between my own, I kissed both of his palms and then held them together, weaving the blue ribbon around his slender wrists.

"Ren," he protested, utterly predictably.

"Shush."

"We can't do this here. Don't you remember what happened last time we tried something in public?"

Hmm. That was an excellent point, and probably one I should be listening to, but I was just so happy that he hadn't complained about being tied up that I chose to completely disregard the rest of it, proceeding to be as inappropriate in front of Viento as I had pretended to chide Mat for.

But the horse just ignored us, shuffling to the side to make room while he contented himself with chewing his hay.

I continued to bind Mathias' hands as the man did his best to distract me, kissing and nosing at my neck with soft murmurs of what sounded like definite interest in what I was doing. When I was finally done – which had taken a ridiculously long time, damn it, because he was indeed *distracting* – I tied the ends of the ribbon off in an elegant bow that made him snort out a laugh, and made *me* want to eat him up.

Then he promptly lifted his arms and hitched them over my head, yanking me towards him and crashing his lips against mine.

"Stop...disrupting my...plans," I gasped against his hot and eager mouth. "I need to talk to you."

"So talk," Mat murmured, nudging my head to the side with his chin so he could run his tongue around the shell of my ear. I shivered. Damn him, he was the one with his hands tied, so why did it feel like I was at *his* mercy?

I pressed my face into his neck, inhaling his scent. That natural Mathiasness, mixed with the trace of my own soap. I liked that, smelling myself on him.

He gave a surprised laugh as I nuzzled deeper.

I couldn't lose this. Not now, not ever. Not when I was so perfectly, indescribably, impossibly *happy*.

"Mat," I began. "What I said about you staying here-"

"Comandante Moreno for you, Your Highness," Ademar called out from the other side of the stall wall where we were hiding, and I shut my eyes, nudging aside the collar of Mat's shirt with my chin so I could continue to kiss my way down the gentle lines of his collarbones, down to-

"Ren," he whispered, unhooking his hands from behind my neck, but I shook my head. My eyes were closed, and the stall door would be staying that way too, and if Ademar didn't want to spend the rest of his life guarding the soldiers' privy at the back of the palace, he would...

"Your Highness! The Comandante says it's urgent."

I dragged my mouth back to Mathias' ear with a groan.

"I'm going to murder him. Both of them. And then I'll do you on their corpses, one after the other."

"Charming," he said with disgust. He wrinkled his nose and I kissed it, garnering a surprised laugh from him. Viento nickered his own amusement.

Earning Mat's laughter or even one of his smiles had become a source of pride for me. He was normally so serious, but I'd discovered that underneath was a wicked sense of humour and a genuine appreciation for life. He made me want more, *be* more.

"My prince," Ad said patiently. "Are you...coming out?"

Mat dipped his head and pulled on the loose end of the ribbon with his teeth, unravelling the bow and freeing his wrists.

"Spoilsport," I whispered, pleased to feel him shiver against me. "You better let me retie that when I get back, Mathias. My mouth has only gotten as far as your neck, and it has a lot more ground to cover before I'm anywhere near through with you."

But I couldn't force myself to step back, to release him.

"I'll just be a moment," I said eventually, but as I made to move towards the stall door, he caught my arm.

"Wait," he murmured, and lifted a hand to smooth my hair down at the side of my head. I smirked at him, noticing his own mussed hair and thinking that I *could* return the favour, if I wanted to.

Funny then, that I had no inclination to do so.

I already couldn't wait the minute it would take to return to him. Or two minutes. Or three, but Dios help me, if the Comandante took any more of my time than that, I'd be asking Jiron to toss him from the palace walls.

"Moreno," I said distastefully as I pulled open the half-height stall door and found him striding through the stables towards Ademar, clearly tired of waiting outside. Both men dipped into bows. "Have you missed my company that badly?"

The Comandante's jaw ticked, but whether it was the glib remark or the sight of Mathias appearing at my shoulder, I didn't know. Nor did I care, because Moreno could have keeled over at my feet and I couldn't have given less of a fuck.

"He can go," he ordered, jutting his chin at Mat.

"He can stay," I countered immediately. "Or must I remind you *once again* that I am charged with his care and not you?"

"Your Highness. The king will be arriving from Máros tomorrow at noon."

I froze at that, the words sending a chill through me that defied the warm, manure-scented air of the stables. I hadn't seen my father since I left for Sesveko several weeks ago, and I'd hoped he'd been planning on keeping his visits to *la Cortina* as blessedly infrequent as usual, despite the negotiations with Mazekhstam.

"I see," I said. "Tattled on me for something else, have you?"

"Ren. Last night there was..." I'd rarely seen Moreno falter, but there it was, a distressed twitch to his mouth that held none of his customary sneer. He cleared his throat and straightened. "There was a coordinated attack along the border. A dozen camps, villages and outposts were hit."

"No," I said, frowning at the impossibility of such a thing. "There's no way Mazekhstam has the numbers for that, or they'd have overwhelmed our border forces and invaded the south a long time ago."

"There weren't many, by all accounts. Just a small strike force in each location. Most of them were killed before they could retreat north, but the damage had already been done."

I hissed out a breath. "Sabotage?"

"Yes," he confirmed with a sharp nod. "But not...my prince, it was targeted assassination of our Blessed."

"*Fuck*. How many?"

"Eighteen. Our forces took out two dozen of their own, but it's hardly a victory when we consider that not every man is created equal. Theirs were ordinary foot soldiers. Ours were magically enhanced resources whose loss could be the edge Mazekhstam needs to finally get through our lines."

My gaze met Ademar's, whose mouth was pulled into a tight, horrified gash. "Breakdown," I demanded of Moreno.

"Nine Touch, six Sight and the remainder with the Scent."

Nine healers, capable of restoring a soldier to full health from a wound that would have otherwise killed him, of staving off infection and fixing up underlying health conditions to ensure our soldiers were as fit and hale as possible. Injured in battle meant nothing as long as a man's comrades could get him off the field and seen to by a healer with the Touch.

Six seers, able to predict the victories and the defeats, their visions not infallible but still providing a clear advantage over whatever snippets of the future they could glean.

And three trackers, whose gift allowed them to find any person or thing wherever they were located on the continent. We used them to monitor enemy movements, locate key opponents for surveillance or assassination, and retrieve lost soldiers, whether captured, injured or deserting.

"And how many Blessed are left?" I asked quietly.

"On the front? *Cinco.*"

Five. By Dios.

There would be more Blessed than that in the country, of course; children and women and the infirm. Those who hadn't yet discovered their gifts, or were hiding them from us in an effort to avoid conscription to Quareh's service. Those whose powers were too weak to be of any use, like that old woman with the Touch in Torrellón, or who had been snatched up by the privileged making deals with the crown, such as Martinez's healer.

But the Blessed weren't innumerable, and they died just as easily as anyone else. With the Voice being grounds for immediate execution, and the

Hearken, the ability to read minds, long since extinct, those eighteen dead souls at our border represented a massive fucking loss for Quareh.

"I've requisitioned your little militia," Moreno told me scornfully. "We need every able body we can find to defend our border, and I've lost my patience for the meaningless errands you keep sending them on."

"They're loaned to me, not enlisted soldiers," I said through gritted teeth, pissed at him getting his grubby hands on them. I'd known I couldn't keep a hundred-strong force secret from the Comandante, but I hadn't expected him to be so brazen as to steal it from me.

"But they are still a *militia*, and military matters are my domain, be it quasi forces or otherwise."

Prick.

"I have Lord Martinez in command of the militia at this time. I ask that he be allowed to remain in that position even if he takes his orders from you instead of me," I said evenly, trying to rein in my irritation.

"Martinez?" Moreno stared at me, brows furrowed in exasperated incredulity. "By Dios, *why*?"

"He's trying to interfere with my engagement to Altagracia," I said, which…wasn't a total lie. He'd once tried to convince me to marry his own daughter, despite Alva Martinez's young age. "It would be preferable for him to be away on the front lines for a while."

Moreno pulled a disgusted face, and thought about that for a long moment.

"Very well," he conceded, and Mathias let out a soft exhale of relief behind me. "But I shall not hold responsibility for his wellbeing. The death of a noble will not be on my hands."

"But ordinary people are fine?" Mat asked in distaste.

Moreno gave him a dismissive look. "You should be familiar with how armies function, Lord *Grachyov*. Do you not know how many thousands of men – and women, because your backwards country puts the fairer sex at unnecessary risk despite their unsuitability for such work – your father has sent to their deaths?"

"*Unnecessary risk?* You fucker. After everything you've done to-"

"Don't indulge him, Moreno," I said, before Mathias could mention Alta's name. I didn't want any attention brought to her. "Mat will get indignant about *anything* if you let him talk long enough."

"Then don't let him talk at all," the Comandante shot back. He looked at my northerner and tilted his head, considering. "Perhaps his tongue?"

I swallowed down bile at the suggestion, but it wasn't an idle one. The king would want blood for this, and the supposed son of the man leading our enemy's army was the perfect outlet for such vengeance.

"You know my father's feelings on tongues," I said lightly to Moreno, even though I wanted to stab him in the Blessed heart. "He always starts with the fingers."

"What the fuck are you both talking about?" Mat demanded.

We ignored him.

"Or their cocks," Moreno suggested, giving me a cruel smirk. "Although that would make it hard to play with your pretty pet, wouldn't it?"

I held his gaze. "You send Commander Grachyov his son's cock-"

Mat blanched. "Excuse me?"

"-and we'll have war by the end of the day," I told the Comandante. "The inability to grasp that delicate balance between threat and provocation is why the politics of Riehse Eshan are best left to people who understand them."

"War? You don't think we're there already?" He spat on the ground. "This is the second act of aggression by Mazekhstam in less than a month, and you're suggesting that we smile and do nothing…again? How many more times would you have us sit idly by as the north fucks us in the ass?" His furious gaze slid to Mathias, and his expression soured even further. "Or maybe that's what you're developing a liking for, Your Highness?"

Ademar's hand snapped to the hilt of his sword. Moreno shot him a nasty smile. "Try it, and I'll see you disciplined for attacking a superior officer."

"It makes no sense," Mat protested, stepping forward to stand beside me.

"Moreno being a bastard? It makes perfect sense," I said. "Maybe you haven't seen past that charming personality of his yet. Give it time."

"If Mazekhstam wanted to threaten Quareh, they achieved that with the massacre in Algejón," Mathias continued, waving a hand and distracting me with the blue ribbon he'd looped around his right wrist. "Why would they wait a few weeks and then attack again for no reason? They would know that would be more likely to provoke you than keep you quiet, and it would just undo the message sent by the first..."

He trailed off and caught my gaze, the growing horror in his blue-grey eyes reflecting my own.

"Fuck, Moreno!" I snarled, wanting to beat the soldier's damn face in. "What did you *do?*"

The man smiled, but there was no humour behind it. Just grim resignation, and a touch of pride. "Unlike you, I refuse to let my country be trodden over by a bunch of barbarians. The insult of Lord Jiménez's death could not be ignored."

By the Blessed. "Who was it?"

"Lord Morozov. He holds lands just across the border from de Leon. Or, I should say, *held.*"

An eye for an eye. A murdered Mazekhstani noble as payback for the death of a Quarehian lord. And where would it end?

Moreno scoffed as he caught sight of my expression. "It wasn't random, my prince. I'm not a monster."

Want to bet?

"Morozov was involved in the Algejón executions," he continued. "It was him who discovered the insurrection and reported it back to his regent. He was far from innocent, if any northerner could ever be called such a thing."

Mat choked in a breath. "Insurrection?"

I'd heard it too. "Comandante?"

Moreno's disdainful sneer turned bitter. "Jiménez, along with his wife and servants, was working with my spies to weaken Mazekhstam's hold on the city so we could recapture it by force. It obviously proved unsuccessful."

Ademar's rapid exhale matched my own.

"No fucking wonder they retaliated!" I snapped. "Mazekhstam put down what it saw as a rebellion – something we ourselves have done dozens of times to maintain peace, and fuck you for getting a sixteen-year-old girl involved in one of your plots – and then one of their nobility is assassinated? They think *we're* the aggressors!" I ran a hand through my hair, agitated and wanting to fucking *scream*.

"Does King Iván know what you did?" asked Mathias, disgust written clear across his face.

Moreno looked him up and down. "Of course. Weren't you chained, little pup?"

Mat held out his wrists, bare but for the ribbon, mocking him. "Clearly not anymore."

The Comandante's eyes flickered lazily to mine and then back to the northerner in front of him. "That's because your master is far too soft. If you were mine, boy, you'd be kept permanently bound, hand to foot."

"And if you were *mine*," Mat hissed, his voice low and harsh, "I'd have you exiled to the icy wastes of the northern tips of the continent, where you could never hurt any of my people ever again."

Moreno laughed, an easy, amused sound that I'd rarely heard erupt from his mouth. "A feisty thing, isn't he?" he said to me, offering a token bow and backing up towards the stable doors. "We'll see where all that spirit goes when the king arrives tomorrow. You know what your father will expect of you to fix this, Ren, and I will enjoy watching you attempt to refuse him."

–

The relentless Quarehian sun beat down hard on everyone gathered in the outer courtyard, and I was glad I'd insisted on Mat covering his exposed skin with the coconut oil before we emerged out here in an effort to protect him from the worst of it. Sweat was pooling at my hairline and the base of my spine, my dark blue coat uncomfortably damp.

"Why don't you take it off?" Mathias murmured in my ear, tugging at the back of my sleeve where no one could see. I smirked.

"I'd have thought getting naked in front of two hundred servants and courtiers was a little too public for your tastes, *mi amor,* but I'm up for it if you are."

His sigh of exasperation was all too familiar.

"I can't," I explained, although part of me – nearly every damn part – would have liked to do exactly what he suggested and remove my coat. "Just like I can't retreat into the cooler air of the palace, or even move into the shade. Appearances are everything."

"Your *appearance* is starting to resemble that of a drowned rat."

I jabbed a sharp elbow into his ribs and he gave a surprised grunt, attempting to smother it with a cough so as not to attract attention to us.

"You don't look any better yourself, brat," I hissed, despite the truth being that Mathias remained irresistibly attractive no matter what he did. The way his hair was plastered to his head, the beads of sweat running down his pale neck…yep, I could get onboard with that, starting with licking every inch of him clean. "And you'll pay for that insult later."

Mat let out an interested little hum in my ear, a noise which made me want to say *screw it,* drag him back to my room, and damn the whole afternoon. But we weren't out here sweltering for nothing. The king would be arriving any moment, and I'd more than learned from last time that having anything less than the entire palace out here to greet him would be a dire mistake.

"If I can't hold firm, why should my people?" I said, knowing Mathias understood but needing to voice it anyway. "I'm asking them to be here. The least I can do is wait with them and not show an ounce of discomfort."

"Then I'll show enough for both of us," he muttered in complaint, keeping his voice low so we wouldn't be overheard. "You know Moreno screwed you over, right?"

I did. It was well past noon, and none of the guards on the walls above us had yet called down to confirm the king's approach. The Comandante had lied about the time of my father's arrival, a fact that was all too clear by Moreno's own conspicuous absence from the courtyard.

I wondered just how fucking pleased with himself he was to know he had hundreds of people, including his own guards, suffering at his whim. The man was a power-hungry maniac.

"Of course," I murmured. "But I couldn't take the risk that he was trying to trick me into not being here when the king arrived by assuming a later time."

"The sangria and pinchos more than make up for it, my prince," Alta said mildly from my other side, where she clutched a glass of cold sangria in one hand and six wooden skewers in the other, entirely devoid of the food they'd once held. I blinked, not having seen her consume any more than two of the snacks, and then let out a fond laugh at my friend's utter adoration for food.

"It's helped to take the edge off everyone's restlessness," I agreed, pleased with my foresight in commissioning the catering. "Perhaps a seventh for my lady?" I flagged down a passing servant, and Altagracia promptly swapped her empty skewers for two more pinchos from the large platter. "Or…an eighth, it seems."

"Don't *count*," Mat chided, and Al gave him an affectionate smile that turned admonishing when she turned it on me. I held up my palms in surrender, and watched her practically inhale the two sets of olive, pepper and anchovy skewers.

"Oh, to be gazed at by someone the way you look at food, *mi querida*, would be a rare compliment indeed."

Alta just raised an eyebrow and tipped her head towards Mathias, who suddenly seemed very interested in the wispy clouds above us.

I fell silent, my joviality abruptly disappearing as I remembered what awaited us this afternoon and why I wasn't all that bothered that my father hadn't yet arrived. Why I'd eschewed sex last night for something far more intimate and precious and not at all like me, holding Mat close until he'd joked about needing to breathe and then eventually fell asleep in my arms when I steadfastly refused to move. I'd lain awake for hours in the darkness, reluctant to let the moment – or him – go.

Lord de Leon wandered into my eyeline with a couple of his usual hangers-on; courtiers and less important landowners who clung to his every word like it was gospel. They gave me bows of varying aptitude and eagerness that I firmly ignored, continuing whatever they'd been discussing as they giggled over their glasses of sangria like it was pure alcohol. Either they couldn't hold their drink, or some *idiota* servant had soaked the fruit for too long. I snagged a slice of orange from my own glass, and plucked it clean with my teeth.

Yep. Definitely the fruit. I flagged down another server, annoyed at how we'd somehow become part of the crowd of people surrounding the border lord as his retinue swarmed into my personal space.

"-and tell me why, despite being married for over fifteen years, I *still* have to explain to my wife that I want her to greet me with a smile when I return home?" de Leon was saying, an incredulous tilt to his brow. "She had the audacity to say she was tired." He shook his head. "I'm away for weeks at a time while she sits her ass at home, and *she's* fucking tired?"

Away playing the life of a courtier, with your meals prepared and your whores ready and waiting, I thought. *While your wife attempts to keep a household together only a few hours from Quareh's contested border.*

"-it's simple really," de Leon continued, in response to something one of his companions had said. "You just have to be clear in your expectations with your woman. It's not their fault if they don't understand. It's on *you* to make sure they do."

I ordered the servant to ignore the drink and just dish me out the wine-infused fruit. Enduring this afternoon less than sober seemed to be a remarkably good idea right now.

"Communication is the key to a healthy marriage. Outline what you expect her to do, and don't forget to correct her when she slips up. She will, of course, but if you handle it properly, she's less likely to forget the second time."

I glanced over at Jiron, and gave him a look. He nodded and dropped one of his huge hands down onto a fuming Mat's shoulder to prevent him from doing anything stupid like throwing himself at the misogynistic, abhorrent lord. Mathias led with his fists far too often: for an accomplished liar, he lost his composure easily in the face of what he perceived as injustice. Alta's jaw was set, but she retained her polite smile as she engaged in small talk with the men.

"You're a fucking idiot," González snapped at de Leon from where he was standing a few yards away. "Do you hear the shit that's coming out of your mouth?"

Mathias' face lit up hopefully, but I shook my head. González was no saviour. The two lords' rivalry meant they seized any opportunity to squabble, and apparently today would be no different.

De Leon smirked. "Considering your wife and a barn door could easily be mixed up on even a sunny day, I doubt think you're in any position to talk,

González. Maybe if you told her to cut down on the meals, you'd be less of an unpleasant prick all the time."

Jiron clamped his other hand over Mat's mouth as he started to hiss indignant curses.

"It's not about what you *say*, but what you do," Lord González countered with an unpleasant sneer to his mouth. "I take on a masculine role in my house so that my wife can properly flourish in her femininity. I keep her soft and plump and healthy, and she's happier for it. *Your* wife looks like a fucking man with those muscles of hers, and that's your fault for letting her take on what should be a male's duty. When did you last-"

Jiron wrenched a struggling Mathias backwards into the shadows of the stables, and I moved to their side. Alta would be fine alone; she'd survived this long in court, and had far more self-control than *someone else* I could name.

"Stop it," I said quietly to my northerner, who was beginning to attract attention. "You're not going to fix Quareh's chauvinism by clawing off two men's faces."

"It would be a good start," he spat, when Jiron finally pulled his hand from his mouth.

"It would," I conceded. "But we have bigger issues to deal with, remember? Namely handling Moreno and my father, and whatever the hell happened at Vitorona."

There was an unexpected yell and we all turned to see de Leon's fist smack into González's jaw.

"Oh, for fuck's sake," I muttered. "Jiron?"

He nodded and waded into the mess, pulling the two men apart with a hand at each of their napes. They spat curses at each other, still trying to hit the other lord despite my guard holding them at arm's length. Alta glided over to us, looking pleased.

"I suppose you will have to admonish them, Your Highness," she said, a mischievous expression on her face. "Can I suggest that to have the punishment properly fit the crime, you order that they be made to give public apologies to their wiv-"

"What's all this?"

Alta promptly fell silent at her father's voice, seeming to shrink into the background as the Comandante strode up in his dress uniform, a hand on the hilt of his freshly polished sword. "Your Highness, if you're incapable of maintaining order, you only had to ask for help."

I swallowed down the bitter taste in my mouth. "You're here. So that means-"

"Prepare for His Majesty's arrival!" boomed a guard from up on the walls, and everyone instantly sprang to attention, the servers vanishing the platters of food and drink to Dios knows where, and the nobles returning to the strict lines they'd originally been allocated to. Moreno grabbed Alta's arm and dragged her back to the centre of the courtyard, placing her at his shoulder as I reluctantly trailed behind and stood beside him with Jiron, Ademar and Mat in a similar position at my back.

My eyes scanned the crowd. I saw the way Clementina's hands shook before she firmly clasped them together, raising her chin with admirable courage. Lord de la Vega wiped his brow with a handkerchief, plastering a jovial smile onto his jowled face as he muttered something to the two Lords Lago. Isobella hung from the arm of an older man I vaguely recognised, tossing her hair when my gaze landed on her and pretending to act like she'd never been happier.

I continued to search the mass of people, eventually finding the person I was looking for hunched at the back of the courtyard, her hands shoved deep in the pockets of her dress. I lifted my chin in acknowledgement, needing to know she was fucking ready for this, but Starling just scowled, dragging her eyes from mine.

The gates drew open, the portcullis was lifted, and then there was my father, stepping from his carriage and settling his unsmiling gaze on me.

*

Chapter Thirty-Two

Mat

The next hour passed agonisingly slowly in the beating sun as the king greeted his subjects and conveyed the news of the mass deaths of the Blessed, although he conveniently left out any mention of Moreno's attack on Mazekhstam that had instigated it. No one else seemed to question why the north had seemingly acted without provocation, and I fumed as the Quarehian monarch painted a gruesome picture of Mazekhstani brutality and irrationality, with more and more accusing faces turning my way as he spoke.

Fuck. It had been barely a handful of days since Alta had convinced Ren to lose the humiliating manacles he'd dressed me in to placate his people, and it looked like we'd be digging them right back out again. If Ren could just explain what had actually happened...

But he couldn't contradict his father. A prince held no power against a king, and contradicting anything Iván said would achieve nothing but swift punishment. I wouldn't ask Ren to brave further lashes at his hands, not for me, even as the muttered hatred swelling through the crowd grew louder.

Would it kill the countries to *talk* to each other? All these politics, one-sided and presumptuous, more focused on controlling the public perception than discovering the truth. Imagine if there was no miscommunication fanning the flames of war, because the leaders of Riehse Eshan stopped shouting and plotting for once, and instead just *listened?*

"Come," Iván said brusquely, and I blinked to find he'd finished his vitriolic speech and was striding purposefully past us, flanked by his own guards with their three-banded coat collars. "And bring the Mazekhstani."

Strong fingers seized my upper arm, and at first I didn't resist, thinking it was Jiron. And then I spotted the guard at Ren's side, and glanced up to find it was Moreno who was dragging me after his king.

"I'm capable of walking unassisted," I snapped, attempting to shrug out of his hold, but the Comandante's fingers just closed tighter around my arm. As his grip turned painful, which I had no doubt was deliberate, Ren fell into step beside me. Worried eyes fell to where the Comandante held me, but he said nothing, just watching carefully.

It was something else the prince couldn't do anything about: the king's order hadn't been to any particular person and Moreno was following it, albeit with far more force than seemed strictly necessary considering I was surrounded by dozens of Quarehians and clearly wasn't going anywhere they didn't want me to. I fumed quietly as I was hauled along, sick and fucking tired of the whole farce.

The king led the way to the throne room, which had been decked out for a banquet since I'd last seen it. Long tables ran the length of the hall, adorned with gleaming cutlery and glassware, and a handful of servants were shooed away from where they had been hanging a banner in Aratorre colours with the family's star-and-blade motif along the side wall. Iván climbed the steps to the throne and sank onto it with a weary sigh.

"If the north insists on speaking only in violence, then we will respond in kind."

"Father," Ren said, pushing his way past us to stand at the foot of the dais. "With respect, I believe that will only escalate matters further. I propose we reach out to the Mazekhstani border lords. They have lands, livestock and families within a day's reach of Quareh; they won't want war any more than we do. They may be able to put pressure on their regent to-"

"How fascinating," Moreno drawled at my side. "The young prince seeks a resolution that is contrary to his initial hostage plan. Perhaps he's let himself get too attached to this?" He gave me a hard shake before turning to his king.

"Your Majesty, the negotiations with Commander Grachyov have undoubtedly stalled. As a military man, he respects strength, and I fear we have not yet sufficiently shown it to him. Your son, Dios bless him, favours a delicate touch in his dealings, but that will not serve us here."

"Juan is right, Renato," Iván said. "The northern commander seeks to test us. It is clear in the way he negotiates, and clearer still in this further brazen attack on us while we hold his son. He evidently does not believe us capable of following through on our threats."

"Of course he does," Ren responded, exasperated. "He hardly believes us a peaceful people. Clearly, the commander has-"

"I don't want to hear it," the king said, and the prince fell silent, fury flashing across his face before he tampered it with a polite smile. "We will send a more impactful message to test the boy's worth."

"In that case, father," Ren offered smoothly before Moreno could speak, "may I suggest we direct this message to the regent instead of Commander Grachyov? Panarina is fond of Mathias, and they're exceedingly close."

I stiffened. What was he playing at?

"My intelligence doesn't report that," Moreno said dismissively.

"Trust me. *Mine* does." Ren gave a mocking laugh as he looked at me, his mouth curled into a sneer. "He buys her confectionery. Isn't that sweet? Once Astrid learns of his capture, she *will* buy his release, and the negotiations will not be hampered by Grachyov's loyalty to his regent, nor his career ambitions."

I flushed, feeling angry and betrayed. Manipulative bastard. He had pretended to care, and now he was using what I had told him against me?

Ren gave me nothing but a faint smile in return. It held none of his usual warmth, and Starling's words came crashing back on me in a vicious roar. *Ren is only nice when it suits him to be.*

"Very well," Iván said. "We will remind them both of the stakes. Guards, we require a finger."

He gestured with his hand out as if expecting one of them to produce a digit from their pocket right then and there. But in the moment it took my brain to get over that absurd thought and process the shock of what had just been fucking ordered, I found myself dragged over to the closest table and pinned down by two guards while a third flattened my right hand against its surface.

Fuck, no!

I cursed and struggled against their hold, sending the nearest plates and glasses to the floor with a crash, but the men resolutely held on. Panic wrapped tight around my chest as a hammer and chisel were placed on the table before us.

Moreno grabbed me by the hair and wrenched my head back. "Which finger shall it be, Grachyov?"

I swallowed.

"Now he's suddenly so quiet," the Comandante commented, shooting a satisfied glance at the prince. "I told you we'd see that fire extinguished, Ren, did I not?"

"Stop playing with the boy, Juan," the king said tiredly.

He looked at me then, really looked, in a way he hadn't done since that first night I was brought before him. "This is not torture, young lord. I do not order people hurt for my own amusement."

I scoffed, and something sour flashed across Iván's face.

"But lessons must be learned. Sometimes once is enough. Sometimes they must be repeated until the message makes it through." His gaze briefly flickered to Ren before coming back to rest on me. "Let us hope that your father and his regent can be taught quickly."

He lounged back against the back of his throne, a small smile playing about his lips. "And that your impertinence does not grow to warrant its own lesson before then."

Liar. He was taking plenty of *amusement* from this. It just suited him to pretend to be above such things. There was no other reason why the king would have Moreno hurt Ren only while he was present, other than that he wanted to be there to watch his son suffer.

And then the Comandante picked up the hammer and chisel, and I stopped breathing. I tugged at the arms holding me but they didn't give even an inch, their holds bruising and unyielding.

I looked to the one person who could help me.

Who *had* to help me.

"Ren!" I pleaded desperately, but the prince didn't so much as twitch, holding my gaze with an icy, dispassionate stare that reminded me uncomfortably of his expression in the vision where he killed me. As if the last few weeks hadn't fucking happened, as if it hadn't been only a handful of hours ago that I'd woken to his arms wrapped tightly around me, his nose nuzzling into my hair. Fuck, had that meant *nothing* to him?

And then as Moreno brought the sharp edge of the chisel to rest below the second knuckle of my right index finger and raised the hammer, the prince's posture stiffened.

"Wait," he ordered.

Hot, intoxicating relief rushed through me, and my legs would have given out had I not been held in place.

The king gave a disappointed sigh. "Renato?"

The word was a growl of warning.

Ren stepped forward and grabbed something from the table, twirling it between his long fingers. From my position, I couldn't make out what it was.

"If you truly want to make an impression, father," he said, and held out whatever it was to Moreno, "can I suggest something a little less clinical?" I frowned as the carving knife came into focus.

"This prick has caused me enough aggravation to want to watch his suffering first," Ren continued, a hitch to his throat as he gazed down at me. But his expression was cruel, eager even, bordering on *enjoyment*.

Moreno gave a bark of surprise and took the knife from him, glancing up at the king with something like approval. Fucked up bastards, the lot of them.

I resumed my struggling, not caring that it was futile, that even if I could shrug them off, there was nowhere I could go to escape the king's order. Because I was not going to give them even a *second* of my compliance.

"I know you get off on this shit, Ren," the Comandante said to him in a low, amused voice, "but this is a new level of depravity, even for you."

"Just get on with it so I can watch, asshole," Ren muttered, his eyes fixed on my hand. I cursed him out in my native language, the world narrowing to that terrifying expression on his face. I'd seen it before when we played particularly roughly, a hunger that never seemed to be satiated, and fuck, he'd always been honest about wanting to hurt me, but this?

This was too real. Too far.

"*No*," I said, straining desperately at the hands that held me down. "No, Ren, please, stop this, stop them, you don't need to do this, Moreno, *please-*"

I continued to babble out pleas as the Comandante pressed the cold blade of the knife against the base of my finger, its serrated edge glinting cruelly in the sunlight streaming through the stained-glass windows at the back of the room.

"Don't you fucking do it," I hissed, my eyes seeking out those of my captors in a last-ditch effort to appeal to their humanity. But none looked at me, too focused on their task of holding me in place as the knife began its gruesome work.

My scream echoed around the hall, white-hot pain lancing through my hand. I flung my head back in agony, smacking it against someone's shoulder and giving me a moment's relief as my vision temporarily swam with black.

But the pain continued to flood through me, relentless and brutal.

As my body instinctively tried to pull my hand back from the vicious mutilation, I somehow found the strength to buck off one of the hands pinning my other shoulder down. I reached out as if I could stop the bloodied knife from sawing through bone, its blade already shrouded in a mass of chewed up skin, but someone caught my uninjured arm, shoving it mercilessly back down to the table.

I snarled at my new assailant, spittle flying from my lips, and caught the narrowed gaze of none other than Renato fucking Aratorre himself.

I had a hundred things I wanted to say to him, none of them pleasant, but words gave way to my anguished cries as they cut through the air once more.

Like the true fucking psychopath he is, Starling had said. Why hadn't I believed her?

I ripped through the final few shreds of remaining skin myself as the guards released me and I finally tore my hand free, cradling the bloodied mess to my chest.

The knife hit the floor with a dull clunk, and Moreno gave me an assessing look, scooping up the abandoned, bloody flesh from the table. I forced myself to draw in breaths through my raw throat, staring at the space where my index finger had once been.

I could hear people talking, but not their words, everything outside of me filtering through as nothing but gentle murmurs and flashes of colour. I let myself sink onto one of the low benches tucked against the tables.

You and I have both seen his darker side.

I'd seen it the very fucking day I arrived, when Ren had ordered Jiron to choke me with his bare hands so he could torture me for the truth of what had happened at St Izolda's Monastery. And then again and again, flashes of his darkness wrapped up in his careless flirtations, those beaming smiles and teasing words.

I didn't know how long I was there, eyes squeezed shut as I wrapped myself around the pain, hurting and hating, but soon I felt hands under my arms, pulling me to my feet.

"Here," someone said, and I heard that because it was *him*. My eyes shot open to find Ren before me, trying to press a bundle of linen to the bloody wound.

"Fuck. Off." I spat, the venom in my voice causing a flicker of tension to run through the prince.

"You need to-"

"Renato," the king called, and Ren hesitated for a moment, seemingly unwilling to pull away from me, but duty won out and he turned away to his father.

One of the guards grabbed the linen from Ren's loose hands and shoved it to the mass of blood and exposed bone that was now my lost finger. I pushed back at them, not wanting anyone near me.

"Keep it there to staunch the blood," said a voice in my ear, and I was coming back to myself enough to recognise it as Jiron. "And stop fighting – we're getting you help."

I knew I shouldn't trust him, knew that he was probably one of the men who had held me down only moments earlier, but I was exhausted and hurting too much to struggle anymore. I let Jiron lead me from the room and through the corridors, my feet obediently plodding along as the guard steered me by the shoulders through the twisting maze of the palace and out into the harsh sunlight of the inner courtyard.

He flung open the surgery door without knocking, but Starling didn't chide him, guiding me to one of her tables in deadly efficiency without even asking what had happened.

"Lie him down," she instructed, and I let out a sharp exhale of breath as Jiron swept me up into his arms to lift me onto the table.

"Star," I croaked, and she met my gaze with one so full of certainty and reassurance that it sent a rush of relief through me.

"I've got you," the healer murmured, gentle fingers taking hold of my right hand. I let her, despite my body crying out with pain and mistrust, and she inspected the wound with her nose barely an inch from the carnage.

I let her work, the now-familiar sensation of her magic soothing my shattered soul.

The pain, I'd get over.

The finger, I'd live without.

But Ren? That fucking *hurt*.

*

Chapter Thirty-Three

Ren

"You fucked up," my father said derisively as the last of the guards departed the throne room, and I swallowed back my anger. Because I *had* fucked up, just not in the way he meant. But with Nathanael, precious Nat, his eyes full of horrified betrayal. Fuck, to hear him scream…genuinely scream, not the surprised yelps I delighted in pulling from his lips, had broken me. I'd endure *anything* if it meant I never heard that sound again.

I swallowed a second time, trying to push back the hot bile that swelled up my throat.

"*Sí*, Your Majesty," agreed Moreno, and just as I was about to snap at him for rubbing it in, he dropped to a knee. "My apologies."

"I don't need fucking apologies, Juan. I need to know this won't happen again. Mazekhstam took out *eighteen* of our Blessed in a single strike; how inept do your men have to be to let that happen?"

"Each outpost and camp will be additionally fortified, and the soldiers reprimanded," the Comandante vowed, his head bowed. "I will see to it personally."

"You will." My father's voice was cold, unyielding. "Take out your knife."

My breath stilled as Moreno obeyed, his eyes downcast and his posture rigid. I would normally have enjoyed him being on my father's shit list instead of me, but my gaze was fixed on the bloody napkin bunched in his left hand. I didn't have fucking time for this.

"Show me you will bleed for your king. Put the blade to your neck."

Mutely, I reached out, and the Comandante obligingly relinquished Mathias' severed finger to me as he wrapped both hands around the hilt of his knife, bringing it to his bared throat.

"My king, *please*."

My father always ignored me when I begged, but Moreno had always been treated differently, even if he wasn't above being subjected to the king's cruelty. The difference was, my punishments were arbitrary and his were reserved for the rarest of occasions when he genuinely displeased his monarch.

"You would ask me for mercy, Juan? Do you think Mazekhstam will show us mercy when they seize the advantage your ineptitude has cost us?"

"No, Your Majesty." The man's voice was hollow, resigned, and I didn't blame him. I'd been in his position far too many times before, knowing the king held absolute power over me and not being able to do a damn thing but endure whatever whims he decided to indulge that day.

"*Hijo,*" my father said abruptly, glancing at me. "You believe the regent will bargain for the boy?"

The implication of what would happen if she didn't was clear in his tone.

"I do, father."

"You did not think that before."

I shrugged, trying to act nonchalant. "That was when we were relying on the information trickling down through our spies. Now that I have him here, Lord Grachyov has been quite forthcoming about his friendship with Panarina."

"You better be right," he said casually, as if there wasn't a man on his knees before him with a knife to his own throat. "Your little kidnapping venture has not proven fruitful thus far."

"Your Majesty," I said tentatively, "I believe we would have a greater chance of success if we were to present our position as solely being the safety of our people in Algejón."

Moreno hissed out a disapproving breath, and the king narrowed his eyes on me.

"And relinquish the city itself? Let the north keep what is *ours*? Are you fucking delusional, boy?" He rose from the throne, padding down the steps towards us, and my hand closed tighter around the bloody cloth I was clutching.

"While we're weakened," I continued, shooting a glance at Moreno to remind my father of whose fault that was, even if I blamed him for pissing off Mazekhstam with Lord Morozov's murder rather than the death of the Blessed, "we should seek to prioritise what is important. And is that not our citizens trapped in the city?"

"Don't get me wrong, Renato, I would not see them dead if I can help it. But Algejón is more than its people, whatever's left of them. It is the city's location and strength that gives it its true value, the placement of our borders. We will not compromise on that!" He turned to Moreno, but his words were for me. "Write to the regent immediately."

"Yes, sire," I said, recognising the dismissal. As I fled the hall, I heard my father's cold voice deliver an additional command.

"Put that knife to your palm, Juan, and *cut*. I will have you remember this failure."

—

The door to the surgery opened before I could reach for the handle, Starling slipping through the small gap and pulling it closed behind her. I frowned, trying to move the tiny woman aside so I could get inside to Mathias, but she held her ground.

"*Move*, Estrella, before I'm forced to make you."

"What took you so long?" she hissed, evidently choosing to ignore my threat. "It's been an hour!"

I gave her an unimpressed look. "Yes, thank you. You may be surprised to learn a prince's education does involve learning how to tell the time."

"Clearly not, as you were gone for *a fucking hour!*"

"Keep your voice down," I ordered. "One of these days, you and I are going to have a chat about the level of respect you're required to show me."

She planted her hands on her hips, equally as unimpressed.

"I couldn't come straight to you," I murmured, watching out for anyone who might spot me here, although I knew Jiron and El had already cleared the courtyard in anticipation of my arrival. I pulled a bundle from my coat pocket. "I had to be seen sending off a messenger to Mazekhstam with Mathias' finger."

"Then stop wasting time, Your Highness." Starling held out her hand for what I held.

I faltered. "Is Mat…is he okay?"

"He's hurt," she said coldly. "And not just physically. He doesn't understand why you'd order him mutilated with a blunter blade."

I felt the words like a blow to my chest.

"But you told him why, right?" I whispered, unable to make my voice any louder.

She scoffed and snatched the bloodied cloth from my hands. "Don't you think I clean up enough of your fucking messes already?"

Starling stepped back into the surgery and slammed the door between us.

I looked helplessly at Elías, who gave me a small smile. "Mathias is in good hands, my prince. You know there's no one more skilled with the Touch than her."

I did know that. But would it be enough? No one could regrow body parts, but the more gifted healers could repair almost any wound. Starling hadn't given me any assurances when I'd gone to her yesterday while Mat was asleep at siesta, other than that she'd try her best to fix what I'd been sure was coming since I'd spoken with Moreno in the stables. My father was cruel, but unimaginative. He'd taken his prisoners' fingers before, and I had no reason to expect this time to be any different.

Except it was different. So fucking different, because it was *Mathias*.

I trudged back to my rooms, replaying what had happened in the throne room again and again. That spark of hope in his expression as he begged me to help him, only to be stamped out by the devastation of his anguish when I didn't.

I'd done that to him.

I'd seen all that life and joy in Mat, and I'd *destroyed it*.

"Your Highness. My prince."

I couldn't breathe. My heart was beating so fast it was painful, loud, heavy thumps that drowned out the world. My chest was encased in a band of iron, squeezing tighter and tighter. My head was swimming, my throat gasping for air, and through it all was that overwhelming, urgent sense of *horror*.

Something firm wrapped around my shoulders, and I clasped at it blindly, unsure if I was trying to push it away or pull it closer, and did it even matter because I couldn't breathe and there was something in my throat and get it out get it out-

"Ren!"

Strong hands clasped my face, warm and familiar, and I breathed in his scent.

"Jir...on," I gasped, and he rubbed his thumbs across my cheeks in that way he always did when I...when I...

"Breathe, Ren," he murmured. "You're okay. Just breathe."

I heaved in huge gulps of air, shaking and sobbing.

"Slower," Jiron ordered.

My breaths deepened, still ragged and painful, but finally delivering enough oxygen to my brain for me to comprehend what was happening.

"I'm fine," I said shortly, when the terror gave way to humiliation. I pushed his hands away from my face. "Who saw-"

"Just El." Jiron's voice was soft. I blinked to find him on his knees before me, settled between my legs where I was sprawled in an armchair in my bedchamber. *Mat's* armchair. "He got you back here without anyone realising."

"Tell him to keep his fucking mouth shut," I muttered, and Jiron rocked back onto his heels, nodding at me. With him on the floor, we were about the same height for once, and it made it difficult to avoid his assessing gaze.

Fuck. I hadn't had a panic attack in years. I'd been getting better at keeping the anxiety at bay, but clearly I hadn't tried hard enough. To be overwhelmed like that; to lose to that part of me, to *fail*...

"Ren-"

"*Prince* Ren."

Jiron dipped his head. "Your Highness. You're under a lot of pressure. Perhaps if you-"

"Get out."

He didn't say a word; just rose to his feet and crossed to the closed doors of the bedchamber, bowing and leaving through them like the obedient guard he was.

And when the silence fell and my breaths quickened once more, I hated him for leaving, wished he'd ignored me and stayed, like Mat would have.

And that made me feel even shittier, but screw Jiron for seeing me like that. For not having the same fucked up thing in his brain that I did, whatever it was that had made me cling to him in the dark of night as a child, cry in his arms as a teenager, and scream myself awake as a man. My anxiety had always rested close beneath the surface, but I'd thought I'd finally beaten it.

Just one more thing I was wrong about.

-

It was four hours before the doors opened again. Mathias didn't meet my eyes, muttering a weary goodnight to my on-duty guards and heading straight for the bathing room.

"I ran you a bath," I said quietly. "And then it got cold, so I ran you another."

He just sighed.

"Mathias. Nathanael. I'm sorry-"

"I don't want to hear it," he snapped, still not looking at me. "I don't want to hear *anything* from you."

I promptly shut up to show him I was willing to do whatever he wanted, whatever it took to make this right between us.

And then because I wasn't very good at staying quiet, I forgot to be so when he unhooked his coat from where it had been draped over his forearm and tossed it over the back of his chair, revealing his right hand...and five fingers.

"It worked!" I breathed, sidling closer and reaching out to reverently touch the digit that had previously been completely separated from him. Mat snarled and yanked his hand away.

"You think because Starling fixed me, that makes everything you did back there *acceptable?*"

"No," I said. "Of course not. But I-"

"No, Ren. No fucking excuses."

"I'm not making excuses. It was deplorable, I know that," I assured him, resting a hand on his hip. "But there was a reason for why-"

"*Naranja,*" he growled, his eyes flashing with unrestrained fury.

I immediately pulled my hand away. "I wasn't trying anything, Nat. I just wanted to explain why I-"

"*Naran-fucking-ja.*"

I fell silent for good this time, not willing to breach a safe word even when it was being used in this context. But damn him, couldn't he just *listen?*

I'd done what I had to do, for *him,* and it was horrible and I wished I could take it all back and put myself in his place. I needed him to know why I'd been so cruel with giving Moreno the knife to take to his hand, and I *really* needed him to not be looking at me like that, all lost and angry and betrayed.

Mathias slammed the door in my face, the second one today and perhaps in my entire life. I rested my forehead against the cool wood, feeling ever so fucking tired.

*

Chapter Thirty-Four

Mat

I'd seen many sides to the second prince of Quareh in the weeks I'd known him: playful Ren, mean Ren, angry Ren and of course, impossibly horny Ren. But a despondent Ren was certainly my least favourite; every time those sorrowful brown eyes turned in my direction, his expression miserable and pleading, it felt like a kick in the chest. Because fuck him, *I* was the one who'd lost a damn finger to his nonsense, even if only temporarily, and I had the right to be fucking mad at him.

"No," I said shortly as he finished his morning prayers and joined me in the corridor outside the chapel. "You're not allowed to talk to me today, either."

Ren gave an over-exaggerated sigh. I'd accuse him of dramatics, but that would be like complaining the ocean was wet.

Yet for all my fury at him for what he'd done, I couldn't deny he'd been on his best behaviour these last few days. He'd complied with my refusal to let him apologise or explain – whatever the fuck he thought he could justify about that day – seeming content to gaze mournfully at me whenever we found ourselves alone, as if hoping I might change my mind at any moment. He also hadn't been inappropriate towards me *once*, which I figured was some kind of earthly impossibility that would probably make the continent explode if it lasted any longer, and despite not being able to get his hands on me in turn, Ren still hadn't returned to ordering floggings or other harm that required Starling to unnecessarily drain her magic to heal. The creative punishments he doled out for his people's wrongdoing continued to be a source of much speculation among the servants and nobles alike, and it seemed, to me at least, that the uncertainty of the resulting penalties had driven down much of the usual misconduct in the palace.

"Your 'ighness!" exclaimed the younger Lord Lago, jumping up from a window seat as we drew close. "Are you…that…are you well?"

The man's curly hair was a mess, his shirt laces loosely trailing past his fingers, and the smell of brandy on him was so strong that I would have worried about him swaying so close to the corridor's braziers had they not already been extinguished with the rising sun.

"Better than you, I imagine," the prince drawled, raking his eyes down the lord. "An early indulgence, or a very late one?"

"Shaven't tushed a drop," Lago declared promptly.

"I see." Ren's tone was polite, if resigned. "Then perhaps Elías can escort you back to your rooms?"

"Ecud," Lago said, in a tone that I assumed he intended to be coy but was ruined by his slurring. "Bud I'd prefer if you did it urshelf, my prince. I would be so increp…uncred…*incredibly* graishful."

"No," Ren said flatly. "I expect your husband is looking for you."

"My *husband*," mumbled Lago, drifting closer to Ren and trailing an unsteady finger down his olive-green coat, "dushent do harf the things to me you can."

"Significantly less than half, I expect," retorted Ren, but there was no life to the words, none of the usual joy he took from flirting his ass off with everyone he encountered.

I gazed past Lago's head and through the open window beyond, the bright blue sky steadfastly cheery despite the mood inside. I could see a lone guard on the outer palace walls, bow in hand, and an enterprising spider had started spinning a web across the open frame in an endeavour that would be ruthlessly destroyed the moment someone closed the window. In my mood, I was tempted to do just that.

But maybe it would be the decent thing to do, to save that hopeful spider the heartache and wasted effort of achieving a mirage of happiness only to have it come crashing down around its head.

Nope, I was not projecting onto an arachnid. Not at all.

"Jush harf an hour," Lago was saying, when I returned my attention to him. "Jush give me something, my prinsh. I need it. I need to *feel*."

Ren glanced at me. "Lago. Go to bed."

"Iv you come with me," he slurred, trying to grasp the prince's hand and missing by a mile. "I'll let you do *anything* you want, jush hurt me, please-"

"A tempting offer," I said shortly. "Seeing as your period of abstinence has ended, Your Highness, perhaps you should-"

"It hasn't," Ren snapped, and it was the most emotion I'd seen from him all morning. "I will remain *abstinent* until its source starts speaking to me again."

"Then you'll be going without for a long fucking time," I retorted, and the lord's head wavered between us both before settling on Elías at his side.

"I fer I may've drunk too much," Lago admitted, and collapsed forward, his head only saved from impact with the tiled floor by Elías darting forward to catch him. "Shank you, good sir."

The guard sighed and folded him up into his arms the same way Luis had carried me up the cliffs of Sesveko all those weeks ago.

"Is he drunk?"

I jumped as I found a sneering Moreno at my shoulder. The bastard had snuck up on us without me even noticing, something he was getting scarily good at.

I glanced down to check my right hand was covered with the black leather glove Ren had procured for me. Me retaining my newly restored finger, and Ren keeping the skin on his back, depended on the king and the Comandante not realising that the glove was hiding an index finger rather than the absence of one.

Thankfully, we only had one of the pricks to currently worry about, with Ren's father having returned to Máros the day after he'd arrived. He hadn't even taken the time to deliver his usual…*attentions* to his son before he left.

Ren gave Moreno a shrug. "Sober as the day he was born. Can't you tell?"

"Ah, moor…moor enno." Lago waved from Elías' muscular arms. "I was jush telling your priddie Alta how she…she…" He frowned, glancing down the corridor. "I thor she was 'ere?"

"Thank you, El," Ren said firmly, and the guard nodded, bearing a giggling lord past us to take him back to bed.

"Your Highness," Moreno began, and by the Blessed Five, I was beginning to hate those words. "I spoke to the king about your herald, and he agreed that she-"

He trailed off, and then unexpectedly dived at Ren, slamming the prince to the floor. His shoulder caught mine with how close we were standing, and I grunted as he knocked me down too, an immense weight landing on my own chest a moment later.

Fuck, was this *it*? Was this Moreno's move against Ren, where he finished off what he'd started with the ambush in the canyon, and re-attempted with the poisoned banquet that had taken out Valentinus? We were so *slow* to catch up, and we hadn't even figured out how and why he'd destroyed Vitorona, let alone what he hoped to gain by killing Quareh's youngest prince…

The dizzy, upside-down nature of the world finally settled, and I heard Moreno seething about the audacity of someone trying to kill his prince in his palace.

"*My* palace," Ren interjected, sounded winded. "But I appreciate your indignation nonetheless."

"Get the fuck off me," I snapped at Ademar, realising it was his huge form that was pressing me to the floor. I shoved at him, but he didn't move.

I managed to turn my head to see Ren similarly pinned by Moreno, the two soldiers ignoring us as their eyes darted around, awkwardly drawing their swords even as they continued to hold us down.

Ren shot Ademar an affectionate smile. "I knew you liked him, really," he said, nodding in my direction, and Ad scowled down at me as I attempted to wriggle out from underneath his suffocating weight.

"Any more of this, and I'm tempted to just let him go," he snarled, and I stilled as I finally realised he wasn't subduing me, but rather shielding me. From whoever had tried to attack Ren?

"Got him!" Elías announced triumphantly, and I strained my neck to see the guard crouched by the open window, one knee on the cushion Lago had been draped across only minutes earlier, and his bow in hand. I couldn't see the lord but I could hear him chuckling to himself at my side, feel the pointed bone of his elbow or knee digging into my leg.

Ademar abruptly peeled himself off me, and was joined by the Comandante a moment later as they peered cautiously out of the window.

"Is the archer dead?" Moreno demanded, but El shook his head, his long hair dancing around his shoulders from where it had come loose from its ties.

"No, sir. In the leg. Figured you'd want to interrogate him."

"Damn straight," growled Moreno, and he looked almost impressed for a moment before he was gone, sprinting down the corridor to get to the downed assassin.

"Lago!" I gasped out the man's name as I spotted him still on the floor, the shaft of an arrow sticking out of his thigh and blood seeping through his left trouser leg. "He needs help!"

Ademar and Elías knelt beside him and worked together to bind the wound with a strip torn from Ad's shirt.

"Get Starling," Ren ordered in a low tone, his eyes fixed on the lord, and Ademar took off running in the same direction as Moreno had gone. Lago giggled, his eyes unfocused and his head lolling against the tiles.

I crawled over and lifted his head into my lap before he could hurt himself. El nodded at me, his hands pressed firmly to the blood-soaked linen wrapped around where the arrow had pierced the man's leg.

"Feelsh funny," Lago said, gazing up at me with a frown. "D'you feel it too?"

Before I could tell him help was coming, he started to scream, the pain finally making it through the shock and whatever liquor was clogging up his bloodstream. As he thrashed wildly, it took all my strength to keep his head protected from the floor, and Elías was required to practically lay on him in an effort to stop Lago from tearing the arrowhead deeper.

"You need to stay still," I begged, but the lord wasn't listening. He keened and tried to pull from my grip, screaming louder as he moved his leg.

"Quintín," Ren snapped, and shivers that were highly inappropriate for the situation slipped through me as I recognised the prince's bedroom voice, the dominance icy cold and yet hot as fuck. "You *will* lie still, do you hear me?"

Lago's eyes widened, and he gave a fervent, submissive nod, staring mutely at Ren as his body tensed and he attempted to hold himself motionless. I brushed the dark curls of hair from the man's pained face, wondering if I had the prince's god to thank for the fact that Lago had taken the arrow meant for him, or if it was no more divine than a drunken lord with an unrequited crush and a pain kink.

"My lord," murmured Starling, as she appeared in my peripheral vision and sank to her knees beside Elías. "We'll have you fixed up in no time, just like always, you hear me?"

Lago gasped as magic sparked from her fingers to his leg, spitting in a red and green glow.

"Now," she said grimly, and El tore the arrow from the flesh with speed but no finesse, sending Lago into another pained scream. I winced, remembering the agony of Star knitting my mutilated finger back to my hand as she'd coaxed the bone, muscle and skin to join together once more. She'd been gasping by the time she finished, the effort of reattaching an entirely severed body part after an hour of separation clearly having taken its toll, but it hadn't stopped the girl from smugly daring me to find 'another fucking healer on Riehse Eshan that could do *that,* Mathias.' It had been incredible magic, and although there was faint discolouration around where the flesh had once been sawed through — thanks again for that delightful bit of savagery, *Ren* — my index finger was almost fully functional.

It was still fucking sore, and it couldn't *quite* bend as far as the others, but considering I'd been convinced I'd lost it for good, I was chalking it up to a positive. And no, I was not planning on thanking the prince for delivering my stolen flesh to Starling for her to reattach it, considering how I'd lost it in the first place.

I glowered at Ren, my fury at him reappearing as Lago's screams died down and the blood ceased to flow from his leg.

The prince's mouth twitched into an unhappy grimace, and his lips parted as if he was about to speak. I hoped it was something that would allow me to tear *his* limbs from his body without his guards trying to stop me.

"Darling!"

I caught sight of a terrible hairstyle and a flash of grey silk before the elder Lord Lago flung himself on his husband, sending me to the bottom of an extremely enthusiastic tangle of limbs and kisses that I would rather *not* be part of. I scrambled free, ignoring Ren's outstretched hand and climbing to my feet unaided.

"All fixed," Starling said, a note of amusement to her voice as she was also forced to disentangle herself from the Lagos. It had been a lot quicker than my own healing, although she looked a little tired. "Perhaps stick to your usual methods of seeking pain next time, rather than taking an arrow to the leg?"

I winced at the words as the elder Lord Lago twisted to glare up at Ren.

"I told you to keep away from him. What the fuck were you doing together?" he snarled, and Ademar's hand landed on his sword in clear warning. The man seemed angry enough to do something ill-advised like try to hit the same prince who had almost just been assassinated, and I knew that if Moreno saw him even try to attempt it, he might be hanging from the walls before lunch.

"Your husband and His Highness were talking state affairs only," I lied. I liked this man and his unwillingness to simper over Ren like the others did far too much to let him be executed.

The younger Lord Lago caught Ren's eye, and the prince gave a small shake of his head to keep him quiet. If he wished to confess to his husband later, that was his decision, but right now, both men needed to stay calm.

And not a second too soon, for Moreno had returned, bearing both an angry grimace and a pronounced limp.

"Fuck me," he snarled, and Ren raised a delicate eyebrow.

"Problem? Or was that an invitation?"

Moreno levelled an unimpressed glower in his direction. "I subdued your assassin, Your Highness."

The prince peered at him. "Are you keeping him in your pocket, perhaps? I can't imagine any other scenario in which my Comandante would return empty-handed without a prisoner to interrogate-"

"He was carrying some kind of poison, my prince. Took it before I could stop him. Damn it!"

Ren ignored the outburst. "-any scenario, that is, other than one where the highest military officer in the country lets the only clue to a thrice attempted assassination kill himself." He shook his head. "It's astounding how you found yourself so promoted, Moreno, it really is."

The Comandante sucked angrily on a tooth, clearly trying hard to restrain himself from smacking his prince. I was half tempted to offer to do it for him.

"He was one of the carpenters here for the Solstice," Moreno gritted out. "Not a resident of the palace, but one allowed through its walls nonetheless. Somehow managed to obtain a guard uniform and the foresight to know where you'd be, yet he wasn't here the day of the first attempt so there's at least one other person still at large. And…wait, *thrice?* Your Highness, is there something you're not telling me?"

"Undoubtedly," Ren said instantly, some of his usual cheer restored as he wound the man up.

An irritated sigh slipped through his lips. "Then you should *tell me*, my prince."

"Okay," Ren agreed. "The exact number of times I've fantasied about smashing your head in with a half-full bottle of wine is…three. With a full bottle, six. No, wait, make that seven now. As for-"

"You," Moreno snapped at Starling, clicking his fingers in her face. She reluctantly dragged her eyes up to his, swallowing the retort she clearly wished to make. "Heal my leg. The bastard got in a lucky blow before I took him down."

Starling gave him a fake smile. "Certainly, my lord Comandante. Please remove your trousers so I can get to the wound."

Ren sniggered, and Moreno's glower could have melted all the ice lakes between Stavroyarsk and Nevimki.

"Your Touch works through clothing, you obtuse girl," he snapped, clearly not as amused as the prince at the idea of humiliating himself by undressing in front of us all. "How else would you have healed Lago with his clothes intact?"

"Tend to him, Starling," Ren said, although a smirk still played around his lips. "Else he'll be intolerable for the rest of the afternoon instead of the five minutes it will take to get rid of him."

She gestured at the window seat but the Comandante ignored her. Rolling her eyes at me, Star dropped to a knee and grasped Moreno's left leg, sending the coloured sparks through the cloth. I knew she could have done it by making contact with any part of his body, but if Moreno knew she could heal through clothing, it was doubly important to avoid him learning of the full extent of her enhanced gift. I'd never heard of the Touch being used in such a sophisticated and indirect way as Starling seemed able to manipulate it into, and I knew without being told that it was beyond anything the king's own healer could do. If they learnt of her talents, she'd be whisked away to the Quarehian capital of Máros before any of us could blink, making it that much harder for her to escape Aratorre control.

I eyed the Comandante, more confused than ever. Who had sent the assassin if not him?

Or perhaps it had been, and the man had only pretended to save Ren when he realised the archer had missed? But he'd acted quicker than either of Ren's guards, and while it was all a blur, I *thought* he'd shielded the prince prior to Lago being hit, knocking us both down so the arrow had come to rest in the thigh of the lord behind us, instead.

Had Moreno acted *too* quickly? Had he known the assassin would be there, and had a change of heart at the last second?

Fuck, a person could drive themselves insane with such thoughts.

"Hurry up," Moreno snapped down at the healer.

"I just healed a man from massive blood loss," Starling retorted, "not to mention the three soldiers you sent to me this morning with flogged backs, Comandante, and the difficult birth I had to handle two hours before dawn. I don't have much magic left."

He let out an irritated noise and shoved her away from him. Starling's head smacked hard against the edge of the window seat, and she yelped in either pain or surprise.

"Der'mo!" I snarled, lifting my fist and preparing to repay the injury to him in kind, but Star shook her head frantically at me.

"Don't, my lord!"

I hissed out a breath and stepped backwards, not failing to notice how Ren's hand twitched as if stopping himself from reaching out to me.

"You northerners are so predictable," Moreno mocked, his gaze not-so-subtly falling to my gloved hand. "Always caving to the whining of women. Let me know if you ever find your balls, little Grachyov, or perhaps we'll ask your regent for them, too."

I turned away, helping Starling to her feet and frowning at the bloody gash across her forehead. She shrugged at me and healed it, the flesh sealing in an instant but not taking an ounce of my rage with it.

As the Lagos hobbled away with an arm around the other's shoulders and Moreno and Ren fell back into serious talk about the assassination attempt, I wandered over to the wall a few feet from them, as far away as I figured I could get without a watchful Ademar dragging me back to the prince's side. I slid down it to sit at its base, too exhausted from both the morning and the shit that was going on between me and Ren to consider standing upright any longer, and tugged at Starling's hand to pull her down beside me.

She rested her head on my shoulder with a weary sigh, yet didn't let go of my left hand. Her fingers were calloused, which always surprised me; I'd expected her to heal the imperfections away. But her hands were nice all the same, tanned and weathered. It was so Starling, all practicality and toughness, and I swallowed down the hard lump I suddenly found in my throat.

"I should have listened to you," I whispered, pitching the words so no one else could hear. "About…the prince. You were right."

"I know," she said without hesitation, her self-confidence in this misogynistic land always another surprise to me, yet so endearingly *her*. "But that doesn't mean it hurts any less."

No, it fucking didn't. The gap between Ren and me felt so achingly wide, and hideously, inexplicably *wrong*. My hand still reached for his at night, despite the fact that I was once again curled in the uncomfortable armchair rather than cuddled up in his bed, and I'd found myself often calling his name to share some amusing thought or interesting sight, only to have to cover it with a cough. I missed his hands on me, his touches both rough and gentle, and his mouth murmuring simultaneously sweet and terrifying words into my ear that could bring my cock to attention in seconds. I missed having him *there*; despite the fact that there was no more space between us during the day than there ever had been, it didn't feel that way. It felt like Ren and I were trapped on opposite ends of the continent, a yawing mass of distance between us, and while I knew that should be *totally fucking fine* considering who the bastard was, it didn't explain why I felt as depressed as he looked all the time.

"Der'mo?" Starling enquired, her lips quirking as if she'd already guessed it to be nothing good.

"I called him something decidedly unpleasant," I admitted, not wanting to meet her eyes. Damn it, why was it always the swearing I had to translate for her?

But she didn't seem bothered in the least, letting out a soft little cackle of delight. "Noted and catalogued, my lord."

Heavy boots passed my eyeline where I was staring glumly down at the floor, and then paused and turned to face me. I sighed.

"I see you're *still* not restrained," Moreno said with no small degree of irritation, and I dragged my gaze up to meet his as he did his best to loom over me and Starling.

"Comandante," Ren said, moving to his side. "The lack of faith you have in my guards' skills really is becoming quite tiresome. Lord Grachyov is not going anywhere, chains or not."

Don't I know it, you bastard.

"Besides," the prince continued, waving an idle hand. "The court seems to think what was done to his finger is punishment enough."

It was true. Despite the murder of the Blessed, the hatred we'd expected to return in force had never arrived. Either *la Cortina's* inhabitants had had their fill of spewing racist comments and disgust in my direction, or they really did see my mutilation as a fitting penalty for my unforgivable crime of being born north of the border.

"And yet you let him hide it," Moreno sneered, gesturing at my gloved hand where it lay on my lap. I noticed the pale lines crossing his own palm, and wondered where the scars had come from and why he hadn't had them healed. "Take that off, boy. Let me see the mess I left you with."

I swallowed, feeling Star's fingers tighten around my other hand in silent support.

No. He would know that Ren had deceived them. That Starling was far more powerful than she pretended to be, and she would become much more valuable to the king as a result.

"Why?" I asked, trying to hide my fear with disgust. "Are you really that sadistic?"

"No more so than your master, Grachyov. Or have you already forgotten that it was him who doubled your agony for his own amusement?"

No, I had not fucking forgotten that. *Thank you, Moreno.*

"Show me," he insisted.

With a grimace, I lifted my right hand to my mouth and began to loosen each finger of the glove with my teeth. My breaths huffed in shallow wheezes, and I couldn't speak, even if I'd wanted to.

"You will not indulge his games, Mathias," Ren said coldly, but his eyes were wide and his expression worried. He glanced between me and Moreno, giving me a subtle shake of his head to tell me to stop. "Comandante, come. Why don't we find-"

The prince fell silent as I jerked my right hand free of the leather glove, the stump of my index finger raw and purple where it sat between my thumb and middle finger. We all stared at the ugly lump of flesh and the gap where a finger had once been.

"You did a terrible job in healing that, girl," Moreno said to Starling condescendingly, but he was smirking as he looked back at me. I held my breath until he nodded at Ren and strode away.

The moment the Comandante was out of sight, I hissed out the screech of pain that had taken my vocal cords hostage, pressing my face into my shoulder to muffle the sound. Starling released my left hand and promptly doubled over, dry retching.

The others stared at us in shock.

"How…?" El began, blinking and shaking his head as if to clear it of what he'd just seen.

"That was a complex piece of magic, Star," I croaked out, my voice hoarse with the agony of what she'd done to me and the strain of appearing unaffected. "I didn't know the Touch could be used to maim as well as heal?"

"And you still don't," she hissed at us all, although there was little force behind it. I scraped back her hair with my good hand as she proceeded to throw up a second time.

"It's a forbidden use of my gift," she muttered, reaching for my discarded glove and tipping it up so my once-again severed finger fell into her palm. I lifted my hand and she pressed the flesh together, muttering a prayer to Dios to give her the strength to complete the heal.

"Starling, if you don't have enough magic left," I began, but she fixed me with a stern look.

"Konchaj bazar," she snapped in clipped Mazekhstani, and then her face softened into an expression of eager hopefulness. "Did I get that right?"

"You did," Ren confirmed from where he was still standing over us. "Although to have any luck in actually getting Mathias to shut up, you should probably start praying again."

*

Chapter Thirty-Five

Ren

The sword came to rest at Jiron's neck, its brutal edge hovering less than an inch from his throat.

"Better," he said approvingly and Elías gave a shy smile, pulling back and twirling the blade in his hand as if its weight meant nothing. I'd have suspected my metalsmith of replacing the sword with one of his lightweight forgeries, except that I knew firsthand how strong each of my guards were.

I'd once insisted on holding one of their swords because I figured it would complete my dashing royal image quite nicely, and had been damn near bent in half with the effort of keeping it aloft. Although, it'd almost been worth it to watch my men struggle to keep a straight face while I reminded them what horrendously gruesome punishments lay in wait for anyone who laughed at their prince.

"Again."

The two guards reset their positions and El ran through the moves that I could have now recited in my sleep, a long and complex sequence designed to improve the footwork Moreno had been bitching about. Jiron acted as aggressor, distraction and victim all in one, moving with him and murmuring corrections as El twisted his blade to protect the other guard in one moment, and defend against him the next.

"Again," Jiron ordered. To his credit, Elías didn't complain, although I expected the repetition must have been starting to grate on him by now.

I murmured the same to Mat beside me, intending to follow it with a suggestively phrased comment about *grating on him* that probably totally sounded better in my head, but fuck it, not everything I said had to be perfectly suave, when I remembered that he wasn't beside me at all. He was sitting cross-legged on the grass a few yards away as he had been since we arrived out here at the training ring an hour ago, watching Jiron and El as he absently shredded daisies between his pale fingers.

"Walk with me," I called out on impulse, and Mat went stiff.

"No, thank you," he said politely, his eyes fixed forward.

Obstinate bastard.

"So you'd prefer to continue murdering innocent flowers instead? That doesn't seem like the sanctimonious Temarian asshole I know."

He glanced downwards with a disdainful sneer and then gave a start, as if the pile of severed daisy petals heaped before him had crawled up onto his lap all by itself.

"It wasn't a request, Mathias. Walk with me." I'd long since learned that *requests* achieved nothing with him; if he didn't want to do something, asking nicely wouldn't change that. And since that day Moreno had taken his finger, he'd ever so coincidentally not wanted to do anything I wanted him to.

Of course, the recalcitrant prick didn't respond well to *commands,* either, at least not ones I framed as a prince. But as a lover? Oh, if I injected *that* particular steely dominance into my tone, I had him shuddering every time.

Mathias feigned indifference, but I could see how his hands were folded tightly in his lap, and he was swallowing rapidly. The influence I had over his body, which I could cheerfully admit I was abusing shamelessly, only went so far, but it was just enough to put him on edge.

"*Khorosho,*" he conceded in a muttered growl after a moment, getting to his feet and brushing petals from his clothes. "Where are we going?"

"Somewhere that isn't here," I clarified, and he sighed.

I waved Elías and Jiron away as they tried to follow, encouraging them to continue their training as the other two guards pulled out of their cooldown stretches and fell into step behind us, as far back as they'd allow me to shoo them.

But if I'd hoped giving Mat as much privacy as we were going to get outside would encourage him to talk to me, I'd been wrong. He just offered me the same frosty silence as he had for the last few days, a judgmental, hostile stillness that I could practically taste on the air. In fact, apart from the handful of exasperated words he'd just shot at me then, Mathias hadn't spoken to me since late last night when I'd been at my desk working on my latest response to Valeri Velichkov. The Temarian prince had recounted by way of a tedious inventory of wheat and sugar how he'd reached out to Mazekhstam's regent about the proposed restoration of the continent's original borders in the interests of avoiding provocation of their shared southern neighbour, suggesting that while her father still lay ill, she focus on matters internal to her country. Given what I now knew of the reciprocal attacks between Mazekhstam and Quareh, I doubted that such a politely framed request would bear any fruit at all, and had been wondering how to best word *try harder, you fucker* in a way that aligned with the price of silk at this time of year, when I noticed Mat had tugged aside the huge tapestry that hung at the back of my bedchamber.

I had watched his hands run along the cracks of the door that stood concealed behind it, admiring the way his shirt lifted to reveal his delicate hipbones as he raised his arms to feel along the top of the frame. There were few people in *la Cortina* that knew that door even existed, but of course the nosy brat had discovered it the very first night he'd been free of the palace's cells.

"Tell me where the key is for this," he'd demanded, without turning around.

I had merely scrawled out another sentence with my favourite swan feather quill, not having the slightest inclination to give him the one thing that would let him into the tunnels beyond and to escape the palace undetected. "Get me naked and you'll find out."

"Hilarious," Mat had deadpanned, his eyes narrowing on me as they finally swept in my direction. "It has to be in the room, otherwise this door would be useless to you in emergencies."

"Logical."

He'd stomped over to me and I had chuckled, leaning back in my chair and stretching out my arms. "Gonna search me, Nathanael?"

He ignored that offer, which was a shame.

"I've seen you undress enough times to know you're not hiding it on you," he muttered, and I cocked my head at that. "But you're always at your desk."

"Because unlike a certain irritating pest I could name, I have an actual job to do," I had sighed out, but I let him scrounge through the papers on the desk's surface and peer underneath it anyway, because I was nice like that. Just not nice enough to give him the ability to run from me.

A WHISPER AND A BREATH

Mathias may have been mad at me, but it didn't mean I cared for him any less. I couldn't touch him, but the craving to do so was just as strong, and when he was standing this close, his alabaster skin so enticing in the flickering light of the lantern, it took everything in me not to fold him into my arms and hold on until he finally forgave me for what I'd done to him.

As Mat had straightened from his crouch next to me, clearly not having found what he was looking for on the undersurface of the desk, I flicked the feathered end of the quill across his delicate neck. He scowled and pulled away, heading to search the bedside table next.

"I imagine you're going to regret that," I'd remarked casually as he yanked open the top drawer. He'd seen me pull oil and rope from it before; did he not expect I might keep equally fun and significantly more interesting things in there?

Mat's eyes had widened as he took in its contents, and I wondered which of my toys had caught his attention.

"*Blyat.*" He had slammed the drawer shut with such force, the bedside table had rocked back into the wall, and hastily crossed the room to search somewhere far from the bed even as I cracked up laughing.

On reflection, maybe that hadn't been the best idea when I was trying to win him back.

Now, I watched him out of the corner of my eye as he dragged his feet alongside me. But the fresh air was doing him good, and even his pissed off mood couldn't stop the interested glances he was giving our surroundings as I led him up into one of the citrus orchards that stretched between the palace and the neighbouring town of Tego. I breathed in the warm afternoon air, savouring the scent of oranges and earth and Quareh.

He pulled ahead, curious despite himself, and I swallowed a curse when he picked the fourth row of the orchard to explore, seemingly at random. I didn't know whether it was Dios guiding him or just Mathias' natural ability to sniff out secrets, but maybe it didn't matter.

I let us wander down the row for a few hundred yards, familiarising myself not with the leafy orange trees around us but the stakes that marked the orchard's growing areas. Then I waved my guards back out of earshot range and called Mat to a stop.

I ground the toe of my boot into the dusty ground, pleased when it brushed against something hidden just under the surface. Watching him from my peripheral vision, I bent to uncover the object, revealing its edges and scraping dirt from an old wooden box.

"What's inside?" Mathias asked, when I didn't immediately open it. As I'd known he would – he was far too nosy to sulk at me forever.

I unclasped the latch and swung open the lid to reveal a knife, around ten inches long and rusted with age. A jewel was set into its handle, but that wasn't why we'd taken it.

"It's Moreno's," I said, a smile playing at my mouth at this part of the memory. "Al stole it from him when she was…eleven? I was nine. He had both mine and her rooms turned over to find it, unable to stand the thought of someone screwing him over even in such a small way. Forced us to stand in the corner of his office for hours to get us to confess where we'd hidden it." I snorted. "Alta made faces at me whenever his back was turned, and I remember I was laughing so much that I ended up smacking my forehead into the wall and damn near knocking myself out."

I dropped the lid and returned the box to where it had lain for the last several years, kicking dirt over its surface to conceal it in the earth once more.

"Of course, we both more than paid for it when we were out of sight of my guards and any courtiers. Alta was limping for a week, and when my father next returned to the palace…"

My voice had turned bitter, and I coughed, trying to infect it with a levity I didn't feel. "Still. Moreno was *livid* when even that failed to break us. It was the first time he managed to convince the king to let him use a whip on me instead of just his fists."

I swallowed down hot bile, trailing a hand along a branch and following it to where it split from the tree's trunk a few steps away, putting space between us so I could breathe. Fuck, it was difficult to say all this out loud; other than to Mat that night he discovered the truth, when the pain had distracted me from the deep-seated shame that held my tongue the rest of the time, I'd never spoken about it before.

"I hate them," I said quietly, running a finger around a knot in the wood. "Moreno and my father. For what they've done to Alta, to me, to Quareh.

But…they're the two people on this continent that I can't stand against. My father would…" I heaved in a heavy breath, returning my hand to my opposite wrist to rub against the leather cuff attached to my left arm. "I hate that I couldn't protect you from them, *mi sol*."

Mat was silent.

I turned on the spot, irritated to find his brow creased in pity. I didn't fucking want *that*. I wanted him to understand what was at stake, to forgive me for playing a part to keep us both alive when it was what we had both been doing this whole time.

"Nathanael," I said softly. "Please talk to me."

"*Nyet*. I'm still pissed at you."

"Then let *me* talk to you," I pleaded. "Let me explain."

He ran a hand through his hair, which I'd noticed was growing long and was now past his ears.

"Fine. Say whatever completely sensible and entirely justifiable thing you're going to say."

I faltered at the unexpected words, and Mathias exploded with fury.

"Why the fuck do you think I haven't allowed you to do so yet?" he yelled at me, his eyes flashing. "You always manage to make me look like the irrational one, because your mind works ten times faster and plots out things that I hadn't thought of. You have an answer for every-fucking-thing, don't you? And I know that once you say it, I'm not going to be able to be angry at you any longer, and damn it Ren, I *want* to be angry! Don't I deserve to be, after everything you've done to me?"

I gave a sombre nod. "You do."

"Don't do that."

I was confused. "Do what?"

"Agree with me. Now I don't want to be mad at you because you think I *should* be mad."

I gave him a sideways grin. "Then maybe you should stop being so contrary."

Which, of course, made him more so.

"Spit it out, Aratorre," he snarled.

"I'm sorry," I said to start with, the most important thing of all.

He didn't look impressed.

I wet my lips. "The reason I told Moreno to use the knife instead of the chisel," I explained carefully, "is because a cleaner cut is harder to heal with the Touch. Don't ask me why it works that way, but I know from experience that jagged edges – ripped skin, splintered bones, torn muscle – that's much easier to repair. Maybe it's because there's more surface area to reattach it." I swallowed. "Although it hurt you at the time, and trust me Nat, I did *not* enjoy that in the way I pretended to, I wanted you to have the best possible chance for your finger to heal."

He stared at me blankly, and I wondered if I'd used words he hadn't understood, replaying it back in my head. I couldn't think of anything: Mat's Quarehian was very good, and he'd expanded his vocabulary considerably since he'd arrived here. Mostly to encapsulate more imaginative cursing, but as I was just as foul-mouthed as he, I couldn't judge.

"Did you hear me?" I asked gently, wanting to close the distance between us to take his hand, and too fucking scared he'd pull away if I tried. "If I hadn't ordered you hurt with the knife, you might have lost your finger permanently."

"I know," Mathias said, crossing his arms. "Starling told me."

I blinked. She had? But...then...

"And, er, the reason I held you down while he did it," I choked out, pained at the memory of him struggling beneath my hands as I condemned him to the Comandante's savagery, "was nothing more than futility. If I hadn't, someone else would have, or you might have hurt yourself more. And if I was seen shying away...well, you heard Moreno the previous day. He was watching me for weakness, for any resistance to the king's orders. It wouldn't have served either of us for me to show it."

"By all means, *knyaz*, keep aiming and missing," Mat snapped. "Don't you think I *realised* all that? Or do you believe me a complete idiot on top of everything else?"

Fuck. This was not going how I'd imagined. I thought that once I told him why I'd done it, he'd realise I hadn't intended to hurt him and that we'd been backed into the same metaphorical corner. That I was still on his side, and-

"Panarina," I breathed, figuring it out. "What I said about Astrid, that hurt you."

"No shit, you prick."

"You said yourself that we needed to say whatever it took to-"

"I said talk shit about me, Ren, not the fucking truth! Do you know what that was like, having my secrets laid bare for everyone to hear? That what I'd told you in private, because I *trusted* you, could be so casually tossed around as if it meant *nothing*?"

I stilled. "I'm sorry. I didn't realise it was so personal."

"Fuck Ren, it's not. It's just..." he trailed off, his nostrils flaring with anger. "It's just that all of those things — not to mention that terrifying expression on your face as you watched him do that to me — *all* of that could have been avoided."

"How?" I asked. "My father wouldn't have let-"

"By fucking *talking to me*!" Mat yelled, nearly shrieking the words at me. "Starling said you'd warned her what would happen beforehand. That meant you *knew*, you asshole, and yet you didn't say a Blessed word to me! If you'd just *told me*, we could have planned it together: I would have been prepared, would have known that you were there for me even if we had to act otherwise...instead of being utterly fucking blindsided!"

"And instead," he hissed, now absolutely livid, "you threw me among the wolves because you wanted to be the only one to *handle it*. Because you didn't trust me."

"No, Mathias," I protested. Did he really think that? Of course I trusted him! "I just didn't want to worry you unnecessarily! To know that was what they had planned for you-"

"Don't you think I could have taken it? After everything I've been through, do you think I'm that weak?"

"I don't think you're weak," I said vehemently, needing him to hear the truth in that statement. "I think you're the strongest, most resilient person I know, and no matter what, you *endure*. But..."

I wanted to tell him that I hadn't wanted to get his hopes up about fixing his hand, that if I'd shared my plan with him in advance and then was unable to retrieve his finger, that I couldn't bear for him to suffer that double disappointment. But the words wouldn't come.

Because they were a fucking lie. I hadn't told him what I knew my father would do, what I knew Mat would be forced to suffer through, for one simple reason.

I hadn't thought to do so.

"Oh, look at that," Mathias said callously. "I was wrong. I am still pissed at you, after all."

I heaved in a painful, shuddering breath. "I'm sorry."

"You keep saying that. But it's just words, Ren."

"No. No, it's not," I whispered, hating the empty look in his eyes. The one that said he was retreating back into himself, taking his smiles and his laughter with him, and that it would be twice as hard to get him to open up to me again. "Tell me what I can do, *mi amor*."

"Let me go."

I froze, and Mat's jaw set into a hard grimace.

"Let me fucking *go,* Ren, right this minute. Tell your guards to turn their backs, and I'll run. *That's* how you fix this."

We stared at each other. And when I didn't respond, he hissed in a breath.

As one, we both looked down at the overturned earth between us. It was closer to him, and the box wasn't buried deep; he could easily get to it first and pull the knife on me, just as he had at Sesveko.

Jiron wasn't here this time – would Luis and Ad be enough to stop him? If it came down to it, none of my guards would risk my life to keep Mathias captive. All he had to do was make them believe he was desperate enough to hurt his enemy, the man who had told him he cared and then hurt him, and Mat was good at lying.

If it even was a lie.

He took a step closer to the box. And another, until he was standing over it.

I hadn't moved. I just watched him, silent and sorry.

Mat kept walking, compacting the soft earth with his boots. He came to a stop before me.

"*Por favor*," he said softly. "You know this isn't going to end well. I want to go home."

"Home?" I echoed. "And where is that? Another country that wishes to hold you hostage, only with sub-zero temperatures and an intolerance for what you like?"

He went still. "And what is it that you think I like?" he asked, his voice like ice.

"Nat, you're gay. Do you really think that the north will allow-"

"Don't you fucking tell me what I am!" he snarled, shoving at my shoulder. "You know nothing about me! Do you think a few weeks of whatever the fuck you did to me will change me?"

I took the blow, my back slamming into a tree. From their respectable distance, Ademar and Luis tensed, but I shook my head to keep them away.

Change me. What you did to me. Fuck, did he honestly believe I had *turned him?* It was who he was, and this Mat, the pretentious, close-minded Mat that I had first met, was a downright asshole.

"Don't you dare," I hissed. "You came to *me* that night at the Martinez estate, don't you remember? You wanted us."

"What the fuck does it even matter?" Mathias asked disdainfully, but there was a flicker of guilt in his eyes. At his horrid words, or for wanting me in the first place? "My brother is working on the treaty, you said. Maybe I won't have to be anyone's Blessed hostage; not yours, not Mazekhstam's. Maybe I can go back to Delzerce to be with my actual family."

"Family you haven't seen in how long? Tell me, other than Valeri, would you even recognise them? Aleksi? Your sister, Mila? You don't know them, Mat!"

He visibly swallowed. "So what, I don't deserve the chance to try?"

I waved an angry hand. "That's not what I meant."

A WHISPER AND A BREATH

"Ren, please. You wanted me to beg? I am. Just *let me go.*"

I took him in, the determined and tenacious man who had dared to stand up to his southern captors, time and time again. Who had fought so fiercely to defend both strangers and family despite what it meant for himself. Who would be utterly fucking destroyed if he returned to the north, where he would either be forced to hide what he was, to rip out that part of himself and live an incomplete life…or risk his reputation, his family, and his safety in defying their laws and their god.

At least here he had someone who appreciated him, who *worshipped* him, even I could only show it behind closed doors when no one was watching.

His demand tore me in two, but how could I let him go, when he'd take my heart with him?

And half my skin, as my father would have me laid raw for such a thing, but I knew I could survive the king's brutal punishment if Mat was waiting for me afterwards. But to return to an empty bedchamber, knowing my wildcat was back in the north where I'd never see him again?

That would fucking *break* me.

Keeping him here would ensure his anger, but surely that would ease in time. Mathias was forgiving by nature. Releasing him meant the end of *everything*, because Dios damn him, he was *mine* and I was *his*. Had I not suffered through enough shit in my life? Did I not deserve this one tiny slice of happiness?

Didn't he?

My eyes fell to his right wrist, where the blue ribbon was still tied. The blood from that day in the throne room had soaked into it, and he should have gotten rid of it a long time ago. He hadn't.

I waved Ademar and Luis closer, and turned back towards the palace.

"No."

*

Chapter Thirty-Six

Mat

"Ren. Just tell him."

"I can't, *mi querida*. He's still so fucking angry at me. It would...it would make things worse."

"Can they really be much wors-"

Alta and Ren's voices drifted through the open doors to the antechamber, abruptly falling silent as Ademar and I walked in. I bowed to the Lady Moreno and steadfastly ignored the asshole at her side.

"Ah, Mathias," Alta said. Her face broke into a smile, although it looked a little strained. "Ren said you were visiting señorita Ortega? How is she?"

Starling was fine. Healing my hand for the second time in the corridor that day had put her out of commission for a couple of days as her magic restored itself, and even Ren hadn't been heartless enough to rush her recovery. Although, as the healer had repeatedly alleged, that was likely more attributable to him not wanting to lose such a valuable asset, than any concern for her personal wellbeing. In turn, I'd told her how defensively the prince had reacted when I'd asked him about his brother's murder of the stableboy, but Starling hadn't looked smug at being proven right. Instead, she'd distracted me with tales of the most outrageous patients she'd treated over the years, delivering the absurd stories with such dry, sardonic wit that she had me in chuckles despite my dark mood.

"Well, thank you. And yourself, my lady?"

"Mat," Ren said, not waiting for her response because he was an arrogant fuckwit that way. "Will you join us?"

I offered Altagracia a regretful smile, not bothering to acknowledge him. "My apologies, Lady Moreno, but it's late and I would be poor company."

"Mat," Ren repeated, his voice irritated. "Could you just-"

Alta put a hand on his arm, and the prince went quiet. Maybe God and His miracles did exist, after all.

"Why don't you retire for the night, Your Highness?" she suggested softly. "I would like to speak to Lord Grachyov for a few moments alone."

Ren's jaw clenched and he stared between us for a long second before nodding stiffly to her and striding into his bedchamber. Luis closed the doors behind him.

"How have you put up with him for so many years?" I asked irritably, and Alta's mouth set into a thin line.

"Sit, *por favor*."

I hastily complied, sinking down onto the lounge next to her. The cushions were still warm from Ren's body, his scent hovering faintly in the air, and shit, even that was enough to make my throat go tight from how much I fucking missed him. I pressed back against the lounge in an effort to capture more of the warmth he'd left, hating myself but needing it more.

"You're mad at him." Altagracia didn't phrase it as a question.

I looked at her, at the carefully sculpted curls that framed Alta's face, the expensive burgundy dress highlighting her figure. At the sadness in her expression. "Aren't I allowed to be?"

Alta blew out a gentle breath. "Of course. But…" She paused, and when she next spoke, it was in hushed Mazekhstani. Clearly, she didn't want Luis or Ademar to hear us from their positions on either side of the bedchamber doors. "But you know he's sorry?"

"So he's said. Repeatedly."

"You don't believe him?"

"I believe him. But it doesn't mean I'm not hurt. I thought he cared, and that we were…" I toyed with one of the buttons on my guard's coat. "My apologies, my lady. I shouldn't be saying this to you."

"Nonsense," she chided gently, articulating the Mazekhstani word with crisp pronunciation like she was learning the language for the first time. I almost smiled when I thought of her and Ren as children, forced to recite basic phrases for their tutors like we had done in Quarehian back in Stavroyarsk. The prince's tale of their mischievous thievery from Moreno had me imagining two tiny miscreants running around *la Cortina* with their hair in plaits, causing messes and generally ruining other people's days. "I've told you: Ren and I are not, and never will be, lovers. We will...engage together once we are married, as we must and no more. But he is my friend, and I can see how this is hurting him. Can you not forgive him, for me?"

"Do you know what he did?"

Her eyes fell to my gloved hand. "He has confided to me many regrets in relation to you, Mathias. But it is not my place to know the details. All I know is that you made him happy, in a way that I have never seen before. I want that for him again."

I looked away. "Not everything exists to serve Ren."

"Indeed. Don't tell him that."

I fought down my smirk, thankful she couldn't see my face. "If *you* don't tell him that I won't be pissed at him forever, my lady. I don't think I'm capable of it. I always forgave Kolya even though I knew he'd turn on me again the next day, even after he tried to kis…" I coughed, trying to cover my slip. That had been a highly personal moment, and the more I thought on it lately, the shittier I felt. "I'm sure the manipulative bastard will work his way back into my good graces soon enough."

"You're very self-aware."

I shrugged. "Not really. I just know I'm shit at holding grudges."

Alta stiffened in her chair. "So you're no longer angry at Ren," she said delicately, her fingers hovering over her mouth and her eyes wide, as if worried what I might say to that.

I blinked. "Yeah, I…no," I admitted, knowing it was the truth when I really stopped to think about it. "I'm not angry at him. I just…don't know what to do."

The confession left me feeling empty, incomplete, like there was something that should be there but I'd been hollowed out. Because if I wasn't mad, what did I feel?

"Do?" Altagracia laughed and stood up, twirling away before I had the chance to get to my own feet for her. "Let him make it up to you, of course. Show him that you need him." She glanced back over her shoulder with a questioning eyebrow, and I nodded slowly.

Fuck, I did need him. I wanted nothing more than to sink into his arms, to hold him close and kiss him until I'd covered every inch of my beautiful, bright prince with my mouth-

"Buenas noches, Lord Grachyov."

I absently repeated her farewell back to her, my mind already on the man behind the closed doors, the one who had captured my heart, body and soul so fucking thoroughly it was unbelievable. How could I have let such a small thing stand between us when the mere *thought* of him set me alight?

Luis pulled open one of the doors for me and I slipped through, several paces into the huge bedchamber before I spotted the prince standing at one of the windows. He was dressed in his grey gown with his hair loose and splayed down over his shoulders, and he had his back to me as he stared out across the moonlight vista beyond the open window.

Ren had barely glanced around before I was on him, my hands flying up to cup his face as I pressed my mouth to his. He gave a surprised murmur and kissed me back, and the taste of him inside my mouth, on my tongue, was every-fucking-thing.

And then he was shoving me backwards.

"Fuck, Nat, I'd rather you *didn't* push me out of the window," he gasped, steadying himself on the wide frame behind him. He looked at me and gave a wicked grin. "Although with a kiss like that to mark my last moment, it wouldn't be a terrible way to go. I've missed you, *mi cielo.*"

"I've missed you," I whispered, and leapt at him again, unable to keep my hands off him for a single second longer. Ren twisted so I was pushing him against the wall instead of the gaping open space with a five storey drop behind it, and then the moments blurred into one long, messy kiss that sent my mind into a drooling blur. Our hands raked up and down each other, too urgent and needy for anything resembling finesse, and I tore at his thin silk gown even as he managed to unlace my shirt with hungry, grasping fingers.

"Mathias," he murmured against my mouth, and then broke our embrace just long enough to rid me of my coat and pull my shirt over my head. I kicked off my boots. "I thought…I thought I'd lost you."

"I was angry," I said. Pointlessly, because I'd more than made that clear, but I didn't know how else to express it. I didn't feel any of that white hot rage anymore, not an inch of it. Just a longing, a desire, a need for this gorgeous Quarehian with his expressive brown eyes and quick wit, his long legs and insatiable sexual appetite. "Now I'm not, so stop talking and fuck me. I *need* you, Ren."

His eyes widened and he let out a sharp exhale, studying my face intently. Seeming to reach a decision, he nodded. We pressed close together once more, and Ren didn't try to stop me as my hands explored south, trailing down the smooth skin of his chest, his stomach, the defined V at his hips. I impatiently tugged the gown away from my prize and stroked even lower, marvelling at the silky softness of his cock and how it instantly hardened at my touch. Murmuring incomprehensible words, Ren walked me backwards, not breaking our contact until the back of my knees hit the bed. Then he shoved me down onto it, turning me over.

"Stay there while I get the oil," he whispered, and pressed a hand to the back of my neck to keep me in place even as the other came down hard on my ass. I jumped at the contact, a startled laugh erupting from my lips, and he made a pleased noise at the back of his throat.

"Hmm. Maybe first I'll do that to you harder," he mused, sounding breathless. "And without your trousers. Remove them for me."

I let my face fall into the blankets, hooking my thumbs into my waistband.

And then I paused.

What the fuck was I doing?

The bastard had known that his father planned to cut off my damn finger, and hadn't said a word to me. He'd smiled and teased and held me the night before as if nothing was wrong, not bothering to utter a single warning. Had let me believe in that throne room, even if it was just for a second while he played the part of the sadistic prince, that I was completely alone, and I had been fucking *terrified* it would prove to be true.

So why, by the Blessed Five, was I letting him get his hands all over me again as if none of that had happened?

Hot rage flooded through me, filling that space inside me once more. It warred with the lust it found there, swirling into a confusing mass of emotions that made everything blurry and bewildering and too fucking overwhelming. I tried to sit up but was immediately shoved back down onto the bed, the blow ruthless and driving the breath from my lungs.

I lay there, winded, and felt Ren's weight shift onto the bed.

"I gave you an order, Mathias." The dominance the prince had been using on me so often lately was back in his tone, and it sent shivers through me even as I fought against it. "Disobey me again and I'll double the number of strikes I lay across that fine ass of yours before I put my cock in it. You won't like that nearly as much."

"Get off me," I snarled, smacking at his hand as he reached for my belt to undress me himself. Ren gave me a delighted yet utterly cruel smile and grabbed my wrist, twisting it until I yelped.

"If that's how we're playing this, then know I plan to make you scream until your voice gives out," he whispered, and I tried to shake him off but he had me held tight. "Protest all you want, Nat, but nothing of mine gets away until I allow it."

Mine. There was that damn possessiveness again, his casual disregard of my autonomy. I was so sick of being owned and imprisoned and *kept.*

Ren ran a hand across my still-clothed ass, his touch almost reverent. "Will you really let me spank you?"

"Why bother asking when you're just going to do it anyway?" I said, irritated. "Isn't that what gets you off? The control? The domination? The *taking?*"

He abruptly let go of my wrist. "What the fuck?"

I found myself rolled onto my back. Ren was kneeling over me, his eyes flashing, and all traces of playfulness had disappeared from his expression. "Are you being serious right now, Mat?"

I glowered at him. "I did tell you to get off me."

He ran a hand over his face, looking stricken. "And that's what your fucking safe word is for! Dios, Nathanael, how am I supposed to *know?*"

"As if you care. You like it when I resist you. When I'm helpless to stop you."

"Of course I do, but only when–"

I pushed up onto my elbows so I could bring my face closer to his. "So just go ahead and do it."

Ren flinched. "Is that what *you'd* like? For me to take you without your consent? So when you return to the north, you can keep your conscience clean and tell them – and *yourself* – that you were forced?"

He snarled and climbed off the bed, his entire body radiating fury. "I will not be the method of your guilty gratification while you get to play the role of hapless victim. Get the fuck out."

"Ren-"

But he was already pulling me to my feet, scooping my shirt from the floor and shoving me towards the doors.

This was not...nothing was...my head hurt and nothing made sense, and what the fuck had I just done? I hadn't seen Ren this incensed since the day he'd torn open my back with a belt, his mouth flattened into a thin, angry line, his shoulders tense. He wrenched open one of the doors and pushed me through it, thrusting my shirt into my arms before slamming it in my face.

I closed my eyes.

"Mathias?"

I opened them again to find Ademar a foot away, peering at me curiously.

"*Blyat*, why are you always *there*?"

My yell startled him and Luis, who exchanged uncertain glances. I heaved in a breath and yanked my shirt back over my head, not bothering to tie up the laces along the sleeves. They were a stupid fucking invention anyway: completely useless, just like the Quarehians who wore them.

Fuck this. I needed to get out of here. I needed to find somewhere to *breathe*.

I strode towards the doors at the opposite end of the room and slipped into the corridor beyond before either of the guards could stop me. As I belatedly realised that they'd simply follow me out here, a vision hit, short and strong. I stepped back into the shadows to stand beside a potted fern, my body angled to reflect the lines of the surrounding shadows.

Luis' head appeared around the door frame a moment later, scanning left and right. I knew he wouldn't see me in this very specific position, as the Sight had shown me as such, although the flimsy hiding place likely wouldn't have held up on any other night. It was a slim set of factors in my favour that had only been identifiable through my gift, and I wasn't questioning it, not now.

"*Mierda*," Luis spat, withdrawing back into the prince's antechamber. "Ad, he's somehow already gone!"

"Find him," I heard Ademar order. "El and Jiron should be back from training soon. I can look after His Highness alone until then."

"I shouldn't-"

"Letting Mathias run free will earn us his wrath more surely than halving his guard will," Ademar said, and I almost felt guilty about leaving Ren vulnerable.

And then I quashed that thought. I hadn't asked to be brought here, and I certainly hadn't asked to be constantly under watch like a wayward puppy. If Ren wanted me guarded, why should I have to be considerate about it?

I remained still as Luis tore off down the corridor. He didn't bother to turn his head, believing me long gone, or he'd have noticed me in the shadows. And when the guard's huge form disappeared, I let out the breath I'd been holding and padded after him, careful to take the stairs up when he'd gone down.

My bare feet slapped the smooth tiles as I climbed, and I relished the coolness against my skin as my emotions started to settle. Careful to duck below any open windows in case I was spotted from the walls, I wandered along the next corridor I found. The palace was peaceful at night, devoid of irritating courtiers and bigoted nobles, and alone in it for the first time, I found a greater appreciation for the elegant architecture and delicate terracotta ornamentations. Stavroyarsk was *heavy,* the castle dark and grim, and while that had an attractive strength to it, it was the light airiness of *la Cortina* that I favoured.

It was strange not to have a single one of Ren's Blessed guards breathing down my neck. I closed my eyes, and let myself enjoy the silence of the halls, a sound I hadn't heard since I was first brought to Quareh. And then a soft chirp drew my attention, and I glanced around in confusion until I spotted a bird nestled up on a beam near the ceiling, its eyes wide and blinking at me in the flickering light of the braziers set along the corridor.

It was the sight of something so innocent, so unaffected by the mess of politics and war and death and *Ren,* that made hot tears prick at my eyes.

Fuck, I was a mess tonight. What the hell was wrong with me?

But I knew there was no single answer. I'd been a prisoner of the Quarehians for weeks now, and the stress of keeping my identity secret along with the worry about what Commander Grachyov intended to do to my friends back home if I didn't, and how to save Ren's people in Algejón when Mazekhstam seemed to be unwilling to trade it for me, and what that *meant*...and then everything happening here, with the massacre in Vitorona and the assassin and Starling's desire to escape and Alta's abuse by her father, and Ren's by *his* father, and, and-

I froze when I realised I was no longer alone in the shadowy corridor.

"My lord," Diego said mockingly as he approached, his footsteps remarkably light for a man of his size. "Funny that a Mazekhstani *puta* like you should have any title at all recognised here, but when you have a daddy like yours, I guess that earns you special privileges, huh?"

The guard prowled closer and I swallowed, determined not to step back or look away. I'd known plenty of men like him back home, and they revelled in their victims' fear. Showing courage didn't necessarily stop them from hurting you – I'd been beaten enough times not to hold out any false hope of such a thing – but it was one less power they held over you while they did so.

"That's twice now you've landed me in trouble, *bárbaro,*" Diego said, his eyes raking up and down my body and making me suddenly crave a bath. Or ten. "Twice you've set back my career with the Comandante. You owe me something for that, boy, and I don't care whether you choose to pay on your knees or your back."

"Keep the fuck away from me," I snarled, raising my fists.

Diego just smiled, a predatory grin that was all teeth. "Both, you say? That'll do nicely."

He reached for me. That was his mistake, opening himself up and putting himself off balance, and I feinted a fist to his face before delivering my real blow, a kick to his groin that doubled him over. I slipped past the guard's grasping hands, getting ready to run, but my bare foot hadn't been nearly as effective as a boot would have been and I heard the scrape of metal as he unsheathed his sword before I'd taken even two steps.

"Stop right there, you little shit," Diego hissed, breathless and angry.

It seemed I was making a habit of leaving furious men in my wake tonight, myself included. Because I was so incredibly pissed at myself: not for what Diego clearly planned to do to me, because that was his fucking problem and I'd make sure he knew it for every second he made it last, but for what I'd done to Ren. It felt like someone else when I thought back on it, my cruel words inflicted to make him bleed, and fuck, I hated that I'd done that. I really was a shitty person, no matter what adoring praises the prince might like to dish out on me.

Liked. I was pretty sure I wasn't going to be getting any of that anymore, not after how I'd hurt him tonight.

"Turn around."

My heart hammered in my chest as I obeyed.

The cold tiles beneath my feet seemed less welcoming at the thought of being pressed against them as the guard took what he wanted. Fear flooded my veins, and I lost the ability to breathe as Diego hobbled closer and brought the tip of his sword to my throat.

Fuck.

He'd have to let go of his weapon if he wanted this to go much further, surely, and then I could try to reach for it, or get away, or…I had no fucking idea, except that I wasn't going to make this easy for him.

His eyes gleamed with wolfish pleasure, and he fiddled at his belt with his free hand. A sick feeling coiled in my stomach. "Get down on your-"

"Diego?"

The guard flinched, only luck drawing the blade back instead of forward and saving me from a slit throat. I staggered backwards as the Comandante strode up to us, his expression inscrutable as he glanced between me and his man.

"What's going on?"

"Nothing, sir," Diego said promptly. "Just found this one wandering the palace unguarded and was in the process of returning him to his master, sir."

Moreno's lip curled. "And you call that nothing?"

Diego faltered. "Uh, Comandante…"

"Get to bed," Moreno ordered, and Diego shot me a look that clearly said *keep your fucking mouth shut* in any number of languages before sheathing his sword and hurrying away.

I heaved in shallow breaths, trying not to let my relief show. Fuck me, with the rate at which Moreno was saving Ren and me, maybe we really would have to take him off the villain list one of these days.

"Where's your escort, Grachyov?"

"Around," I said.

Moreno's cool gaze ran over me; not in the same way as Diego's had, but careful and calculating. He took in my bare feet, the trailing shirt laces, and hair that might not have screamed *just fucked*, but certainly suggested its closely-related companion of *was maybe about to be fucked, but ruined it all with his stupid temper and idiotic mouth and is now wallowing in self-loathing over how callously cruel he can apparently be.*

"You like being out here alone?" Moreno asked, and I frowned up at him.

"What's that supposed to mean?"

He shrugged. "I just know how being surrounded by people – guards – all the time can be. Maybe I can arrange for you to have more time to yourself. Get you your own room while you're staying with us. Proper clothes," he added dryly, eyeing again the overly large shirt and trousers I'd borrowed from Elías and Ademar.

"Why would you offer that?" I asked, suspicious as fuck of his intentions even if that all sounded wonderful. *Especially* because that all sounded wonderful.

"I was just hoping we could talk, little lord. You've been in Ren's company for several weeks now, have you not? In my role, I have to be aware of everything that could compromise the people I'm sworn to protect." The Comandante spread his arms. "There must be something you've noticed about the prince that could let his enemies get to him. Tell me, so I can stop it and keep him safe."

I thought of Ren's coded messages with my brother. His anxiety, something that he thought he hid from me, but sleeping in the same room with him for months – some of that, in the same bed – had gifted me an insight into his mind that I often didn't get from his conscious self. I thought of Ren's tears at Vitorona and how he'd do *anything* to protect those he loved.

"If not him," Moreno said softly, "the people around him, perhaps?"

Alta's wilfulness. Starling's plans to flee the palace. El's secret.

I shook my head. "Can't think of anything."

"Try harder," he immediately spat back, and when I let my expression slide into a sneer, he grabbed me by the collar and shoved me backwards.

I was sick of being manhandled tonight, but Moreno wasn't a bossy, slender prince messing around in the bedroom. The Comandante's hold on me was immovable, and no Blessed safe word would get him to stop as he half dragged, half pushed me over to the nearest window, unlatching it and flinging it open.

"*Blyat!*"

Now my hands, one bare, one gloved, were grabbing at him instead of trying to push him away, while he used his grip on my shirt to lever my torso out over nothingness. We were on the highest floor of the palace and I could feel the cool night wind nipping greedily at my hair and shirt as he held me out further. I clawed at his hand.

"Moreno, you wouldn't!"

He just raised an eyebrow.

I hissed out a harsh breath, glancing down over my shoulder at the courtyard six storeys below and immediately regretting it. The angle he was holding me at had lifted my feet from the floor, and my bare soles scrabbled at the wall under the window in a desperate attempt to secure myself. Finding nothing, I hooked my ankles around the back of his knees, hoping the idea of mutually assured destruction would be enough to stop him from dropping me, but knowing the man would be able to shake me off with ease if he wished.

We stared at each other, the wind flicking my too-long hair into my eyes, and terror took a tighter hold on my heart at the idea that fate would end me over the walls of *la Cortina* as it had always promised to do, albeit at the hands of a decidedly less handsome Quarehian.

At least if the Comandante killed me here, I'd never have to face Ren's knife in my gut, or the impassive look on his face as he yanked it out and I fell over the edge of the terrace. Hell, with the shit I'd just pulled on the prince, I wouldn't have been surprised if that was the death that awaited me once I returned to his rooms.

If I returned.

Damn it, no one knew we were here but for Diego. And if I was found dead on the cobblestones below, the guard was unlikely to rat out his master for the murder. I'd really screwed up every single second of tonight.

I held back a whimper with my remaining shred of self-control, and offered him a scornful expression instead.

"Last chance, Grachyov," Moreno said softly. "Or I let go, the prince finds a new obsession, and my king finally authorises me to take Algejón back by force instead of playing these stupid fucking games."

*

Chapter Thirty-Seven

Ren

My kinks may have been relatively broad, but they were one-directional. I liked inflicting pain, not taking it, so why was I suddenly such a fucking masochist when it came to Nathanael Velichkov? Nothing about the man was *painless* – from the excruciatingly lengthy chase to get him into my bed, to his acerbic, sharp-edged self that only thawed with exceptionally hard work on my part, the daily arguments and scowls I had to put up with in his company, and now whatever he was doing to me that made my chest feel tight whenever I was away from him for more than a few moments.

Being without him hurt, but it seemed that being *with* him was just as dangerous, if what he'd just done was any indication. Had he seriously been about to let me fuck him when he didn't want it? By the Blessed Five, I'd drummed into him the importance of his safe word until he'd been rolling those pretty little eyes at me, but it seemed that not even that had sunk in.

I slid down the wall, my head in my hands.

Mat could be as sweet as fuck, but he was also occasionally capable of immense cruelty, to both himself and me.

I wouldn't be his villain, his way of indulging his own desires without being forced to confront them. I may have been less than perfect myself – just a smidge – but I had *never* lain with someone who was less than willing.

How dare he foist his shame about what he liked onto me?

"Your Highness," Ad said urgently from the doorway. "Luis found him."

I pushed to my feet, refastened the tie on my gown, and made sure to plaster an appropriately infuriated expression across my face as I joined my men in the antechamber.

Ademar was in his position by my bedchamber doors, while Jiron and Elías hovered behind one of the lounges, their cheeks flushed from another training session. But I only had eyes for my fourth guard and the man he was holding onto: a paler than usual, barefoot Mathias.

The northerner looked uncharacteristically subdued and he wasn't even *trying* to pull out of Luis' grip on him, which was downright fucking weird.

"You look rough, little one," Jiron said, his brow creasing as he noticed the same. "Are you alright?"

"He's going to look rougher in a minute," I snapped. "First you pull that shit on me in bed, and then you run from my guards? Where the fuck did you find him?"

I shot off that last part to Luis, who hadn't yet let go as if worried Mat might take off again if he did.

"Halfway out of a window," Luis said, "with-"

"*And* trying to escape, you idiotic, brain-dead Temarian?" I yelled, realising belatedly that the antechamber doors still stood open to the corridor where anyone might overhear me. Jiron swiftly moved to close them. "Must you piss me off any *more* in a single Blessed night? What is it with you and-"

"With the Comandante trying to push him out of it," Luis finished loudly, cutting over my words in a way he knew he must never do.

I fell silent. "What the fuck? Mat?"

Luis let go of his arm and Mathias staggered, almost falling down onto the guard's feet until Luis caught him again and wrenched him back upright. Maybe his continued hold on my man hadn't been to stop him running, after all.

"He wanted information on you," Mathias said hoarsely, not looking me in the eye. "Weaknesses. Secrets."

My anger changed targets in the breath it took for him to utter the words.

"That *fucker*," I snarled, crossing the room to him and taking him into my arms before I could think about what I was doing. Mat wrapped himself around me as much as I did him, Luis stepping politely backwards, and we became a tangle of limbs as we tried to hold onto each other tighter than was physically possible.

I breathed Mathias in, that intoxicating and familiar scent of my wildcat, and I didn't give a damn about what he'd done earlier, not when he was clinging onto me like this. Like I *mattered* to him.

"The Comandante wouldn't have actually pushed you out a window," Ademar said softly, clearly trying to be reassuring. Ad didn't *do* reassuring, so it came out in his usual caustic, sardonic way, but I appreciated the attempt until the moment Mathias stiffened in my arms.

"I think he might have," he muttered into my neck, but the room was so quiet that I expected everyone else could hear him too. "He implied that he'd prefer to take back Algejón himself rather than obtain it through politics."

Shit. Mathias had value here, but only as a hostage. Once that was overlooked, as was what Moreno now seemed to be doing in favour of bloodthirsty methods that would leave thousands of my people dead in a full city-scale assault, then Mat became no more than an enemy to be disposed of.

"Bastard," El hissed unexpectedly. It was rare for him to show such emotion. "We won't let him get to you, Mathias."

Mat lifted his head. "Thank you," he whispered at my men, his voice raw. I rested my own head on his shoulder, savouring his closeness and wanting to keep him safe in my arms, forever.

"What did Moreno say when you found them?" I murmured, and Luis let out a low snarl.

"Some bullshit about trying to prevent a suicide. I don't know of many men who jump out of windows backwards with their final words being 'don't you fucking dare', but that was the story he was sticking with."

"Asshole," Mat muttered, the bite in his voice almost back to its usual levels.

"I'll carve him into pieces so small they'll be mistaken for dust," I threatened, but I knew I could never touch Moreno without proof of what he'd done. My father would have my head for it, and then where would my northerner be?

Mat spat something in angry, rapid Mazekhstani and I flinched.

"What was *that*?"

He pulled back, not letting go but enough to look me in the eye, and wet his lips, frowning in a way that made me want to execute every single person who had ever hurt him, myself included. It was an expression of fear and resignation, and of all the adjectives on the continent, *resigned* was not one I'd ever thought I'd use for him. But the words I'd caught from his furious snarl had made me realise there was more to the story, a more that I suspected was going to make me explode with rage.

"I just said that I'm lucky Moreno didn't decide to wait until after Diego was done before holding his impromptu interrogation," he repeated quickly, trying to brush me off.

But I caught his chin, not letting him duck away again. "Diego?"

"Yeah. It's not important-"

"What did Diego do to you, Nat?"

I felt him shudder, the vibration passing through us at each spot we were joined, and as we were practically plastered together, it shook me too.

"He didn't do anything," Mat whispered. "But he wanted to."

I'd been wrong. My anger wasn't an explosion, but rather a quiet sluice of ice that shot down my veins and froze them solid.

A growl resonated from behind me, deep and animalistic. I'd only heard Jiron make that sound twice before, and each time it was when he'd found me seriously hurt. He'd sworn vengeance on each of the culprits then: he hadn't been able to do anything about the huge piece of masonry I'd fallen off and broken my collarbone from when I was seven, but the drunk courtier who had backhanded me into a glass window and would have left me permanently blind if not for my father's healer...well. Let's say the king's justice had been too slow for Jiron, and there hadn't been enough of the man's neck left for it to find its way into a noose.

"I want his head," I told my men coldly, and they each met my eye before nodding, steel in their gazes. Diego would feel the full consequences of his actions. I may not have been able to touch Moreno, but his guard? Diego was fucking *done*.

"Food," I said. "And alcohol. You, *mi sol*, are taking a bath."

Mat, unexpectedly, laughed at that.

"*¿Qué?*"

"Nothing," he said, but his eyes were bright with some joke I wasn't getting. After a moment, he took pity on me and shrugged. "I think it's the first time since that very first night that you've encouraged me to bathe instead of complaining about it."

"Yes, well, you're lucky it's spring. There's not nearly enough rain in Quareh during the summer months to keep up with your insatiable bathing habits."

I guess we'll just have to share.

The words were on the tip of my tongue but I forced them back. Mathias didn't need me flirting, not now. Not with Diego having tried to…by Dios, I was going to beat the guard's fucking face in with my bare hands.

"Unless we share," Mat said dryly, leaving me gaping after him as he extricated himself from my embrace and wandered into the bedchamber. He wrapped his arms around himself, still looking vulnerable and lost despite the recovered strength in his voice.

"You think wine is going to fix that?" Luis asked quietly, watching him leave.

"No," I said. "That's why you're fetching us brandy."

-

Looking after Mathias was just as difficult as I'd expected it to be. He'd shooed away any attempts to help him eat, chastised me when I tried to wrap him up in blankets, and just gave a long-suffering sigh when I offered to barricade all of the windows.

"Ren," he'd said in exasperation, after turning down yet another a mug of cocoa and fishing out his boots from where they'd rolled under the bed, "nothing actually happened. I'm fine."

"You will let me take care of you," I'd said determinedly, and *that* order had gone down about as well as stale bread. Not that I'd ever eaten such a thing, but I'd heard it said by those with the inherent lack of common sense that consuming stale bread required.

But he had conceded to joining me in a game of pitarra, where I delighted in annihilating him multiple times in a row until it was pointed out that I clearly hadn't explained the rules properly if I was going to start giving myself three turns to each of his one rather than the two turns I'd told him were standard for a board game of this type. Yet the teasing glint in his eye said that he knew exactly what bullshit I'd been spouting from the start, and I counted my plan to distract him from the events of the night successful as his concentration steadily deepened, the stubborn prick evidently determined to beat me in a round despite my blatant cheating.

"Have another brandy," I coaxed, prodding the bottle towards him across the desk with the tips of my fingers. "Maybe it will make the overwhelming losses easier to bear."

"Stop trying to get me drunk so I lose track of whose turn it is," Mat retorted, setting down an ebony marker in the corner of the wooden board. He frowned at the corresponding ivory counters set out in front of me. "Did you always have fifteen pieces?"

"Always," I lied. I nudged one of them into the very centre of the board.

"*Svoloch*. You told me the middle wasn't a playable position."

I tsked and shook my head. "I don't think I did."

"There isn't even a line that goes to it!" Mat protested, but his tone was mild, mellowed by drink.

"Ah," I explained. "See, when the black player has at least seven markers off the board and the white player has captured more than one but less than three corners, then the centre becomes playable. It corresponds to any two other pieces on the board, which means…oh yes. I win, again."

"You're fucking unbelievable," he complained, but he leaned back in his chair with a fond smile, downing the rest of his brandy.

I reset the board just as his expression darkened. "I get why you couldn't…why you couldn't let me leave the palace. It wasn't fair of me to ask."

I clicked my tongue. "Don't do that."

"Do what?"

"Don't be so *Mathias*. Selfless and forgiving and shit, because I don't deserve that."

"Ren. If you'd let me go, it would have been your ass on the line-"

"That's exactly what I'm talking about," I pointed out.

"-and Luis and Ademar's. I didn't think of what I was demanding at the time, but of course they would have been punished too. Maybe even the others?

A WHISPER AND A BREATH

Five people for one, it was no question. That's not selfless. That's pragmatic."

"Mat. I didn't refuse because I was scared of my father," I told him. "I refused, because I was scared for myself. For you. For all the things that would happen if you went home, and what...what I wouldn't have anymore."

"What?"

"This," I said quietly. "Us."

His face twisted into greater agony. "Ren, I didn't mean what I said to you earlier about you taking-"

"First rule of pitarra," I interrupted, splashing another inch of golden liquid into his glass and refilling my own. "No talking about any serious shit, kay?" I met his eyes, ignoring the fact that I'd let us discuss my mistakes, but not his. "Not tonight."

Mathias swallowed and then nodded, chewing on his lip. And by Dios I wanted to be the one to do that for him, his flushed face and sprawled limbs making him extra sexy, but that wasn't what this was about. I subtly adjusted myself under the desk and then dumped three ivory markers onto the board in quick succession.

"Bonus round," I explained patiently, in response to his raised eyebrow. "They occur on the prime numbered rounds commencing after twenty-three, and allow the white player to immediately place..." I quickly counted out my markers, ignoring the one hidden in my coat sleeve. "...a fifth of their total counters down in a single turn. Oh, look, three in a row. I guess that's another win for me."

Mat reset the board with a soft chuckle, shaking his head at me.

There was a knock at the door a few minutes later and I responded absently, only glancing up when Jiron appeared behind Mathias.

"Churros," he said, waving a plate of them. Mat snorted good-naturedly, his eyes bright from the brandy, and twisted around in his seat.

"Jiron, you did *not* need to wake the poor kitchen staff to make me churros. And do you seriously think I can eat...however many there are? Twenty of the damn things?"

"Lightweight," I teased, leaning forward and resting my hands on the board.

"Alta can put away thirty without breaking a sweat."

Mathias, without turning around, held up a finger in my direction. "I saw that."

I grinned, and moved my piece back. "Can't blame me for trying."

"Actually, I can," he retorted, "seeing as it's the third time you've cheated."

"Only the third?" Jiron asked mildly, and I stared at him in astonishment. Jiron did *not* gang up on me.

"This *round*," Mat clarified, and my guard chuckled, setting the plate of heavenly scented fried dough beside the flickering lantern on the desk and backing out of the room. I eyed the three black counters I'd just noticed lined up along the right-hand side of the pitarra board, and my northerner smirked at me as he noticed the direction of my frown.

"Nathanael," I said, reaching for one of the churros and earning myself nothing but burned fingers. "Did I tell you about the extremely well-known and not at all fabricated rule where on the thirty-first round, the white player gets to knock two black pieces from the board whenever he wishes?"

"Oh yes, I had heard that one," he teased, watching me from over the rim of his glass. His posture was unusually relaxed, his smile broad, and fuck, how I adored this man. "It's just a shame for you we're on round thirty-two. Three in a row, you prick. I win."

*

Chapter Thirty-Eight

Mat

I scrubbed at my hair with a towel as I toed open the bathing room door and reached for my shirt, which was lying across the back of my armchair.

"Leave it," Ren said from where he was cutting up – oh, how predictably – an orange on the side table near the main doors. "Sit." Without looking, he waved the knife towards the straight-backed chair behind his desk where he'd sat last night as we played board games and gotten drunk well into the early hours of the morning.

My cock twitched at the assertive command. I was tempted to defy him – I was *always* tempted to defy him – but I was still feeling guilty about what I'd said about him forcing me, and wanted to prove to him that it had been utter bullshit.

Shirtless and with my towel draped around my neck, I padded towards the chair and obediently sat down, not taking my eyes from him. Ren was never predictable, and I loved how exciting it made things like this.

Even if it was probably incredibly unhealthy for us to jump back into bed together without talking it over first, considering we'd spent most of the morning unproductively dozing next to each other and fighting through the murky haze of the alcohol. At least it had been the expensive shit that didn't produce too terrible hangovers.

Ren finally turned around, sucking juice from his fingertips. He smirked when he met my gaze.

"Lose the bedroom eyes, Mathias. It's not me who's getting their hands on you."

There was movement in the corner of my eye and I flushed as I realised we weren't alone. Had I been so blind for the prince I'd failed to notice a whole other Blessed person in the room?

Camila, setting a comb and a pair of shiny scissors on the edge of the desk, circled around me and tugged at the towel to settle it over my shoulders. At least she didn't flinch in my proximity anymore.

I glanced at Ren. "Do I get a say in this?"

He shrugged. "Considering you now know I want it cut, that means you'll probably insist on growing it out just to spite me, so...*no, mi amor*. I prefer your hair short."

"You've never seen it long," I pointed out. To be fair, neither had I. It was rare to find a northern man with hair more than a couple of inches in length, which was what mine was now nearing.

"It's long enough already," he said dismissively, and waved a hand. It was obviously a signal for Camila to begin, as she began to comb through my hair with methodical grace, snipping at my locks. After watching her preen and groom Ren for weeks, I knew the servant was competent, and any mistake on her part would be deliberate. It would also be suicidal, as Ren had an unhealthy obsession with my hair — almost as much as his own — and wouldn't take kindly to such a thing.

So instead I watched the prince, whose expression not only turned sly when he noticed my interest, but the way he devoured the rest of his fruit became downright pornographic.

A while later, my head feeling lighter in more ways than one, I wandered out into the antechamber. Ademar entered the room from the guards' bedchamber at the same time, a tostada shoved into his mouth as he roughly tied up his hair.

He tore off a mouthful of his breakfast and swallowed. His expression seemed to soften as he glanced over at me, but I was surely only imagining such a thing, as it quickly devolved into a scowl.

"Still here, *bárbaro*?"

"Sure am, you prick," I shot back. "Who else will keep you on your toes?"

Ad scoffed, but my attention was caught by Jiron swatting Luis' hand away from the mostly empty platter seated on the recently replaced table.

"Mathias," Jiron said, nodding at it. Two slightly squished tostadas were bunched up at one end.

"Uh, thanks?" I said. What was it with him and feeding me?

"The gratitude," Luis grumbled, shooting me a dark look. I didn't mind; it was reassuring to know that the guards didn't intend to treat me any differently despite them going all soft and gooey on me last night. "If you don't want them, give them to someone who does." He flung himself down on one of the lounges and turned the glare on Jiron. "How's he going to eat *two*? He's so tiny, one bite would probably double his body weight."

"Exactly," Jiron rumbled, folding his huge arms as he looked down at me with mock severity. "Little one, you are too small to miss meals."

"Besides," Ad commented. "I expect the prince had you work up quite an appetite this morning."

I gave him a look that was decidedly unimpressed. "I know we've talked about how shit you are at your job, Ademar, but even you couldn't fail to notice Camila has been in there for the last half hour."

Like I fucking had.

"I noticed," he said with a smirk, emphasising each syllable, and I pulled a disgusted face at him before scooping up the two tostadas under Luis' greedy gaze.

"Ren said I could visit Starling."

"*Did* he?" drawled an amused voice from behind me.

I shrugged, not bothering to turn around. "Something along those lines. You know I don't really listen to you."

"Fine," the prince said. "I'll be down shortly. Luis?"

Luis groaned, heaved his bulk up off the lounge with another wistful look at the now empty platter, and accompanied me down to the courtyard.

"*Gracias,*" I mumbled quietly to him as we walked. "For…you know." If he hadn't arrived to stop Moreno when he did, I didn't know where I'd be right now. A sheen of blood and brain matter on the cobblestones, I presumed.

The guard shrugged like it had been nothing.

"Seriously," he said, nodding at the tortillas in my hands. "You gonna share those?"

"I am, actually," I confirmed. He reached for one, and I held them out of reach. "Not with you."

I made Luis knock on the surgery door as my hands were full, and Starling greeted us with a tired smile that quickly perked up when I offered her the second tostada. We wandered into the middle of the courtyard to eat our breakfast on our usual bench, Luis hanging back to roam around the edge with his eyes on us.

I took a bite, hoping the food would settle a stomach full of fried dough and alcohol, and leaned back on one hand as I caught Starling up on what had happened last night. My throat tightened as I spoke, and I scowled, not having realised how badly the memories must still be affecting me, even outside in the sunlight.

"And then he – *fuck*," I hissed, bringing a hand to my throat to scratch at whatever unseen force was holding it closed. I couldn't breathe. My limbs felt impossibly heavy.

I choked in desperate spurts of air as I slid from the bench.

Strong arms caught me before my head hit the ground, and Luis' concerned face peered down.

"Mathias?"

"Move," snapped Starling, and then I felt the soothing rush of her Touch on my neck and chest, easing the pressure and allowing me to gulp in grateful lungfuls of oxygen. "Is that better?"

I nodded, briefly closing my eyes before clambering to my feet. Maybe I should rethink my distaste for being guarded all the time, especially if shit like this was going to keep happening.

"Luis, how many did you eat?" I eyed the tostada in my hand with suspicion and more than a little panic. Whoever had sent these assassins clearly wasn't giving up; the food had once again made it within *feet* of Ren. How many of his other guards had been taken out?

"Eat? More than half a dozen," he said, brow furrowing as he made the same connection as me. "Maybe it was just yours?"

That made no sense. Why go to the trouble of contaminating a single serving when there was no way to know who would eat it, or if it would even be touched at all?

"Was it the same poison as that which killed Valentinus?" I asked Star. The healer gave a helpless shrug of her shoulders.

"I was too busy healing you to notice. But it felt like...no, I'm not going to guess."

"Okay," I said. "Take a look at the poison first this time, okay?" And then I took another huge bite from my lethal breakfast.

The two of them had just enough time to deliver their enraged protests before my tongue prickled unpleasantly and the tightness around my neck returned with a terrifying and invisible noose. I dropped to my knees, the food falling from my loose fingers as I choked and gasped on nothing.

Starling ground her teeth, crouching beside me and running her hands along my throat and under my shirt for a moment before the red and green sparks of her magic stole the discomfort away once more.

"Well?" I wheezed, once I'd recovered my breath.

"Well," she repeated, her expression dark, and then suddenly she was hitting every inch of me she could reach. "You're. A. Fucking. Moron!"

"Estrella, darling. I'm the only one who gets to do that."

I lowered my arms from where I had them wrapped protectively around my head, blinking up against the sun to where Ren was silhouetted with Ademar and Jiron at his back. The prince shifted his stance slightly, shading my face so I could see.

"Do I have to ask what the hell happened *every* time I see you, Mathias?"

"He was poisoned," Luis said promptly, and Ren went rigid, his face transforming into something terrifying to watch. His eyes bore into me where I was slumped on the ground.

"Is that true?" The prince's words were like steel, splittingly sharp edged.

Starling rocked back onto her haunches, gave me another filthy look, and then picked up my discarded tostada, making sure to brush the dirt from its surface before biting into it. I yelped and tried to bat her hand away from her mouth, but I was too late.

"No," said the healer.

She continued to chew as I stared at her in horror, making us all wait until she'd swallowed before elaborating. "It's peanut oil. Harmless to anyone without an allergy to it."

Ren cocked his head at me. "You're allergic to peanuts?"

"Yes," I said.

I hadn't recognised the symptoms, but then I hadn't gone into anaphylactic shock for over a decade. The Panarins' kitchen staff knew to be careful, especially as King Oleg's wife suffered from the same affliction.

"Why the fuck didn't you say anything?"

I gave the prince a sardonic smile as I pushed myself to his feet. "Oh yes, the cell guards who were giving me stale bread and mouldy fruit to eat *really* wanted to hear about my preferences for fine cuisine."

Ren scowled. "*After that*, you fuckwit."

I shrugged. "Peanuts don't grow in Riehse Eshan; they're imported. Are they not as much of a delicacy here in Quareh as they are in Mazekhstam?"

Ren inclined his head. "They are."

"Then I hardly expected to be here long enough for it to matter."

My words had a weight to them I hadn't intended, and the silence that fell upon us was once again my fucking fault for speaking without thinking. I gave a laugh that sounded far too forced.

"No harm done, thanks to Star. You know, some people might think she deserves a promotion."

But the prince didn't rise to the bait. Nor, unfortunately, did he agree with me. He was staring off into the distance, frowning, his expression somewhere between smug and concerned. That wasn't a great combination, not where Renato Aratorre was concerned.

"Go back to my chambers, Mathias," he said quietly, and I was about to protest when he added, "Starling, stay with him just in case there's any lingering symptoms. I won't be long." He turned and disappeared back into the palace without another word, leaving Jiron to accompany us.

The guard's hand rested on his sword hilt like he expected to run into the assassin at any moment, and the tension in his posture distracted me from immediately realising that Alta was in the antechamber when we arrived back at Ren's rooms.

A WHISPER AND A BREATH

I bowed. "Lady Moreno," I said warmly. Beside me, Starling gave a shallow curtsey and murmured the same. Alta smiled broadly at me.

I took a seat and patted the lounge to encourage Starling to sit with me. She immediately curled up among the cushions, in stark contrast to Alta's prim, straight-backed position opposite us.

"I was looking for Ren," Alta said to me in Mazekhstani.

"He said he's on his way." I glanced at Starling, who was looking lost. "Can we speak in Quarehian?"

Alta dipped her head politely, but her tone was cool as she spoke. "My father is in a terrible mood this morning. I wished to advise the prince to stay out of his way before something regrettable happens."

Starling snorted, kicking out at my leg.

"You could *advise*," I said, grimacing as the blow landed, "but it may not do much good. Ren is…worked up." I tried to smother the flash of guilt I felt at the thought of what might happen if the prince encountered Moreno today. I liked to think he was less impulsive than me, but the look on his face last night when Luis told him what had happened had been chilling.

Alta eyed me thoughtfully. "I see," she murmured, and shifted slightly in her seat, instinctively pressing a hand to her side when she winced at the movement.

Oh, now *I* wanted to turn Moreno into dust particles, or whatever the fuck Ren had been going on about. *Bastard.*

"Well," Starling said brightly in an obvious effort to clear the mood of the room, "I'm just happy that I didn't have to perform an autopsy on my best friend this morning because he was stupid enough to eat food that could kill him. *Twice.*"

Jiron tensed even further, and I rolled my eyes at the terrible change in topic.

"You love autopsies," I accused with affection. "You'd have been happy either way."

She grinned. "You got me. Although being unable to torment you with bloody organs and slimy entrails would have taken most of the fun out of it. You were just lucky I didn't make you hold *other* parts of Valentinus."

"Fuck, Star, you're really going there?"

Her eyes sparkled with mischief. "You weren't even a little bit curious what a vindictive old man like him had under-"

"*No,*" I said quickly, although I was laughing. And then I realised that Alta's mouth was set in a thin line. The woman was clearly uncomfortable, either with the talk of sexual organs or dead bodies, or both, and I hastened to find a subject of conversation that she'd be interested in. I didn't know her nearly as well as Ren did, but there was one thing that got the Lady Moreno talking, every time.

"I've now eaten enough churros to be confident in saying that they don't hold a candle to ponchiki," I said. "I don't know what you Quarehians were thinking, making dough into lines instead of balls, but your churros are missing the best part: the ricotta cheese."

Alta gave me an indignant look, and I knew I had her. She exploded into an in-depth analysis of the two cultural desserts, ripping apart everything I loved about ponchiki in favour of her overly-sweet, beloved churros, and I watched her with delight. And an occasional controversial comment to keep her fire alight.

But Starling was now looking bored, her chin tucked on her arm as she draped herself over the back of the lounge. Damn it, whatever subject I chose, one of the women felt excluded.

Star caught my expression and pulled a face of her own. "I don't exactly get five course meals prepared by the palace kitchen like you two. I wouldn't know a churlo from a pomchicky if it danced on my ass."

"Then by all means," Alta said graciously. "Continue to speak of the dead."

"The dead." The healer snorted. "Has Lady Moreno ever killed so much as a spider?"

"Why would one need to kill an innocent spider?" Alta asked stiffly, her mouth turned down in disdain.

"Cos they're always crawling over you while you're trying to sleep?" Starling retorted with a raised eyebrow, like it was the most obvious thing ever. "Don't you just..."

She smacked her leg, hard, and the responding slap made the noblewoman flinch.

"No!" Altagracia exclaimed, evidently horrified. "Why would you not catch them in a jar and have them released into the bushes in the courtyard?"

"The courtyard outside my surgery? So *that's* where all the fuckers come from."

Alta's mouth twitched slightly.

I let out a breath. "I'm sorry this is so awkward."

"You don't have to apologise," Starling said.

"Señorita Ortega and I are just different people," Altagracia added cordially, "from different...circumstances."

Starling, who was watching the woman closely, exhaled slightly, and I realised Alta had passed whatever test she'd set up for her in her head.

"We have nothing in common, that's all."

"You do," I said quietly. "You've both been nothing but nice to me. No one else here can say the same."

"You're easy to be nice to, Mathias," said Alta.

"What she said," Starling agreed, jerking her thumb at the other woman, whose eyes widened, although I wasn't sure if it was due to the unexpected acquiescence or the lack of manners from the pointing. "Unlike the rest of the bastard men here."

And *that* got them talking, enthusiastically ranting and bonding over the position of women in Quareh. Alta and I were nodding along to Star's ideas about educational reform when we heard the prince's voice in the corridor, and she fell silent.

"Dios, don't tell me you're starting a fucking revolution in here," Ren drawled as he appeared in the doorway. Starling rolled her eyes. Alta bit her lip. I leaned back against the lounge and folded my arms.

"You don't even know what we were talking about," I said.

Ren smirked at me and held up three fingers.

"One, none of you have greeted me appropriately, which tells me it was nothing good." The two women immediately got to their feet, Alta rather more gracefully, and offered hasty curtsies. Ren snorted and dropped a finger.

"Two, I know the three of you," he said, eyeing us in turn as he tucked a second finger under his thumb, "and I know *exactly* what you're all like."

"And three," Ren finished with a broad grin, glancing over my shoulder. "Jiron heard everything, and he's just informed me of the important parts."

I really needed to teach Starling more Mazekhstani.

"Have you seen my father today?" Alta asked, worrying at the sleeve of her ice-blue dress. "I was just telling Lord Grachyov that you should be avoiding him if you can."

"He should be avoiding *me*," Ren said shortly, "as Diego seems to be doing. Mat, come here."

The prince held out a hand to help me to my feet, and thinking it was just a courtesy, I allowed it. Only he didn't release me afterwards but yanked playfully on my hand to haul me against him and then kissed me.

It was soft, and sweet, and utterly inappropriate.

"*Ren,*" I hissed, pulling away and staring awkwardly at the floor as I tried to avoid catching anyone's eye. The two women may have already known about us, but with Starling voicing her wish for Ren's death not so long ago, and Alta being his fucking fiancée, I wasn't comfortable with engaging in such displays of affection in front of either of them.

Besides, we *still* hadn't talked things through between us.

"Ladies," the prince said in clear dismissal, his voice tinged with authority in that don't-fuck-with-me tone he sometimes took. The one I mostly ignored, but Alta and Star both dropped into another curtsey and hastily left the room, the latter shooting Ren a death glare as she did so.

"You know," Ren mused, head cocked as he regarded her departing form, "there was a time when Starling used to at least *pretend* to be obedient."

"Don't start," I told him. "Did you find the other assassin?"

He shook his head. "No, but I don't need to. I figured it out."

We all waited patiently for the prince to finish looking smug.

"Your Highness?" Luis prompted, giving into the anticipation, and Ren's grin broadened.

"It took a while, I'll admit," Ren said. "Being me, it was hard to get past…well, me."

"Is this love letter to yourself going somewhere?" I asked.

"I wasn't the target of the assassination attempts." The prince held up a finger, dramatically swirled it through the air, and then dropped his hand down to point at me. Luis hissed in a breath, but I just raised an eyebrow.

"Don't you see, Nat?" Ren asked, spreading his arms. "The peanut oil was for *you*. The perfect poison, deadly only to someone with an allergy. Maybe they've been tainting my guards' food for weeks, unable to get to mine, which is what you've been eating. I expect it was the same the day Valentinus died; perhaps he was also allergic to peanuts, or-" he added, brightening as he added more ideas to his absurd theory, "-maybe the poison was in the stroganoff. A foreign dish no one else would touch but the token Mazekhstani guest, or a greedy herald making his way through the entire banquet."

I scoffed. "You're saying someone tried to kill me twice, and I didn't notice?"

Ren shook his head and held up three fingers, chilling me with the implication that the arrow that had ended up in Lago had been intended for me. We'd all been standing so close that no one had considered it anything other than an attempt on the prince's life.

Then Ren pulled a face and added a fourth finger.

"The ambushes at the canyon. The northerners weren't some clever plan to redirect our suspicions; they were a desperate, hasty attempt to take you out, Mat – with an added bonus of the rest of us, I'm sure – before we returned to the protection of the palace."

It had been my horse that reared, saving me from the first arrow. The last attacker alive had given up his chance to flee to come after me, not Ren.

Could it really be true that I'd been the intended target all along?

"Who sent them?" Jiron asked, in that rumbling, deep voice of his.

"Well," Ren said. "At first I wondered if it was one of the people Mathias has pissed off here in *la Cortina*, and I was really not looking forward to having to draft *that* list. Quareh would run out of ink first." He gave me a fond, exasperated look. "But no one would risk their life to end yours over petty racial distaste, Mat, not when they know you're not really at fault for Algejón or the massacre of the Blessed. Killing you wouldn't bring them anything but temporary petty satisfaction…and a beheading."

The prince paused, glancing around to catch the eye of each person in the room. "But you know who would benefit from your death, *mi amor*, and have knowledge about an allergy even I wasn't aware of?"

We all stared at him.

"Mazekhstam."

I tsked and rolled my eyes. The guards were silent.

"I'll just keep going," Ren said to the room, brushing invisible lint from the shoulders of his navy coat. "Feel free to chip in with praise and adoration when you all finally catch up, yeah?"

"Why would my own people want me dead?" I asked in exasperation.

"Because they're not your people," Ren said, his tone as harsh as his words. "You're their political hostage."

"Exactly. So it's in Mazekhstam's interests to keep me alive, or they lose their leverage over Temar."

"Oh, because they've been trying *so hard* to get you back?" Ren asked sarcastically, and I had to concede that one. "Capture and death by a foreign nation would be admittedly difficult to explain to Temar, especially when Mazekhstam have prioritised their territorial expansion into Quarehian lands over retrieving you, but an accident? Nathanael Velichkov drowning after saving a bunch of adorable wolf cubs from an ice-encrusted lake?" He gave a dramatic sigh, fluttering his hand at his forehead like a swooning noble lady. "How tragic and blameless an end."

"I don't—"

"Such a regrettable incident would require a grovelling apology of course, but if the Temarians ever found out that Mazekhstam not only lost one of their own royals to the south but refused to give up Algejón to recover him, that would be far worse, politically speaking. Hence, taking you out before anyone realises you were ever here." Ren let out a breathy laugh. "They obviously don't know that your brother is already aware."

I chewed my lip, remembering the threat delivered to my friends in the north that had ensured I stay silent about my identity.

"And no one would ever recognise it as a lie," he continued, "because for all Quareh knows, it's never laid eyes on Nathanael Velichkov. Mazekhstam holds a sombre funeral – no body of course, or else it's cremated before your family arrives – and arranges for a new Temarian hostage to be shipped to Stavroyarsk."

Ren paused, giving me a significant look.

"And then Mazekhstam laughs at Quareh, produces the real Lord Grachyov from wherever he's been hiding, and says *sorry, looks like you captured a servant with delusions of grandeur, you idiotic southerners*. Quareh is left with nothing more than a corpse, never knowing the true identity of who it held, and the continent's status quo is preserved. Everything goes back to how it was. Including Algejón remaining in northern hands, with not a single concession made to the south."

We all gaped at the prince.

I found my voice first. "That's convoluted as fuck."

"That's your objection to this? *Complexity*?"

I shook my head. "No. You're wrong."

"Your Astrid didn't just leave you here to die, Mat," said Ren, his expression pitying. "She sent men after you to make sure it would happen."

Not Astrid. She wouldn't. She…wouldn't, right?

But it all made a sickening kind of sense.

"No," I said with a disbelieving laugh, but it sounded hollow. I started to pace. "I don't get assassinated. I get ignored, and teased, and occasionally locked in sheds in the middle of winter, but I don't get *assassinated!*"

"Who the fuck locked you in a shed?" Ren growled, stepping closer to me.

"That's not the issue here."

"It's exactly the issue, Mat. Be it assassin or asshole, I'm not letting anyone near you."

My breath fled my lungs with the possessive protectiveness of his words. The prince eyed me intently, his body tense as if trying to stop himself from crossing that final couple of feet between us.

"How will we stop the assassin without knowing who it is?" Jiron asked.

Ren tossed his head, his hair cascading around his shoulders. "By taking away the motivation to kill Mathias, of course."

I sucked in a breath as I followed that statement through to its conclusion. "No. You can't tell Mazekhstam that you know who I am. They'll kill Zovisasha and Lilia!"

"If I didn't, they'd have killed *you*," Ren snarled, and finally gave up on any pretence of self-restraint, eating up the distance between us and cupping my face in his hands. His palms were warm against my skin. "But I doubt Commander Grachyov will follow through on that, regardless. The threat was to keep you quiet, not stop anyone else figuring it out on their own."

"I can't take that chance."

"I know you couldn't," he said. "Which is why I asked your brother to protect your friends." The prince tapped the breast pocket of his coat. "He sent someone to keep an eye on them and get them out of the capital if things turned bad."

Oh. Ren had...he'd used some of his precious bargaining power with Valeri to help two northerners he didn't even know? Just because he knew what it would do to me if they died?

And then the tense of his words sank in.

Didn't. Couldn't.

"You asshole," I snapped, pulling free as he tried to take my hand. I stalked into the bedchamber and shut the doors when Ren followed me in, not wanting the guards to witness what was going to be another of our truly epic arguments. "You've already done it, haven't you? Sent a messenger to Stavroyarsk?"

"I have," Ren confirmed, and then paused. The almost guilty expression on his face told me I wasn't going to like what came next. "But I knew that would take days for the stand down order to trickle down to the assassin, and I couldn't take the risk of something happening to you before then. So I've made sure that everyone here knows too. Now any attempt on your life will reflect badly on Mazekhstam, whom I conveniently pointed out would stand to gain the most from your death."

The words sounded funny to my ears, like I was floating underwater. I'd kept my identity a secret for so long, and then he'd just…just…

I stared at him.

"What part of *stop making fucking decisions for me without talking to me first* did you not understand?" I yelled after a long moment of stunned silence, wanting to hit him, strangle him, kiss him… fuck, maybe all of the above. "You've fucked me over *again*, Ren!"

"I saved your life."

"At the cost of my country! Who knows what your father's now going to try to extort from Temar? You've given him leverage over my family!"

"Leverage he always had, Mathias," Ren said quietly.

"While he didn't know who I was, he had nothing," I hissed.

The prince swallowed. "If you died, *I* would have had nothing."

All my anger seeped out of me at the admission. "What are you-"

"I knew you'd say no, Mat," Ren told the floor, his head bowed. "And I couldn't let you die. Even if you hate me for it, because I'd rather have your hatred than your corpse." At that, he looked up, and I saw his eyes were glassy with tears even as his mouth was set into a stubborn line. "I will give you *everything*, Nathanael, even when you fight me on it. Because there's nothing on this whole fucking continent that I care for more than you."

*

Chapter Thirty-Nine

Ren

Baring your soul to your sometimes-lover, sometimes-enemy and always-pain-in-your-ass, turned out to be surprisingly cathartic. I think I even cried. I'll deny it, of course, but Mat's borrowed shirt definitely had wet patches on it by the time I finally pulled out of his arms, and they weren't the fun kind.

Mathias said something in softly murmured Mazekhstani, his ungloved hand stroking through my hair and down my back. The words, too faint for me to hear properly, were comforting. I always liked hearing him talk in his native tongue.

"Okay," I said, thankful my voice had finally steadied. "Enough of the overly dramatic, maudlin crap. Lay it on me."

He blinked, delicate eyelashes fluttering. "What?"

"Everything you want to yell at me right now. How I was selfish, and arrogant, and all those other delightful adjectives you have for me. How I had *no right*, and *fuck, Ren, what were you thinking?* and *for an impossibly handsome prince, Aratorre, you really do make stupid decisions, don't you?*"

Mathias let out a long breath, and his hand stilled on my back. "For an impossibly handsome prince, Aratorre," he began, and I braced myself. "You're really quite hard to stay mad at."

I faltered. "An interesting tactic. Will the yelling come later, or is it just going to be disappointed, judgmental stares for the next week? Because I'd rather you shout at me, Nat. I *hate* not talking to you. It's like a day without sun, or a meal without dessert, or a night without…"

"Sex?" he finished, raising an eyebrow.

"Sure," I said. Because that was easier than what I'd been going to say.

Without *you*.

"I was angry," Mat murmured. 'But then you…no one has ever put me first like that."

I frowned, twisting around on the bed to look at him. He gave me a hesitant smile, and laced his fingers in mine.

"It *was* a stupid decision," he said. "Because it didn't benefit you or your people at all. Now knowing who I am and that Commander Grachyov never truly intended to negotiate for me means your father will probably allow Moreno to try to take Algejón by force, and we both know that will only end in mass bloodshed. You chose me over a city full of fucking people, Ren, and no one else on the continent has ever done that. Not Grachyov, not even Astrid."

I swallowed. "Mat-"

"It was wrong of you to decide my fate," Mathias growled, but he didn't let go of my hand, his thumb drawing gentle circles on mine in contradiction to his less than tender tone. "And controlling, and downright foolish. But I…I can't fault you for that, as much as I know I should. Because it's so *you*, and I can't expect that to change."

His mouth curved into a rueful smile. "And fuck, Ren, I don't want to die either. I don't know if your ridiculous assassin theory is true or not, but if it could take me away from you, then I'll believe it. I'm…"

He leaned in and kissed me. His lips were soft, searching and tentative.

He tried to pull back after a moment, but I didn't allow it, curling my hands around his shoulders to hold him in place until I'd had my fill of him, that heavenly, bittersweet taste of Nathanael Velichkov on my tongue.

"What I'm *trying* to say, you asshole," he finally gasped out, shoving me back with a fond smile on his face, "is that I care for you too. I know we weren't supposed to let it get that far, but damn you, you're in my head and you won't leave."

"I won't," I agreed. "I can be annoyingly persistent that way."

"Don't I know it."

"Nathanael, your vexing ass is in my head too. Not a bad image to have stuck there, all things considered," – he rolled his eyes – "but you were about to say something really sweet about me? Continue."

Mat bit his lip. "You fucked up that day you let them take my finger, but I fucked up last night. That doesn't make either thing okay, but maybe it makes it easier to deal with them, because we're still learning about each other. Neither of us are perfect."

"But-"

"*No,* Ren. You're not."

I sighed deeply and clutched at my heart. "You wound me."

He offered me a wry grin. "To the bone, I'm sure."

I manoeuvred us on the bed so we were sitting cross-legged, facing each other, our hands clasped and our foreheads touching. "I don't want perfect," I said seriously, seeking out the truth in his eyes and hoping he could see it in mine. "I want *you.* I want my acerbic, irritable, adorable northerner, who gets into far too many fights and puts his ass on the line for strangers simply because he believes it's the right thing to do."

Mathias' mouth opened, surprised, and then closed again.

"I've rendered him speechless," I crowed to the empty room. "Hark this moment, for I doubt it will pass by again."

"Shut up."

"…and there it goes."

"Well," Mat said, scowling at my ear when he seemed unable to meet my eyes. "I want you too, you idiot. You may be arrogant and melodramatic and flamboyant-"

"Don't forget my hair," I added, worried that he may indeed, forget my hair. "It's pretty perfect all by itself."

"It's okay, I suppose," he teased, releasing one of my hands to tug on it. "But I'll dye it green if you don't stop interrupting."

I stopped. *Immediately.*

"I think we should try again," said Mathias, flooding my soul with pure happiness with those six words. "Us, I mean. What we had. And…by the Blessed, Ren, I don't think we're ever going to *not* argue."

"It doesn't seem like us," I agreed.

His eyes lit up. "Was that an interruption?"

"More like a confirmation," I said hastily, waving my free hand. Mathias caught it and kissed each of my knuckles, brushing his lips over the suddenly sensitive skin, and I marvelled at *this,* at having him touch me so casually like it meant nothing.

But it meant *everything*. I'd never had this before, not this gentle…affection. I'd fucked, and kissed, and given aftercare when it was required after some of my more intense play sessions.

But I'd never just *held* someone like I found myself doing with Mat, touching his hand, his leg, the dimples in his back, because it felt right and I couldn't bear to have even air separate us.

"Whenever I try to remember what my life was like before you, Ren," he murmured now, his mouth twisting, "it feels…empty. Shallow."

"Absolutely fucking boring?" I suggested, and he gave me a dry look.

"Infinitely less exasperating."

"That's what I said."

Mat knocked his forehead gently against mine.

"So, what do you say?" he asked, the soft words barely a whisper. I could have answered with a single word – *yes, fucking yes!*…admittedly, that was three, but prince's prerogative and all – yet, it didn't really feel like *me*.

Winding him up to the point where he tried to take a swing at me? That was more my style.

I inspected my fingernails. "Say to what?"

"What I just…you know… "

I cocked my head. "Your Quarehian seems to be getting worse, Mat. You now appear incapable of finishing your sentences."

"*Svoloch!*"

"See, *that's* Mazekhstani," I pointed out. "You can tell because it's all growly and hissy, not the smooth, dulcet notes of the south."

"I take it back. Life without you was bliss, Your Highness," Mat said, a dangerous glimmer in his eye that told me he was up to something. I just didn't know *what.*

I winked at him. "Well, don't let me ever be accused of leaving someone feeling *empty*."

"Renato. You're quickly losing your privileges."

"I'm a fucking prince of Quareh, Nat. I *am* privilege. If I want to take my sweet time in answering your question, what are you going to do to stop me? Beg me again? Bat those pretty little eyelashes of yours?" I gave him a heated look, letting what I was imagining for him show on my face. "Kneel for me?"

He let out a ragged breath. "Very well. No more joining me in the bath."

"I'll join you wherever I like." When he merely raised an eyebrow, I scoffed, and then paused. "Wait, you're actually-"

"And…that's morning cuddles gone."

I hissed out a breath. "You're fucking ruthless."

Mathias opened his mouth, but I slammed my hand against it before he could say another word.

"Okay!" I said hastily. "Yes*, mi sol.* Yes, I want us. I want to hold you again, and kiss you until you're breathless, and I *really* want bath time and cuddles back on the table."

I withdrew my hand cautiously.

"*Thank you,"* Mat said smugly. "Was that so hard?"

Oh, the fucker.

"I have one more question," he added because he was so damn irritating like that, and I groaned, throwing myself backwards. My head hit the pillow and I let my arms lie where they fell, splayed out at my side. Maybe if I stayed still enough, he might think me dead and leave me alone.

But my northerner just laughed and crawled up me, gifting generous kisses to all the interesting parts of my body. As I glanced down at him and saw how his face was pressed into my crotch, I regretted that I hadn't undressed before dramatically flinging myself to my death.

"Mmm," I groaned, as my cock came alive at him nosing at it. Not making any sounds seemed to be a fatal flaw in my corpse plan: I wasn't as loud as Mathias – no one was capable of making that much fucking noise, and I couldn't *wait* to hear what he was like when I was finally inside him – but I wasn't exactly capable of being silent, either.

"I'm not dead," I told him.

"Didn't think you were," Mat murmured back, his words muffled from where he spoke them into my trousers. "I wouldn't be that lucky."

"But I am gravely injured, such that parts of me – my ears, for example, which I expect are fairly vital to your incessant need to ask *questions* – are completely out of commission."

"Any other parts of you suddenly not working?" he asked, and then laughed softly. "Because everything seems fine down here."

He began working his way further up my body, unbuttoning my coat so he could push up my shirt and lick at my stomach, before swirling his warm tongue higher to gift attention to each nipple. I shivered under his touch.

"All good so far, *moy knyaz*," Mat murmured. "Why do you not want me to ask if you-"

I made a noise of warning. "Because I expect your question is riddled with serious nonsense, like *how can we possibly have a future together?* or *what do we do about Mazekhstam?* or *why are you always stealing the fucking blankets, Ren?*"

Mathias scoffed, like he hadn't asked that last one at least a dozen times before, and in *exactly* the same whiny voice I'd just used.

He put a finger to my lips as if to silence me, and I promptly licked it.

"Fine," I said. "Ask your damn question."

I licked his finger again because I could, and because it tasted like him. I revelled in the way it made his eyes widen and shift his hips above mine.

"Never mind," Mat murmured with a devilish look on his face as he gazed down at me, and I hissed out an indignant splutter.

"No, you brat, after all that you don't get to-"

We both stiffened as we heard raised voices; angry, almost shouts, and then a feminine shriek of outrage. Something heavy thumped into the wall between my bedchamber and the antechamber.

Mat's eyes crinkled in concern, and we frowned at each other in an unspoken question. He dropped a hand to push himself off me, but the doors burst open before he could, making us both flinch and pull closer to each other.

With his sword drawn, the Comandante strode into the room, his eyes raking into each corner.

"What the fuck?" I snapped as he marched to the bathing room door and kicked it open, peering inside before turning back to us. His mouth formed its customary sneer at the sight of Mat on top of me.

I wondered what he was going to say now that he realised Mathias had been lying about who he was this whole time, for surely the news had reached his ears by now. But his words weren't anything like I'd expected.

"Where is she?" the Comandante demanded.

I ignored him like I ignore all rude and armed men who come stomping into my room uninvited, lifting Mat off me and setting his ass on the bed before getting to my feet.

"Jiron?" I called out.

"Your Highness!"

"How dare you?" Mathias hissed at Moreno in an echo of my own thoughts as I strode towards the doors, which were still swinging on their hinges from the force of the man's entrance.

What I saw in the antechamber beyond made me absolutely livid. Camila, a smashed plate at her feet, had pressed herself flat against the back wall, her eyes wide and terrified as she stared at the rest of the men crowding the room. One of Moreno's palace guards had his sword to Ademar's neck, and the murderous look on Ad's face said he was about two seconds from ramming it down his opponent's gullet. Jiron, bleeding from his forehead, was pinned against the wall by four other guards who still seemed to be having trouble holding him in place. And Luis, a biscuit stuffed half in his mouth, was in a standoff with another two of the Comandante's men, his huge fists raised to defend against their swords in a move that was so stupid I was surprised Mathias hadn't yet tried it.

Cowardly traitorous bastards. To get the drop on my men like that, they must have entered the room under the guise of peace, and then drawn their weapons when it was too late to stop them. I couldn't help but notice that the palace guards more than twice outnumbered my own.

A WHISPER AND A BREATH

Ademar stepped neatly backwards, flicking up a knife I hadn't even seen him draw to swat the sword away from his throat. One of Luis' attackers rounded on him, and the two guards backed my man up towards Camila, pressing too close to allow him to free his own sword. Ademar gave them a patronising sneer and adjusted his grip on the knife.

"*Stand the fuck down!*" I ordered, practically spitting the words as hot fury raced through me. "Or I'll have you all hanged for treason, you fuckers."

The palace guards glanced at each other and then backed off, allowing Jiron to turn around, Ademar to breathe, and Luis to take a bite of his biscuit. I rounded on Moreno.

"You better have a damn good explanation for this," I warned in a low snarl, "although I'm hoping you don't so I can finally fit your neck for a noose."

He didn't look remotely bothered, which meant he was confident in whatever Blessed excuse he had for raiding my rooms like this.

"Security of the realm," he said imperiously, and Mat scoffed. "We're looking for someone who has infiltrated your ranks through guile and deceit, my prince, a gender traitor who deserves-"

"Camila!" I exclaimed loudly, crossing the room and pulling her into my arms.

Because *fuck*, there was only one person whom Moreno could be talking about. I didn't know how he'd found out about Elías, but I could only thank Dios that the guard wasn't here.

"*Mi querida*," I murmured, wrapping my arms around Camila and feeling the girl tense under my grip. "Are you alright? You're not harmed?"

"The servant was never in any danger," Moreno said irritably.

I cupped my fingers under Camila's chin and turned her face from side to side, as if inspecting her for injuries. But I needed to get closer, and I could only hope Mat would understand that I couldn't ask him about this one first.

"Hmm," I said, dropping my voice into a seductive purr. "Still as beautiful as ever, I see."

Camila raised an eyebrow. Sure, we'd had one memorable night together a while back, but then I'd realised that toying with her too much would lose me an excellent servant, and she'd admitted that her tastes ran in the other direction, and we hadn't played together since.

Now, I leaned in and kissed her, pressing my body to hers to hide us as I moved my mouth from her lips to her cheek, and then her ear.

"Oh, that's just fucking great," I heard Mathias complain loudly, and there was a dull thud like he'd smacked his hand against the door. Camila flinched, but I held her tight.

"Find Elías at the training ring," I whispered to her, the tension that whipped through her body the only indication she'd heard me beneath my northerner's indignant yelling. "Tell him to *run.*"

I released my servant and stepped back, realising too late that it would look far too suspicious for her to leave so abruptly and without permission. I opened my mouth to dismiss her, hoping Moreno wouldn't read too much into it, when Mat appeared at my side.

"Are you utterly incapable of thinking with your head instead of your cock?" he accused me with a hard jab to the chest, his expression irate. "Your men are literally being held at swordpoint, and here you are, two seconds from screwing your servant into the wall! *You* can fuck off now," Mathias snapped at Camila, and she dropped into a hasty curtsey before scurrying from the room.

"You don't need to be jealous, *mi amor,*" I said dismissively. "There's plenty of me to go around."

"I'm not *jealous,*" he hissed back. "I just don't know why we must be subjected to watching you jump every warm body you see. Or is even a pulse optional for His Royal Highness?"

I gave a cold laugh. "Just because you put out doesn't mean I owe you anything, Temarian. Get out of my face."

"I'll *break* your face, you arrogant fuckwit," Mat snapped, and we both settled into a solid round of what we did best, arguing so loudly and vehemently that it took the Comandante several minutes to get his voice heard through the mix of Quarehian and Mazekhstani insults we were flinging at each other.

"Your Highness," Moreno growled, his hand coming down hard on my wildcat's shoulder. "Do you need me to teach him to respect you?"

"I'll take care of it," I said lazily, and gave them both a suggestive wink that told them in no uncertain terms how I planned to achieve that. "You were...saying something earlier? An apology, perhaps, for barging into my private quarters like this?"

The Comandante bared his teeth in the terrifying approximation of a smile. "I'm here to protect my prince from a nefarious threat within," he said. "Tell me where Elías is."

"El?" I asked, screwing up my nose in confusion even as my heart raced. Had we bought him enough time? "Pulling a shift at the privies. Why?"

At a nod from their master, Moreno's men hastened from the room. My own guards bristled.

"It has recently come to my attention that your so-called guard is nothing more than a woman in disguise."

I saw Ademar and Luis tense from the corner of my eye, not nearly as composed as Mat's convincing look of surprise. Jiron wore his straight-backed professionalism like a mask, as usual.

"I'm unequivocally sure that's not true," I said. "Elías has been with me for years, and has served me loyally for that entire time. There's nothing *so-called* about him."

"I won't argue the point, Your Highness. I know there's no possibility in which you were not aware of this, and I find that exceptionally disappointing."

I gave him a bland look. "I really have no idea what you're talking about."

"We'll see what she says when I arrest her, won't we?"

"Speaking of guards who need arresting," I said testily. "I want Diego brought to me."

The Comandante clicked his tongue. "You may be waiting a while. I sent him on an assignment to south Quareh late last night."

I sucked in an angry breath.

"A dangerous one, of course, my prince," he continued. "I'd assumed you wanted him punished after what he nearly did to your boy." His eyes flickered to Mathias, and his expression turned sly. "Lucky I was there, really."

We were both silent. Because he *had* saved Mat from being raped, but he'd also tried to throw him out of a fucking window. It was difficult to be grateful to him, and impossible not to be.

"Nathanael Velichkov," Moreno said to him slowly, as if tasting the name on his tongue. I wanted to cut it off. Hearing the words spoken so freely after them being a secret for so long; *our secret,* mine and Mat's, felt unbearably wrong. "To think, we had royalty in our hands all this time."

Then he smirked at me. "And in our beds, apparently. What I'd give to see Queen Zora's face when she finds out what you've been doing to her son. The vengeance of a Commander is one thing, but Temar's ruler might just demand your head, my prince."

Mat visibly stiffened.

The Comandante gave him a cruel smile. "Well, Temar can go fuck itself, boy. The south answers to no one."

He squared his shoulders as one of his men returned and shook his head.

"Where the fuck is she?" Moreno rounded on me, his humour abruptly disappearing, and I shrugged.

"I find it *exceptionally disappointing* that you can't apprehend one person," I said. "I do hope El doesn't evade your attempts to catch him. That would prove to be rather embarrassing for you, wouldn't it?"

The Comandante's glare came to rest on Ademar. "I'll ensure your sister is dragged before the king to face the price of her deception," he threatened in a low voice. "And when I'm proved right, I'll have you arrested as well, on the charges of conspiracy to break Quareh's gender laws and endangering a royal."

"I don't have a sister." Ad's voice was cold, but his knuckles were white around the hilt of his knife.

"You won't for long, certainly."

With that, Moreno marched from the room, and it felt like everyone left behind let out a collective breath.

"Fuck!" swore Luis, banging his fist against the doorframe. "How in Dios' name did he find out?"

Jiron caught my eye, and I shook my head at his silent question. It hadn't been Mat.

But Ademar wasn't as subtle in his accusations. "You," he snarled, catching Mathias by the collar. "How could you do that to El?"

The northerner smacked at his hand. "It wasn't me, you asshole. Why would I tell Moreno shit?"

"No?" Ad shook him, as if he might rattle a confession loose. "Elías' secret was kept hidden for years, and then less than two weeks after *you* find out, suddenly that bastard knows! What did you really talk about last night?"

Mat gaped at him. "I…"

Luis came to his rescue, laying a hand on the other guard's arm. "Leave him alone, Ad. The Comandante tried to kill him, remember?"

"Or so they made it look. What did he offer you to give up my brother, *bárbaro*?"

"This is ridiculous," Mat hissed.

"Ademar," I said loudly. "What did I tell you about not putting your hands on Nat? If he says it wasn't him, it wasn't him."

The guard let go, but clearly reluctantly, shooting daggers at the northerner. They were returned with interest.

"This isn't helping El," I said, feeling sick. "We can only hope Camila warned him in time for him to get away, but he can't ever return to the palace. He'll be on the run for the rest of his life."

We fell silent at the words, at their finality, and I cursed Moreno and my father in every language I knew.

"You did well to keep the Comandante distracted, Your Highnesses," Jiron murmured, and Luis shot him a surprised look, perhaps not having realised our bickering had been an act. Mat's lips curled into a half smile at the address, but Ademar's scowl didn't ease in the slightest.

Fuck. It was all unravelling. Mat's secret, any hope we had for Algejón or discovering the truth about Vitorona…and now we'd lost El. I was useless, and exhausted, and I'd never felt less worthy of my title. What was the point of being a fucking *prince* if I was so helpless to stop everything coming apart around me?

"I've got you," someone murmured into my ear, and I didn't have to look up to know it was *him*. The light in the interminable darkness, the only good thing about this whole fucking mess, because Mathias was here, holding me, and Dios, this was the second time today I was going to break down on him, wasn't it? He'd think me useless too when he realised, when he saw how truly incapable I was of holding it together. Some royal I was. I couldn't even *breathe*.

*

Chapter Forty

Mat

It was late afternoon when the prince finally roused from sleep, his hair tousled and his face drawn into pained lines. His eyes were dark and hollow.

"Hey," I said softly from where I was seated next to him on the bed, and Ren flinched, twisting over onto his side to stare at me.

"I didn't know you were still here," he whispered, his voice little more than a harsh rasp. I leaned over to pass him the glass of water from the bedside table.

"I haven't left. Drink."

"So bossy," he complained, but a glimmer of his usual spark crossed his face and he downed the whole glass before handing it back to me. "Don't go stealing my role."

Then he surprised me by wriggling closer and laying his head on my lap. I leant back against the headboard, running my hand through his hair and not saying a word, letting the silence bolster his courage or give him an out, whichever he preferred.

"You shouldn't have had to see me like that," Ren said quietly after a long moment, so faint I could barely hear him.

"Like what?"

"Losing control," he mumbled, his fingers tracing the stitching of a darned-over hole in the right knee of my trousers. "Helpless."

"Renato Aratorre," I said firmly, "that is the last of my 'delightful adjectives' I'd ever use to describe you."

"I can't...that's the second fucking panic attack I've had in a fortnight," he snarled, and I felt him tense. I moved my hands to his shoulders and pressed my thumbs against the base of his neck like Lilia had taught me, rewarded by a soft groan. And then he immediately stiffened again.

"Relax," I murmured. "I'm not going to hurt you. Unlike a certain prince we could both name."

That earned me a half-hearted chuckle, and he turned his head to press a chaste kiss to my leg.

"Thank you for...you know," Ren said awkwardly. "You're even better than Jiron at talking me through to the other side."

"You did the work yourself." I massaged deeper, and this time I felt his body properly relax under my hands. "And don't think like that. You have a lot going on."

"So do you. More. And yet I don't see *you* breaking down and hyperventilating."

Oh, *this* one. He could be so fucking obtuse at times.

"You are kidding, right?" I said in disbelief. "I went *psychotic* when I was down in the cells. I'm pretty sure manic delirium is worse than a bare half minute of breathlessness. And if we're talking about losing control, are you forgetting how much I screamed when Moreno mutilated my hand? I was fucking *crying*, Ren." I smacked his arm. "So stop feeling sorry for yourself and own it. We all have our highs and lows, and those pieces of ourselves we'd rather weren't there, but are. Don't let your anxiety take away from everything you've achieved despite it. Perhaps even because of it."

Ren shifted in my lap until he was looking up at me, brown eyes wide and adoring.

"You really are a walking contradiction, Mat," he said, and I was relieved to find his voice was already clearer, stronger. "You spout such Blessed wisdom sometimes, and then you also come out with shit like *'I'm straight.'*"

I scowled, playing with a lock of his hair. "That was a long time ago," I said haughtily. "Before I-"

"Realised how good it feels to have my fingers shoved up your ass?"

That cheeky grin was infectious. Heart-warming. *Soul-infusing.*

Infuriating as hell.

"Careful, prince," I warned. "Or you'll find that's another privilege that can be revoked."

"Pfft. You love that too much to give it up."

I raised an eyebrow at the sheer arrogance. "Says who?"

He pulled me close, fisting a hand in my hair as he bent me double to bring my head down to meet his. Because raising his own head would be too much fucking work, apparently.

"Those delicious noises you make when I do it," Ren murmured against my mouth. "The way you wriggle around on my fingers, fucking yourself on them, panting and squirming and crying out my name."

His words shot straight to my cock, and my face went hot. "I don't-"

"Oh, you *do*," he assured me, and when I made to straighten, he kept me in place with surprising strength considering his position in my lap. "I adore it, Nat. I've never been with anyone as expressive as you in bed. It's like you're rewarding me for every single little thing I do to you; every twist of my hand, the smallest curl of my finger." He pulled me down further, ignoring my grunt of discomfort as my spine stretched painfully, and then nipped at my ear. "I love being inside you."

"Fucking hell," I whispered, lost to that seductive tone, his hands on me, and-

I cleared my throat, shaking myself free of the temptation to surrender to him, to let us both escape our heads a while. "We can't," I said reluctantly. "We don't have time."

Ren frowned, scrambling up to seat himself next to me. "Time?"

"Yeah. I'd prefer not to make the day worse, but I have some bad news."

"Fuck! They caught Elías?"

"No," I assured him, watching his shoulders sag in relief. "There's still no sign of El. Seems he got away cleanly, thanks to you and Camila."

Ren leaned forward and abruptly licked my face from chin to forehead. I spluttered and pushed him off me.

"Hey, don't sell yourself short," he said, as I wiped my face clean on his pillow. "You and your accusations of me being a fucking necrophiliac helped distract Moreno. By the Blessed Five, how do you even come up with that shit?"

I shrugged. "It felt suitably dramatic for the moment. Maybe you're rubbing

off on me."

His eyes gleamed with filthy promise, and he lunged for me.

"Not an invitation!" I yelped, sliding off the bed before he could take my ill-advised words to their inevitable conclusion. The prince followed me, and I backed up as he prowled closer. "I saw something earlier."

My tone must have clued him in that I was being serious, as Ren's expression sobered and he gave me a curt nod to warn me against trying to deliver the news softly.

"Your father's on his way to the palace again."

Ren groaned. "Can't the bastard just stay in his own? How long do I have?"

"He's arriving today," I told him. "At dusk."

Ren digested that for a moment, his mouth tightening into that harsh line I only ever saw when the king was around. He ran a hand over his face and glanced at the window, where the sky was just beginning to darken.

"Fuck, Mat, it's nearly dusk now! You let me sleep well past siesta, you prick. We have to get everyone ready for his arrival!"

I lay a hand on his arm. "Clementina has taken care of it. She's gotten word to everyone who needs to be there."

Which was everyone. Fucking kings.

"I even sent Jiron to ask Alta to handle the catering to keep them happy, seeing as it helped last time," I added.

"Alta?" The prince's face was surprised.

"Can you think of anyone more perfect?" I grinned, pleased with myself. "And I got your...um, piano teacher to arrange some live music. If you merge with the crowd rather than announcing your presence when you arrive, they should be distracted enough to believe you've been there the whole time. You just need to get your ass dressed, *ahora*. I'll send for Camila."

He eyed me suspiciously, and more than a little fondly. "You're terribly crafty."

"I've got nothing on you," I said carelessly, and then sighed. "Damn it."

Ren let out a shuddering breath. "Mathias, your double entendres *alone* are making me hard. Tell me we can play together soon."

"Funny," I mused, leaning in to brush a kiss against his lips. "That's what I was going to ask you earlier, but you didn't want to hear it. Something about not having ears."

Ren's howl of protest followed me to the door.

—

"Lord Grachyov! I mean…Prince Velichkov?"

I turned at the corrected address, finding Alta at the bottom of the stairs Luis and I had just climbed on our way back to Ren's rooms. She was worrying at a curl of hair, just like Astrid did when she was stressed.

"My lady?"

"I…may we speak?" she asked hesitantly, ascending the steps with an effortless feminine grace that was so different to Starling, who stomped everywhere as if the tiled floors of *la Cortina* had somehow personally offended her. When I inclined my head, Altagracia gestured to a side door, and I followed her through the doorway to find it was a music room of some kind. It was only lit by a single brazier now, but I expected that in the daytime it would be a light and airy room, the floor to ceiling windows lending themselves to spectacular views across the huge lake that bordered the back of the palace.

I diverted my eyes from the grand piano and fixed them on Alta instead.

"Please wait outside," she was saying to Luis, her words slightly muffled by her hand hovering hesitatingly over her mouth, as if shocked to be making such a request. And maybe two decades ago an unmarried man and woman alone together might have caused a scandal, but not in current times. And certainly not in Quareh, where extramarital encounters were not only permitted, but encouraged. Quarehians were free with their sexuality and promiscuity in a way that I was still trying to wrap my head around, and yet they remained remarkably and obnoxiously outdated in their views on women's rights. It felt like a paradox, and yet the north was almost the exact opposite in its views. How could the two halves of Riehse Eshan have evolved such distinct and contrary cultures?

Bigotry, isolationism, and sheer pigheadedness, obviously. It was becoming more and more clear the longer I lived on the other side of the divide that neither the north or the south *wanted* to change, nor sought the friendship of the other. While Temar and Mazekhstam had reached a reluctant truce, bought by bloodshed and the ransom of children, Quareh was seen – and saw itself – as set apart from the other countries on the continent. A ridiculous, pointless rivalry over land, belief, and the lust for dominance.

Luis frowned at the Lady Moreno, but he obediently closed the doors on us, remaining outside.

"About that kiss," I began, because damn it, Ren doing that in front of her was still playing on my mind. "I didn't know he was going to-"

Altagracia waved a gracious hand. "I am happy for you. It seems your amorous entanglement has been restored, then?"

I blinked at her, the complex Quarehian words not landing properly in my head. "My what?"

"You and Ren. Your…*relations*. Amativeness, and what it leads to."

By the Blessed Five, was she really asking me if I was having sex with her fiancé again?

I didn't answer, because that was as awkward as fuck, but it seemed she took my response from the heat spreading across my face, because Alta had a little secretive smile on her face by the time I stopped choking and had composed myself enough to look back at her.

"I am glad you took my advice, my lord. Your Highness."

Another thing I didn't respond to, because although she was being impossibly accepting and nauseatingly nice about the whole thing, her words sent an irrational flare of irritation through me. Alta's *advice* had been nothing more than to magically forgive the bastard and throw myself at him, and look how well *that* had gone. I had no idea why I'd even listened; it had just made things worse.

Although, maybe they'd had to get worse in order to get better. To make me realise that it wasn't only Ren who was capable of fuck-ups, and holding onto my fury with him was just making us both miserable.

Because it wasn't an exaggeration that I found myself missing him every second he wasn't at my side. And it was even worse now, knowing he was on his way to his father's chambers while Luis returned me to the prince's, that sick certainty that Ren wouldn't escape the whip for a second consecutive royal visit. Not when Iván's gaze had sought mine before he'd even fully descended his carriage steps half an hour ago; it was unclear whether he'd encountered the messenger on the road, or his own seers had given him advance notice of what the whole of *la Cortina* now knew about my identity, but the way the king's eyes had then narrowed on his son next to me had been far less ambiguous.

I swallowed down bile. "Please forgive me, my lady. I wish to retire for the night."

I needed to be there when Ren got back to his rooms. Take care of him, help him see that he didn't deserve a single second of his father's abuse. Smother him in blankets like he'd tried to do to me. I'd even let him win at pitarra, if that would make his cheating little soul happy.

"How is Elías?"

Once again, Lady Moreno surprised me.

"He's…fine, we believe," I said, taken off guard by the unexpected question. "We know the Comandante hasn't yet caught him, and El will only have more advantages the further away he can get from the palace. He had his bow and sword with him, but likely little money, so Ren is trying to work out how to get some to him. Did you know him well?"

"Oh, no," she said hastily, but there was tension in her posture, an even greater stiffness than usual that told me she wasn't…lying, exactly, but there was certainly some hidden truth she wasn't disclosing.

"Then why would you care?" I asked, unconcerned about how rude I knew I must sound. Ren would be suffering tonight, at the hands of his own family no less, and I was not in the mood to dance around words.

"He's…been with Ren for a while," Alta said in a soft voice. "The prince cares for him."

There. That flash of guilt that crossed her face.

"Your Highness. We are not equal in rank after all, it seems." She sank into a curtsey and turned to leave.

"It was you." My voice echoed harshly around the beautiful room. Alta flinched. "You told Moreno about El."

She didn't turn around, silhouetted against the flickering flames of the brazier. Carefully sculpted hair, a delicate neck, an elegant dress that was nearly half her height in width where it met the floor. I watched her shoulders cave in, shaking silently.

I didn't care. Why shouldn't Alta deserve to feel bad, when Elías was on the run for his fucking life? Not to mention what would happen to Ademar and Ren if El was caught and his alleged crimes were proved. What would that even entail? Being stripped naked in front of the king and his court? As if his body meant *anything* to his ability to guard the prince?

"How could you, Alta? Don't you understand that Elías is *never* going to be able to come back here? He'll have to spend his whole life in hiding, avoiding the Comandante's men and unable to live any type of normal life! You knew that, and you still *gave him up?*"

I was yelling now, something else I didn't care about. Let the whole damn palace hear.

Altagracia hissed out a breath and reached for the door handle. But there was no way in hell she was leaving like that, not without a fucking *explanation*. I caught her arm.

The way she recoiled at my touch made me release it just as quickly.

Fuck.

"I didn't want to," she whispered, finally turning to face me. Her eyes were wide and wet, but she'd stopped the tears from running, as the rouge on her cheeks remained unstreaked. She clasped her chest, over her heart. "He didn't…he was in such a horrible mood, and I don't know what had happened last night but he just kept talking about it and how he hadn't…I'm so sorry, I can't-"

I lunged forward just as she collapsed, catching her in my arms. She was warm and soft, with delicate limbs and a beautiful face. A perfect noble lady. But Altagracia Moreno was so much more than that, despite Quareh insisting on shoving her into the neat little box it wished to categorise her with. Alta was passionate. Loving. Clever. Ren's best friend, a quiet advocate for women's rights, a saviour of spiders.

A WHISPER AND A BREATH

And the Comandante's frequent victim.

"Moreno made you tell him," I murmured, remembering how she'd been holding her side this morning when she visited Ren's chambers, her insistence on warning the prince to stay out of her father's way today because of his mood. One I'd put him in last night by giving him shit all on Ren, or maybe Luis by stopping the man from killing me.

Alta nodded frantically, trying to push herself out of my grasp to stand upright again. I didn't fight it, letting her reclaim her dignity.

"He was *furious*, Mathias. Nathanael, I mean."

I gave her a small smile. "Either is fine."

"Ren said you were good at sniffing out secrets," she said, biting her lip. "But I never thought to question if you had one of your own. I'm normally quite observant, which is how I figured out Elías, but you are…quite the actor."

"An unfortunate necessity of my life. Altagracia, tell me what happened."

"He wouldn't stop," she whispered, staring past me. I knew if I turned my head to look, there would be nothing there. "He just kept kicking me, over and over…he said I just had to give him something. Something on Ren. I didn't know what to do."

My heart broke for this poor woman. Ren had hidden his abuse from her, but it seemed she hadn't been entirely forthcoming with him about the extent of her own. Ren had implied that Moreno occasionally hurt her when he thought her too outspoken, but fuck, for him to…

"You have to understand," Alta said hollowly. "I couldn't tell my father about *you*. About what Ren really feels for you, how far he'd go to protect you. That would be… Elías was all I had."

I swallowed, feeling guilty at that. Maybe it was my fault El was out there, all alone, because despite everything, Alta had protected us.

"Come by the prince's rooms later," I told her. Ren would hate having visitors when his back was still in agony, but this couldn't wait. "We'll tell him together."

"No!" She clutched at my arm, teeth almost bared in a wildness I had never seen in her. "You can't tell him! I don't want him to look at me like he's…like he's disappointed."

"He won't."

"He will. He's always so strong, and I'm just…"

I resisted the urge to shake her. It was exactly the same bullshit Ren himself had been spouting earlier this afternoon. So concerned about fucking *appearances,* even to those closest to them, who they had to know didn't give a damn.

"Stop it," I said, letting a touch of ice seep into my tone. "You were in a shitty situation, and you did what we all would have done."

"You wouldn't have," she said quietly, and I didn't know how to respond to that.

"There's no reason to tell him," Altagracia added after a moment, raising her chin and looking more like the force of nature she'd been this afternoon when we'd arrived down in the courtyard to find a half a fucking banquet had been laid out for the palace denizens waiting for the king's arrival. I'd led us to Alta's side and raved over her organisational skills until she'd blushed. Ren had told me to stop looking so smug.

Now, Lady Moreno wasn't blushing. In fact, she looked paler than I'd ever seen her. "Telling the prince doesn't change anything," she insisted. "It won't help Elías. It won't help Ren. All it will do is make him look at me differently."

Like Ademar was looking at me. He'd been cold towards me all afternoon; not that exasperated, irritated treatment he normally doled out to me, but actual dislike. It wasn't hard to guess that he still blamed me for outing El. Here was my chance to prove him wrong by pointing the finger at the person who was actually responsible.

Except Ren was right about me, wasn't he? I was a soft-hearted *idiot.*

"Fine," I said. "I won't say anything. But I still think you should."

Her mouth snapped into a line that told me she wouldn't be following that suggestion anytime soon.

"Your Highness," Alta said softly, and then slipped from the room.

I took a moment to compose myself and allow her to leave the corridor by the time I entered it, but one look at Luis' stony face told me he'd heard my yelling. *Blin,* we should have been speaking in Mazekhstani.

"Ademar deserves to know," he said shortly.

I shook my head. "No. We can't do that."

"It's his brother-"

"And telling him won't bring El back," I said, hating that I was parroting Alta. "What if Ad gets angry enough to do something to Altagracia? That would *kill* Ren."

Luis huffed out an indignant sigh, but his expression told me I had him. He was a man used to following orders, and in the absence of his prince commanding him otherwise, he'd follow my lead.

"Prince Velichkov?"

How did *Ren* stand it every day? If I ever made king by some random chance of luck – hell, maybe I'd declare sovereignty over a tiny island somewhere, because I was certainly sick of the rest of Riehse Eshan – I'd ban all fucking titles. They could use whichever of my names they liked, but there wouldn't be a single *prince* or *highness* or *sire* in earshot. Ren would hate it.

"What?" I snapped.

The guard that came hurrying up to us was younger than me, smooth-shaven and sweaty. He eyed me nervously. "Um, I've been sent to collect you?"

"Oh, have you now? You can tell His Highness that after all these weeks, I do know my way back to his fucking rooms."

The guard shook his head so fast that the beads of sweat came rolling off him like a post-bathed dog. I tried to surreptitiously wipe my cheek.

"Not His Highness, Your…um, Highness. It's His Majesty who has summoned you."

I looked at Luis. He looked at me.

"Collect away," I said.

–

Ren was talking to Clementina in the corridor when I arrived at the king's rooms. The prince seemed like his usual self, waving his arms in that physically expressive way he always talked, and I released half of a relieved breath when I was realised he was unharmed, only to inhale it right back in when I noticed Starling and Dr. Sánchez standing stiffly a few feet away, not talking to each other. I hadn't seen the doctor since that evening I'd nearly died down in the cells shortly after my arrival, and in all honesty, that had been too much. He was a plain looking man, his clothes doing the most to distinguish him, and I wondered why I hadn't previously figured out he was Iván's spy. The fabrics he wore were far too fine to have been earned on a doctor's wage, even one on the Aratorre retinue, and they made Star's plain brown not-dress look even shabbier in comparison.

Their presence here meant nothing good. In fact, I was fairly fucking certain that it meant Ren's predictions about how the night was going to go were absolutely spot on. A healer with the Touch, to undo the damage inflicted by the king upon his son. And a doctor, magicless but male, to soothe Quarehian egos by assuring them all that he was, in fact, the one to work such miracles.

But the prince didn't seem the least bit fearful, laughing as he told his herald a story that I was sure involved far too many lewd jokes and inappropriate innuendoes. To him, this was just another day of daddy's fucked up affections; his tale in the orchard had told me it had been going on for nearly a decade, with the beatings even longer than that.

My breath felt tight, and I wanted to scream.

If only I could steal him away. I'd stab any of the fuckers who tried to stop me. *Moy knyaz*, my bright prince with such light and life in his eyes. We argued, sure, and I may have wished to punch him in his pretty face at least once a day, but I couldn't imagine wanting him *hurt*. To take away his Ren-ness, that easy smile and teasing wit...

He hadn't yet noticed me, waving his hands animatedly as he spoke, and it was rare I had the opportunity to catch him off guard. Too rare to pass it up.

I stepped up behind him and murmured into his ear.

"I do hope you're not flirting, Aratorre. You *know* what that will cost you."

Ren whirled around, startled, and his raised hand nearly caught me across the temple. He pulled it back just in time.

"Mat? What are you...what are you doing here?"

"Summoned by your father," I said, shrugging at my guard behind me, who had dissolved into the shadows of the corridor with the rest of them. Unobtrusive, yet watchful. For being young and prone to stuttering, the man now held himself like any of the king's other guards; careful, silent and stoic. Luis had been stopped a corridor back, as I assumed had the guards who'd accompanied Ren here. The king didn't trust any but his own to be in the proximity of his rooms, it seemed.

Ren's expression turned sad, and he shut his eyes briefly. "I see."

"Your Highness," Clementina said, and there wasn't a trace of her former hostility in her expression as she addressed me. Had time dulled it, or was the revelation that I was Temarian, not Mazekhstani, enough to remove my label of 'enemy' in her eyes? She curtsied. "Apologies. I didn't know who you were, before."

"No one did," I said. "I expect that's why we're here."

Ren blew out a breath. "Clementina, you should take the evening. I can handle the address."

The herald studied him for a moment, probably longer than protocol allowed, and then lifted her chin. "I'm fine, my prince."

His mouth twitched in something like approval.

But my mood soured further when I noticed Moreno approaching Ren, a sadistic curl to his lips. "I wouldn't want to be in your shoes," he drawled by way of greeting.

"Probably a good thing," the prince said with a faked smile. "I'm not sure your webbed feet would fit into those boots of mine that Mathias loves so much."

By the Blessed Five, the very sight of the Comandante set my blood boiling. I was physically shaking with fury, and I knew that if I opened my mouth, it wouldn't be to say anything nearly as civil to him. I wanted to claw his fucking eyes out for what he'd done to Alta, to El, to every single person on this continent that he'd trod under his heel.

Before Moreno could respond, the two guards flanking the doors to the king's rooms reached out and pulled them open in a synchronised, practiced move. Clementina blanched, and then seemed to pull herself together, sweeping through the doors and leaving the rest of us to follow. Ren's fingers deliberately brushed against mine as I forced myself to move.

The king apparently had two antechambers; the first looked almost like another corridor, long and thin with a bench tucked against each wall, but with no windows. It was clearly a waiting area. The second was where Iván Aratorre sat, in a high-backed chair nearly as grand as the throne downstairs. His family's heart-and-blade emblem was stamped into the seat's back above the king's head, while the arms bore decorative carvings that were typically Quarehian: pretty, but useless.

We moved closer to the seated king in that second room, the noise of our boots echoing. I glanced around. The space was decked with low seating and tables like Ren's antechamber, but I couldn't imagine any of Iván's guards lazing around in here with their feet up, or engaging in a bout of wrestling. It felt formal and austere, and I didn't miss the way Ren had tensed as he crossed the threshold ahead of me. This place was not a comfortable one for him.

"Your Majesty!" declared Clementina, plastering a huge smile onto her face as if there was nothing she'd rather be doing on this rainy evening than introducing the king to his own damn son. She sank into a deep curtsey before him.

The prince grabbed my arm and yanked me down into an awkward bow, evidently guessing that I hadn't been inclined to join the rest of them in theirs. Bless his suspicious little heart and its correct assumptions.

"You two are in so much fucking trouble," Moreno said to us under his breath from where he stood beside Ren, sounding positively ecstatic about the thought. I resisted the urge to slam his head into the nearest wall.

Clementina cleared her throat. "May I announce Prince Renato of the sacred Aratorre line, second son of Quareh."

The herald glanced at the Comandante, bit her lip, and then looked at me. "Prince Nathanael Velichkov, third son of Temar."

Moreno's face was a satisfying mix of indignation and irritation. Yet he was unable to protest the way she'd pushed him down the line because he was naturally outranked by a prince, even a foreign one. It was probably the only time in my life I'd ever taken enjoyment in my title.

"Comandante Juan Moreno of His Majesty's own, defender of Quareh. Dr. Alonso Sánchez, healer, and his assistant, señorita Estrella Ortega."

The king dragged his eyes to Clementina, and his lip curled.

I watched the Comandante's expression turn smug, and then back to pissed as Iván did nothing more than dismiss her. Sánchez and Starling retreated with the herald from the room without saying a word, evidently well familiar with their expected roles. I swallowed as the doors closed behind us, wishing I could take Ren's hand in mine.

"Renato. Tell me how long you've known who our prisoner really was," Iván ordered, skipping any greeting or sentiment.

"Your asshole son finally figured it out this morning," I told the room, dragging my eyes from Moreno and making sure to offer the king a dismissive sneer. "Took you all long enough-"

"Shortly after he arrived," corrected Ren, because of course he had to show off *now* of all times. I gave him a disbelieving look and he immediately averted his eyes to the floor, looking guilty. Damn straight he should. He could have been as sneaky and dishonourable as his usual difficult self, but no, he had to go and be *honest*. Idiot.

"I see. Nathanael," Iván said quietly. His eyes were a paler brown than Ren's, washed out and cold. "You've caused me a lot of grief with your deception."

I scoffed. "Do you expect me to apologise?"

Ren winced at my side. If he'd known I'd be called here, I expect I would have received a fresh lecture about holding my tongue, but I didn't give a shit. Anything that took his father's attention away from him was a win.

"I see you don't learn lessons well, after all," the king said, reminding me of what he'd said to me in the throne room on his last visit. His piercing gaze dropped to my gloved right hand, and I hoped he wasn't going to make me remove it like Moreno had. Starling was on the other side of those doors, maybe further, and couldn't help me this time.

"Never mind," Iván continued, waving a careless hand that was evidently a signal of some kind, for Moreno moved towards a cabinet on the side wall. "I'm sure this one will sink in much faster."

I tried to hold my composure, but my palms were slippery with sweat, and my heart was pounding so loudly I was surprised no one had commented on it.

"Your Majesty," Ren said smoothly. "This is a positive development. Nathanael's family can put pressure on Mazekhstam to relinquish Algejón to us, and the combined force of both Quareh and Temar will leave them no choice. His worth has become more than just a lost son – it's the threat of civil war amongst the north if Mazekhstam does not concede."

His father's gaze slid from mine to settle on his son, and his lip curled in disgust. "You have fucked this thing up from the beginning, Renato," he accused. "And now I discover you've been lying to me for just as long. I will handle the negotiations from here."

The words made my blood run cold. The way he said them, heavy with meaning, made me suspect that I'd been right in thinking that the king intended to recover their occupied city through other means, and that he had different plans for my ransom. Fuck, what would he demand from my family? Just money, or would it be some of *their* lands? Or worse…Temar's submission to Quareh?

I wasn't worth that much, surely. Certainly not to my mother, who hadn't visited me once in the time I'd been kept in Stavroyarsk. But a prince was more than a person; he was a figurehead. Regardless of any familial loyalty or love that Queen Zora Velichkova may or may not have had for me, leaving one of her own line in enemy hands would be an unwise move. It undermined the lie spun by royals that they were chosen and protected by God, and that their value was far beyond that of any ordinary person. Allowing Quareh to execute her own son would be a sign of weakness, a concession to the strength and audacity of the south…as would paying any ransom too great in cost.

It would be a careful political game the two countries would play, balancing a value and a worth, judging what would be best regarded by their respective peoples. I didn't want a single part in it.

But once again, what I wanted *didn't fucking matter.*

My gut churned as I caught sight of Moreno kicking the cabinet door closed and coiling a vicious leather whip in his hands as he stared almost hungrily at Ren. The prince ignored him, keeping his posture relaxed and his eyes on his father, and I hated that he'd endured this enough times to be able to act so casual about it.

The Comandante's eyes flickered to mine as he realised I was watching him, and he gave me an unpleasant smile, stroking the whip like it was a Blessed cat. "Both boys, sire?"

At that, Ren's tension finally seeped into his stance, and his shoulders straightened as if preparing to do something incredibly stupid.

Back off, Aratorre. That's my job.

But Iván frowned. "Juan."

"Your Majesty?"

"You have no subtlety, Moreno," Ren said, and let out a long sigh, like he was disappointed in him. The Comandante's mouth tightened.

"He's the son of Zora Velichkova," Iván pointed out, looking exasperated. "A real chance to turn Temar to our side against those war-mongering Mazekhstani fuckers. I'm not going to risk his life under the lash or some girl's Touch, Juan."

He looked to his son. "Renato?"

Ren peeled off his jacket, and held it out to me.

"*No*," I said. "You're not doing this."

We stared at each other for a moment, his eyes searching mine, and then he shrugged and dropped the coat to the tiled floor. The navy fabric with its gold edging landed in an undignified heap, and I blinked at it, too slow to stop the prince as he pulled his shirt over his head and dumped it on top of his jacket at my feet. He tied his hair up into a messy top knot, exposing his bare back.

"Ren!"

But he ignored me, moving closer to the king and sinking down to his knees on the tiles before him. Naked from the waist up, head bowed, he already looked so fucking defeated.

"The one that hurts," his father said.

"*K chertu eto*," I snarled. *Fuck this.*

As Moreno let the end of the whip drop to the floor in anticipation of the first swing, I put myself between him and Ren. I was not going to let this prick, or any other, harm my man.

"Mat! Stand down!" The prince's voice was harsh, a barked order like those he gave to his men. Too bad for him I had no intention of obeying.

"You don't want me hurt?" I asked the king, hot fury coiling through me. "Then you better tell Moreno to back off. Because I'm not moving."

The Comandante stepped forward, reaching for me, but Iván waved him back. He didn't look angry.

He was...smiling.

"Is that right, boy?"

I squared my shoulders, knowing that I couldn't do shit against a trained soldier like Moreno, but not willing to join Ren in his submission. I'd wondered who held Ren in place when the king ordered him hurt, but it seemed that the prince did it all by himself.

How could he just let them do such things to him? Maybe I couldn't win this, but I was damn well going to *try*.

"Fuck. You," I spat at the king of Quareh. "I won't let you hurt him."

"Mathias, no," Ren whispered from the floor. "Father, please don't, I'll be good-"

Iván looked down at his son, his expression cold. "Nathanael Velichkov," he said, when his gaze finally shifted to me. His mouth looked odd. "Come here."

I had no intention of moving. I had planned to stay in that exact spot, guarding Ren, until the bastard let us leave. I knew I was the only thing standing in the way of Moreno's whip tasting royal blood.

None of that explained why, without a second thought, I abandoned Ren and moved to stand in front of the king. I was breathing heavily, like I'd run there.

That didn't...I hadn't meant to...it was...

"Kneel," Iván said.

I knelt.

"What the fuck-"

"You really are a slow learner," the king commented mildly, and this time, as he spoke, I saw his tongue flicker between his teeth. It was as black as pitch. "Stop breathing, Nathanael."

My throat instantly contracted, cutting off my air, and it was like the peanut oil all over again. My hands clawed at my neck, seeking to release whatever pressure was wrapped around it. A hand, or a cloth…but nothing was there.

Vaguely, I heard Ren yelling, as if from a distance. His father telling him to stay where he was. The crack of a whip through the air and the noise of its impact…that seemed significant, somehow, and brought a roiling sensation to my insides, but I couldn't think clearly, just needed to breathe, if I could just breathe, I could think, or maybe I needed to think to breathe and-

I fell forward onto my hands, as if the changed position might help to dislodge whatever was clawing its way down my throat. But it held on tight with a fierce ferocity.

More words. More noises. More terrible, heart-wrenching sounds of leather hitting flesh.

Something that might have been a rasp of pain, ever so quiet and drawn from reluctant lips.

I couldn't get my mind to focus on anything. My lungs burned, my thoughts blurred, and I was going, going…

Iván murmured something and suddenly I could breathe again, a cure more instant than even Starling's healing magic. I drew in gulps of air, my forehead pressed to the cool tiles beneath my hands, cursing the human need for oxygen considering it had been screwing me over so delightfully lately.

"Stay there," the king ordered, keeping me in place at his feet with nothing but his words.

"Mathias!"

Ren's voice, so urgent and pained. I lifted my head as much as the magic allowed, and met his agonised gaze.

"Mat?"

I couldn't get any words out, but I could nod at him. The prince's expression turned to relief and he almost smiled, and then his face flooded with distress as Moreno flicked his arm and brought the whip down across his back once more.

But again, he made no noise but for a small hiss.

Oh, my beautiful, brave prince. How many times did they hurt you before you learned how to keep quiet?

I'd resented Ren for submitting, but now knowing what his father could do…what he *was*…it all made sense.

There was no need for threats or restraints, because no one could disobey the Voice. If the king Told him to take it, to kneel on the floor and allow Moreno to carve his back to bloody pieces, there wasn't a Blessed thing Ren could do about it. His rebelliousness had probably died years ago, straining uselessly at Iván's command over and over until he'd been forced to accept that the power his father had over him wasn't just in the form of a crown.

And he'd obeyed him tonight without the need for such orders, to save me from witnessing him brought low by the king's magic. Perhaps in the hope that his father wouldn't use it on me if he complied…fuck, what was it that Ren had said? *I'll be good?*

But as another blow landed, and another, the prince's gaze losing its sharpness, his bare shoulders hunching further forward with every strike and the Comandante growing visibly frustrated despite the damage he was inflicting, I realised that Ren was still holding onto a shred of defiance against his abusers. The only thing he could refuse to give them.

Satisfaction in his suffering.

Lips pressed together, Ren remained almost silent as the flogging continued for what felt like an eternity, my heart clenched so tight in my chest that it hurt. Moreno pulled no more than a faint grunt or the lightest of gasps from him, and was clearly disappointed in the lack of response. Maybe he hit him harder because of that; maybe he would have put his all into it regardless.

It was no wonder Ren took every opportunity to wind the Comandante up and undermine his plans. A soldier should never have this much power over a royal. Licence to hurt the man he was sworn to protect, to take *pleasure* from the act?

This was so fucked up.

A WHISPER AND A BREATH

The prince's face twisted in agony, his palms landing flat on the tiles before him as he tried to hold himself up. Blood ran thickly down his torso, soaking into his trousers and steadily dripping from his elbows.

But although his gasps of pain came more freely now, there were no tears in those stricken brown eyes.

Ren had cried for Miel. For Vitorona. For me.

But he wouldn't cry for the two men who had abused him for his entire life.

The end of the whip sliced across his back again, and again.

This was…this was beyond anything I'd seen a man survive in Stavroyarsk. This was more than punishment: it was a fucking death sentence.

"Please," I begged the king, unable to see him even without his malignant magic holding me still. Because I couldn't look away from the prince who had been full of smiles only hours ago, gently teasing me and laughing so easily. How had he endured this for *years*?

"Please, *por favor*, stop this. You're going to kill him!"

Silence from above me. A grunt from Moreno as he swung again, starting to tire.

"Please, Your Majesty! He's your son!"

Ren swayed on the spot, his expression unfocused.

"Fuck you all!" I screamed, not caring what Iván could do to me. Losing my breath again seemed so small a thing compared to losing *him*.

The whip fell once more with that horrifically wet noise it had been making when it landed on already bloody, torn-up flesh.

"Ren! *Dorogoi!*"

Moreno glanced at me, his mouth curling into a sneer, but I didn't fucking care what he'd heard me say to the prince. Because his grip had slipped, and the precious second it took him to adjust the handle of the whip was a second my lover wasn't being tortured.

Ren gave me a half smile. And then I finally got to see the utter fucking mess made of his back when he proceeded to collapse bonelessly to the floor, and lay there, unmoving.

A WHISPER AND A BREATH

*

Chapter Forty-One

Ren

Soft warmth, against scalding fire. The prickle of sparks, lost within raging bolts of lightning. A gentle caress, overwhelmed by the biting, burning, throbbing, *sheer fucking agony* of the web of gouges carved deep into my skin.

But those little sensations were the most important, the most welcome. Because they were bringing me back to myself, inch by excruciating inch.

Back to Mathias.

I could feel him, even through all the pain and Starling's magic. Feel his hand in mine, squeezing tight, yet slippery with something I expected was blood. His other hand on my face, smoothing loose strands of hair back and stroking my cheek. I leaned into the small touches, seeking him like a moth to a flame.

Despite it all, I smiled.

Dorogoi, he'd called me. *Darling.*

Fuck, he was adorable.

Another wave of pain hit and I shuddered out a tormented breath. Mathias murmured soothing nonsense to me in Mazekhstani, and I tried to focus on that instead of Starling's fingers on my back as she healed away the mess of churned up skin with her Touch.

"There. That one. Work faster, girl."

It took me a while to recognise the voice, my thoughts having to be dragged through a thick haze before they made any sense. It was Dr. Sánchez, doing his usual thing of pointing out the lacerations on my body as if the healer couldn't possibly see the bloodied wounds on her own, satisfying himself and the other men in the room with his show of being in charge.

Starling's magic swept through me, that bittersweet taste of relief mixed with the knowledge of what was next. When I had enough strength to squeeze Mat's hand back, I immediately did so, and was rewarded by his sharp intake of breath.

"Ren! Oh, thank fuck! You scared me, you *svoloch.*"

I lay sprawled on the floor, bleeding and semi-conscious as the Touch pulled me from the death that would have otherwise taken me. Estrella patched together my skin, repaired the muscles underneath, and restored the blood in my body through magic that was worth more than its weight in gold. If I ever lost her, I was done for.

Eventually, I opened my eyes, pleased that the first thing I saw was his grey-blue ones peering back at me from barely six inches away.

I licked my dry lips and stretched them into a smile. Despite the hurt, it was a genuine one. "Such concern in those pretty eyes of yours, *mi cielo*. Be careful. You don't want anyone thinking the northerner has gone soft."

"Dios help me," Mat teased, but there was also something dark in his expression, a deep, ferocious hatred that terrified me with the fear of what he might do with it. Surely he'd learned his lesson when my father turned his magic on him? When he'd worked out why there hadn't been even a single guard present in the chamber, why I'd gone to my knees willingly in the hope that the king would leave Mathias alone if I was compliant?

Surely even Nathanael Velichkov knew a lost cause when he saw one?

I winced with the final sweep of Starling's calloused hands over my now uninjured, yet sticky, skin. The Touch didn't take away all of the pain, nor any of the blood.

"Your Highness," she murmured, which was a surprise. She didn't normally say anything to me in these encounters, nor I her. Was it Mat's presence that had changed things?

"*Gracias,* Starling," Mathias said quietly, and the doctor harrumphed from above us, clicking his fingers to order his assistant away. As the doors closed behind them, I allowed Mat to help me back to my knees, but no further.

"Ren," he said, impatient and frustrated as he tried to tug me to my feet. "It's over."

I shook my head.

"Ren?" He pressed a kiss to my forehead, soft and sweet. It grounded me, brought a sense of calm I hadn't known I could feel while kneeling and helpless like this.

"You see, Your Majesty?" Moreno's slimy voice always sent shudders through me during these sessions. "Just as I told you."

"I see, Juan. And heard." They laughed softly together, mocking and disdainful, and I winced as they poked their claws into Mat's moment of vulnerability. Oh, how I wished they hadn't heard what he'd yelled out at me in his pain. *Dorogoi*. Mat didn't say such things, not like me, who tossed out pet names and affections like grains of rice at a wedding.

And that meant it had been sincere. A rush of warmth filled me, a pleased and giddy elation that had no business being felt in this room where so much pain had been dealt.

"So, Nathanael," my father said. "My son was successful in his manipulations, I see. Your bitch of a mother will not be pleased."

But he sounded incredibly so.

"Manipulations?" Mat's voice was cold.

"His plan to make you fall for him, you foolish northerner. Or did you imagine it real? Why would he care about *you*, out of all of those he's had before, and will certainly have after?"

"It's-"

"Quiet, Renato."

His command, hissed on a black tongue, ensured my silence. I could only squeeze Mathias' fingers tighter, trying to convey that it was a lie, a manipulation of the king's own, but why would he believe me? Fuck, if my father managed to push that wedge back between us, to lose Mat's trust in me once again…would I be capable of earning it back a second time?

We were such a fragile thing, tested but not yet proven, and Mat's insecurities were his weakness. I'd seen how easily he'd caved to the idea that Astrid had ordered his death, despite giving his own life for hers at the monastery all those months ago. The fear that I'd turned on him the last time my father visited had been enough to break us.

Mi gato montés shifted beside me, also on his knees even though my father's compulsion on him to stay down must have already worn off if he'd been able to crawl over to me. Fuck, the memory of that snapped order, like Mat was a dog to be brought to heel, sparked a new wave of fury in me.

"It is real," he said, not an ounce of doubt in his voice. His Mazekhstani accent was particularly pronounced as he spoke the Quarehian words, and affection flooded through me.

Moreno laughed the loudest this time.

"Boy, if you knew how many lovers your *dorogoi* has had, you wouldn't be so damn naïve."

Mathias gave an easy shrug. "It doesn't matter. I care for him."

Oh, my heart.

I held his hand tighter, suspecting that I might be in the range of hurting him, but he didn't seem to mind, so I didn't either.

"I see," my father said, his face impassive, and then leant back in his chair. "The one that reminds."

I stiffened at the all-too familiar words, his stupid ritual.

The one that hurts. A flogging so brutal I wouldn't survive it without Starling's Touch.

The one that reminds. The lashes that I would keep with me for days, the pain reminding me of my bastard father and his man each time I moved. I wasn't permitted to have those healed by magic, and I'd more than learned my lesson for my disobedience the one time I'd attempted to subvert his rules.

I tried to push Mathias away from me as the Comandante stepped forward, uncoiling the whip once more. He'd cleaned it of my blood while I'd been unconscious. A small mercy.

But the king held up a hand, an unexpected interruption to our usual routine.

"Nathanael. It seems appropriate, as a symbol of restitution for any grievance that your own mutilation may have caused Temar, that you be the one to lay the marks across my son's back."

"Absolutely fucking not," Mat said immediately, stupidly, and uselessly.

"I'm not asking. You will take that whip, and you will use it on Renato. Twenty lashes."

My father's tongue, black and ugly like a diseased, necrotic snake, peeked out from behind his teeth. The Blessed manifested their ability through colouring of the five senses. But while Mat's was a beautiful and perfectly fated navy and gold, the king's looked like death itself. It was one of the reasons those with the Voice didn't survive execution for long: either their visible magic, or their victims' knowledge that they'd been forced to do something they didn't want to, made it difficult for them to hide from the law.

Yet my father had been clever. He only used his power in private, as he was now, or when he could get away with ordering all witnesses to kill themselves before they could disclose his secret. Like the day he'd 'won' the Quarehian throne from King Adalberto Padilla through beating him in melee combat…by Telling his opponent to leave his chest unguarded when they shook hands prior to the duel. For so long, I wished I could share that story with my father's Council, have them execute him for the traitorous coward he was, but as I grew older, I realised that even if they believed me, they were too spineless themselves to move against him. A bunch of old men who loved the power my father had given them too much to risk unseating themselves.

While it would be incorrect to say the king didn't abuse his ability – the hapless and stricken northerner stumbling towards the Comandante right now being a prime example of that – he did only rely on it in limited circumstances, unlike many of those with the Voice who immediately exploited the will of everyone in reach.

Moreno held out the whip to Mat with something unreadable in his expression. Maybe even he didn't know whether he would enjoy this or not; while the Comandante loved being the one to make me suffer, I imagined he found a vicious pleasure in the thought of me being additionally demeaned through torment delivered at Mathias' hands.

Oh, if I could get a knife to either his or my father's throats, I'd cut them without hesitation.

"I'm so sorry," Mat whispered as he moved to stand behind me, guilty horror flooding his expression. I shook my head, giving him a soft smile. He was no more responsible for what was about to happen than he was for the sun rising each morning, and just as helpless to stop it. The Voice was a cruel, twisted thing, and with every one of those Blessed I killed or ordered executed, I knew I was making the continent a little safer. It was just a fucking shame I couldn't add my father to that list.

"Proceed," the king Told him. "But make every effort not to break the skin."

So there are no scars, he'd explained, that first time. Couldn't have his son permanently maimed, right?

Yeah, fuck you too, daddy.

I tried to ignore the bite of the leather tail of the whip as it sliced across my skin, almost feather light compared to what I'd endured earlier, and instead listened to the noises Mathias was making behind me. Little grunts of effort; not as he swung, but as he pulled back, as if he was trying his damnedest to break through the compulsion on him.

You sweet, adorable little kitten, Nathanael. No one had ever, in the entire recorded history of Riehse Eshan, been able to resist the Voice when they'd heard its words. It couldn't be done. But my fierce, contrary wildcat thought *he* would be the one to prove that fundamental truth of magic wrong.

He didn't, of course.

Nineteen strikes. Nineteen strikes in which I didn't cry out once, my silence guaranteed for the first handful by my father's order to be quiet, and when that ran out, as it always did within a few minutes – while the length of time differed between each person with the Voice, just as the strength of all of the Blessed's magic varied from person to person because no one could create infinite obedience – the rest was by my own obstinacy.

And after the nineteenth swing, Mat stopped, and dropped the whip as if it had burned him. Moreno sucked in an anticipatory breath as I glanced over my shoulder and winced at the movement.

"Nat," I said quietly. "Just do it."

I didn't give a shit that the final lash would be under his own volition now that the compulsion on him had waned. He had to do it. He *had* to, because else my father would-

Mathias shook his head, eyes flaring with defiance. "*No.*"

"Break the index finger on your left hand," the king Told him casually, and then swiftly compelled me back into both silence and stillness to cut off my horrified protests. "And then you'll deliver *three* more lashes to Renato."

Fuck, fuck, fuck!

Mat obeyed instantly of course, his gloved right hand snapping down on his index finger. The crack of the bone was overshadowed only by his cry of pain, although it was significantly less visceral than the way he'd screamed in the throne room. His breathing came out in harsh pants.

He glared up at my father through lidded eyes and clenched teeth as he cradled his injured hand to his chest and bent to pick up the whip.

My heart shattered as I watched Mathias be hurt by Quareh *again*, and in that moment, I made a long overdue decision.

I couldn't keep him here.

No matter how empty the continent would feel without him by my side, no matter how much it would tear me into pieces for him to leave. It was something I'd been too selfish to agree to even when he'd begged me, but now I had no choice, despite it guaranteeing me another excruciating session on my knees before my king.

Because fuck, I think I loved him.

-

Mat's unbroken hand swept the damp cloth down my arms and then dabbed it gently against my injured back, wiping off the blood so we could return to my chambers without drawing attention. The waistband of my trousers was soaked, but I could hide that with my coat.

I heard my northerner growl as a pair of boots moved into my vision, and I reluctantly glanced upwards to find the Comandante standing over us.

"Your Highness. I seem to have found you on your knees once again."

"I quite like it down here," I told him. "It makes it easier to avoid looking at your ugly face."

Moreno seethed. He could never take insults, despite regularly dishing them out.

"As Elías will not be returning to your retinue, I've appointed you a new guard."

I sighed and got to my feet, trying not to wince as my back screamed in protest. Mathias rose with me.

"I do hope it's Diego," I said. "Completely inexplicably, I feel in the mood for slicing someone's skin off."

The Comandante's smile was all teeth. "I'm sure Diego will be comforted by the fact you no longer order men flogged."

I paused, wondering if Mat was going to offer an exception for the soldier who had tried to fuck him.

When he didn't, I just shrugged. "He'll wish it was merely a flogging."

"I told you, I sent Diego away," said Moreno. "Cirilo will be your new man. He's waiting for you in your rooms."

"Well, *Cirilo* can wait all he likes," I told him sweetly, taking the shirt Mat was holding out to me and pulling it over my head. I tried not to flinch as the fabric brushed the raw and wounded skin. "I'm not taking him on. Keep your spies out of my chambers, Comandante."

Moreno nodded, but not in acceptance. More in wicked, anticipatory glee, as if he'd been hoping for that answer. "The king may refuse to see it, but I always knew you better than he did, Ren."

I dragged my eyes to his. He was too much of a coward to have said any such thing while my father was still in the room.

"Is that so?"

The Comandante looked at Mathias then. "You were right," he said, and his hand shot out, fingers twisting in the front of Mat's shirt. He yanked him close, and Mat hissed in surprise.

I reached out to help him pull free but my back cried out in agony, and I stumbled.

"Ren does care for you," Moreno said with amusement, watching me work through the pain and ignoring how Mathias' nails clawed at his hand. "It's an absurdly unenviable position you two find yourselves in. Doomed fucking love between enemy princes." He barked out an incredulous laugh, hauling my lover backwards with him as I staggered closer. "How in the name of the Blessed Five did you think *that* was going to work?"

"Get your fucking hands off him, Moreno, or I swear to Dios I'll-"

"Any further acts of aggression from the north, and the king will be cutting off more parts from dear little Nathanael here," he interrupted, shaking Mat. My boy hissed out curses and continued resisting his hold on him, but the

Comandante was twice his size and too tough to be fended off by a few scratches. "And what a terrible shame that would be. After all, we've seen how easily the northern countries can be...*provoked* into violence."

I stilled.

"So, Your Highness, considering I hold your heart in my fist..." He tightened his grip on Mat, jerking him even closer to his own chest, and then reached out to take hold of my collar too. I let myself be pulled forward until we were all sharing the same air, Moreno bent over us both so we were forced to look up at him.

Mathias slid his fingers into mine.

"I expect you to prove less...troublesome," Moreno warned, his voice a low growl as he delivered the threat. "*Both of you*. Cirilo stays."

He abruptly let go and I rocked back onto my heels, Mathias' warm hand the only thing saving me from falling back to the floor. Then Mat snatched up my coat, helped me into it, and without a word to the Comandante, led me from my father's rooms.

It was both easier and harder to keep up the pretence to my guards with the northerner by my side. I barely had to do or say anything when I was in the company of such a talented liar who was able to spin a convincingly intricate tale to Luis and Jiron about the imaginary lecture and threats the king had issued on us both, sighing and shaking his head like he'd really had to sit through an hour of such tedious nonsense, but it just gave me more time to seethe on what had been done to him.

His left hand was now fixed, thank Dios. I'd been worried that my father, in the spirit of his 'lessons', would have insisted on the finger remaining broken, but Starling had apparently been permitted to heal him as she'd been waiting for us outside the king's chambers.

When she had seen Mathias' mangled hand, her expression had blazed with a fury so intense it had almost rivalled my own. I'd never been fond of the girl, unable to stomach how she saw me at my weakest so often, but that look on her face softened my distaste, somewhat, as did the gentle way she cradled Mat's broken finger as she set it back into place and mended the shattered bone.

I wasn't, however, overly happy with what the healer had done next, which was to rise to her toes and whisper something into Mathias' ear that made him bite his lip and then give her an affectionate smile.

As I opened my mouth to demand that if she was flirting with my lover right in front of me, she should at least have the decency to say it out loud like I did, he'd taken my hand in his gloved one. I didn't bother to hide my smug grin at that, but Starling didn't look the least bit daunted as she continued to run her fingers lightly over the knuckles on Mat's other hand, despite the fact that it was clearly already healed.

Okay, I wasn't opposed to the idea of a threesome, but if I was sharing my precious Mat, it would be on my fucking terms. And I got the impression that little Estrella was not someone who followed orders in bed, and I wouldn't tolerate that from anyone other than Mathias.

Just as I'd been about to snatch his other hand from hers, appearances be damned, a flood of warmth had rushed down my back. I'd bitten back a curse as I realised Starling was healing my secondary lash wounds, the ones we both knew she wasn't allowed to touch. I had to force myself not to react in front of Dr. Sánchez or the king's guards, even though the shock of her blatant defiance and the realisation that she could heal by the Touch *through another person* was hard to keep off my face.

Mat had laughed like Starling had whispered something funny to him, keeping up a one-sided conversation as the healer and I fell silent with our shared concentration, and I once again marvelled at how effortlessly he fell into the role of saviour of others, even if he was falling dangerously close to the line of making everything fucking worse, as usual. He knew what we risked if we were found out, and his involvement in this act of rebellion would only damn him too. And after everything he'd just suffered, how could he be so stupid to jeopardise himself for me?

To have me healed within spitting distance of my father's open chamber doors was downright reckless, although I couldn't help but admire the audacity of the two of them. They were an unstoppable force; highly destructive, utterly chaotic, and if it had been a little less dangerous, I might have praised Mathias for bringing Starling out of her shell. But her increased outspokenness and tenacity made her more vulnerable as a female in Quareh, and the way he'd encouraged her to push back and speak her mind had only increased the complaints I'd received about the healer since-

A WHISPER AND A BREATH

I blinked as something tugged at my shoulders, rousing myself from my reverie and realising we were now alone in my bedchamber.

"You're in your head, Ren," Mathias said, as he pulled off my coat. "Nasty place to be."

"Depends on your definition of *nasty*," I shot back automatically, but I didn't have the energy to wink at him as I usually would have. Still, he gave me a smile, and then abruptly lost it.

"I'm so-"

"Don't you *dare* say sorry," I warned. "Besides, your lashes are much lighter than the Comandante's." I smirked. "You've never flogged anyone before, have you?"

Mat blinked at me, and then exploded into that righteous indignation of his.

"Of course I fucking haven't, Ren! What kind of Blessed question is that?"

He muttered more under his breath, reaching for my shirt.

I let him peel it off me, grateful that he did it one arm at a time so I didn't have to lift my arms above my head. And then I realised that I could do whatever I fucking well liked, because I could barely feel the hurt. It was an odd sensation, to be cut to the core and feel it only on the inside.

"It shows," I said quietly. "When my father Told you not to break the skin, you didn't know how much force that would take. So the orders required you to err on the side of caution. You were practically tickling me, *mi amor*."

He sighed, clearly not buying it, and scowled at the floor. When he next spoke, his voice was cold and furious.

"What kind of sick fucker gets off on his own son's suffering?"

I swallowed. I'd hoped that he'd been too distracted to notice, but of course Mat was too observant to have let the bulge in my father's trousers escape his attention. The first time I'd seen it myself during one of my...*punishments*, I'd been terrified that he'd been planning to take matters further, but there had never been even the suggestion of such a thing. It seemed whatever else my father was, he wasn't *that*. He just seemed to enjoy the scene; whether it was watching me hurt specifically, or anyone he brought to their knees before him, I didn't know. I didn't especially care to find out.

"Well, that's one way in which we're alike, me and him," I said bitterly. "Inflicting pain turns us on. As you said, Mat. Sick fuckers."

I headed for the bathing room and pulled the chain to release the water into the bath. A moment later, I heard the door shut behind me, and let out the sigh I'd been holding.

Mathias didn't want to be around me after I'd pointed out that little fact, and I couldn't blame him. Seeing what my own father was capable of – what I knew *I* was capable of, sans magic – wasn't an easy thing to face.

I was messed up and I knew it, but it felt so *good* to indulge that I'd rarely tried to stop myself, repeating the lies in my head that it was okay, I was better than him, just because I only enjoyed hurting people who let me. Like it made me any less depraved.

A light touch at my hip made me jump, and I glanced down with a frown to find pale fingers grazing my bare skin.

Mat had shut himself *in* with the monster, rather than putting the door between us like he should have. Idiotic northerner.

"Were you hard when Moreno sawed off my finger? When you held me down and he made me scream?" he asked quietly from behind me, running his hand along the top of my trousers to brush along my stomach. Then he moved lower, as if looking for evidence of arousal at the memory of those sickening events.

I stilled.

"Answer me, Ren."

Horrified, it took me a moment to find my voice. "Of course not! Mat, I told you-"

"What about when Jiron was beating me at Sesveko?"

I let out a breath. I could see what Mathias was trying to do for me, and I didn't deserve it. Bless his stubborn little soul and his insistence on seeing good in people that didn't exist.

He tsked when I didn't respond, and began to repeat himself. "When Jiron-"

"No. Fuck no."

"When you had me tied to your bed and you used the belt on me?" There was a slight tremor in his voice as he said this one, and he was clearly not as confident of the answer as he had been with the others.

I could have lied. Confirmed that I was the freak I knew myself to be and sent Mathias running from me, like he should.

But as I turned my head to deliver the words to him, there was something in that steady blue-grey gaze that pulled the reluctant truth from my lips.

"No."

It wasn't the idea of doing that to Mathias that had kept my cock flaccid that day – Dios knows, it would have been hot in any other circumstance – but it hadn't been for enjoyment. It had been to knock some long overdue sense into him, and while I regretted my actions, getting off on his pain hadn't been why I had done it. It had only been anger that had sustained my blows to his back.

"And the floggings you used to order on your people as punishments?" Mat asked softly. "Do they...do it for you?"

"No," I said again. Those things were brutal, and not sexy in any damn way. "But the people I hurt personally, the ones I *want* to hurt?" I turned in his arms to face him, but I didn't touch him. Not now, not like this. "That *does* do it for me, Nat. I'm not just talking about the bites and scratches I give to you. I really hurt them."

I let my lust at the idea shine through into my expression. He deserved to know. Fuck, I should never have let us get this far without telling him what I was.

Mathias' eyes were wide. "Do you want to-"

He fell silent, but the question was as clear as if he'd voiced it.

Do you want to hurt me?

And the answer was just as unequivocal. *Fuck yes I do, Mat.*

To hear my northerner scream for me, feel him flinch, watch his shoulders heave as he fought through the pain?

On nights other than these, when I hadn't been kneeling at my father's feet, I normally wasn't ashamed about what I liked in bed. Everyone enjoyed *something*. The fact that I was a prick who occasionally enjoyed beating his lovers until they bled? It fitted my persona quite nicely, if one thought about it.

But here, in this moment, when we'd just gone through what we had, it felt sick to even voice such a fantasy. How could I hurt Mathias after everything he'd been through? It would be so Blessed wrong.

And yet still I craved it within the darkest parts of myself.

Thank fuck he'd be leaving soon. The man was temptation itself, and I feared that any longer in his presence, and I wouldn't be able to stop myself from taking what shouldn't be mine. Mathias was too *good,* too pure for me, and I'd already damaged him enough.

*

Chapter Forty-Two

Mat

"Tell me about your mother," I said, feeling Ren tense up under my hands. "You said your father killed her. You meant with the Voice, didn't you?"

A twinge of guilt shot through me at raising such a sensitive subject, but clearly pampering wasn't doing it for the prince tonight. I'd had wine and oranges delivered to him, which were both lying untouched under his trailing left hand as it hung limply over the side of the bath. He hadn't reached for me when I'd joined him, tucking up his knees to give me space at the other end of the tub instead of sprawling all over me like he usually did. The water had grown cold, which was downright heresy, but he hadn't let me drain and refill it after I'd hastily escaped its chilly embrace, just lying there with his expression blank and his eyes distant as I lathered soap through his dark strands of hair.

And that wasn't right. Ren practically *purred* whenever he talked me into washing his hair, leaning into my hands like a touch-starved puppy and making demands for obscenely long scalp massages. Once, my fingertips had gone numb by the time he finally stopped whimpering whenever I tried to let go.

But the prince before me was a shadow of his usual glowing self. Dull and lifeless.

So if sweetness wasn't helping to ease the wounds his father and Moreno had left on him tonight, I planned to open them back up myself and scrape out whatever lingering infection remained. I'd have him *talking*, damn it, screaming and crying if he must, but anything other than that terrifying numbness he'd descended into over the last hour.

"Ren," I prompted. "Your mother."

"Mathias…"

"So I'm right?"

Ren sighed. At first I thought he wasn't going to answer me, that I'd have to climb from my chair back into the bath and start throttling him until he reacted with anything other than apathy, but eventually the words seeped from him, quiet and reluctant. "I don't know what he said to her. Could he make her organs shut down by merely saying it out loud? Or did he just Tell her to stop breathing, like he did to you?"

My chest felt tight at the memory of that. Of being helpless to the bastard's power, of my body and my life able to be controlled with a fucking *word*.

"How?" I pressed, feeling uncomfortably heartless with the questions. "She died the day you were born. How would you know what happened?"

"My brother said he saw our father lean in and whisper something to her, just at the end. It meant nothing to Horacio at the time, of course. Until father started hurting me and we realised what he was." Ren swallowed. "One day we decided to confront him, thought that if we just...if we just made him admit what he'd done to mother, it would be...I don't know. Better?

"I was eight, Horacio thirteen, and we walked hand in hand *right* up to our father to demand justice." Ren's right hand sliced up out of the bath, water cascading from his fingers. "We were foolish, idealistic idiots who thought we could fix wrongs by shouting at them loud enough." He barked out a short, unexpected laugh. "Kind of like you, Nat."

"What happened? Was that when he sent you here?"

"Yeah," Ren said quietly. "After I'd healed."

I sucked in a breath. "He beat you?"

This time his laugh was bitter, devoid of humour. "No. My father has never laid hands on me a day in his life. *Horacio* beat me."

Fuck.

Ren was silent for a long moment, his hand dropping back under the water. "I remember feeling angry, helpless, but mostly I remember my brother's face." His shoulders rose then fell in a slow shrug. "He was screaming at our father to let him stop, tears streaming down his face...and of course that made the king even madder. Father never tolerated tears from us, nor defiance."

He heaved in a breath. "I didn't see what happened after I lost unconsciousness, but I heard about it."

Then he looked up, a smile on his face that didn't meet his eyes. The mask of a man who'd had to hide for a long time.

"The stableboy," I whispered. The one that Horacio had beaten to death in front of dozens of witnesses, earning himself a gruesome reputation across the continent. Ren's fury at me for raising the rumours made a lot more sense now I knew who had really been responsible for the murder.

The prince nodded, standing so abruptly the water sloshed carelessly over the side of the bath. He held out an arm, and I didn't even bother to mock him for the imperious gesture, mutely handing him a towel to dry himself. "Horacio's closest friend," he said quietly. "Our father broke my brother that day, Mat, and ensured he'd never stand up to him again. And then he separated us. Our mother was dead, our sisters were married off and sent from the continent shortly afterwards, and Horacio, he just…"

Ren climbed out of the bath, wrapping the towel around him as he made his way back into the bedchamber, fiddling at the leather cuff on his left wrist he always kept dry when bathing.

"Despite it all, my brother is still a good man, Mathias, I have to believe that. I *do* believe that. Once he's out of our father's shadow, I think he'll be good for Quareh. That's what keeps me going, anyway. The promise that one day, it will all be better."

He heaved in a breath and released it in another long sigh, before grabbing my hand. I thought he was seeking comfort and I squeezed his fingers, before realising that he'd loosened the cuff and was now strapping it around my own wrist. "Or am I being idealistic again?"

He shot me a crooked smile, but it had just enough Ren-ness in the expression to make me return it.

"You don't need to give me that," I protested, as he fixed the buckle of the thick bracelet in place. "It's yours."

"It is mine," he agreed. "And you are mine. Hence, it is yours."

I glanced down at it. It was heavier than I'd expected for such a simple design: the Aratorre symbol stamped into the band of brown leather, which was a few shades darker than Ren's own golden skin. I'd never seen him take it off before; it was the one thing he kept on him no matter what else he was wearing at the time. Including when he was wearing nothing at all.

"*Gracias,*" I said, touched by the gesture. "Although if we're using that logic, that heavenly bath back there is mine, so you never get to complain about me using it ever again."

"I sharn't," Ren promised, and I rolled my eyes at the infeasibility of such a thing, but he didn't look amused.

"Mat, it's not just-"

I leaned in and kissed him, tasting him on my lips. Despite not touching the oranges I'd ordered, he still tasted of citrus and saffron, that heady scent that made my mouth tingle and my cock stir.

Ren let out a soft noise. "*Mi sol,* you are making this harder than it needs to be."

I snorted at his careless phrasing, and he groaned.

"Yes, *thank you*. But I made a decision tonight, when my father was…you know. And I-"

I kissed him again. I didn't want to hear about where his mind had gone while he was being tortured for no fucking reason. I hated that I hadn't been able to save him from the king's cruelty like I'd hoped, and I would not have him dwelling on what had happened. Talking about his mother – his *brother* – had brought Ren back to himself, and now I intended to spirit him away from bad things entirely.

Because if I really was his, then that made him mine.

*

Chapter Forty-Three

Ren

I lost myself in the man before me, in the feel of his hands on me, the taste of his tongue, the firm press of his thigh as he forced a leg between mine. Dios, Mathias was everything.

Too fast for me to stop him, he reached out and untucked the end of my towel from where it was folded around my hips. It slumped to the floor, followed a moment later by his own, and I gazed at his nakedness with reverent hunger. His smooth skin, the sharp curve of his hips, that glorious cock I'd tasted so many times and yet still couldn't get enough of.

Mat gave me a shy smile, and all I wanted to do was eat him up, inch by fucking inch.

But I'd been trying to let him *go*, damn it.

With reluctance, I pulled back. "Mat. You need to-"

"No more talking, *knyaz*," he said, and then dared to clamp his hand over my mouth.

I yanked it away immediately, delicious heat sparking through me as I closed my fingers around Mathias' delicate wrist and forced it down. I tried to ignore the way it made my breath hitch with excitement.

"*Excuse you?*"

"They took away your power tonight, Ren," Mat said quietly. "Your autonomy. Your control." He tugged gently against my hold on him, not really trying to pull free. There was a challenge in his gaze. "Take it back."

I growled my appreciation of *that* gloriously enticing idea, and then reality hit.

"No. Not with...Nat, you were also-"

"So let me submit because I want to," he said stubbornly, and for once, there wasn't a trace of embarrassment on his face when he spoke of such things. "Not because I have to."

A WHISPER AND A BREATH

I swallowed. "We shouldn't-"

Mathias shoved me in the chest, hard enough to make me stumble backwards and release his arm.

I stared at him. "What the fuck was that?"

He shrugged. "Incentive. Unless you don't want this, in which case tell me so, there's nothing you can say other than yes."

"Mat-"

He shoved at me again, making my blood pound.

"You're really pushing your luck here, *mi cielo*," I snapped.

"Good," he shot back, with a wicked smile that spoke right to my cock. "What are you going to do about it?"

"I'm going to-"

"*Sí* or *no*," said Mat, once again provoking me with that cruel mouth of his. By the Blessed Five, had he even let me finish a sentence yet? "It's pretty simple. Even a southerner should understand."

Prick.

When he stepped forward to push me again, I caught his arm and used his momentum to twist it behind his back. Not painfully, just enough to stop him in his tracks.

I held him there for a moment, enjoying the feel of his bare skin under my hands but holding myself back from pressing any closer. I just had to let him cool off, and then I could tell him everything I'd been trying to when he kissed me.

Mathias cocked his head without looking around at me.

"What are you doing?" His tone was exasperated.

"Teaching you to-"

"You're not teaching me a damned thing," he said with a feigned sigh, interrupting yet again. "Except, apparently, how boring you're capable of being."

The taunt set my cock alight in a way that shattered all of my self-control, slipping through my defences like only Mat could. Oh, the brat was fucking *done for*.

Grabbing the back of his neck with my free hand, I threw him against the nearest wall, keeping his face shoved against it so he couldn't move. I wrenched his arm higher up his back, the sudden physical resistance under my fingers announcing the moment I hit his body's limit.

Then I pushed his arm up a quarter inch further, and Mat let out a pained gasp.

And fuck me, it was such a different sound to the ones he'd made when my father had forced him to break his own fingers. He was hurting, sure, but there was a delight behind it. Exhilaration. Arousal.

The noise, and the way he pressed his bare ass back against my rock-hard length, loosened the chokehold on my heart that told me I was perverted for wanting this, for wanting to bruise and cut him until he cried.

Fuck, *no*. I couldn't go that far, not with Mat.

But maybe…maybe I could indulge the way we had before, one last time. Nothing that would harm him, but enough to give us both pleasure.

Because I'd been right, all those times I'd teased my northerner about enjoying being hurt. I had suspected it ever since that first night I'd had him in my rooms and I'd slammed him against the wall a little like this for a reason I couldn't even remember now, and he had let out a little noise of pleasure, so soft I'd wondered if I'd imagined it. Mathias himself certainly hadn't seemed to notice.

But there was a big difference between a suspicion and a truth, and it hadn't been until I'd had the chance to sink my teeth and nails into my boy that I'd proven my theory correct. Mat came alive under pain – not as much as what Lago craved, and he still seemed to enjoy protesting against being hurt, but it was an absolute delight to watch. And *feel*.

Now, Mat shuddered in my arms, his breathing ragged.

"Still bored, my difficult Temarian," I purred, "or would you like to wind me up some more?"

I pulled back slightly, and then as he started to speak, reapplied the pressure on his arm. He was louder in his shout this time, more affected, even though

I hadn't pushed him any further than before. It would have just felt like it as a result of the growing soreness in his muscles.

"Fuck," Mathias gasped, his lips scraping against the plaster as I held him in place against the wall. "You've proven your point, Ren."

I laughed in his ear.

"This isn't a point. This is me making you submit, just like you told me to." I licked the back of his neck before playfully biting into it. He shivered. "And you? Are you enjoying yourself, *mi amor?*"

I thrust against his hip, pressing him further into the wall and grinding his cock hard against it. Mat gifted me with a pained whimper.

"What was that?"

"Yes," he reluctantly admitted on a strangled breath. My lover simply hated agreeing with me about anything, even his own pleasure.

"Good." I let go of him. "Because you have a lot of entirely illegal assaulting of a royal prince to make up for."

"As do you," he grumbled, rotating out his shoulder.

"Tell you what, just because I'm nice," I offered, dropping my voice, "we'll punish *you* for both transgressions. How does that sound?"

Far too many delectable ideas for such punishment ran through my head, quickening my pulse, but I smothered them all when Mathias sucked in a quick breath.

"Or not," I said quickly, worrying I'd gone too far. "We can play nicely, if you'd prefer."

But when he turned around to face me, I found his eyes were blazing with excitement at the idea.

"You don't have to be gentle with me, Ren," Mathias murmured, looking up at me from under his delicate eyelashes with an expression that practically *smouldered.* "Not if you don't want to."

I considered him. Gentle would be safer, at least until I knew I could trust him in bed again, but fuck, I was impatient. This gorgeous man made me want to throw *safe* out of the window, common sense and responsibility be damned.

"Are you sure?" I asked, knowing I was being an idiot to even consider letting him do this, but also having the self-control of a fucking tsunami in the face of such temptation. Mat nodded, that sultry *come-fuck-me* look still on his damn face.

I clicked my tongue. "And my brat has learned the importance of his safe word, and will fucking *use it* if he feels at all uncomfortable?"

Mat's expression dropped into a scowl. "*Yes,*" he said petulantly, and then winced, as if realising how pathetic he'd sounded. He cleared his throat. "I will."

I smiled. "Good. Then beg me for it."

He stared at me, delightful pink flooding his porcelain cheeks at the suggestion. "Uh..."

"Eloquent as always, Nathanael."

Riling him was too easy. His jaw clenched, and that obstinate defiance of his flashed back into his gaze.

"Fuck you—"

I backhanded him across the face. He was surprised enough that I managed to make him stagger back into the wall.

Mathias rounded on me with a snarl, his fists rising. I cocked my head, enjoying the way my hand tingled from the impact and how his normally pale cheek was already blooming with colour.

"I told you to *beg*, Velichkov, and 'fuck you' does not sound like begging to me," I said, keeping my tone mild. "Want to try again?"

Mat's lips curled into a smile, and he dropped his hands. "I see you took *don't be gentle* as *be twice the asshole you usually are*," he accused. "Not that I thought it was possible with you, prince."

"If you think this is mean, wait until I get my hands on you," I said idly, examining my nails. "I plan to take every act of insubordination out on your flesh."

He bared his teeth at me in a wild grin. "You'll have to catch me first."

I laughed in delight as he lunged to the side, my fingers grazing his arm but unable to gain leverage on his bare skin. He dived around the back of my desk, his eyes darkening with lust.

"Mathias," I breathed fondly, a thrill racing through me. "You really know the way to my heart, don't you?"

"It's not your heart I'm aiming to win tonight," he shot back suggestively, biting down on his lip and directing a pointed look at my crotch.

A growl burst from my throat, unbidden, and I stalked closer to him. Fuck, this man was something else. He set every nerve ending alight even when we weren't touching, and the mere thought of him could send me breathless.

My heart pumped faster in anticipation of the chase as I drew close, and Mathias gave me a cocky grin, ensuring to keep the desk between us as I rounded it. I feinted left and then darted around to the right, rewarded by his surprised grunt and the brush of his elbow under my fingertips. But the bastard was quick, ducking beneath the desk and out the other side in a surprisingly graceful move, and my hands slammed down onto the wood a moment too late.

Mat shot me a teasing grin as he backed away, circling around the end of the four-poster bed.

"I guess if you're not really trying, Aratorre, you clearly don't want me that badly," he taunted. "Shall I leave?"

This one really had no sense of self-preservation, because when I got my hands on him, he was *fucked*.

I wet my lips. "Do you know wh...?"

The sentence was nonsense, designed to keep him listening instead of fleeing, and sure enough, his reactions were a split second too slow when I lunged for him instead. Mathias made it onto my bed and had half-rolled off the other side when I caught his leg, but *half* wasn't good enough.

I grinned as I dragged him backwards by the ankle, his clawing hands pulling most of the blankets with him, and I let my full weight fall onto his back to pin him in place.

Got you.

*

Chapter Forty-Four

Mat

"Stay *still*," the prince snarled from above me, and I obeyed that as well as I followed any of his orders, which was to say, not at fucking all. He made a cute noise of irritation as I wriggled out of the hold he'd attempted to put me in, and then proceeded to strangle me with a blanket. We fought desperately as we each tried to get the other underneath us, a tangle of limbs and warm skin and Ren's long hair, strands of which seemed to get in my eyes and mouth no matter our position.

We were evenly matched in size, although I was being careful not to hurt him. Ren had no such compunctions.

He scratched and he bit, his grip on my arms and hips much firmer than mine on his, enough that I knew he'd leave me with bruises. I didn't bother pointing that out. The fucker knew perfectly well what he was doing, and every time I cried out when he sank yet another part of his body into mine – his teeth or nails into my skin, his fist into my stomach, or once, when I was starting to get the upper hand, his fingers hooked around the side of my mouth – he gave a small, approving growl, clearly getting off on it all.

And I had to admit that I was too. Grappling naked with someone as effortlessly attractive as Ren was more than a little distracting, and he took every opportunity to feel me up while trying to dominate me. He was an enterprising multi-tasker, I'd give him that, but his efforts made him an easy target and I soon managed to force the prince down beneath me, my forearm pressed to his chest and my other hand fisted in his hair to keep him in place. We stared at each other, panting heavily and fighting to catch our breath.

Ren rubbed himself against my eager cock, and I loosened my grip on his hair as a shiver ran through me.

"You like that?" Ren purred, falling still where he was trapped underneath me. "You win. Just tell me what you want, my prince. I'll be *ever* so good for you."

His voice had gone meek, subservient, and I smirked at him as he slid his hand down between my legs in a clear effort to please me, only to freeze as his fingers instead closed in a vice grip around my balls. *"Idiota.* Will you ever learn?"

I groaned and dropped my forehead to his chest. *"Ty gryaznyy grebanyy moshennik."*

"I am indeed a filthy fucking cheat," he confirmed happily, humming with pleasure as he tightened his hold. "Emphasis on *filthy*."

Testing his resolve, I tried to pull away, but he simply tsked and squeezed harder. I winced at both the pain and the threat, and finally fell still, my heart pounding with exhilaration. I didn't know why this was so fucking hot, but a glance downwards told me we were both getting off on this.

It made no sense. I shouldn't be aroused by Ren's rough handling of me, his casual cruelty, the way he forced my submission…but *shouldn't* had nothing to do with the way my cock twitched, leaking pre-cum over his stomach and ever so clearly fucking *here for this*.

"Now, Mathias, you're going to be utterly compliant and faultlessly obedient for me," Ren added sweetly, and I gave him a look that told him exactly how much I wasn't going to be doing that.

The one he shot back said *oh, I know.*

He lifted his head and pressed his lips to mine, gentle and soft. I savoured it, because I had a feeling I wouldn't be receiving any such tenderness in a moment's time, and sure enough, when he pulled back, his fingernails sank deep into the soft flesh of my balls.

Ren grinned as I yelped, tucking his free hand under his head as if he planned to settle in for the night and keep me in this Blessedly painful position. "I believe you owe me something?"

"*Fine,* you sadistic bastard," I breathed, although I couldn't stop my own smile. There was something about him that made me almost drunkenly happy, my mood latching onto his and flying high. "Use me as you wish."

As he smirked, I added, "but this time, you let me touch you."

"You could have been touching me when we fought," Ren pointed out, dropping his chin and shamelessly running his eyes down my body. I squirmed under his gaze, and he raised an eyebrow as he tightened his grip and forced me to still. "Instead, you went and squandered the opportunity on trying to *win*."

He said it like I'd never had any chance of beating him. Perhaps, knowing him, I hadn't.

I licked dry lips. "Still."

"Naww, you want to take care of me, *mi sol*?"

"I do," I said, my breath coming out in fast pants. I drank him in beneath me, wishing I could move against him for the friction I so desperately craved. "I insist on it."

"Words like 'insist' won't get you anywhere," Ren chided, lifting his head to free his hand so he could smack my ass, and then punishing me for my resulting flinch by ruthlessly digging his nails deeper into my balls.

"Ow! Fuck, Ren! You're going to tear them off!"

"Better speak quickly, then," he suggested, his eyes sparkling with mischief.

"I'd like to take care of you," I pleaded. "Please, Ren. I need to. Will you let me?"

Then I scowled when I caught sight of his expression. "Oh for...why are you looking so smug? Is it the fucking begging?"

"It's the fucking begging," Ren confirmed with a cruel smirk, writhing beneath me but thankfully, finally, *mercifully* letting go. "Having the proud and indomitable third prince of Temar say *please* clearly does it for me. Do it again."

"No." I glowered at him and rocked backwards to keep my bruised and tormented balls out of his reach. "It was a second of weakness."

"Actually it was a carefully cultivated two months, but whatever."

"What?"

"Nothing," Ren said innocently. I wasn't fooled.

"Out with it, Aratorre," I growled.

"You want to get me off?" he asked, a grin broadening on his face that I didn't trust one bit to be as honest as it seemed. "You *need* to?"

"I didn't say get you off. I said take care of you." I shot him a nasty look. "Read into that what you will."

Yet Ren's overly-pleased expression didn't falter. "All I'm hearing is how desperate you are for me."

Oh, the bastard. I'd thought him a generous lover with the way he seemed content to bring me to climax as often as he could get his hands on me without asking me to reciprocate…fuck, without *letting* me reciprocate. But it seemed I'd confused 'generous' with 'sly and utterly underhanded' in what was such a Ren move, I was surprised I hadn't seen it coming from a mile away.

Giving me pleasure over and over without taking it from me, keeping my hands and mouth off him for weeks, because he knew I would eventually insist on returning the status quo? Or rather, that I would *beg for it?*

"Yes," the prince crooned with undisguised glee, apparently reading my face. "With your concern for equality, I knew all it would take to break you was to expose you to some injustice…and set you loose upon it. Dios, you're adorable."

He put his hands on my chest and lightly pushed. I reared back off his hips, letting him up, and he pulled me to my feet beside the bed before setting his mouth to mine. The kiss was raw and wild, our banter clearly not having taken the edge off his arousal, and the prince moaned into my mouth as his tongue explored mine with a fervent, frenzied energy as if this was his last night on the continent. His hard length brushed against mine, and we swallowed down each other's gasps.

And then Ren pulled back, his lips wet and swollen and his eyes glittering.

Fuck, he made for one hell of a sight.

He swayed backward as I tried to chase his mouth with mine and instead offered me a teasing smirk, shaking his head.

"Get down on your knees."

"Why?" I asked, stupidly, my brain not having caught up.

Ren's smile became wolfish. "Because tonight, Nathanael Velichkov, you're going to learn how to suck cock."

His voice was a rough growl, an octave lower than usual, and I shuddered at the thick flush of heat that passed through me at the filthy words.

Ren only used my full name when he was feeling particularly cruel, and there was a dark gleam in his brown eyes. And yet, when he snaked a hand onto my shoulder and pressed down sharply to send me to the floor, I let him.

He let out a keening sound at that, a noise of wantonness and raw need.

The prince's hand moved from my shoulder to my face as I knelt before him, tracing my cheek, my jaw, the seam of my lips. He dug two of his fingers into the latter, prying my mouth open and pushing them deeper. He tasted of spice and citrus. Of Ren.

"We both know your teeth are sharp, wildcat," he murmured. "But let's keep that for another time, hmm?"

I made sure to catch and hold his eye before deliberately biting down on the fingers that were in my mouth. Ren sucked in a breath but didn't pull away.

"Oh," he groaned, stroking my tongue with his fingertips even as I increased the pressure. "You're going to be the most dangerous thing I've ever stuck my cock into, aren't you? To risk your teeth would be terribly foolish, and yet I find myself unable to resist. You've got me all tangled up in knots, Mathias."

Same, I thought. Why else would I be kneeling for him for like this? What else could explain why I had pulled my teeth from his fingers and started sucking on them instead, wanting to please him, to see him come apart for me?

At Ren's soft moan, I bobbed my head forward to take more of the two fingers I had claimed as my own, my mouth closing over his rings. My tongue explored their chamfered edges, and I licked playfully at the webbing between his fingers.

"Fuck, Mat!"

The prince's breathing was ragged, his eyes lidded, and I absolutely adored how I could have such an effect on him. Arrogant, cocky Ren, barely able to stand.

It was intoxicating.

He gasped as I sucked harder. "I need...I need to get my cock in that delectable mouth of yours before I come from this alone. Down, boy."

Ren's other hand shot out to hold my shoulder as he tried to ease his fingers from my mouth. I growled around them, letting him know I wasn't done, but he moved his grip to my throat to force me to release them. He didn't let go when I did, his thumb pressing against my windpipe to cause my breathing to be as strangled as his.

"I should have known that with a tongue that vicious, it would be talented in more ways than one," the prince purred, not taking his eyes from me.

I just snapped my teeth at him.

That earned me a hard slap across the face, Ren letting go of my neck as he hit me. I fell to my hands, snarling curses at him even as I flushed with heat and want, but he took hold of a fistful of my hair and hauled me back up against him. I froze as my burning cheek came to rest within an inch of his erect cock.

It looked…absolutely fucking *huge* this close, thick veins running up the length of it to where beads of pre-cum rested at its tip.

Ren lifted his right hand to inspect my teeth marks.

"*Mierda*," he said on a breathless groan that was almost obscene. "Please tell me you won't actually bite me, Mat."

I didn't answer. I was too busy staring at his cock, and wondering how I was supposed to do this if my mouth was impossibly dry and swallowing suddenly seemed so difficult? Sucking on fingers was one thing. Zovisasha liked it when I did that for her, although her delicate fingers hadn't been anything like the demanding ones of the prince. I knew how to eat out a woman.

But I'd certainly never had my mouth so close to one of *these*. How the fuck was it even supposed to fit? How did Ren do it?

The prince turned towards the bed, stopped, turned back, and then twisted around again. Each movement tugged hard at my hair.

"I see His Highness is being appropriately decisive this evening," I offered, trying to keep my tone casual and utterly failing.

"It's your first time," Ren said, falling still. "I've decided I won't tie your hands."

A shiver ran through me. I was so messed up, but it was hard to care when I was aching so hard for him, for *this,* that all sense seemed to have left me.

"*¿Estás bien, mi amor?*"

I started, glancing up at Ren, who was watching me carefully with an almost tender look to his expression. He grazed his knuckles over my cheek.

"I'm alright," I confirmed in answer to his question, and dropped my attention back to his leaking cock.

I tried to remember how Lilia and Zovisasha had blown me, but I hadn't exactly been taking notes at the time. I'd never expected to ever be in a position where I was doing it myself. And the prince was so fucking talented at it: what if I disappointed him?

Scratch that. I *would* disappoint him. Why had I asked for this? I had no clue what I was doing, and he was so…*experienced.* All I wanted was to show him what he meant to me, but when he realised how terrible I was at pleasuring him, he'd move on to someone else, and then I'd lose him, lose his arms around me when we slept, his laughter and his teasing and…

Oh, fuck.

"Watching you plan it all out is really quite something, Nat," Ren said with a laugh.

I wet my lips. "It's complicated."

"No," he said. "It's really not." And then he tightened his grip on my hair and shoved my head down, forcing himself between my lips.

Fuck, Ren! I'd planned on…I didn't know, licking it first? Taking it slow? Teasing him like he had me?

But I should have known that Ren wouldn't relinquish control so easily, and my hands flew to his thighs as he drove himself deep.

*

Chapter Forty-Five

Ren

How was it that the more I had of him, the more I wanted? Mathias was so fucking *satisfying*; water after a drought, the sun on an overcast day, a cool breeze in the summer heat.

And yet I knew I'd never be content with what I had. I wanted every square inch of him, to hold him close enough that no one else could ever get to him, to crawl inside his damn skin if I could, just so I could keep him safe and close and with *me*.

And oh fuck, his tight, hot mouth was something else. My cock had found a home it never wanted to leave, a perfect haven where it was cherished and cared for and Dios-damned *worshipped* by the man on his knees before me.

Camila, bless her thoughtful little soul, had cut Mat's hair just enough for me to still be able to take hold of it, and now I left my hand fisted in his hair so he could tie his disobedience to his lust for pain. And as I'd expected, he was pulling hard against my grip, but not to get away.

He glanced up at me, and the sight of those beautiful eyes of his as his mouth took my length made my legs weak. I fought to stay upright, worried I was going to embarrass myself by coming too soon, but by the Blessed, he was making it hard to hold on.

I smoothed out the frown lines I found on his forehead. "Relax your throat, Mat," I encouraged, my voice ragged. "Breathe through your nose. And for fuck's sake, stop overthinking this."

But of course he was. My uptight northerner couldn't just *enjoy* himself.

That just meant I'd have to take away his ability to think entirely.

I pulled back and thrust again, amused when his shoulders heaved as he struggled to take me. And when he finally followed my advice and relaxed, I watched his expression soften as the movements suddenly made more sense for him. I groaned as it let me go deeper, sinking my cock into that wet and eager mouth that despite his earlier threats, offered not even a graze of teeth.

I'd had people kneeling for me before. Men and women, so delightfully submissive, willing to obey my every command and desire.

That was not Mat. I couldn't imagine that he'd *ever* be docile and demure for me. Yet from the aroused state of him, he clearly enjoyed going to his knees as much as I liked seeing him on them: I just had to put him there. And the work it took to do so – be it emotional manipulation or physical force – made it a hundred times more exhilarating.

Wrestling for dominance on the bed, feeling him writhe and buck against me as we tested his strength against mine, had awoken a primal desire I'd never had the chance to explore before. I'd been rough with many of my other partners, but they never dared to fight back like Mat did. And by Dios, I adored it, being able to bring him to heel with my own body…and maybe a few sneaky tricks when that hadn't entirely worked out. The sense of triumph I felt as I now thrust between his lips, claiming my fucking prize with my handprint blazed across his cheek and his eyes bright, made this the best head I'd ever received.

I felt the muscles of his throat contract as he swallowed against me, loving how tight he felt.

But after a few minutes of letting me fuck his face like I'd fantasied about so often, my eyes closing from the sheer pleasure of feeling him around me, Mathias unexpectedly reached up and tapped my leg. Three times.

I pulled back instantly, easing myself out of his mouth and peering down at him in concern. Had I hurt him? Was it too much? Did he hate doing it?

Shit. I've messed up.

"Mathias?"

He nodded, almost as if to himself, and then caught my eye. "Sorry," he muttered with a rueful grin. "I just needed to know."

And then he lunged forward, pulling against my hold on his hair as he swallowed my length again, and I understood.

He hadn't tapped out because he couldn't take it, but rather to prove to himself that he still had control, unlike what had happened with my father. That it wasn't that he *had* to do this, but that he *wanted* to, and all my remaining doubts about whether he could be trusted to play with me fell away.

I blinked as Mat slapped aside the hand I'd knotted through his hair. Surprised, I didn't immediately return it to its rightful position, although it was awfully tempting to grab the brat and drive myself right to the back of his throat, bringing tears to his eyes that I could enjoy kissing away later.

But all thoughts of putting him back in his place disappeared as Mat brought his hands up to join his mouth in lavishing attention on my cock, and I groaned as he wrapped his fingers around the base of my length and brought his mouth down deep.

He was messy and completely without skill. His lips glistened wetly with saliva, and he was making obscene noises as he licked and sucked, his enthusiasm more than making up for his lack of experience.

I fucking loved it.

Groaning, I grabbed hold of the bed post to steady myself, and murmured heartfelt words about how amazing he felt. Mathias let out a soft noise of contentment.

And then I looked at that pretty mouth of his, the one that was capable of such deceit. I'd thought it fuckable the first time I'd laid eyes on him and as usual, I'd been unequivocally correct. The way his lips wrapped around my cock and how his tongue explored me without hesitation? It was divine. The man was painfully shy at times, but when pushed beyond the limits of what he'd otherwise have set for himself, it seemed he truly shone.

I'd never made Mat do anything in bed before other than to let me take care of him, partially to avoid freaking him out while I got him used to the idea of being with another man. But the other reason, the other glorious reason, was now I knew I'd gotten my lover over the line, I was going to do everything I could to keep him on its edge. I adored tormenting Mathias, exploring his boundaries and bringing out a side to him that I suspected no one else had ever seen before.

"Stroke yourself," I ordered, and Mathias flushed so furiously that I was surprised there was any blood left in the rest of his body at all.

He mumbled something around me that was probably *"no thanks"*, or *"I can't"*, or something equally and ridiculously stubborn.

"You damn well can," I said, injecting a growl into my tone to let him know I wasn't fucking around. "And you will."

A WHISPER AND A BREATH

I couldn't reach him from where I was standing, but I wasn't going to let his beautiful cock go untouched. And if I couldn't take care of what was mine, I'd make sure he did.

Mat blushed harder, but he dropped one of his hands. I let out a heavy breath as I watched him wrap pale fingers around himself and give a tentative tug.

"Faster," I commanded, and although I'd only meant his hand, he sped up his mouth too, until forming words became the most difficult task I'd ever attempted. Watching him jerk himself off as he continued to suck and lick at me was pure Blessed ecstasy, and I almost missed the tell-tale signs of Mat getting close – that haziness in his eyes, the slight arching of his back.

"*No*, Nathanael," I whispered. "You don't get to come until I say so."

He frowned around me, but let go of himself.

I tsked in disapproval. "Did I say stop? You will continue to work that glorious cock of yours, but you'll not come without permission."

I let myself enjoy the flash of panic and frustration that passed across his expression and reached up to gently tousle his hair as he took himself back in hand and stroked slowly, his whole body quivering.

"I know. I'm mean."

Mathias growled out his agreement, the noise muffled through his mouthful, and the vibration made me pant. I wanted him to do it again.

"Do you know how gorgeously sexy you are?" I said breathlessly. I wished he could see himself at my feet like this. Maybe I'd have mirrors installed in the room so he could watch us from every angle. "Kneeling for me, taking my cock down your throat like a good boy?"

Mat closed his eyes, moaning around my length. His eyelashes fluttered.

"Will you swallow?"

His eyes shot open again, wide but not alarmed.

"I want to be inside you, Mathias, deep inside," I murmured, stroking his throat and feeling him shiver beneath my touch. "Please say you will."

He looked up, a pleading expression on his face as his hand sped up once again.

"Yes, *mi sol*. You've earned it," I said, and his mouth clamped down tighter around my cock as I allowed him to come, drops of warmth splashing onto my bare leg. His throat worked to take more of me, and watching him struggle sent lines of bliss through my veins, pulling my balls up tight.

In a split-second decision, I pulled out, coming over his face instead of in his mouth. I didn't have time to warn him so he could make the choice himself, and while I'd asked if he would swallow, he hadn't been able to answer. Despite his inexpertise, his besotted expression made it difficult to remember that this was new to him.

But fuck, this was almost as good. His eyes drifted closed again as I marked his face, lines of cum catching on his eyelashes and cheeks. I cried out my pleasure, the sight of him wrenching every last drop from me, and as Mat's tongue shot out to lick his lips clean, I choked, leaning a hand on his shoulder to steady myself.

Dios mio, this man was going to be the death of me.

*

Chapter Forty-Six

Mat

Ren was curled around me like a cat, one knee tucked behind mine while his other leg rested heavily on my thigh. He held me tightly, murmuring compliments into the back of my neck while I tried to fight my smile. He was always so *clingy* in the morning, something I'd never expected from a man who'd seemingly had as many lovers as I'd had breakfasts, and it gave me a little thrill each time I considered the possibility that he wasn't normally like this.

That it was something special, just for us.

He sighed happily, peppering my bare shoulder with indulgent kisses, and then rolled onto his back. I took the opportunity to reach out and smack him in the stomach with the back of my hand.

Ren let out a grunting, pained gasp, far too dramatic considering how lightly I'd tapped him, and brought his knees up to his chest to protect himself. "What the fuck was that for?"

"You know perfectly well what," I said, pressing my fingers to my cheek where the sting of his blows had admittedly long since faded, but Ren's shit-eating grin didn't hold even an ounce of remorse.

"You love it when I'm rough with you," the prince declared as he laid his hand over mine, and I didn't contradict him. I didn't need to: we both knew I wouldn't have put up with half the shit he'd pulled on me last night if I didn't.

Then he yawned and stretched, his face suddenly sombre. "I should get dressed before Camila arrives if I'm going to keep up the pretence for Moreno."

I reached for my discarded trousers. Ren might enjoy parading around naked when he wasn't feigning an injury, but if the bedchamber doors were going to be opening, I was not lying here unclothed.

"You're a prince," said Ren a little sadly. "Feel free to dress like one."

He waved a hand at his wardrobe as he pulled on his own clothes. When he caught me watching, he slowed his movements, giving me a reverse strip tease. I'd never known anyone who could make covering up sexy, but Renato Aratorre somehow achieved it with ease.

"If you're offering me those ridiculous boots of yours, I'd rather go barefoot," I finally managed to choke out as he finished pulling on his coat with tantalising seduction, "because I-"

"Will throw them out of the window? I got that."

I shot him a sly look. "Nah. You converted me. I like them now."

"So you'll wear them?" the prince asked with a laugh. "I'm having trouble imagining my grumpy Temarian in something so pretentious."

I shuddered. "No. I want you to wear them. Tonight." I headed towards the wardrobe, pausing only to whisper in his ear. "*And nothing else.*"

The hungry look that brought to his face sustained me while I picked through his outrageous outfits, eventually settling on the plainest cream shirt I could find. I'd been hoping for grey or black trousers, but everything seemed to be in *colour,* and cobalt blue was the least offensive of them. I knew I'd seen Ren in simpler clothing in the past, but wherever it was stored, it wasn't in this wardrobe, which seemed designed solely to give me a headache.

At least when it came to choosing my own clothes, although I'd found several ostentatious items that were so utterly Ren that I looked forward to seeing him in them.

And out of them.

"Very well, *mi cielo,*" purred Ren, slipping behind me and taking hold of my hips so he could tug me back against him. He ground his hard length against me, and palmed my cock through my new trousers as if to assure himself that our suffering was mutual. I tried and failed to hold back my groan. "As long as you remember that you're still due for punishment. Don't think you can distract me with that delectable mouth of yours for a second night in a row."

I grinned.

Challenge accepted.

—

Starling sank into a deep curtsey as she opened the surgery door for me, her head bowed and her skirts spread so wide in her hands that I could see daylight between the folds, the hidden feature of the dress that wasn't actually a dress at all.

"Oh, fuck off," I said by way of greeting, and she straightened with her face screwed up in silent laughter.

"I see why you didn't tell me," the healer chuckled, before I could apologise for not doing so. "I'd be embarrassed too."

"For being Temarian?"

"For being a fucking prince, you asshole," she said, flicking her fingers at me dismissively. "And there I was, thinking you were actually a decent person."

I snorted. "Hello to you too, Star."

"Do you have a crown?" She poured water into two chipped glasses and handed one to me.

"No."

"A shame," Starling said. "I've always wanted to smack a prince around the head with his own crown."

"I'll steal you one of Ren's and you can go wild," I offered, and the healer shot me a mischievous grin.

"I'm sorry I didn't..." I trailed off helplessly, biting my lip and feeling like a shit friend.

"We all have secrets," Starling said, her tone lightly casual. Surprisingly, she didn't sound bothered that I'd been lying to her since we first met.

"It's just that I couldn't tell *anyone*."

"That's generally how a secret works, yeah," she teased. And then her shoulders sagged, and she put her glass down before wrapping her arms around herself. "But *la Cortina* has a way of dragging them out into the light regardless. Poor Elías."

I set my own glass on one of the tables before pulling her close to me. We held each other tight, seeking something that wasn't the blood and betrayal that seemed to perpetually infect the palace.

"Did you know about him? Before, I mean?"

Starling nodded, stepping back and brushing down my shoulders as if worried she'd gotten dirt on Ren's fancy-ass clothes. I didn't give a shit if she had, but they *were* admittedly very soft, and it was nice to wear something that fitted me for once.

"He never told me, but he didn't have to. The bodies of everyone I treat are laid bare to me as soon as I Touch them, and I've healed everyone here at least once. I could tell you who has the hairiest chest, the weakest heart, the biggest cock – and it's not your precious prince," she added with a smirk, and I snorted.

"It felt plenty big last night."

Star exploded with spluttering laughter, smacking me on the chest as my cheeks warmed. "Oh, you filthy thing. You look so innocent, but you're really not, are you?"

I let out a breath. "You're not going to chastise me again? Warn me away from him?"

"I don't get it," Starling admitted carefully, tucking a stray lock of frizzy hair behind her ear. It immediately sprang free again. "But everyone has their own thing, and if His Craziness is yours, then..." She spread her arms, screwing up her face as she spoke. The words were clearly reluctant ones. "I can be happy for you. And I'll never be the prince's biggest fan, but if you believe he's for real, then I'm willing to give him the benefit of the doubt. For your sake only."

I eyed her, amused.

"But if the prick breaks your heart, I'll return those stripes I took from his back. All of them. *At once.*"

The threat, delivered by the tiny, fierce girl before me, made me smile. "*Gracias*, Star."

She hmphed. "Just don't let him take advantage of you, kay?"

"I don't think he'd let me let him," I said. "He's taken to asking permission six times before he even touches me."

Starling made an approving noise.

"It ruins the mood," I complained, and she smacked me again, this time on the arm.

"Consent is nothing to whinge about," the healer chided. "Besides, His Viciousness *should* come with a warning label." Starling gave me a wicked grin, showing crooked teeth. "I'd be happy to tie it tight around his neck for him."

I bit back a chuckle.

"With a bell," she added thoughtfully. "So you always hear him coming."

I couldn't stop my laughter that time.

*

Chapter Forty-Seven

Ren

I was bored. Never mind that I had a thousand things I should and could be doing: Mat wasn't with me – he was at his daily catch up with that annoying healer friend of his because I was too fucking soft – so I was bored. Everything seemed grey and lifeless when he wasn't there to share it with.

Thief. He'd stolen my crown, my heart, and now all the damn colour from the world.

"Your Highness?"

"No," I told the voice, my arm draped over my eyes while I in turn was draped myself over one of the lounges in the second ballroom. "Whatever it is, it's not going to help."

"My prince, we were supposed to be discussing the colour scheme for the next Solstice?"

I sighed. "That's half a year away." The previous one had been a dull affair in any event. I'd been forced to dance with various courtiers and nobles, unable to take the one person into my arms whom I had *wanted* to spend time with. Mathias had sulked in Jiron's shadow the whole night, glowering at anyone who dared to approach their corner of the hall.

"Good preparation cannot be understated-"

"How do you know when you're in love?" I asked, interrupting whoever it was at my side. I'd probably greeted him and held half a fucking conversation with him before flinging myself dramatically onto the lounge became the more appealing option, but I was damned if I could remember who he was.

"Uh, love, sire?"

"Yes," I snapped. "Stop talking shades of burgundy and tell me the difference between love and lust."

There was a long silence.

"Well, I've never been in love, my prince, so I can't-"

"Get out," I said, waving my free hand and continuing to wave it until I heard my guest shuffle away.

Useless. They were all useless.

I wondered if I should ask Alta. Just because she didn't feel sexual attraction didn't mean she hadn't ever been romantically attracted to anyone, although I was sure she would have mentioned it to me before now if she had.

I opened my mouth to order that new guard bring Al to me, and then remembered she'd left the palace two days ago with her father for another of their *trips*. As much as I enjoyed Moreno being out of my hair for a while, it came at the cost of Alta's absence, and it didn't get rid of my father, who, to my *absolute fucking delight*, had remained at *la Cortina* while he waited for Queen Zora Velichkova's reply to Mat's ransom. I wish I knew what he'd demanded for *mi gato montés*, but it seemed he'd meant it when he said he was taking over the negotiations.

A twinge of guilt hit me as I thought of mine and Alta's last conversation before she'd left. Her wide eyes and soft voice as she enquired once again if I'd yet spoken to my father about setting a date for our wedding. She had been asking me that each time the king had visited *la Cortina*, and each time, I gave her the pathetic excuse that I hadn't had the opportunity to do so. Because fuck, I'd promised her that I would, that day out on the terrace. The same day that Mathias had almost died down in the cells and I'd brought him into my life to keep my political interests safe, only for him to weasel his deceitful little self into my heart and settle there, contented, like a cat with its belly full of cream.

But this time, my father was still around. I could have gone to him that very minute and demanded he marry me and Al, and yet the silence stretched awkwardly between us when I didn't make the offer to do so. Alta had given a huge sigh, wearing such a disappointed expression that I couldn't look at her, and I felt like an incredibly poor friend. She needed our marriage for protection from Moreno, and I'd always been fully on board with that plan.

But now...if I saved Altagracia, I lost Mathias. For I could easily imagine how he'd react if I invited him to be my piece on the side to fill the sexual hole in my marriage: with a rude gesture, a sneer, and a cold bed.

And oh fuck, I'd give anything to keep him, to repeat the past week and a half over and over again. Feeling him relax as he fell asleep in my arms. Often waking up in his. Watching him dress in my clothes, and peeling them off him at the end of each day. Making him go down on me in the bath, not bothering to lift my hips so he had to do it in bursts, ducking below the surface of the water and emerging a minute later, choking and spluttering, which I'd found both amusing and downright fucking arousing. I'd taught him how I liked to be stroked, what rhythm and firmness worked best, and he'd spent a long time exploring my body with a thoughtful expression that turned pleased when he found a spot that made me laugh or buck against his hands with breathless moans.

"I've found that love is when everything makes sense in her company," Clementina said softly. "I mean...*his*, Your Highness."

I cracked an eye, lifting my arm just high enough to bring my herald into view. She wasn't looking at me, but was rather gazing down at the far end of the ballroom, where I knew Camila was helping to replace the window drapes.

Did things make sense with Mathias?

In a way.

And in many others, he just made things more confusing, more chaotic. More exciting: a heart-pounding, exhilarating thrill that made me enjoy my life for the first time in a long time.

Oh, yeah. I was fucked.

*

Chapter Forty-Eight

Mat

The prince wandered over to where I was sitting in my armchair, plucked the book I was reading out of my hands without a word of warning, and replaced it with a hairbrush. Then he slid down to the floor to sit between my legs, his back to me and his pose expectant.

I gave a surprised laugh but obediently began to brush his hair, drawing the bristles through the thick locks. Ren laid a red ribbon across the page of my book to mark it, being fucking considerate for once in his damn life, and moved to put it aside.

"Read to me?" I asked.

"Read to you?"

"It's hard reading for pleasure in Quarehian," I admitted, carefully combing out a knot. My time in *la Cortina* had improved my grasp of the language, but it was still exhausting to have to work through so many foreign words on a page.

The prince opened the book and obligingly started reading. He was only two sentences in when the story took a distinct turn from the dry reflection on class warfare I had understood it as, with the main characters — three elderly servants who had previously been waxing lyrical about the hardships of life — starting to eagerly fuck in a variety of inventive ways.

"Funny how the first ten pages had no sex at all, and now it's devolved into nothing but orgies," I said, when this had continued for quite some time.

"You were reading it wrong," Ren remarked without pausing for breath, and then proceeded to read aloud a paragraph that graphically detailed the large tits of a character he'd evidently made up to progress his…uh, *plot*.

Enjoying the warmth of him between my thighs, I laid the brush aside, playing absently with his hair as I listened to his melodic voice detailing various acts of increasing obscenity. I'd separated it into three and started plaiting the soft strands before I realised what I was doing, my fingers falling easily into the familiar pattern. But it wasn't Astrid's blonde locks in my hands now, or Lilia's gorgeous red mane: Ren's dark hair wrapped around my fingers, his head resting heavily against my knee, evoked a sensation of not just fondness but an aching hardness between my legs that the prince couldn't fail to notice in his position.

I cleared my throat, shifting in my seat to try to ease the pressure, but Ren just leaned his shoulders back against me more firmly to keep me still.

Fuck. He played this game far too well, but I refused to be the first to give in.

I focused on the strands of hair in my hands, not saying a word.

When I reached the end of the braid, my cock hard and wanting, the prince handed me the ribbon he'd used as a bookmark without looking up from the page. The silk slithered through his fingers into mine.

I'd been intending to tie off his hair, but I paused, remembering something I'd Seen a couple of days ago. It had just been a flash, an image of *moy knyaz* lying on his back on the bed with my hands around his neck, and at first I had been horrified, hating that my Sight was still favouring visions of us killing each other.

But after hours of rumination, I kept coming back to the look that had been in Ren's eyes as vision-me squeezed tighter.

Not fear.

Something much more intoxicating.

Curious, I lay the ribbon across the smooth line of Ren's neck and pulled it tight. The prince's head was forced back into my lap, and the book fell from his suddenly limp hands. I stared down at him, at his bared throat crossed with the red slash of the ribbon, and his lidded, hazy gaze.

Ren's eyes closed, his lips parting, and from my position looking down at him, I could see *exactly* what I was doing to the rest of him.

"Fuck," I breathed, revelling in the ecstatic expression on my *dorogoi's* face. "You really like that."

I loosened my grip and the prince's eyes shot open as he heaved in a breath. His fingers curled around my ankles, holding us both in place.

"Why did you never say anything?" I asked quietly. "We could have…"

Ren swallowed and wet his lips. "I've never-"

Whatever he'd been about to say was chased away by a firm knock on the door. As the prince cleared his throat and bade entrance, I tied the ribbon off around the back of his neck. Loose enough for him to breathe, but tight enough to remind him that it was there with every such breath, taut against the muscles of his throat. From the way Ren stiffened between my legs, his nails digging painfully into the top of my bare feet, he was enjoying that. A lot.

"Ademar," he said curtly as the man entered.

"My prince. I've been advised the king is looking for you."

Ren groaned, pressing his face into my knee as if not being able to see the guard meant the problem he'd brought with him would miraculously disappear.

"Have you checked the terrace?" I suggested to Ad. "His Highness sometimes takes his meals there."

"Or the stables," the prince added, his voice muffled by the fabric. "I believe Mathias had something he wished to collect from Galo."

Ademar glanced between us, frowning, and then shrugged and bowed. "Very good. I will advise His Majesty's guards to check those places next."

"Do that," Ren said, his voice soft as he lifted his head. "And then come back here. It's…time."

Ad's eyes flickered to mine, and he squared his shoulders before nodding sharply and backing out of the bedchamber. I tugged on Ren's braid to make him look up at me again.

"Time for what?"

But he jerked his hair out of my grip and had gotten to his feet before he answered me.

"You need to leave."

He did up the remainder of the buttons on his high-collared coat to conceal the ribbon around his neck and keep it a secret only for us.

I rolled my eyes. "Afraid I'm going to crack your little coded letters while you're gone?"

"Not my room. The palace. *Quareh.*" When he finally turned around, I saw the prince's eyes were wet with tears. "It's time for you to run, Mathias."

*

Chapter Forty-Nine

Ren

Every time I started to think of Mat's stubbornness as *endearing*, he reminded me of how fucking annoying it was.

"Ren, I'm not leaving you alone with your father," he said for the sixth time, folding his arms and scowling at me.

"This is not up for debate," I hissed, shoving him towards the tapestry hanging on the back wall of my bedchamber. "You need to get out, now. Boots and coat, Nathanael."

Dios, I should have sent him away *days* ago. But once again, I'd proved how selfish I was, keeping him at my side despite my plans to get him to and across the border being finalised within a day of that horrible evening when my father had hurt Mathias for trying to protect me.

Because *what was one more night?* I'd asked myself time and time again. One more night of seeing his shy smiles, hearing his breathing soften as he fell asleep, feeling the warmth of his body against mine in bed.

Until here we were. And now it was too late.

"Nat, my father wants to speak to me. Considering he doesn't give a shit about what's happening in my life, I'm guessing it means he's received the response from your mother about your ransom. And we both know that's not going to be good, regardless of which way it goes."

Mathias fell silent at that. Because either Queen Velichkova had conceded to Quareh's demands, in which case Mat would feel guilty for the rest of his life for whatever he had cost his country. Or she hadn't, and…no. I wasn't going to think about that possibility.

"You're taking the tunnel," I said firmly, wrenching aside the tapestry and revealing the door behind it. "It will get you out of the palace without being seen by the guards. Ad is going with you; he'll get you to the Mazekhstani border, where one of de la Vega's trading caravans will be waiting to take you north."

"I can't ask-"

"Ademar wants to do this," I told Mat, tugging at his collar to bring his chin down so I could press a kiss to his forehead. "He's going to look for El on the way back. You just need to worry about *you*, you hear me? Maybe take the opportunity to convince Ad that it wasn't you who outed his brother, instead of those half admissions you've been making lately for whoever you've covering for. Starling, I can only assume."

Mathias swallowed, looking up at the door as he shrugged on one of my coats and annoyingly ignored me as he always did when I tried to press him on who he was protecting. He clearly hadn't told Moreno about Elías' secret and I was sure Ademar knew that deep down, but Mat wasn't making it easier for either of them by suggesting that he had. My northerner had a selfless heart bigger than the continent, and not one of us deserved a piece of it.

"Are you finally going to show me where you keep the key for this door, prince?" he asked instead.

I grinned, grabbing his left wrist and wrenching it towards me with more force than was necessary, but the perfect amount to leave us both breathless.

Mat's sly look of interest turned into a frown as I slid the small piece of metal from a hidden slit in the leather cuff. "Oh, fuck me. This whole time?"

"This whole time," I confirmed, unlocking the door and returning the key to its place in the leather band before letting go of his arm. "You'll need it to get through the door at the other end. Take this-" I yanked a satchel out from under the bed and thrust it into his arms. "Money, cloak, water. Food," I added, throwing in a wrapped loaf of bread and half a dozen oranges into the bag from the platter on my desk. "Fuck, Mat, don't die."

He heaved out a breath. "I can't leave you."

"I don't want you to either, *mi sol*." I leaned in close, wrapping my arms around him and breathing in that scent of *home*. "But if you stay, you'll get hurt, or worse, and I can't lose you like that. At least this way, I know you have a chance to survive."

*

Chapter Fifty

Mat

I scowled into the dark space behind the open door, a series of steps descending into gloom and illuminated only by light filtering through cracks in the walls that were too evenly spaced to be accidental. The air was musty, and it held an anticipatory type of silence.

A silence Ren was rapidly filling with muttered commands and warnings, his voice gaining in pitch as he started to spiral.

"Hey," I said, pulling back to look him in the eye. "We can figure out another way."

"No," he whispered. "I've risked you enough. Please, *mi amor,* let me do this for you. Let me fix at least some of the mess I made by having you brought here."

I kissed him then, savouring his lips on mine, the warmth of his skin under my fingers, and feeling a part of my soul detach and stay with his as we parted.

"Maybe when you get home, we can do this properly," Ren said quietly. "You can invite me to Delzerce, assuming Velichkov comes through on the treaty and you can return to your family."

"Would you come if I did?"

"I would," he answered without hesitation. "Although I expect your brother would have me shot full of arrows the moment I stepped foot in Temar."

I swallowed down my retort, knowing that even if that wasn't true, it wasn't like we could court each other properly anyway. Not in the north.

And then we both froze as Iván Aratorre's voice thundered from the antechamber beyond the double set of doors at the other side of the room.

"I know my son is here! Move aside!"

Ren swore, shoving me onto the staircase and wrenching the door closed, shutting me into blackness. I blinked, letting my eyes adjust, and not daring to move a fucking muscle as I heard the tapestry pull back on its rails a second before the noise of the familiar loud thumps of the main bedchamber doors hitting the wall.

Like father, like son, I thought wryly, and then stamped down on that disgusting thought before it could take root. Ren was nothing like the king: I'd told him that, and I'd meant it.

"Renato!"

"Father," Ren said smoothly, like he hadn't just been helping foreign prisoners escape from under his nose a moment earlier. "It's rare you visit me in my rooms."

"Renato," Iván said again, and this time I could hear his voice crack, even muffled through the door. "I've just received word from Máros. There's been an...incident."

Good, I thought savagely. Whatever rebellion or mayhem had occurred back in the capital, hopefully it would call the king back there and give Ren a few more days of peace. Hell, something as small as mould getting into the royal wardrobes would please me, knowing it was inconveniencing this bastard.

But his next words stopped me cold.

"Your brother and his sons are dead."

*

Chapter Fifty-One

Ren

"Dead," I repeated numbly, the words not quite making sense in my head. Horacio couldn't be dead. He was...he'd *always* been there, in each one of my earliest memories.

And my nephews?

They were just children!

My father stepped forward and I flinched as he wrapped his arms around me. I blinked at his shoulder, surprised. He'd never hugged me before. I couldn't even remember him touching me.

It was that, more than anything else, that made his horrifying words real.

"I...how's Laurita?" I whispered. Fuck, how was *she* dealing with this?

"It's hard for a wife to grieve her man when she's also a corpse." My father's words as he delivered the additionally devasting news were callous. He didn't give a fuck about my brother's wife but for her ability to bear children...oh Dios, *dead children*...

I pulled out of his arms, turning my face away so he couldn't see how close to throwing up I was.

"All of them?" I croaked. "How?"

"Horacio's guards. They slaughtered them – cut them down where they lay in bed, by all accounts, and then took the cowardly way out before they could be questioned as to why. Fuck, Renato, it's..."

He trailed off, sounding lost. But the usual steel was back in his tone a moment later.

"I've interrogated my own guards to ensure this treachery doesn't run deeper. You should do the same."

I turned back to him, angry. "I'm not torturing my men."

The king gave me a weary look. "Nothing permanently damaging, Renato.

Do you think I wanted to hurt mine? Just apply enough pressure to be sure they're not involved." He waved a hand. "Fuck, give them a pay increase afterwards to soothe any injured feelings, I don't care. And make sure you're only using those who have been with you a while. You have a new guard, no?"

"Luis," I said. "He wouldn't be involved in something like this." Then I remembered Moreno's spy, my even newer guard Cirilo. Him, I definitely didn't trust.

My father gave a hollow laugh. "That's what I thought about Horacio's men. Take Luis out of your roster, at least until we find out how far this reaches. Post him to the gates or something."

"I can't," I said, focusing on the absurd conversation in an attempt to distract myself from thinking about Horacio and Laurita lying dead in their bed, their sheets soaked with blood. The cot next to them... "With Elías gone, I need at least a third man to rotate out shifts."

"I'll assign you some of mine when I've finished screening them," he said, and barely were those heartless words out of his mouth than he started talking about something else, something that washed through my head at dizzying speed until an unexpected word snagged my attention.

"Did you say *marriage*?"

"Yes," my father said impatiently. "You must wed Altagracia Moreno so you can produce heirs as soon as possible. Surely even you must understand the precarious position our line is now in, with you and I the last of the Aratorres?"

This man. Oh, I would gladly be the *very last* of the Aratorres, if I didn't know that he could stop me before I would ever get a blade into the heart that was as black as his tongue. His son and grandchildren had just been *murdered,* and all he could think about was making more?

"Where's the Temarian?" he asked abruptly, glancing around the room as if he expected to find Mat lounging in one of the armchairs. And to be fair, if he'd arrived five minutes earlier, he just might have.

"Oh," I said, waving a hand and doing my best to look dismissively unaffected even as my heart raced and my breaths sped up. But the feel of the ribbon, tight around my throat, helped to ground me. "He got...*clingy*. I had him returned to the cells."

"Good. Let his next breath of fresh air be the one the noose takes from him."

I swallowed. From the corner of my eye through the open doors, I saw Jiron's chin raise a quarter of an inch. For him, while on duty, that was akin to a surprised yell.

"You...you plan to execute Nathanael?" I asked, choking on the words.

"The north killed my son!" my father snarled, spittle flying from his lips as his fury abruptly enveloped him. "If Zora thinks she's getting her boy back after she took mine from me, I'll be happy to send his corpse to Delzerce to correct her. That bitch will know my pain *twice over* before I am done with her and her fucking people."

"Do you have proof that Temar was responsible?"

"Temar and Mazekhstam have been in bed together for the last forty years, Renato," the king said with a sneer. "It was one or the other of the northern pricks, and I'm not giving them another Blessed inch of Quarehian mercy. Come," he added brusquely, ushering me from the room and snapping his fingers at Jiron and Ademar to make them follow us into the corridor.

I faltered, catching Ad's eye.

"Ademar," I said, "I want you to stay guarding my rooms to ensure-"

"*No,*" my father snapped. "They'll both remain in your company – and within eyesight of my own guards – until we know the extent of the web of traitors." He collected his men at the door and led the procession down the stairs.

I resisted the urge to look behind me. I could only hope Mat realised Ad wasn't coming and didn't wait for him, but how would the northerner survive the trip to the border on his own? Fuck, he wouldn't even know where to look for de la Vega's caravan.

I sent up a hasty prayer to Dios to watch his back until I could sneak someone out of the palace to look after him, focusing on the pull of the ribbon against my neck to stave away the swirling darkness inside me that was reaching up to tug me under.

Oh fuck. Horacio, I should have tried harder to save you. To get back to you. Maybe it wouldn't have happened if I'd just...if I...

"You'll accompany me to Máros for the funeral," the king was saying, "and then will remain there. You have a lot to catch up on."

He glanced at me, caught sight of my wet cheeks, and then slapped me hard across the face without warning. My father had never cared for tears.

"Wipe your face, boy," he snarled coldly as I straightened, careful to avoid the gaze of our guards. "My heir does not demean himself with *crying*."

His *heir*. It was something I hadn't ever let myself imagine, not as a second-born son.

But now? One day, I would be the fucking king of Quareh.

*

A WHISPER AND A BREATH

Chapter Fifty-Two

Mat

I stumbled in the gloom, my feet expecting more stairs where there were none. Scraping a mass of webs from my face – there wasn't enough light to see if there were any spiders attached to them, so I was going to choose to be an optimist about it – I cautiously picked my way along the tunnel, the sound of my boots slapping against the stone echoing back at me despite my efforts to be quiet. Ren hadn't given me directions, presumably because Ademar was supposed to be accompanying me, but I was sure that the way out was not up the second set of stairs to my right. That likely led to the king's quarters, and I had no desire to get any closer to that prick than I had to. I'd heard his intentions for my death all too clearly.

I shivered. I'd known things had gone south for me since the moment Astrid and I were alerted to the approach of a group of Quarehians at the Mazekhstani monastery all those months ago, and since that time, my death had remained a real possibility. But hearing those words uttered from Iván Aratorre's lips, his snarl of pure hatred as he spoke of taking from my mother what he thought she had taken from him?

I couldn't even say for sure that she wasn't responsible. I didn't know Queen Zora Velichkova. Despite her birthing me, I didn't have a single memory of the woman, and I certainly couldn't speak to whether she'd have the first prince of Quareh murdered in retaliation for the south threatening her with the ransom of her son. If she had, she'd have to know she was guaranteeing my own death, which would make it three for three in terms of countries in Riehse Eshan who were apparently quite fine with me not taking another breath.

I scowled at the dark around me.

Fuck them. I was determined to survive, if only to piss everyone off and make it twice as difficult to play their games with human lives.

Maybe not *only*.

I hadn't said a proper goodbye to Ren, and I was not going to have that be the last time we saw each other. By the Blessed Five, I was pathetic, because being alone already *hurt* so much…not seeing his smile, being out of earshot of his incessant commentary and good humour. He'd have taken the opportunity in the darkness to have felt me up and then denied it entirely, I was sure.

But if I stayed, I was dead. It wasn't a hard choice to make.

So why did it feel like I was making the wrong one?

I reluctantly pushed on, the path taking me beneath the heart of the palace if the noises filtering through the slight, perfectly straight cracks in the stone ceiling was any indication. *La Cortina's* inhabitants were on edge, high pitched exclamations dotted with the bustle of people moving quickly above me.

But I didn't give a shit about any of them other than Ren, and maybe Alta, and definitely…

"Star," I whispered, spotting another set of steps recessed into the left-hand wall. These were short enough, maybe two storeys' worth, that I could just see up to their zenith where a door sat, innocuous and quite clearly not where I was supposed to go. Ren had said the tunnel would take me *out* of the palace, and this was evidently not far enough.

But there was no fucking way I was leaving Starling behind.

I climbed the stairs and pressed my ear to the door. If my sense of direction was worth anything, this exit would emerge near Star's surgery, if not inside it. It felt like luck was on my side for once, but I supposed it was just pragmatism: having a tunnel network that could allow a healer to service their royal without being seen would avoid a lot of unwanted rumours about ill health, unorthodox pregnancies and embarrassing diseases.

Slipping the little key from the cuff, I felt around in the darkness until my fingers located the keyhole. The turning of the lock seemed impossibly loud, and I cringed, waiting for a horde of guards to descend on my position.

But when no one dragged me through the cracked door, I nudged it open wider, coming face to face with a sheath of stiff material.

Original, I thought wryly, batting at the tapestry until I found its edge and peeled it back.

But it wasn't the surgery I found myself in. It looked like someone's private quarters, a neatly made bed sitting across from a spotless desk.

I glanced at the door. Hopefully whoever lived here was caught up in the chaos of the palace, and I could-

"Give me one reason why I shouldn't have you hauled before the king for trespassing," a voice warned, and I froze, turning to find Dr. Sánchez rising from an armchair in the far corner of the room. His mouth was turned up in a sneer. "*Bárbaro.*"

*

Chapter Fifty-Three

Ren

My father laid a heavy hand on my shoulder, forcing me to stop and look at him.

"You are...well?" he asked, his narrowed eyes giving the words a pointed meaning.

"Yes." Enough days had passed since his latest round of cruelty that I no longer had to feign discomfort in my back, but I didn't appreciate the reminder of the monster who stood before me. This bastard had tortured Mathias because he dared to stand against him, and there hadn't been a damn thing I could do about it.

"Good. I'm sure all that nonsense can be put behind us now, *mi hijo.*"

"Of course," I said stiffly.

No, over a decade of abuse could *not* be fucking forgotten, but what else could I say? Being his heir suddenly made me his favourite son simply by virtue of being his *only* son, and knowing I'd never be forced to endure another of Moreno's vicious floggings felt hollow in the face of what it had cost.

A deranged laugh threatened to bubble to the surface when I thought of how Mat was undoubtedly out of the tunnels by now and fleeing north. Oh, my father's face when he discovered he was gone would be absolutely priceless. His desire to take out his fury and frustration on my flesh as he usually did would be thwarted by the risk of losing his only male child to a stroke of bad luck.

"If we're talking about men we can't trust to have *our backs*," I said meaningfully, but the king didn't twitch. "Comandante Moreno should be at the top of the list."

I was given a wry smile. "How did I know he'd be the first thing you'd use your improved status to attempt to remove? Dismiss or execute him in your own reign, Renato. The Comandante is an extremely capable man I need on my side."

"And if he's not on your side?"

"Juan is a power-hungry cocksucker," said my father in an idle tone, and I blinked. He'd never spoken so candidly about him before. "Why do you think I delayed your marriage to his daughter for so long? The promise of unity with our family kept him in line, while the lack of follow through prevented him from asking for more in fear he may lose my blessing for it."

"I see," I said slowly. If I was honest, I'd never suspected that my father's reticence to set a wedding date had been anything more than purely not giving a shit.

"But he's not fool enough to make a move against us," he continued. "Two more dead Aratorre men, and that leaves one of your sisters' foreign husbands on the Quarehian throne. He loves his country far too much to ever let that happen."

"Or he takes it himself," I growled.

But my father shook his head. "The line of succession would still be there, and any usurper wouldn't be able to kill both of your sisters in their homelands. Why do you think I sent them so far away? They may no longer be Aratorres by name, but with our blood extending past the reach of the continent, our claim to Quareh will always hold strong."

I frowned. There was something not quite right with his logic. Something Quintín Lago's husband had once said about...

But my father just clicked his tongue. "No, *hijo*, Juan is not our concern. Whoever this is, whatever this is – if it's not the northern bastards, it may be revenge for something your brother had done. You will go through his decrees and records on our return to Máros and identify any possible perpetrators."

I would. And if I found even the vaguest reference to Moreno on the tiniest slip of parchment, I'd hang him with it.

For practicality, I hoped it was a larger piece of parchment. Preferably rope sized.

I liked to consider myself above fabricating evidence against him if I couldn't find anything, but only because that would let the real murderer go free. Who would dare take out the heir to the south? Could the northern royals really be so brazen and well-connected to have done this?

Perhaps it wasn't so far-fetched. After all, Astrid Panarina had tried to have Mat killed while he was at my side. The palace in the capital was better guarded than this one, but both endeavours would have been equally as dangerous and ambitious.

At a wave of the king's hand, his guards pushed open the door before us and he strode purposefully into *la Cortina's* throne room, me at his heels like a good little dog. Two thirds of the room were crowded, with the stench of sweat wafting from the hordes of nobles and landowners suggesting they'd all had to make their way here pretty sharpish. The confused yet cautious expectation on their faces as Clementina drew attention to our presence and they turned as one to look in our direction said they had no fucking clue what had compelled their monarch to summon them all here unexpectedly in the middle of the morning, but they didn't think it was anything good. Court-dwelling folk might be back-stabbing social climbers, but they were rarely stupid.

I swore under my breath as Moreno peeled away from the wall and fell into step beside me as we crossed the unoccupied portion of the hall towards the dais and its throne.

"How convenient the timing of your return," I muttered, and he threw me an exasperated look.

"To the contrary, little prince. It was me who bore the unfortunate task of riding back from Máros to deliver the tragic news to your father."

Oh, even more fucking convenient. How had the king not found it suspicious that the Comandante had been in the capital at the exact time Horacio had been killed?

I searched the crowd for Alta, spotting her in the front row. Her face was pale, and she was biting her lip so hard I could see blood welling under her teeth.

Fuck. What had the bastard *done?*

As my father started to ascend the dais, Moreno nudged me with his elbow. "Where's your little pet, Ren?"

"Sleeping me off," I said with a forced grin. "I wore him out, the poor thing."

The Comandante wasn't sure whether to look disgusted or smug at the reminder I'd taken a Temarian prince to bed, and settled for a non-committal huff instead. Knowing how I felt about him, Moreno would never believe I'd sent Mat back to the cells, and my father knew he wasn't in my rooms. I just had to hope neither of them spoke to each other until Mathias had gotten far enough away from the palace that they had no hope of catching him.

"This is where I leave you," I said, emphasising the point as I walked up the dais' steps after my father and left the Comandante at the bottom of them. His scowl at the reminder of his rank was almost worth the pain of his presence.

I stood to the side of the throne, hands clasped, and tried to emulate Dios-damned stone as the king informed his people of the untimely death of the first prince of Quareh.

*

Chapter Fifty-Four

Mat

"Well?" Sánchez asked, heaving himself out of the armchair and skittering across the room towards the bedchamber's entrance door, moving sideways like a crab so he didn't turn his back to me. I reined in my snigger. "No clever comments this time? Got you good, haven't I?"

"Sure," I said agreeably. "You were very cunning, lying in wait for someone to happen to emerge from tunnels that haven't been used in years. In your own rooms."

"Don't you move," the so-called doctor warned me, holding up a shaky finger as I took a step towards him. "I'm fetching a guard."

"I'm not here for you. Where's Starling?"

At that, the man's expression soured. "Señorita Ortega is *working*. You distract her far too much these days, with your...your..."

He gestured with both hands, forming a circle that was apparently meant to point out whichever of my features was so distressing to him, but which was wide enough to capture me head to foot. "You'll not come around here anymore if you know what's good for you."

"I don't intend to ever return here again," I said truthfully, "but I have to speak to her. *Ahora.*"

"*No*, you're staying right there until someone comes to collect you," Sánchez spat. "And then I'll tell His Majesty how you broke into my rooms and tried to steal my valuables."

I sighed. Imaginative, this one was not. What the fuck would imprisoned Temarian royalty need with a couple of silk scarves and a pocket watch?

"Then I suppose *I'll* have to tell him about your deal with Renato Aratorre," I pointed out. "About how you lie to the king to maintain your cushy lifestyle here."

The doctor's eyes bulged from his head. "You...you...!"

"Me," I confirmed. "You're going to sit quietly in your chair until I'm gone, *sí?*"

But I'd underestimated the man: either his propensity for indignance, or his faith that his prince would protect him from the consequences of his treachery, because Sánchez drew in a breath, squaring his shoulders in preparation to scream for help.

I leapt forward to silence him, knowing I'd never reach him in time, but-

Sánchez's eyes rolled back in his head and he collapsed to the floor in a graceless heap.

Starling stood in the doorway behind where he'd been, head cocked and a single finger outstretched. Red and green sparks still flickered around her fingertip.

"I thought I heard your voice up here, Math…Nathanael," she remarked, withdrawing her hand and looking down at her master with nothing more than mild indifference. "Are you cheating on me with him?"

"The Touch of the most powerful Blessed I've ever met has nothing on the healing capability of leeches," I teased. "You better pick your game up, Star."

She grinned, and stepped over Sánchez. Well. Stepped *on* him, but the man was out cold and clearly wouldn't be feeling it for a while.

"What can I do for you, Your Highness?" she asked, her eyes shrewdly darting over my shoulder. "And does it have anything to do with that tantalisingly open door behind you that I never knew was there?"

"It does. Escape with me?"

"Fuck yes!" Starling yelled happily before the words had finished leaving my mouth, and I blinked in bemusement as she wrapped her arms around my neck, planted a swift kiss on my cheek, and then disappeared back the way she'd come. I heard her boots pounding down some unseen stairs and a moment later back up, a cloak slung around her shoulders.

"Is there anything else you want to-"

"Nothing. I have nothing," she said, grabbing my hand and leading me through the hidden door as if it was her rescuing me. Her eagerness was intoxicating, but not surprising. As far as I could tell, she'd been looking to escape her life here for a lot longer than I had.

We tugged the tapestry and door closed behind us, and raced down the steps hand in hand. My heart beat loudly in my ears. Starling laughed joyfully.

"How the hell did you get away from His Snarliness and those barnacles he calls guards?"

I swallowed, suddenly finding it difficult to breathe and blaming it on the stale air and the pace we were legging it along the tunnel. Clearly the healer had far less reservations about spiders and broken ankles than I did, as she was dragging me through the darkness at something more than a jog and only just less than a sprint.

"He let me go."

Star was quiet for a long moment, and then I felt her shrug through our joint hands. "Fuck it. I'm not going to question it. I'm just so glad you can finally be free."

"We," I corrected, and I caught the flash of grinning white teeth in the gloom.

"I'm going to go *fishing*," she declared as we ran, and I laughed at the random statement. "I'll probably hate it, but I don't care. I've never been fishing before, and now I can. Oh, and rock climbing, Nathanael! I'm going to sleep late every morning and learn to swim and use a bow to catch rabbits and get lost in a field somewhere. Preferably one full of wildflowers."

The delight in her voice was infectious, and she only slowed her relentless pace after about ten minutes when the tunnel seemed to come to a dead stop.

"Here," I said breathlessly, extracting my hand from hers and fishing around in the cuff for the key to the door I knew would be there. How she stayed so fucking fit when she'd been confined to the palace as much as I had, I had no idea, but I was wheezing and not doing a very good job of hiding it.

Star clicked her tongue when I fumbled the lock, wrenching the key from my hands and doing it herself. I snorted, stepping back to let her work.

That was when the vision hit me.

"Nathanael?" Starling was saying, and I shook my head, clearing it of the fog. Light was streaming into the tunnel now, highlighting how fucking filthy both it and we were, and I brushed a huge, fanged spider from my sleeve with disgust. "Are you okay?"

"Will you carry this for me?" I asked, shrugging the satchel from over my head and looping it over hers. She raised an eyebrow, handing me back the key and planting her hands on her hips.

"Naww. Is it too heavy for your precious shoulders?"

"It is," I agreed. "Everyone knows how pathetic princes are."

"Damn straight."

I gestured for the healer to go first, and she stepped through the door, blinking at the sunlight as it fell on her face. I watched her for a second, at the smile that spread across her lips, at how she inhaled the air as if it tasted different when steeped in freedom, and the way she ran her fingers gently along a half-collapsed stone wall that edged out from beyond the doorway.

"Go north," I told her. "Stay safe, Star."

And then I pulled the door closed between us, shutting myself back in the darkness. There was a moment of stunned silence, curses and furious banging erupting from the other side a second later.

I was an idiot for this, I knew that.

But the vision had shown me Ren writhing on the floor of the throne room in the same clothes I'd left him in only half an hour ago, Moreno standing over him. *Moy dorogoi* was howling in pain, clutching at his leg, with blood trickling down his temple.

And there was no Blessed way I was letting that be his fate.

*

Chapter Fifty-Five

Ren

There was crying. Wailing. Fucking *bawling*, and really, had any of these sycophant assholes even known Horacio? How dare they use his death as an excuse for clawing their way into the king's attentions, each seeking to be the loudest in demonstrating their false misery?

Mathias would have instantly called them on it. For a moment, I let myself imagine how the huddled nobility and courtiers would respond to the northerner's acerbic comments about their sickeningly fake sympathies, revelling in the way their eyes would widen, their teeth would grit, and their pathetic protests would flow thick and fast while he just rolled his eyes.

But Mat wasn't here. Never would be again. And I wasn't brave enough to do what he wouldn't have even hesitated at, because Mathias didn't think of things like consequences or reputation or the deadly ire of one's father when we were once again behind closed doors.

He just...acted in whatever way he thought right, and I was so fucking envious of how beautiful that was even as I despaired at it.

Because how could a man like that survive in a world like this?

Fuck. How could a man like that even survive the journey to the northern parts of the continent, alone and vulnerable?

I took a breath, refusing to let my thoughts go so dark.

Ademar would find him. Mat wasn't El – he wouldn't be able to cover his tracks nearly as well, and then Ad would get him to the border and de la Vega's caravan would escort him to Stavroyarsk, and then *mi gato montés* would be free to not be free, wasting away in the dark confines of Panarina's fucking castle while Riehse Eshan's royalty continued to play games with his life...

I should have found a caravan heading to Delzerce. But that might have put him in even more danger, if he was discovered fleeing the treaty's terms before they were officially dissolved, and-

"Your Highness," said a voice I was already not very fond of, and I dragged

my gaze to the left to catch sight of the top of a balding head as Cirilo rose from his bow. "I'm reporting for my shift at your side." Cirilo stepped aside, gesturing for Jiron to swap places with him and relieve himself of duty.

"No," said Jiron, in that quiet, assured way of his. "With the first prince dead, I will not leave His Highness' side until I am satisfied he is in no danger."

"As long as I get to be the big spoon tonight," I joked, but the words felt hollow when there was no Mathias to tease with them.

"Jiron-"

"No," my guard said again, and exasperated, Cirilo turned to my other side. "Then Ademar, you should get some rest."

Ad ignored him, crossing his arms and giving me a perfect view of his muscles straining against his shirt.

Fuck, even *that* wasn't cheering me up.

"Ademar, you can't just pretend I don't exist."

It seemed like he could indeed do that, judging by the way Ad's eyes swept the room as if the guard wasn't even there.

Cirilo gritted his teeth. "What happened to your brother wasn't my fault."

I frowned, wondering if this was the opportunity to get Ademar away that I'd been looking for. And then I glanced over at where the king was holding court a few steps away from the dais, surrounded by a thick cluster of his own guards, and realised he was watching us.

"Ademar, Jiron, just give me a chance to prove-"

"Shut the fuck up, all of you, unless you want my father to remember that he intends to torture you to test your loyalty," I muttered from the side of my mouth, plastering on a suitably sombre expression as I pretended to accept more fucking condolences from another of the nobility. Cirilo ducked his head and moved behind me, flanked by the other guards.

I swallowed, feeling the looming threat of panic bearing down on me when I thought again on everything that had happened. Without Mat, without Horacio...fuck, I couldn't do this alone.

But as my throat swelled, I felt it press against the tight band of ribbon underneath the high collar of my coat. The pressure brought comfort, something to focus on that wasn't the chaos swirling both inside my head and out of it.

I tugged down my collar to trace a finger along the red silk ribbon, tied by Mathias what felt so long ago now. As the last thing he'd given me, I was never, *ever* taking it off.

*

Chapter Fifty-Six

Mat

I crept onto the archer's balcony, surprised to discover it deserted when the throne room below was occupied by king, prince, and what looked like most of *la Cortina's* residents. At least the rich ones – but there were enough servants in attendance to ensure that whatever happened would be common knowledge by lunch. It had been a nerve-wracking trek from Ren's rooms, but thankfully the corridors had been drained of most of their usual denizens, and those who remained moved and spoke loudly enough that I'd been able to easily avoid them.

And then the stupidity of my plan – that was too generous a word for what I was doing. *Intentions,* perhaps? – had hit me when I arrived at the throne room to find each of its entrances crawling with the king's guards, none of whom I recognised. Certainly no one who would hesitate to toss me into the cells for real, or put steel through my heart, or whatever else Iván might have ordered for me, all without anyone inside the room being any the wiser.

I'd looked for Ren's guards after emerging from the tunnel, but the prince's chambers had been empty. And if Moreno was about to make his move…fuck, there wasn't time to do *anything* but get as close as possible to warn *moy knyaz*. Which is why my desperation had driven me to three floors up, to the balcony used to guard the king from above. Whenever royalty was in attendance in the throne room, it was occupied by an archer, a further layer of protection for the Aratorres.

And yet today, as I slowly pushed open the door and peered onto the balcony from the brightly lit corridor, I'd found it completely empty.

Dread hit me like a lead weight forced down my throat.

I swallowed, silently moving closer to the edge so I could peer down below. There was a murmur of chatter rising from the ground floor, nothing pitched in urgency or panic, and I could only take that as a sign that the Comandante hadn't yet struck.

And perhaps he wouldn't. The Sight wasn't absolute: was I panicking needlessly? Maybe it had shown me an outcome that wouldn't come to pass in this lifetime, just as it had promised that one day Ren would fatally stab me and let me fall from the palace's walls.

That wasn't going to happen. The fucker was as soft as butter underneath, all those hard edges tempered by his love for his country and his friends through a tender vulnerability he rarely let anyone see, but I'd been lucky enough to do so. Ren wasn't going to just *kill* me, not after risking his own Blessed life to set me free. After everything else we'd been through.

So if that wasn't our future, maybe this one wasn't his. Maybe it had been triggered by a rogue flash of resentment and ambition from Moreno, an imagining of a possibility where he was foolish enough to attack his prince. Nothing real.

Or maybe it would happen, but on the king's order. I'd hoped that with his elder brother dead, Ren would be protected from his father's cruelty, and had even justified stealing Starling away on the basis that without the healer, Iván couldn't afford to be so harsh with his only son. But perhaps Ren's pain at Moreno's hands hadn't stopped, wouldn't do so until-

I let out a breath at the sight of my lover beneath me, hale and whole, greeting the nobles gathered around him with clasped hands and kissed cheeks. Jiron, Ademar and Cirilo watched the interactions with wary expressions, and I was never more glad that Ren had men who would protect him, who would die for him.

I was being ridiculous. What could I have done, even if my vision had proven to be true? Dropped three storeys into the middle of the hall without breaking every single one of my bones, avoided the guards and defeated Moreno in single combat while forcing him to reveal his intentions to hurt his prince? Intentions that he might not even have?

Fuck. I really was as rash and impulsive as Ren liked to tease me for, and I was doing nobody any good here, crouched at the edge of a darkened balcony in a palace full of people who would happily see me dead. I shouldn't have come back. Perhaps if I took the tunnels at a run, I could catch up to Starling before nightfall.

And then the crowd heaved as the king moved, people bowing and ducking out of the way of their monarch as he made his way to his son's side. I tensed, but the words they exchanged seemed polite enough, even if I couldn't hear them from up here. Ren nodded, dropping into a bow and easing his collar away from his neck as he straightened.

The king's face darkened.

The people gathered around the two of them seemed to tense, and Ren's stance became guarded. He shook his head at something the king was saying, his untied braid flicking to the side, but the king was suddenly reaching for him, wrapping one of his hands around his son's neck.

All three of Ren's guards stiffened, but the prince waved them back. Defying their monarch would be suicide, and he knew it.

He fell still under his father's hand, and I froze. My assumptions about Ren's increased value to Iván had apparently been wrong, but would the king really hurt him in front of his whole court? If he did, what could I possibly do to stop it, when even Jiron couldn't stand up to him?

The king's fingers twisted, and he drew back, crimson splashed over his fingers. I couldn't breathe.

What had he…how had he…

But it wasn't blood. The streak of red was the ribbon I'd tied around Ren's neck, and now his father tossed it to the floor, his mouth curling in disgust as he turned on his heel and deliberately trod it into the stone. Ren had his back to me, so I couldn't see his expression, but the fists he had curled at his sides told me more than enough.

Ren didn't lose physical control, not like me. If he dared to stand against the king, without thought or planning, he would be struck down where he stood-

Something hot and heavy yanked my head unexpectedly backwards and I yelped, the noise stolen by the meaty hand that was clasped across my mouth. I kicked out, but another arm snaked around my waist, dragging me from the edge of the balcony and back into its shadows.

"Now, now," a man murmured into my ear, his arms tightening around mine to hold me in place against his chest. "We both know how this is going to go."

Fear took hold of me, because that was a voice I recognised far too well.

Diego had returned to *la Cortina*.

A WHISPER AND A BREATH

*

Chapter Fifty-Seven

Ren

Hot fury burned through me, a hatred that had been building for nearly two decades as I stared at my father's retreating back. After everything, *everything* he'd taken from me, how dare he interfere with my last memory of Mathias too?

It wasn't about the fucking ribbon, although it also *was* about the fucking ribbon: what harm had it been doing anyone? It didn't make me look *weak*, like my father had sneered at me just loud enough to be overheard by the handful of nearby nobility who'd quickly glanced away, and what did it fucking matter if I had indeed been collared, like he'd accused?

Nathanael Velichkov had my heart, my body, and every second of my thoughts. I would scream that from the palace roof if I didn't know that such a thing would ruin his reputation back home, and I certainly had no issue with wearing something that claimed me as his. Perhaps he hadn't meant it that way, but it had felt possessive all the same, how he'd tugged the silk tight across my throat to steal my breath with a fascinated gleam in his eyes. I had no clue how the fuck he'd known about a desire I'd kept hidden from every single one of my lovers, but that was Mathias. He never could leave a secret unexposed, and it seemed my interest in being choked had been just one more of his impossibly acute discoveries.

Movement caught my eye; a familiar shape and smile. Alta glided into the space between me and my father and lowered herself, not in a curtsey but to scoop the ribbon from the floor, her skirts folding gracefully around her. She rose and pressed the silk into my hand, and I stared at the slash of red crushed between our joined fingers.

"Al," I whispered, horror rising in me as she pressed a chaste kiss to my cheek.

Fuck, no. I should have stopped her; I should have fetched the fallen ribbon myself and taken the hit: anything, *anything* but what was about to happen. Because even if most of the room hadn't witnessed what had just occurred between me and my father, enough had done so, and it meant there was no chance of him letting her defiance stand.

"Altagracia." The king's voice was as cold as the expression he turned on her. He didn't have to beckon her closer for everyone in the room to know what he wanted but did so anyway, one long finger curling towards himself where he stood.

My best friend's fingers pulled from mine.

I was frozen with indecision. Should I throw myself on my father's wrath in an effort to redirect his attention from her? Or would that make it worse? Surely he wouldn't risk exposing his Voice in front of so many people, but would that make her punishment any less terrible?

Yet Alta moved without hesitation, sweeping up to the king and presenting in a curtsey, her head lowered demurely. What the fuck had she been thinking? She'd always been far smarter than me at avoiding his attention, so to do something so incredibly foolish for…what? A scrap of silk?

No.

It was for me. For Mat. Because Al, with her perceptive ways and quiet loyalty, had probably guessed exactly what that shred of fabric meant to me, and had put herself in harm's way for it.

I looked helplessly towards the Comandante. Was he not as scared for his daughter as I was?

But Moreno's face was impassive. *Unfeeling bastard.*

My father put a finger under Al's chin and forced her to rise, leaning forward to whisper something into her ear. Words meant for her alone, apparently, and it did nothing to ease the churning in my gut. Was he using the Voice on her? What the fuck was he going to make her do?

Alta's mouth moved, her lips forming a response too quiet to hear, and king and victim exchanged a few murmured words before she sank back to the floor in front of him, falling to her knees with her head bowed and her hands clasped in her lap. The silk of her emerald dress was crumpled, and my friend's usual put-together appearance seemed to shatter before my eyes as her shoulders shook with unseen tears.

Fuck you, father.

"How lucky for the Lady Moreno that she is required to perform her marital duties to my son tonight," the king announced loudly, side-stepping Alta and leaving her on the floor. "A bride may be forgiven for her brazenness with the excitement of upcoming nuptials, but I expect her husband will keep her in line moving forward."

His pale eyes caught mine, making the glaring threat even more obvious. I inclined my head, barely breathing, and thankful that our impending wedding had protected Al from physical injury. Yet it was a sickening reminder of what else awaited us later today; a forced marriage, an unhappy bride, and a cold bed while we worked out how to handle the expectations laid on us both.

"But there is something more important than a wedding to address," my father continued, flicking his fingers impatiently at one of his guards, who were, as always, only a step behind him. The man leaned forward, and upon a whispered command from his king, obediently slid his knife from his belt and handed it over. The world stilled around me again.

Was he going to use it on Alta after all? Or had someone else earned his erratic ire?

"My lords and ladies," the king said steadily, every eye in the room on him. "I have failed you, my people, and I have failed myself. Consider this my penance."

And without warning, my father drew the knife across his own throat.

*

Chapter Fifty-Eight

Mat

I could taste his sweat, a bitter tang from where his palm was still wrapped tightly across my mouth. Diego's hand was large enough to also cover my nose, and I thrashed in his grip as I grew light-headed from the lack of air.

Not that he seemed to give a fuck.

He hauled me mercilessly against him, his belt digging into my back. Diego may not have been as large as Jiron, but he had no trouble dragging me backwards into the corridor, his thick arms like steel as I pounded uselessly against them with half-clenched fists, each blow weaker than the last.

"Shush," he murmured into my ear, and in my oxygen-deprived state, the words sounded delicate, gentle. Comforting, almost.

Light flickered, my eyes drifting shut, and then the world slammed back into focus as the guard dropped his hand from my face to close the door behind us.

I heaved in a breath. By the Blessed, Quareh was determined to suffocate me. First Jiron, then the peanuts, the king, and now Diego? I didn't know what the hell Ren could find so enjoyable about losing his ability to fucking breathe, but I certainly didn't share the sentiment.

The click of a lock brought me back to myself. I stamped down hard on Diego's foot with the heel of my boot and then threw my head back in the hope of catching his chin, but the first blow did nothing to him and the second was caught before it landed, his hand coming down hard on the back of my skull to hold me in place.

Diego tsked, walking me further into the room he'd brought me to. There were no windows, but it was lit by two braziers, the charcoal glowing softly in the iron trays. It was a schoolroom, or it had been once: half a dozen desks were arrayed in three rows facing the large slate tile hung on the far wall. But it was difficult to take in the ordinary décor of the space when it had clearly been utilised for an entirely different purpose today.

A WHISPER AND A BREATH

A slaughterhouse.

I shuddered at the sight of the five corpses slumped gracelessly in the corner. Arms lay over legs, slit throats dripped onto boots; whoever had piled them here hadn't cared where or how they'd fallen. All five were wearing the uniforms of the palace guard, one man with a bow still strung over his shoulder, and while I was thankful I couldn't see most of their faces, the one that was turned in my direction looked vaguely familiar. His blank, unseeing eyes stared at me, his expression so different to the one I was used to seeing on his face as he held watch in the corridors or exchanged a joke with Luis as we passed by.

"What happened to them?" My voice was hoarse.

"Some men just can't see the obvious," Diego said cryptically, and then gave an unexpected bark of laughter. 'Don't worry. You're not going to be joining them just yet."

I grunted, struggling against his hold, but the guard still had my arms pinned to my sides.

"Get off me!"

"I don't think so," Diego murmured. "Not after you so thoughtfully lost your guards again and wandered right by my post. Did you miss me, *puta*, is that it? Are you so desperate for what I'm going to give you?"

He shook me hard, and fear coiled in my gut.

"The prince wants your head after last time," I snarled at him, continuing to fight. "What do you think he'll do to you if he discovers you tried again?"

"I think you'll find the *prince* has far bigger problems right now than worrying about what happened to his whore."

The icy, petrifying feeling inside me grew with each ominous word.

So it was true. Something was going to happen to Ren, and while I was at this bastard's mercy, I couldn't stop it.

Diego let go of my arms, only to spin me around and slam me ruthlessly against the wall.

"You're his guard," I accused, gasping out a breath. "Your duty is to protect him!"

"My duty is to the ruler of Quareh," Diego shot back. "Maybe that's your boy, maybe it's not."

I frowned at that. "What do you mea-"

Diego's hand found my face again, but this time his fingers didn't press across my lips, but between them. I choked, bucking against him, and gagged as his fingers forced their way to the back of my throat. The acrid taste of sweat flooded my tongue, and he pulled back before pushing deeper again, fucking my mouth with his huge fingers. I tried to bite down, but the thumb and forefinger of his other hand pressed against my jaw to keep it open while he used his weight to pin me to the wall.

He seemed only amused at my efforts to fight him off.

"You're so…*small*," he commented idly, not sounding an inch out of breath despite me putting all my strength into trying to escape him. He finally tugged his fingers free and held them up between us, a smile curving his lips as he took in the saliva-coated digits. I coughed, choking. "Can that delicate little mouth even take me? What about the rest of you?"

Snarling, I worked an arm free and jabbed my fist into his gut.

The guard merely shrugged. "I guess we'll just have to find out."

*

Chapter Fifty-Nine

Ren

I stared at my father's corpse as the last of the nobility and servants were shooed out by guards. Moreno directed it all with ruthless efficiency.

My father looked...unimpressive, in death. Pale fingers still wrapped around the hilt of the knife, eyes frozen wide, skin bleached of colour.

Alta rose on unsteady legs, looking sick. The hem of her dress was soaked in royal blood.

Fuck me, the bastard was really dead?

Despite the evidence before me, it was hard to believe. We were all mortal, but I'd expected my father to leave this world as late as possible for the mere inconvenience of it, hating and cursing and taking as many others with him as he could.

Not...not by his own hand. Not so *needlessly*.

"Al," I murmured, holding out a hand to her. She faltered, glancing between me and the body on the floor before her, and then knelt at its side, closing the king's eyes and pushing at his limbs to rearrange him more gracefully from where he had fallen.

He didn't deserve it. He didn't deserve a single moment of her thoughts, but Altagracia Moreno had always been a better person than me.

The doors at the end of the throne room finally closed, and a smattering of palace guards headed back towards us with sombre expressions. The Comandante ran a hand through his hair, jaw set.

"Jiron," I muttered, my mind already running through everything that would have to be done. The logistics, the politics, the reassurances, the security, the funeral preparations for my entire fucking family to be laid to rest in the capital. The king's suicide had been well-witnessed, but rumours would fly across the country if the palace's residents weren't properly managed. "Arrange for..."

I blinked as I caught sight of the Comandante's hand at his side, two fingers outstretched and the others tucked behind his thumb. A signal of some kind?

"Wha-"

I felt something nudge my shoulder, sending me staggering forward, and spun around to find Jiron sheathing his sword in Cirilo's neck.

He tugged it free with a calmness I certainly wasn't feeling, and gave me a short nod, flicking blood from the blade. Cirilo slumped to the ground, dead, and a knife fell from from his limp fingers.

"Moreno," I said in disbelief, turning to stare at the Comandante even as Ademar hauled me behind his bulk with one hand and drew his sword with the other. "Did you just try to have me killed?"

"Of course not, my prince," Moreno said with a frown, his own sword drawn. He strode closer, his tone and posture relaxed, and I let out a breath as I realised he was just checking Cirilo was dead.

Which is why it was a good thing I'm not a Dios-damned soldier, because he had me fooled.

Yet even if my guard was down, Jiron's never was, and as the Comandante's blade swung around towards me and Ademar, Jiron was there to meet it. Their swords collided less than a foot away from me.

"*Mierda!*" Ad hissed, his free hand falling to the back of my neck. He shoved me forward, putting his body between me and Moreno, and guiding us in a run towards the closest door.

"No," I snarled, trying to twist away. "Jiron!"

But Ademar didn't let go of me, his grip unyielding. I couldn't see what was happening behind us; I could only hear the clash of steel and the grunts of exertion as the men fought, my heartbeat racing in my ears. I was shoved and tugged into place, numb at how *quickly* everything was happening.

We reached the side door and my guard cursed as he found it locked. The heavy wood and steel combination couldn't be compromised by brute strength, yet Ad tried anyway, giving it a firm kick and then a second, but it barely even rattled in its hinges.

And then he was pulling me away towards the main doors, and I was still trying to get a glimpse of the fight, but Ademar's broad arm was around me, keeping me as small a target as possible.

Fuck, fuck, fuck!

Moreno was capitalising on my father's death to steal the Blessed throne? Had I not seen this coming a mile away, and yet here I fucking was, running for cover as my oldest friend put his life on the line to stop him?

Worry churned in my gut, but I stamped it down. There were dozens of guards in the palace; I could send each and every one of them to help Jiron cut the fucker down. Like the two standing between us and the main doors. But why weren't they trying to...

Ademar finally let go of me, shoving me to the side. "Don't do this," he said to the palace guards in a low voice, hefting his sword and proving that his instincts were just as good as Jiron's. "Your duty is to the crown."

"Which will soon be him," one of them said with an absurd amount of confidence, nodding over our shoulders at where the fight still played out. I turned to see Jiron parry a clever swipe from the Comandante, only for his own blow to be blocked just as effectively.

What the fuck was Moreno playing at? A coup? Had he been behind Horacio's death, or was this all opportunity?

No, the possibility that this was a coincidence was rapidly draining away with the locked door and the two guards closing in on Ademar as if they'd known exactly what was going to happen.

Ad made a shooing gesture behind his back, and I obligingly backed away to let him swing his sword without fear of accidentally decapitating his prince.

"Alta," I hissed, holding out a hand as I spotted her huddled against the wall, and wide-eyed, she hurried over to take it.

"Ren! You-"

"It'll be okay," I murmured, trying to hide my flinch as the two guards descended on Ademar with the horrific screech of metal on metal as all three swords clashed. I offered her a wry grin. "At least now I have an excuse to execute your father."

She stared at me, her face pale.

A WHISPER AND A BREATH

"Altagracia!" Moreno yelled, as he swung a vicious strike at Jiron's head. The guard staggered backwards, narrowly avoiding the blade. "Don't let Ren leave this hall! Do your duty to your family!"

"Do yours, and die!" I spat back at him. "And hope it's at the merciful edge of Jiron's blade rather than what I have planned for you if he lets you live."

Al tugged me back against the wall as Ademar's blade flashed through the air to block one guard and feign a blow towards the second, and the man's skill was evident in how he held off his two opponents. Fuck, I was so proud of both him and Jiron, but it should never have come to this, not in my own palace, not in my own Blessed throne room.

And while my men were holding their own, they weren't winning. I glanced back over at where Cirilo lay, blood pooling from his body, and his still-sheathed sword at his side.

I wasn't a swordsman, but how hard could it fucking be? I'd watched enough of my guards' practice sessions to know the basics. Besides, I didn't intend on making it a fair fight: if I could catch one of the palace guards unawares from behind, Ademar could do the rest.

"Stay here," I urged Alta, but she clutched at my hand.

"No, Ren, what are you doing?"

"Ensuring we win this," I said, giving her a smile I didn't feel as I prepared to race for the sword. "Keep your head down, okay?"

"Ren," she said again, and now she was crying. "Don't leave me."

I paused, and blinked at her.

Alta squeezed my hand tighter, pulling me back against the wall. "I can't lose you."

"No," I said, terror curling through me. "No, it's not-"

Jiron grunted as Moreno's blade caught him across the bicep, and I watched helplessly as the Comandante pressed his advantage, driving Jiron back three steps before the guard recovered his footing.

"Al, I have to help them!"

"You'll get yourself killed," she fussed, reaching over to tuck a lock of hair behind my ear. I stared at her.

There was an appalling squelching noise, and we both turned to see Ademar slicing open one of Moreno's guards from sternum to groin less than six feet away from us, ducking under his still outstretched arm to continue his fight with the other.

Yes. Ad could take him, and Jiron was already regaining the lost ground, his blade moving so fast I could barely see it. Moreno was bleeding from at least half a dozen shallow cuts; nothing fatal, but enough to slow his movements, and his lips were pulled back into a snarl as he fought for his life.

You underestimated Jiron, you fucker. He'll tear your Dios-damned head off.

And then it was over: Jiron pulled a complicated move I had never seen before in my life, a twist of his wrist that sent Moreno's sword flying from his grasp and his own pointed directly at the Comandante's throat.

I let out a breath, my palms slick.

"Your Highness?"

"Finish him," I snarled, but as Jiron made to press the tip of his blade into Moreno's neck, Alta leapt forward.

"Stop!" she cried, and my guard jerked his gaze to her, startled. A second, no more, but that was all the time it took for Moreno to palm a knife and stab Jiron in the heart.

*

Chapter Sixty

Mat

"I told you when we met that you weren't my type," Diego drawled, his face inches from mine. "And it's true: you're not." He raked his gaze down me. "I don't do fragile little boys like you. They have an unfortunate habit of breaking."

And then he reached for his belt, undoing all of the pathetic shreds of hope his words had given me.

"But if no one needs you alive, *pequeño bárbaro*, then it becomes considerably less of a problem."

I hissed out a sharp breath, tasting bile.

"Ah," the guard breathed, leaning even closer until his breath warmed my cheek. "There it is. That terror in your eyes? That's what I wanted from you, you conniving prick. Do you know what the Comandante did to me for failing to bring back the Mazekhstani princess thanks to your little ruse?"

I didn't give a shit. This man hadn't been getting near Astrid, and what was happening now only confirmed that I'd made the right choice to keep her from him. I tried to jerk my hands out from his grip and he promptly struck me hard across the face, my cheek smacking into the wall.

It didn't matter that Ren had done something similar to me while we were playing, and more than once. It wasn't about the gentleness that neither man showed to me: it was about the ability to stop them whenever I wanted.

And Diego wasn't stopping.

"And then I learn," he hissed, tightening his hold on my wrists where he held them against the wall above my head, until it wasn't just uncomfortable but *painful*, the bones in my hands crunching together, "that you're not as much of a consolation prize as my punishment warranted, but actually a little princeling in your own right? You hid that from them, and I suffered for it."

"Yes, Diego," I said sarcastically, baring my teeth at him. "I kept my identity a secret for months just to inconvenience *you*."

It seemed he missed my tone, for he made a noise that sounded like indignant agreement and proceeded to slam his fist into my face. Everything darkened for a second, and I felt a warm trickle of blood ooze from my nose.

"Diego?"

The door rattled, but didn't open.

"Diego, you in there?"

"Yes," the guard snapped, glaring at me as if it was my fucking fault someone was looking for him. "What?"

"The king's dead," the voice on the other side of the door said, and I froze. *Dead?* Iván Aratorre was *dead?*

How?

What did that mean for Ren? Was he…was he now Quareh's king?

"And the prince?" Diego asked in an echo of my thoughts, except he seemed a lot less shocked that his monarch was no longer alive.

Oh.

Oh.

The murdered guards in the corner took on a whole new meaning. Fuck, Diego was part of a Blessed plot to kill the king? Was he behind Horacio and his family? How far did this go?

The unseen man sniggered. "Crying for his mummy by now, I expect. The Comandante had suggested we find the Temarian to help things along – you seen him?"

"No."

I heaved in a breath. "Help-"

Diego's hand slammed down over my mouth again, cutting off my yell. Neither man seemed an attractive option, but I'd take a stranger over this monster any day, especially if the one outside was planning to take me to Ren. Because it seemed I was already too late to stop the horrific circumstances of my vision coming true.

"What was that?"

"Nothing," Diego snarled out.

"Have you…have you got someone in there with you?" the voice asked, trying the door handle again.

"Yes. Can you give me some fucking privacy?"

"*Dios mio,* Diego, we're in the middle of a Blessed uprising here! Your timing is absolute shit."

Diego's eyes bored into mine, not an ounce of mercy in their depths. "There's something I needed to take care of," he said meaningfully. I struggled in his grip, but he held firm. "Cover for me, and I'll owe you one."

The voice sighed. "You owe me two, asshole." There was a shuffle of boots down the corridor. Diego cocked his head, a smug grin creeping over his face as he looked me over once more, and he dropped his free hand to his trousers.

"I've never had royalty before," he purred, once he'd freed himself from his clothes. "I wonder how sweet you'll taste."

*

Chapter Sixty-One

Ren

"Hey, prince." The man holding me gave me a hard shake, trying to dislodge my attention from my friend's dead body. "He's talking to you."

I didn't give a shit.

"You killed Jiron, you fucker," I spat at Moreno, but he merely raised an eyebrow.

"I did. And Ademar will follow him into Dios' embrace unless you give me what I want."

"And what was that again?" I asked carelessly.

The guard who held my forearms pinned together behind my back growled in my ear.

"The fucking throne," Moreno snarled, sick of repeating himself. To be fair, I had made him do so several times, for the first few I genuinely hadn't been listening. It was hard to focus on the bastard when Jiron lay dead on the floor, blood seeping from his fallen body.

Fuck. *No.*

But denying it didn't make it any less real. Hadn't stopped the knife from plunging into his chest as Jiron's attention was on Alta. Hadn't stopped my oldest friend from collapsing to his knees without a word, clutching at the hilt, and then falling heavily to the tiles as Moreno put his boot on his shoulder and kicked him down. Denial didn't make Jiron's body any less still, even if in his curled up form, his face turned away from me, he could have almost been sleeping.

"We always knew you were a piece of shit unworthy of your title, *Comandante,*" Ademar snarled, and the two palace guards flanking him were forced to seek the assistance of a third to keep him on his knees. I'd been stupid to think that the entirety of our opposition had been in the hall with us — as soon as Jiron had fallen, Moreno had brought more men into the throne room to subdue Ad, and it hadn't taken long for my other guard to be brought down under the weight of so many disloyal palace guards.

Cowardly fucker. He couldn't even beat Jiron without Alta's help, and she…

I shot her trembling form an accusing look as she hovered over by the far wall. Four bodies were strewn between us. It was a fucking bloodbath in here.

Ademar grunted as someone hit him, and then I heard him laugh.

"If that's as hard as you can punch, *cabrón,* I feel sorry for you."

"Ren," Moreno said, cutting through Ad's bravado bullshit. "Stop acting like a fucking child, and cede the Dios-damned throne to me. You're not leaving here until you do."

I held his gaze, fury simmering through me. "Then you'll be waiting a long time, traitor."

"Will I?"

The Comandante flicked a hand and the guards surrounding Ademar immediately backed away, leaving my man alone on his knees. Ad grinned up at Moreno, his face bloody and his eyes slightly unfocused. "His Highness is worth a thousand of you," he said disdainfully, and Moreno drew his sword with an irritated set to his jaw. "You're not worthy to lick his boots-"

I choked out a cry as the Comandante's sword swung through the air and separated Ademar's head from his body, the room silent but for two dull thumps as they hit the floor. Alta's hand flew up to cover her mouth.

"You see," Moreno said idly, almost as if we'd been in the middle of a conversation about the fucking weather, "there are plenty of people who I know you care for, Ren. Sooner or later I'll find one whose death will take that so-called wit from you."

He wandered closer, his naked sword dripping Ad's blood onto the tiles. I stared at it numbly.

"I can have my men bring your other guard to us. Lady Isobella. That room servant you're so fond of."

I said nothing.

"Ren. Look at me."

I didn't, so the impatient bastard grabbed my face to force my eyes to meet his. His hand was still slick with Jiron's blood.

"You can survive this, little Aratorre. Just hand over the throne before I'm forced to end your entire family line to take it myself. You'd be doing Quareh a favour: do you really think you, with your whoring, and your petty sarcasm, and your little *outfits* are fit to rule? You'd run our country into the Blessed ground!"

"My outfits are fabulous," I said automatically, but the words were dull, lifeless. I jerked my chin from his grasp. "And if you think I'll believe a promise to let me live when I'd be a threat to your pitiful monarchy even with a secession of power, you've underestimated my intelligence somewhat."

He gave me a rueful smile. "I've never underestimated you, Ren. Unlike your father, I've always known how clever you are. But a king needs more; he needs to be *tough,* and you, little *príncipe,* have never been that. So yes, I will kill you. But if you help me save Quareh by giving it back its strength, by returning everything Iván leached from it over the past quarter century?" He patted my chest. "Then your death will be quick and honourable, and you will save the lives of those you would otherwise condemn with your stubbornness. Do this not for yourself, but for your people."

I scoffed and pulled against my captor's hold, but his hands on me were unrelenting, keeping me in place for the Comandante's taunts.

"Father, I could just-"

"Quiet," Moreno snapped at his daughter, and Al fell silent, her eyes flickering uncertainly between us. "No. I will have his true co-operation, no matter how long it takes…or how *bloody* it gets." He leaned in, his whispered words landing in my ears like daggers. "Because I know you, Ren. I know how to break you."

The thought of the whip he'd used so often on me chilled me to the bone, but I raised my chin, refusing to give him anything other than my defiance. I'd taken the pain of his floggings before; I'd survive another now.

Yet Moreno just clicked his fingers at the men near the doors. "Fetch me the other prince."

He turned back to me, his mouth lit up in a cruel smile. "Will you give me what I want when I take the rest of precious Nathanael's fingers? Or will it be when I carve those judgmental eyes of his from his fucking head?"

I was silent. Rationally, I knew he wouldn't get his filthy, treacherous hands on Mat: my lover was long gone.

But I also knew how stubborn Mathias was. And a part of me couldn't help the horrible thought that crept up my spine, freezing my blood even in the warm Quarehian air.

What if he's still here?

*

A WHISPER AND A BREATH

Chapter Sixty-Two

Mat

Spit ran down one side of my face and I clamped my lips shut to stop it dribbling into my mouth, turning my head to the side in disgust. Diego chuckled, and spat on me again, smearing his fingers over my face a moment later to collect the moisture. I averted my eyes as he dropped his hand and began to work himself over, the choppy movements rocking us both where he lay on top of me. He didn't have all of my limbs pinned, but he didn't need to – his weight on mine was sufficient to keep me in place.

I tried to wipe my face on my shoulder, and surprisingly, the guard let me.

"If that offends your delicate sensibilities, boy, I don't know how you're going to go with this next part."

Diego tugged at my belt, having to let go of his cock to undo the clasp, and I took advantage of his distraction to kick out, my right foot catching one of the legs of the nearest brazier. He flinched at the noise the metal made as it hit the floor, the light in the room flickering as the charcoal fell to the tiles, sparked, and simmered.

And then he laughed when nothing else happened, patting my cheek with a nauseating fondness.

With the hand he'd just been using to get himself ready for me. I fought the urge to heave.

"Roll over for me, little princeling," he ordered, his fingers raking under the waistband of my trousers as he lifted his weight slightly to allow me to do so.

I swallowed, and nodded, obediently shifting onto my side and feeling him start to tug at my clothes. And that's when I reached out, wrapped my left hand around a lump of fallen charcoal, and pressed it to his face.

Fuck, it burned. It hurt like nothing I'd felt since the day Moreno had sawed through my finger with a Blessed carving knife, and while my right hand would have been protected by its leather glove, the world didn't work that way. It was my left hand that could reach the burning charcoal and my left hand that shoved it into my would-be-rapist's face, but the pain against my skin was *nothing* compared to the piercing scream that erupted from his mouth.

Diego reared away, falling backwards, and I dropped the charcoal as I drew my knee up and kicked at him, catching him in the chest. He was still screaming, clutching at his face, and through his frantic fingers, I caught sight of something absolutely horrific.

Red and white and black. Gruesome and melted. I hadn't just caught him in the cheek, but also the eye.

"You fucker!" he screeched as he lunged at me, a hand coming up for my throat. And even half-blinded, he was a formidable enemy, his strength outweighing mine several times over. If he got hold of me, I was dead.

I scrambled backwards, the hems of my loosened trousers catching under my boots, and I cursed as I accidentally put weight on my injured hand and collapsed under its weight. But the misstep saved me, my back hitting the floor just as his fingers closed around the space where my neck had been.

"*Otvali*," I snarled, kicking out again, but he caught my ankle and dragged me across the floor back towards him, hissing out threats. I scrabbled at the tiles, my fingers finding nothing but air.

Just as he dragged me back into his arms, my gloved hand closed around something solid and I swung it with every inch of strength I had left.

Diego's grip loosened as I caught him around the side of the head. Blinking back blood, sweat and spittle from my eyes, I stared dazedly at what I held, and then pulled it back and stabbed it through his throat.

He wavered, for a moment, on that precipice between life and death.

As did I, because *fuck*, I'd never killed anyone before. And yet here I was, a dying man sitting on my ankles, blinking, his body ruined and shattered because of *me*.

And then Diego slumped sideways, the brazier poker still jutting from his throat. When he landed, his weight pushed the tip of the metal further through his neck.

I stared at it for a moment, at that glistening shaft, the light from the other brazier giving the bloodied tip a peaceful, almost serene quality. There was silence now, other than the drip of blood and my ragged breathing. And the sound of me throwing up.

*

Chapter Sixty-Three

Ren

I spat out blood, the crimson spittle marring the gleaming tiles of the throne room in what had to be the most perfect analogy for the Quarehian ruling class I'd ever accidentally created.

"Ren," Moreno said again, his pretend patience long since drained away. Now, his teeth were gritted and his eyes wild. "Stop being so fucking stubborn!"

"It's funny," I mused. "Having been on the other side of this conversation so often, I now realise those words achieve nothing but to make one even more so."

The Comandante's hand shot out and I closed my eyes, expecting him to hit me again. But the blow never landed. Instead, I felt his fingers close around the collar of my coat, nails raking my skin. The painful grip the palace guard had on my arms abruptly eased, and then I was falling, thrown to the floor and only just aware enough through the haze of blood and pain to prevent my head from smacking against the tiles.

I rolled onto my back, groaning quietly. Everything ached.

"Do you really want this to get more unpleasant?" Moreno asked from where he was standing above me, sword now sheathed and his hands on his hips. "You've seen me break our enemies before – does your love for pain extend to having your limbs broken on the rack, or your skin peeled from your bones, little Aratorre?"

"He likes inflicting pain," muttered the guard who had been holding me, shooting me a cruel look. "Not taking it."

"Just because you were begging for your daddy after only a little slap," I said carelessly, now recognising him from a drunken dalliance a couple of years ago. In all fairness to him, he had taken much more of my sadism before he safe worded, but hey, traitors didn't deserve fairness.

"And I'm guessing there's a reason you haven't already had me dragged away to your adorable little torture chamber," I slurred at Moreno, "and it's something to do with the fact that we're still tucked up in here. You only have a limited number of men on your side, and dragging a beat-up prince through the palace would not be particularly supportive to your narrative of me willingly ceding the throne to you because what...my ass gets uncomfortable sitting on it all day?"

"The tragic deaths of your family broke your heart," the Comandante corrected, "and you knew you could not be the ruler Quareh requires. Realising we needed strength on the eve of war with the north, you named me king so I would lead our country through these terrible times, before voluntarily following your father and brother into the afterlife." He gave me a wicked half-smile. "Piss me off any further, Ren, and your legacy will be of a scared boy attempting to abandon his duties, not a great act of extreme selflessness."

Apparently he caught my eye roll, because he sighed, shrugged, and stamped down hard on my right leg.

I screamed as the bone shattered, blinding pain shooting up my leg and bathing my entire body in unceasing waves of agony.

"Father!"

"Altagracia, stay out of this," Moreno warned, not taking his eyes from me as my screams dulled to grunted moans. "I've lost patience for your jokes, prince."

And I'd lost the will for them. Sarcasm was the last thing on my mind as the sheer fucking *hurt* of it all continued to roll through me without warning.

"I've taken your brother from you. Your nephews and your father. Dios help me, Ren, I will take your northern lover too, if you don't cede. The. Blessed. *Throne!*"

"Fuck you," I said, but far from the proud snarl I'd intended it to be, the words came out as more of a breathless, pitiful groan.

"Father!" Al screamed from somewhere, but it sounded distant, muted by the fresh wave of pain as Moreno brought his foot down on my leg once more.

"Father, please-"

"Shut up, girl-"

"You said you wouldn't hurt him-"

"That was before he-"

"You promised-"

"I don't give a shit-"

"Stop hurting him!"

The words, clear and authoritative, ran through the hall. Moreno grunted, and lifted his boot from my shattered leg, turning to his daughter.

"Altagracia..."

"No," she snapped, and I raised my head, red and black blurs racing across my vision, to see the Morenos facing off against each other. His huge form, sword at his hip, against her dainty one, where the pool of Jiron's blood lapped at the hem of her dress.

Al raised her chin as the Comandante closed the gap between them. "No," she said again, swallowing. "Don't you take another step."

Her next words were almost a plea, whispered and desperate.

"Jiron. Kill him."

Everyone in the room with a heartbeat watched in utter fucking disbelief as the man we thought dead uncurled from the floor, stabbed his sword through Moreno's heart as he stood frozen and shocked, and then turned to offer me one of his calm, reassuring smiles.

"Jiron?" I whispered as he dropped the blade and staggered forward, pressing his hand to the gush of blood easing from his chest. "You're alive?"

"I'm not leaving you that easily, my prince," Jiron murmured, and then he fell to his knees and collapsed unconscious over Moreno's corpse.

*

Chapter Sixty-Four

Mat

I raced down the stairs, but my heart was pounding even quicker than the pace at which my boots slapped the steps. Glancing over the edge of the archer's balcony into the throne room had shown me a dozen bodies, Jiron's huge bulk slumped among them – fuck, what the hell had *happened?* – but no Ren. No Alta.

As I rounded the final spiral of the stairs down onto the third floor of the palace, several things happened at once. I caught sight of Altagracia's green dress through the open terrace doors, and my eyes were drawn to her side, where a weary and bloody – but quite definitely alive – prince of Quareh leant against the table.

Something solid arrested my motion as I ran towards them, and I found myself tangled in a guard's arms for the second time today.

And the name I'd been meaning to shout became strangled by said arms wrapping around my throat, so all that came out was an incoherent grunt.

"Get off me," I snarled, batting at the hands holding onto me, and to my surprise, they did.

And then I saw Ren and Alta's faces turned towards us and realised it wasn't me the guard had been listening to at all.

"Ren," I breathed, ducking under the guard's arm and charging at the prince, pulling both him and Alta into a group hug that I'll admit was a tad too Quarehian-touchy-feely for my usual preferences, but fuck it, Moreno had been *torturing him* if my vision was to be believed.

Altagracia laughed, and I felt her shoulders shake against my arm. "Nathanael! This is unlike you."

"I..."

I didn't have words to express the sheer relief I was feeling, but some of that soured as Ren remained stiff under my touch. I drew back, swallowing my gasp as I looked at him properly and caught sight of the bloody handprint stamped across his face. Something I'd seen all too often in the vision of him killing me, but it was *over*, Moreno and the king were dead on the floor of the throne room, and something either of us had done must have changed the future that had once been laid out for this moment.

We were safe.

Yet Ren's expression was twisted in pain as he looked at me, saying nothing, and I cursed as I noticed how he was favouring one leg.

"Shit," I said, alarmed. "What did he *do*?"

"The Comandante betrayed his prince," said Alta with barely restrained fury, and I didn't miss the careful way she titled him instead of naming him father as she usually did. "He hurt him."

Her words didn't tell me anything I hadn't already Seen.

"Ren," I muttered urgently, catching his hands. They were cold and unresponsive, despite the warmth of the evening air. He stared back at me, silent and still. "Ren, say something!"

"He's in shock," Altagracia told me, and her tone was gentle. "All that death, so suddenly. Give him space."

I shook my head, remembering how the prince responded after being hurt by his father and Moreno. "I've seen him like this before, and space just makes him retreats into himself further. We need to pull him out of it."

"Nathanael." Now her voice was angry. She tugged the prince's hands out of mine. "I've known Ren longer than you. Go back to his rooms and get cleaned up, and he'll join you when he's ready."

I folded my arms. "I'm not leaving him."

"Just...go. Please. I'll take care of him."

"Alta, he's been fucking tortured!" The guards behind me shifted, and I lowered my voice. "I'm not leaving his side until we know exactly who was involved in the plot to kill the Aratorres."

"Ren," Alta said with a sigh, ducking her head. "Tell Nathanael you're fine and that he should rest for the siesta."

"I'm fine," Ren said to me dully, the sun reflected in his unblinking eyes. "You should rest for the siesta."

Oh, hell fucking no. Whatever creepy shit was going on here, I was having no part of it, and neither was *moy dorogoi*.

I grabbed his hand with my good one and started dragging him towards the terrace doors. I'd carry him up the stairs if I had to, but I was getting him alone so I could figure out what the fuck Moreno had done to him and *fix it*.

"Prince Nathanael," Alta murmured. "Come enjoy the view with us, won't you?"

My feet started to move of their own accord, not into the palace, but back out towards the terrace walls. I tried to stop, to stay *still*, but it was like I'd been caught in a tide, swept after Alta and Ren with no say in the matter.

"You're-"

"Don't say anything," Altagracia ordered softly, glancing back over her shoulder at me as she tucked her arm through Ren's to prop him up as he started to struggle to stay upright. Her smile was broad, but it was her tongue that held my attention, flickering out from behind her teeth with a yellowish hue.

Alta had the fucking Voice.

*

Chapter Sixty-Five

Ren

On the outside, I was numb. Al had taken away my words, my resistance, everything that stopped me from doing anything other than limping obediently beside her.

Yet inside me, it was messy and loud, and I felt utterly helpless. When Mathias had turned up on the terrace like a Blessed ghost, covered in nearly as much blood as me and beaming broadly at us as he fell for the same lie I had in thinking Altagracia was our friend, I'd wanted to scream at him, *beg him,* to run, but where had that gotten me? No one could defy the Voice. It was a magic beyond comprehension, a force of unnatural strength that had me standing docilely beside the woman who had, only a few minutes ago, Told all of her father's guards who remained in the throne room to take their own lives, just as she had the king.

Just as she'd apparently made Horacio's guards kill him and his family. It might have been the Comandante behind the plot to take the throne, but it had been *Alta* who made it happen; sweet, precious Altagracia who stole treats from the kitchen and lay with me under the stars and made up stories about the constellations. Alta, who had always been at my side, who had always had my back in this dark and fucked-up world…

No. It couldn't be her. I was missing something, I *had* to be, because for my friend to be that cruel meant-

"I don't understand," whispered Mat, sounding as lost as I felt. He stumbled behind us, forced along by Alta's compulsion, and what the fuck was he doing here, anyway? He was meant to be miles away by now, fleeing north, not running around my palace drenched in blood!

It didn't look like his, at least, although if he thought I hadn't noticed the vicious burn on his left palm, he was in for a rude shock when I was allowed to speak freely again. I was going to wrap him in a blanket and never, *ever,* let him out of my sight. If that was the trouble *mi gato montés* could get into with less than an hour of freedom, I planned to tie him to my bed forevermore, bound by both ankles and wrists and-

Oh, but by the Blessed, it was good to see him. Although I hated that Alta had him on the same invisible leash as held me, Mathias' presence was a comfort I so desperately needed after everything that had happened. He caught my eye and gave an almost imperceptible nod.

Together, we could find a way out of this.

Together, we felt unstoppable.

Al didn't say anything other than to bid me dismiss the guards hovering around the terrace doors and have them shut the doors to leave us to enjoy the sunlight – and the privacy – alone. She'd declared them loyal when they found us outside the throne room and practically carried me up here to get away from the stench of death, and while I didn't know their names, I vaguely recognised them from around the palace.

But they weren't Jiron. They weren't Ademar.

The memory of my guards choked me in a way I couldn't express out loud. I had to keep the same neutral fucking expression on my face that Alta had Told me to adopt when Moreno's guards had fallen on their own swords, after she'd compelled Jiron out of unconsciousness to kill her father despite the way it had aggravated his injury – an injury *she'd* caused by using the Voice to stop Jiron from killing Moreno in the first place.

Fuck, it was so messed up. Al had saved her father then, and subsequently had him killed? Because what...he'd hurt me when he'd promised not to? Could she really be that naïve? If she had the power of the fucking Voice, why hadn't she stopped him a long time ago?

"You can speak now," she said softly, those brown eyes looking at me so pleadingly, pained in a way that she had no right to be. "But neither of you can hurt me, try to run, or warn anyone. Ren, you have to believe me, I didn't want-"

"You killed them," I accused, the words not feeling *enough* for how I felt. "All of them. My brother, his wife and children. Vitorona too?"

Al flinched. "That was...that was my father. He wanted to see how...how it worked. How many people I could control at once. He burned the village afterwards to hide the evidence."

And had the one survivor murdered when he discovered the child had escaped, I realised. A deaf child, immune to the Voice but not the horrors he'd witnessed his own family and friends commit upon each other because of Alta's words.

"By the Blessed," Mathias hissed, disgust etched across his face. "You didn't have to say *yes* to him!"

"He would have killed all of the villagers anyway!" she protested, and Mat scoffed. "I hoped if I could refine my gift, make their deaths mean something so there wouldn't be as much collateral damage when I used the Voice to…for what he wanted, then I could save lives." She swallowed as the northerner's lip curled in disdain. "You don't get to judge me, Nathanael. You didn't have to endure him, *every day.*"

She looked at me. "I thought if I got him what he wanted, he'd leave me alone."

I felt sick. I'd *known* that had been the reason for her recently renewed interest in our marriage: an attempt to escape her abusive father, although I hadn't realised how much of a last-minute hope it had been. Yet I'd just brushed her off in favour of getting Mat into bed, not knowing I was forcing her closer to the edge of agreeing to Moreno's plot.

And maybe she could have used the Voice to keep Moreno off her, but not for long. A momentary triumph would have seen her punished for standing against him later, unless she'd used it to finish him off permanently. And as I'd seen in the throne room, she hadn't been prepared to do that until it came down to me or him. She'd plotted from the shadows, running circles around everyone but the one man who thought he owned her.

And in Quareh's eyes, he had.

"He caught me using my power to save a woman from being raped by a courtier," Al said softly. "I think his…plan took shape from there."

"The plan to take the Quarehian throne by having you kill the rest of my family and force me into ceding the throne?"

She was silent, but her expression confirmed all of my worst fears.

"Fuck, Al!"

"The thing about the Voice," Alta said softly, "is that you either use it or you hide it, but not both. But I *wanted* both."

"How?" I asked, my voice barely a croak. "People know when you use the Voice on them."

"He didn't," she said, glancing at Mat with surprising eagerness, yet the withering look he gave her was so full of hatred that Alta flinched.

I felt the blood drain from my face. "What did you make him do?"

She lifted her chin. "Something he already wanted to," Al told me, and Mathias hissed out an angry breath.

*

Chapter Sixty-Six

Mat

"I discovered that was the trick," Alta continued, almost excitedly now. We both stared at her in horror. "Give the person a little nudge into something they may do themselves, instead of the full push into something completely out of character, and they won't notice they were Told to do it. You can easily phrase it as a suggestion, or even a request *not* to do that thing, because the Voice doesn't care about inflection or superfluous words."

"Al. What did you *do*?" The prince's tone was cold, an ice to it that he'd never previously directed towards his friend.

"Nathanael said himself that he would forgive you in time. I just brought that time forward, that was all."

Oh, fuck her. It had been *her* that night.

The night that could have ruined everything, and had given Ren such a haunted look on his face that I never wanted to see again. She'd taken away my anger at Ren and then *suggested* that I show him I needed him. Whether Alta had intended her command to result in me throwing myself at the prince and shamelessly begging him to fuck me, I didn't know.

And I didn't much care.

She'd forced us both into that situation, and if the compulsion hadn't worn off before we'd gone too far…did she even understand what that meant?

Ren would have taken me without my consent, and neither of us would have known that until it was too late.

"No one realised," Alta said, and there was a touch of pride in her voice now as she spoke. "A guard mused out loud about jumping from one of the palace walls, so I Told the idiot to indulge his whim. I got Lago drunk and coming onto you to make Nathanael jealous enough to get over your spat. I escalated de Leon and González's bickering into a brawl, and they thought it was their own idea."

She shook her head. "I used the Voice on multiple lords in the middle of the

Blessed palace, and none of the stupid fools even *noticed*."

"I don't give a fuck," Ren snarled, and the vulnerable, hurt look in his eyes told me that he'd worked out what she'd done to us despite her best efforts at changing the subject. "Dios, Mat, I could have...."

"Don't be angry, Ren," Alta snapped, and her tongue flashed with yellow. "Stop looking so darn horrified. I had no power in this backwards country, and thanks to my gender, never would. But now? Dios has blessed me with a gift; a chance to bring *change*."

Ren's furious expression instantly eased, flattening into something neutral, disinterested, and so utterly unlike him that I wanted to shake her. But I was unable to do so while Alta's command not to hurt her remained effective.

"Stop it," I growled. "Can't you see how wrong it is to take away free will like that?"

Altagracia's lips thinned, and she turned away, the wind nipping at her dark hair where it was tucked into a careful bun. Ren's own hair, the braid I'd never sealed when I'd found a much more inventive use for the ribbon, was rapidly unravelling in the ferocious breeze that whipped across the terrace.

Al looked out over the orchards, at the swathe of verdant greenery stretched out between us and the horizon.

"Free will," she said bitterly. "When have any of us had that? Ren's role was to be nothing but a spare heir, to exist at the whim of the king. My life was dictated by my father's, as is every other woman's in Quareh. And you, Nathanael? The child who was raised as Mazekhstam's hostage, only to be captured by yet another foreign power as an adult? When was the last time you were able to do something for yourself?"

"About an hour ago," I snapped, running a hand through my hair in irritation, "when I returned to the palace to help stop a coup and discovered that you were behind it all along."

Alta's shoulders tensed, and she whirled on me, anger and indignation dancing like wildfire across her normally serene face. Behind her, Ren sat down heavily on the low wall that surrounded the terrace, slumping forward and letting his right hand drift down to his foot. It looked like he'd finally succumbed to the pain of his broken leg, but as I saw the glint of a blade pass between his boot and his fingers, I realised he was getting ready to make his move.

Neither of us could fight Alta while the command not to do so remained active, but it wouldn't last forever. I just had to keep her distracted.

"You may not have been the one physically hurting him," I snarled back in response to her protests that it had been her father, "but you knew it would happen. You *let* it happen. You had the power to stop Moreno, and-"

"And I did!"

"Only when you realised you couldn't have them both," I accused, not having a clue what had gone down in the throne room but knowing I'd hit the mark when she paled. "Just like how you wanted to both use and hide the Voice, you wanted to please your father *and* save Ren, didn't you? You want everything?"

"Is that so wrong?" she demanded, voice rising in pitch. "I've been denied so much in my life, Nathanael!"

"Haven't we all? But what gives you the right to decide who lives and dies?"

"Dios granted me this power-"

"Dios didn't do shit," I interrupted, letting the sneer in my voice shine through into my expression. Blaming gods for human mistakes was an ancient excuse, and I had no patience for it. "It was chance or ancestry that landed you with the Voice, not an imaginary omnipotent entity. And instead of using it to help people, you *slaughtered* them!"

Alta crossed herself and then twisted her fingers in the folds of her dress. "Do not blaspheme! It's not as easy as you would believe, Nathanael, or do you imagine me so cruel? The king and the first prince were monsters who were sucking the soul from this country! Vitorona had to happen in order for my father to trust me, to let me influence his plans for Ren and convince him to keep him alive-"

"Which he was never going to do. Keep justifying your horrendous acts to yourself, my lady, but don't think for one *second* they're going to work on us."

"No," she whispered, shaking her head. "No, no-"

"You murdered hundreds of innocent people!"

I needed her to see it, to understand what she'd done. How could that be for the greater good? With the Voice, she could have told the citizens of Vitorona to run, to fight off Moreno's men – hell, to make his men stand down with no more than a word. But she hadn't. She'd forced husbands to cut down wives, mothers to kill their children, and I could never, *ever*, forgive her for that, regardless of whose idea the massacre had been.

"Altagracia," I said coldly. "Do you think you're any better than the men whose lives you took today? Or back in Máros? Do you believe any god, Dios or not, will ever permit you entrance to heaven for the murder of Horacio's *children*?"

"Shut up!" Alta screeched, pointing a finger at me, and I could speak no more, but she was so riled up, she didn't seem to notice.

She whirled, skirts flaring, her hands shooting up to cover her ears. "Shut him up! Stop him from talking ever again, because I *didn't*, shut him up, don't let him say such-"

Ren stepped forward, compelled by the Voice's wild commands, and thrust the hidden knife he held into my gut. For a moment, I stared at him, and he me.

My breath hitched.

And then the pain tore through my body and reality synced with the scene I'd witnessed dozens of times before.

Only this time it was fucking real.

"I'm sorry, Mathias," Ren said, but still subject to Alta's thoughtless words to not *look so horrified*, his face was expressionless, unbothered, as if my death at his hands meant nothing.

He pulled the knife free, blood and my insides spurting out with it, and in a pain-infused daze, I looked up. There they were, the three flags I knew would be flying at half-mast in commiseration of a royal death. And Ren was turning and the world was spinning, and I felt the back of my shins hit the low wall of the terrace and then I was falling, falling, falling...

Agony enveloped me as I hit the ground, followed a moment later by the blissful nothingness of the dark.

*

Chapter Sixty-Seven

Ren

I stared at the place Mathias had fallen from, the smear of glistening blood on the pale stone the only indication he'd once stood before us, alive and wild and indignant.

"Fuck," I croaked, the bloodied knife slipping from my limp fingers.

What had I done?

"Stay there," Alta said hoarsely, freezing me in place even as she tentatively peered over the edge of the terrace. I waited for the gasp of surprise, the frown...*anything* that would tell me my boy was somehow, against all the odds, not lying dead and broken at the bottom of the outer palace wall three storeys below. But the way Al staggered backwards, retching, her expression drawn into horrified dismay as she glanced back at me? The last of the faint vestiges of my hope as to his survival drained away.

"Fuck."

The word, uttered by a girl who never swore, mirrored mine in its utter emptiness.

"No," I whispered. "Alta, I didn't mean..."

"Neither did I! He just made me so...mad! Everything he was saying-"

"He's Nathanael Velichkov," I said, wanting to scream it at her and unable to do so while the command that bound me to a neutral expression was still active. "He makes *everyone* mad, but he survived the rest of them. Why couldn't he survive *you?*"

Anguish tore at my soul, pieces of it fluttering away as the sheer pain of it all ripped through me. I wasn't whole; could never be again.

Al straightened. "Come," she ordered, tears welling in her eyes, and although I didn't know if I wanted to stay or run from this accursed place as fast as I could, I didn't have a choice but to limp in agony after her as she swept from the terrace back into the shadowed halls of the palace, my father's dried blood encrusted on the bottom of her emerald dress.

"We have to fetch his…"

I couldn't say corpse. I couldn't even *think* the word, because a dead Mathias was an oxymoron, so at odds with the way he fought and rebelled and lived so fiercely with each breath.

Not my Nathanael, with his dry humour and exasperated sulkiness, the sleepy blinks he always gave me when I woke him in the mornings, and the way he came alive under my touch.

Why had the idiot come back?

He'd been *free,* free to escape every curse my family bore, and instead he'd returned only to die by my own hand. The man I would have given *anything* to protect, and I'd…I'd…

"I'll have it dealt with," Al said, but her voice was cold now, her expression closed off, and I watched her retreat into the protective shell I'd helped her build as a child as we passed into the quiet corridor, the palace's denizens either resting for the siesta or still processing the king's suicide.

Not suicide. Fucking *murder.*

And Mat was gone too.

I felt the rest of Al's compulsions peel from me one by one as we walked, but she was too clever to miss it. With only a couple of murmured words, she forbade me from doing anything contrary to her interests before I could act on any intention to do so, including forcing me to hobble along on my broken leg with agony racing through my body with each step. Is this how she expected us to live? Me in her magical thrall, unable to warn the guards who dutifully trailed after us as if nothing was wrong?

"Hold strong, Ren," she whispered, and slipped her hand into mine. "Just a little longer, and then you can grieve for him, I promise."

"A little longer?" I hissed out, the pain dulling my thoughts. "For what? Everyone is dead."

Her fingers squeezed mine, almost painful, but they brought me back to myself. "You're not. You're the next king of Quareh, Renato Aratorre, and you're going to do *amazing* things." Her eyes lit up. "We're going to fix it all."

No, we weren't. Because nothing fixed the broken body of my Temarian, or the absence of Horacio and his family, or the knowledge that the girl who stood beside me was responsible for the horrors we'd seen hints of in the ashes of Vitorona.

"It will be worth it, in the end," Alta said softly. "We're going to make the cost one that was worth bearing, no matter how steep it feels now, because we can save thousands of lives by delivering Quareh the rulers it needs."

I scoffed. "Do you think you can possibly justify what you've done? Nat was right: nothing you do will *ever* make up for the evil you've already committed."

"I did what I had to do," she said, "and you don't get to judge me for that! All those difficult decisions you've had to make over the years, and you would condemn *me?* Dios, Ren, I've cleaned blood from your very hands! We were subjected to unspeakable cruelty over the years, and we *survived,* you and I, by doing what needed to be done. Now, that all changes. We're going to make things better for *everyone.*"

I didn't answer. I couldn't. Because of the only people I'd ever loved: Horacio, Jiron, Mathias and Alta…three of them were dead and the fourth was responsible.

Maybe it was just as well that Al had kept me from the edge of the terrace, because I wanted nothing more than to throw myself over the edge of it and join my lover in oblivion.

*

Chapter Sixty-Eight

Mat

Fingers traced over my cheek, familiar in their callused feel and no-nonsense brusqueness.

Well, this was awkward. I'd spent at least a decade denouncing God and heaven as being nothing but reassuring platitudes and convenient narratives, and yet here I was, rousing to consciousness in the afterlife. Whether it was heaven or hell remained to be seen: I wasn't exactly a pinnacle of goodness, but I'd always figured Starling a decent enough person to pass through the pearly gates, and if she was here…

I shot upright. "Fuck, Star, you can't be dead!"

The corners of the healer's mouth twisted upwards in amusement. "A terribly good thing I'm not, then," she said, and shoved me back down. I howled in pain, and she tsked, pressing a hand over my mouth to muffle the sound. "With that noise, anyone would think you'd been stabbed and had each of your bones shattered in falling from the fucking palace walls. Oh. Wait."

It wasn't funny, but it was hard not to smile at the way Starling affectionately rolled her eyes and continued to run her hands over me. I blinked away the green and red sparks that flickered from her fingers and flared against the darkness that surrounded us, taking in the new reality of not being dead.

I coughed. "How did…how am I alive?"

"I pulled you back from the brink, and held you to life until it was dark enough to bring you back here to heal you properly," Starling said, her bushy eyebrows folding in mock admonishment. "You're lucky I was able to get close to you without being seen by the guards on the walls."

Luck likely had less to do with it than the fact that at least a dozen of the palace guard were dead as a result of the coup, but I was thankful nonetheless. I lifted my left hand and inspected the smooth skin I found on my palm, as if Diego had never happened.

"How did you know where to find me?"

"You told me your vision, remember? Three flags at half mast was when His Fickleness would stab you and push you off the terrace."

"He didn't push me," I began weakly, but she shushed me with a wave of her hand.

"Regardless, when I saw the flags in the distance after you left me here, you prick –" I frowned, finally putting together the broken masonry around us and realising we were in the ruins at the end of the tunnel "– I couldn't leave without checking you weren't about to cork it. And a fucking good thing I did," the healer said sternly, and I nodded, chastised.

But I still had far too many questions to stay silent.

"How did you get me all the way out here? Or is super strength another hidden talent of the Touch?"

Starling slapped her bicep. "You've never seen my muscles. I could carry six of you."

"No doubt," commented an amused voice. "But I convinced señorita Ortega to focus on healing you and leave the carrying to us mere mortals."

I blinked at the man before us who seemed to have materialised from the night.

"Elías! You're...you're not in eastern Quareh?"

"Did Ademar think I would be?" He shook his head fondly and clicked his tongue. "That brother of mine is getting soft in the head if he really expected me to flee across the country just because the Comandante got himself a little worked up."

That seemed like a gross under-exaggeration, but his words triggered memories of what had happened before I was stabbed. I struggled to sit upright, causing Starling to half sit on me to keep me prone.

"Star, El, Moreno is dead!"

Their shared glances of amusement faded into seriousness.

"What?"

"And the king, and all the Aratorres in Máros and some guards – I didn't see – Jiron, fuck, they killed Jiron!"

Elías knelt by my side, a graceful movement belied by the way his knuckles were white as they clenched into fists.

"The prince? Ad?"

"Ren's still alive," I whispered. "But I don't know about...I didn't see him..."

I fell silent, yet any hope I'd attempted to inject into my words fell flat. If Ademar or Luis were alive, surely they'd have stayed with their charge. And yet the guards Ren had been with when I found him had been strangers to me.

"How?"

Starling and El asked the question at the same time, and I swallowed, putting together what I'd figured out.

"Altagracia Moreno has the Voice. Her and her father attempted a coup, only she had him killed when he broke his promise not to hurt Ren. Now she's controlling him, and I don't know what-"

My voice broke.

"I'm going in." Elías stood, unhooking his bow from his back and testing the string. He tugged the cover off his quiver with a deft movement, striding through the ruins without another word.

"Wait," I gasped, but the guard didn't pause. "Star, get him to wait for me! I have to help!"

She shrugged. "What help can a half-dead prince offer the fucking warrior over there? Rest up, you goose."

"Starling," I hissed. "What use is a sword and a bow against the Voice? Alta killed the king with a *word*. She made Horacio's guards turn on him, and even murdered her own father!"

Her expression was grim. "If she rounds that off by finishing off His Oppressiveness, I'll throw her a fucking parade."

I smacked her hands away. "You said you would give Ren a chance!"

"That was before he tried to kill you, Nathanael. That *was* his chance."

"Under magical compulsion. Surely you understand the power of the Voice?"

She sighed, rocking back onto her heels. "His fiancée. His palace. His problem, no?"

"*No*," I said firmly. "Quareh's problem. *My* problem. Alta has Ren trapped in his own body," I argued. "She's controlling his every word and action."

Now the healer just looked sad. "What do you expect to do about that? We're just *us*. We can't fight. We can't...whatever you envision yourself doing."

"It's *Ren,* Star."

She paused for a long moment, reading my face. Whatever she saw in it made her blow out an exasperated breath. "*Blin.* Fine. But whatever you do, for now you need to lie still so I can restore the rest of your missing blood. Unless you have a particular fondness for the corpselike look you're currently resembling?"

*

Chapter Sixty-Nine

Ren

A guard approached us where we were seated in the second dining room, and bowed. "My king," he said, and the words sent a fretful shiver through me. "Word has arrived of a matter of great concern. The-"

"Be discrete with such information," Alta said sharply, startling Lord Lago on her left. The guard fell silent, and Alta smiled benignly at him. "We don't want to cause a panic when it's probably nothing but fuss, do we?"

She had a point. Announcing a *great concern* in front of all the nobility gathered to eat with us was terribly bad judgment, but the young guard probably hadn't had the training to teach him the necessary political subtlety. The thought that he might be one of the most experienced of my guards left alive was a terrifying thought, but at least he was loyal. Al had asked each of the men to re-swear themselves to me, and the way she'd phrased it along with the subtle use of her gift meant none of them could lie when doing so. The one who had tried to had been swiftly dealt with, his eyes still bulging in shock at the way his own mouth had betrayed his treachery.

"*Mi querido*, would you please let me take this?" Alta asked, pretending to wipe her mouth with a napkin as she hid her tongue and compelled my submission, her fucking *please* be damned. "If I'm to serve you, Your Majesty, I wish to start by easing your mind of such matters."

I was forced to agree and Al rose from her chair, waving a graceful hand at the confused guard to usher him from the room ahead of her.

"Very...progressive of you, my king," the elder Lord Lago muttered at his husband's other side.

"Indeed. Although some may describe it differently. There are even those who would view giving such autonomy to a woman as heretical to Dios," Lord Hierro said, giving me a significant glance as he raised his wine glass to his lips.

I took a long sip from my own.

"I am not my father," I told them, staring into the depths of the dark liquid. "And as the future king, I am the appointed voice of Dios, am I not?"

Quiet murmurs of assent floated around the room, although not all were convinced. I wish I could explain more, but Alta had repeatedly applied conditions on what I could and could not do and say, and I was bound to follow her commands. At her will, I'd given a sad speech about my father's suicide and the Comandante's heroic death in saving me from a handful of traitorous guards who sought the opportunity to dispose of a further Aratorre. I'd given reassurances and promises I may well have offered myself, but they felt hollow and distorted when compelled from my lips. I'd made small talk when all I wanted to be was alone, laughed when I felt like screaming, and flirted to *keep up appearances* when in reality, every glimmer of playfulness had died with Mathias.

Al had even made me assign Luis away from my side when he'd turned up beaten and bloody, having fought off more of Moreno's guards sent to subdue him as he slept off shift. The look on his face as I'd ordered him to the walls...fuck, it told me that he thought I believed everything I didn't.

That I didn't trust him, just as my father had told me not to.

That I was punishing him because he hadn't been there for me when it all went down.

That he was as dispensable as he'd always feared.

And yet, it was exactly because of how valuable Luis was that Alta had separated us, evidently fearing that he'd realise something was wrong with me, just as Mat had.

And I'd smiled and joked as he trudged away. Fuck me.

I hated this feeling of helplessness. My father may have used the Voice on me to make me obey, to bow before him, to allow him to take his pound of flesh...but he'd never kept me in his thrall like this.

Resentment was festering inside me, cancerous and dark.

"And may Dios continue to speak through you and your heirs," someone said, and others took up the toast. "May the Lady Altagracia, our future Queen Consort, be as fertile as your late brother's wife, rest his soul."

"And hers," I added, and they murmured their assent even as the reminder that I still faced a wedding tonight made me want to stab each of their simpering, overly red faces in. How much shittier could this damned day get?

*

Chapter Seventy

Mat

A blade in the gut, another spider-strewn trip through the tunnels, and now a cast-iron frying pan to the shoulder. The things I endured for ridiculous southern princes was confounding even me.

"Ow!" I hissed, clutching my shoulder as I crawled further out of the hidden door – this one, unfortunately, being more of a cupboard – and when I emerged into the palace kitchen, I could see why. Tapestries didn't exactly work down here, and I supposed I should be glad that the architect of *la Cortina's* hidden tunnel network had some imagination after all, otherwise this entrance might have been found long ago.

"*Lo siento!*" hit my ears with a gasp, and tiny hands clutched at my dusty clothes to pull me to my feet. "I'm sorry, señor, we thought you were a monster!"

Covered in filth and dried blood as I was, I supposed that was a fair first assessment.

I looked down at the body attached to the hands, finding the wide eyes of the young kitchen hand who'd stolen from the palace and risked Ren's wrath all those weeks ago. Next to him stood Consuela Sanz, the frying pan hanging loosely from her fingers like its weight was nothing.

Fucking hell. She'd swung that thing with the force of someone three times her size, and my shoulder was throbbing.

Starling had refused to sever my pain receptors: her *no way in hell* had been the more polite version of her response, accompanied by a dozen reasons why that was a *terrible fucking idea, Nathanael*, but had begrudgingly agreed to strengthen some of my muscles so I'd tire less quickly, and might even have a chance of fending someone like Diego off next time. Not that I'd told her about the first time.

I couldn't blame her for not coming with me – hell, I was relieved I hadn't had to fight her on it. Starling wasn't risking her life for this, not when she finally had the chance at proper freedom. But as sure as I was about that, I'd been equally certain of my own direction when we parted: down the tunnel and into the palace.

Our fight about my stupidity in returning had continued throughout the remainder of her healing, but she'd hugged me when I'd left, tears glistening in her eyes as she gave me a lecture about being careful, interspersed with the few Mazekhstani words she'd learnt from me as if that might hammer it a little further home. And fuck if I hadn't said the same things to her in turn, although I was far more confident about her ability to escape Quareh than I was about mine to somehow get Ren away from Alta.

Star was clever, resourceful, and she wasn't going back to the man who had stabbed her in the fucking stomach last time she'd seen him.

Was I crazy?

Perhaps. But I also knew I wasn't leaving him. Ren was stuck with me now, and he'd soon learn that my stubbornness didn't just extend to *no*, but also *yes*.

Yes, you foolish man with your pretentious clothes and impossible smirks, I'm staying.

Yes, I care for you.

Yes, I love you.

Swallowing that thought, I glanced around.

The kitchen was empty, but the plates stacked high on the nearby counters and the suds in the boy's hair told me why the two children were still here. There had been a large evening meal, it seemed, although I didn't know the occasion. Perhaps Ren was still in the hall? I hoped not. I wasn't exactly inconspicuous, and catching him alone was my only chance to get close.

"I'm looking for Ren," I told them in a hushed whisper. "His Highness – Majesty?" Damn, that title felt odd. "It's very important that I find him."

Consuela beamed at me. "He's so pretty."

"He is."

"He was smiling," the boy said, knotting his fingers together, "but he looked sad. Are you going to fix that?"

I thought of Horacio and Jiron's deaths, Alta's betrayal.

"I'm not sure I can," I said honestly. "But I'm going to try. Where is he?"

"His Majesty has returned to his rooms with his new wife," Consuela said softly. "The wedding ceremony finished an hour ago, señor."

I went cold.

Wedding? But that was...that was the old king who wanted...

He was smiling, but he looked sad.

Fuck.

*

A WHISPER AND A BREATH

Chapter Seventy-One

Ren

I stood awkwardly in the centre of my bedchamber as I had been Told to do, politely averting my eyes from my new wife as Camila stripped the outer gown from Altagracia's form. My body was exhausted from being magically tugged and shoved around all day, not to mention the injuries Moreno had inflicted on me earlier. Starling was missing from the palace – a major inconvenience I had no doubt Mathias was to blame for – and the local healer someone had found had barely been able to set my broken leg so it wasn't quite as agonising to walk on. Not exactly the sexy-as-fuck image I'd hoped to project on my wedding day.

But the ache in my bones and muscles was nothing compared to the one in my soul. I felt utterly depleted, drained of will, and it was only the memory of *mi gato montés* that kept me putting one limping foot in front of the other whenever Alta wasn't compelling me to do so. Mat wouldn't have given up so easily. He'd have been fighting to his last breath, and I was determined to honour him in the same way, even if my attempts so far had been useless.

Al knew me too well to fall for any of the cajoling or trickery I'd employed to date, tutting fondly as she dragged me to the chapel. Those moments standing before Dios and the most senior members of my court as I proclaimed marital vows I had no intention of holding were agonising, and I'd half hoped that He would strike me down for my falsity.

But whatever Dios had planned for me seemingly did not involve divine intervention, as I was left with a fake smile on my face, a brand-new wife in my arms who was as scheming as she was beautiful, and a brief dinner I couldn't eat for fear I'd simply throw it back up.

And then amid cheers and catcalls we were both ushered from the hall, and the implications of what would happen next made me wish more than ever that there was a way to resist the Voice.

"Ren," said a soft voice, familiar and so heartbreaking, and I turned my head to find Al throwing her arms around me. The doors were shut and we were alone: unfamiliar guards stood watch outside, and I was as helpless as all those times my father had ordered me beaten.

"Hold me," Alta whispered, and I brought my own arms up to embrace her and the thin undergown she wore, the movement wooden and entirely not my own. "Tell me it's going to be okay."

"It's going to be okay," I repeated as required.

"Not like that," she muttered into my chest, pulling back with glassy eyes. "Like you normally say it to me, Ren."

I swallowed. "I'm not me, Al. You made sure of that."

Her gaze narrowed and she detached herself from me, glancing away but not before I caught sight of the tears running down her cheeks.

"You think I wanted this?" she hissed, swiping angrily at her face. "If you'd stop resisting me, I wouldn't have to..."

"You mean if I obeyed you without magic, you'd stop using magic to make me obey? That's no choice at all, *Queen Consort Aratorre*."

"Ren," she begged, catching my hand. "Please. Don't make us enemies."

I choked on the retort I'd been about to make, because fuck, this was *Alta*. My best friend.

"I didn't mean for Nathanael to die," she whispered, squeezing my fingers with each word. "I didn't know you had a knife. He was supposed to...when this was over, you and him would have had your happily ever after. A hacienda in south Quareh by the beach, the two of you forever. Horses, wine, sunshine. Would that not have been perfect?"

My voice was just as soft. "When this is over? How do you think this is going to end, Al?"

"With a baby," she said, and the words, spat out, shocked me back into silence. "Our baby, Ren, your male heir. Then you can abdicate, live your life finally as you please and away from the expectations of your father."

"While you take regency on behalf of the child," I said slowly, working it out far too late. Fuck, that was messed up. "Are you so desperate for power? You have the Voice!"

Alta stilled. "And that might have been enough for your father. All he had to do was use it to claim the throne, and then Quareh *listened*. Me? Even if I force you to crown me right now, no one will care! I can make them do things for what, half an hour?" She shook her head. "That's not enough to command armies. Keep the nobility loyal."

"Al."

"Save *generations* of children from the oppression and bigotry that infects this country," she hissed, her eyes wide and her tone passionate, like it always got when we'd talk about such things in private.

I swallowed, feeling shitty, yet also a touch hurt.

"You don't think I would have-"

Alta laid a cool hand on my cheek. "No, Ren. I love you and I'll protect you until the day I die, but I don't think you would do what really needs to be done. Because you're still male, and you don't understand what Quarehian women go through."

Mat did. He'd been here a matter of weeks, yet had highlighted issues I hadn't even thought of, drawn my attention to inequalities I took for granted, been insistent in his demand for change. How could he do all that, and yet I, prince and now king, could be seen by my people as no better than my father? *Fuck*.

I turned away, disgusted at myself.

"Don't waste your energy," Al said tiredly. "My father had it sealed to prevent you from escaping in the event you made it back here."

I blinked, realising she thought I was heading for the tunnel behind the tapestry. And maybe I subconsciously was, reaching for one of the last places I'd seen sweet Nathanael, his pale eyebrows set in their customary frown that I loved kissing away.

"*Mi querido*," Alta murmured, and slid her tiny hands around my waist, resting her cheek against my shoulder blades. Her thumb sought out the missing cuff on my left wrist: while even she didn't know what it really meant, she'd worn down the leather over the years with that same familiar gesture.

Finding it missing, she sighed against my back.

"It'll be okay," she said, her voice soft as she spoke the same consolation she'd demanded from me earlier. "Soon, it'll be okay."

A WHISPER AND A BREATH

*

Chapter Seventy-Two

Mat

When Ren's voice finally hit my ears, it immediately soothed every anxious part of me. It was like stepping into a hot bath, that enveloping of warmth and comfort and the certainty of *rightness*.

But only for a moment. For his voice was raised in anger, a tone I knew all too well and felt oddly possessive of. *Moy dorogoi* was permitted to shout at me; I enjoyed winding him up as much as he did to me in turn, but no one *else* was allowed to upset him. After everything he'd been through, Ren deserved happiness and sunshine and long cuddles, where the asshole could act the sadist dominant all he liked but quickly turned into the little spoon when sleep overtook him. The number of times this past week that I'd been woken by his semi-conscious self snuggling into my side, practically mewling for my arms to be wrapped around him? I'd been saving the disclosure of that revelation for a particularly satisfying moment.

Alta's softer voice drifted after Ren's, and I frowned, continuing to feel my way along the tunnel. I knew I had to be close to the prince's rooms to be hearing the two of them, but night had fallen and there wasn't an ounce of light making its way into the passageway. I'd been hoping to grab a lantern from the kitchens, however that plan had been thwarted by the arrival of several Quarehians in the kitchens shortly after Consuela's revelation about the wedding, and it had only been the hasty toss of a frying pan across the stone floor that distracted the arrivals long enough for me to throw myself back into the secrecy of the tunnels.

"...have to consummate the marriage," Altagracia was saying, and I scowled at the darkness. Like fuck they would. All those weeks ago when Alta had mentioned having more control over her fate than I might have expected, I had assumed she was plotting a way out of their marriage.

Not into it.

"Al–"

"I know, Ren! But I don't see another way of making an heir! If you do, by all means tell me, because I'm as thrilled about this as you are."

I mouthed curses at her as my outstretched fingertips finally met wood and impatiently traced my way down to the keyhole, more than ready to burst in there and stop this nonsense by doing whatever the fuck knew what – a problem for later, with later being about three seconds from now – but there was nothing.

No sharp edge of wood, no gap, no recess, nothing.

Fuck, was the door not built to be accessed from the outside? I supposed that would make sense if it was only intended as an escape route, but it seemed a little short-sighted to...

My fingers explored further, and I swore some more as I felt a rough hardness down the edges of the door and lumped around where I guessed the keyhole should be.

It had been mortared shut.

"Ren. Stop making this harder than it needs to be."

"Alta! You're better than this!"

Ren's plea was desperate, choked. What if he went into a panic attack while I was on the other side of this Blessed door?

I gave it a solid kick, but it did nothing but hurt my toes. Ren's boots were far less durable than those I'd borrowed from the guards.

Alta and Ren's voices continued uninterrupted from the other side as I started to panic.

This was *not* how it was going down. Alta did not get to destroy the remaining shreds of my beautiful prince after taking so much from him: not just his family, not just Jiron, but his oldest friend, the Lady Moreno herself. He loved her, for fuck's sake, and this was how she repaid that?

I considered shouting out, guessing they'd hear me as well as I could them if I did, but what would that achieve? Alta could freeze me in place with a word, make me throw myself down the steps, stop breathing...just as the king had done.

I couldn't do anything from here.

Silently snarling some further graphic curses in a combination of languages,

A WHISPER AND A BREATH

I tore down the stairs, trusting my feet to bear me to safety.

Light sparked ahead, and after so long in the dark, even that single glow through one of the tunnel's cracks was welcome. It lit up the dreary space enough for me to find the door to Sánchez's quarters, and then blinking in overly-bright lantern light, I leapt over his still prone form – I should really turn him onto his side so he didn't choke, but I also didn't give a fuck – and raced down the stairs. Across the deserted courtyard, where I paused at the foot of the western tower.

If I took the proper route to Ren's chambers, I'd inevitably run into guards. I doubted any of them would let me barge into the newly-weds bedchamber with no more than a wild allegation against the new Queen Consort, and maybe with time I could have come up with something better.

But I had to get to them *now*, damn it!

It was stupid. It was probably fatal. But as I started to climb the wall, thanking Star for the strengthened muscles and Ren for the supple boots, the only explanation I could give myself was one that made no sense at all.

I'll do anything.

Because it was one frustration after another – Diego, Alta, the blocked door – if they thought they could keep me from my man, they were wrong. I may have been beaten, burned and stabbed, but I wasn't dead, and that meant I wasn't stopping until something got me that way.

My fingers slipped and my breath caught in my throat as I hung from one hand for a moment. The walls of *la Cortina* were rough, but hardly suitable for climbing. There was barely any surface for my fingers or feet, and the pockmarks that did exist were too far apart. It was suicidal to try.

Swallowing, I regained my handhold and continued.

Two storeys up, three.

I could see Ren's open window above me.

Four storeys.

My fingers brushed the windowsill.

And then without warning, my left foot slipped from the tiny jut of stone it was resting on. My weight dropped, my fingers slid free, and for the second time that day, I was falling from the palace's walls.

And this time there was no Starling waiting to save me.

Just the merciless cobblestones five storeys below.

*

Chapter Seventy-Three

Ren

"*Stop.*"

We stared at each other, breathing harshly, and then we both glanced down at where I'd grabbed Alta's wrist the moment I felt the cessation of her command not to move against her. The orders were running out more quickly now as she tired from using her gifts on me all day, and the panicked flutter of her eyelashes told me that she'd worked that out as well as I had.

But she could still utter a word quicker than I could stop her from doing so.

"Let go," she Told me, enunciating both syllables, and I did, loosening my fingers without thought to allow her to pull herself free. Her tongue flickered with the sunflower yellow hue that revealed her magic, and she licked her lips nervously.

"Ren, we have at least nine months in which we will have to work together before you can leave this all behind," Al said, reminding me of her distasteful intentions for us and our future son with an expression that I could only describe as *disappointed* with me. "I do not want to have to keep you bidden the whole time, but I will if that's what it takes."

I wanted to point out that she had to sleep in that time, but I knew from the occasions we'd napped in the shade of the orchards as children that she was a light sleeper, and I feared she could stop me before I would even make it from the room. As my new wife and Quareh's Queen Consort, it wouldn't be unusual for her to accompany me everywhere unless I otherwise ordered her from my side – and of course, with Alta in my ear, I would never do such a thing. Would she really hold me in her thrall for her entire pregnancy? Surely there had to be *sometime* we'd be apart, some moment of opportunity I could seize?

She sighed, playing with her thumbnail in a gesture so heartbreakingly familiar, I felt a lump form in my throat. This was *Altagracia,* and yet in that moment, I hated her for doing this to me, to the others, to…no. I hated the Voice. It had corrupted her with its promise of power, and I hated *myself,* for causing her to think that this was the only way she could take it.

"I'm tired," she said, her voice barely above a whisper. "Tired of being polite and humble and *obedient*. I can't do that anymore."

I closed my eyes in the hope it would stop my tears from falling. Instead, they welled behind my eyelids, spilling free a moment later when I felt the caress of fingertips against my cheek. "I'm so sorry."

There was a long silence, the air so heavy I felt it trying to smother me. When I couldn't stand it anymore, I opened my eyes to find her swallowing rapidly, her delicate throat working to keep her own tears in check.

"Undress," Alta whispered, but the words weren't a compulsion. "Please, Ren."

I took her hands in mine, hands I knew as well as my own. How many times had we held each other like this for comfort? For bravery?

I lifted her hands to my mouth and kissed them, catching her eyes in wordless conveyance of everything I needed to say in a single look and a lifetime of shared fears.

And when she didn't answer, I resorted to words after all.

"You're a good person, Al. I know this isn't you."

"It has to be," she murmured, so quietly that I strained to hear her even standing so close.

"Don't," I pleaded, my voice choked with something unfamiliar. Fear. "Please, Alta, not tonight. Just give me a day?"

Her commands were wearing thinner with every hour that passed, her magic draining with each use of her power. She'd need time to recover it, just as all the Blessed did when they overtaxed themselves. If I had that time, I could make her see how wrong this was, escape the helplessness her Voice inflicted, show her that I would-

But she shook her head. "I can't."

"Al!"

"You think I want this?" Her voice was high-pitched and terrified. "I'd rather carve out my own heart than hurt you! But I have no choice: this is the path that has been laid, and I must follow it to its end. I have a chance, Ren, a real chance to make my country better. Do I not owe it to Quareh to try, even if it's at the cost of you and me?"

Sighing, she slipped her hands from mine, the loss of her warmth against my skin more than physical. "I think we could have been happy together. But my happiness cannot be more important than that of *thousands* of Quarehian women."

"And we can make it better," I promised. "Just not like this! Altagracia, I'm not my father. You know that!"

She let out a shuddering breath. "I do. But you're also not what we need. We need real reform, Ren, equality and liberation, and your family has messed it up too badly to give you any more chances."

Swallowing some more, Alta reached for the tie of her undergown and tugged on it, letting the cloth slide off her shoulders and to the floor. She stood awkwardly, bare shoulders hunched.

I looked away before I could see anything.

"We've always known this was coming," she said brusquely, turning my face back towards her. I made sure to keep my eyes high. "Don't pretend it's not easier for you."

"How, exactly, is it easier for m-"

"Because at least you like being with other people," said Alta, a sob muting her words before she lifted her head defiantly. "Ren, we always knew we'd be here someday. We talked about how we'd do this, remember? Quickly, professionally, and quietly."

I let out a choked noise, and she shushed me, tucking a loose lock of hair behind my ear.

"I could Tell you to enjoy it," she said bitterly. "At least then one of us would."

I froze, terror creeping through my veins at such a thought. How would it feel to hate what you were doing but be compelled to like it? How could I ever forgive myself for such a thing?

But she only tugged at my coat. When I refused to let her pull it off me, Al sighed, retreating back into that protective shell I'd helped her build up over the years. Colder, fiercer, one of the best and most terrible people I'd ever known. A woman whom Quareh and my father had wronged, leeching the life and hope from her until such desperate acts were all that were open to her.

"You will get me pregnant, Ren," Alta Told me, golden yellow flashes swirling around her tongue as she sobbed out the words. My tears, running silently down my cheeks, matched those of my wife. "And you will-"

A knife appeared at her neck, familiar and wrong. A remnant of another time, not necessarily happier but certainly freer, where Al and I were on the same side instead of forced apart.

She opened her mouth to speak. But the blade slid across her throat, taking my best friend's life in the silence between one heartbeat and the next.

"Mat…" I croaked, unable to believe what I was seeing.

But then Mathias was there, his arms around me, and nothing made any sense but I didn't care because he was *here*.

*

Chapter Seventy-Four

Mat

I dropped the knife and eased Altagracia's lifeless body to the floor with a gentleness born out of both the necessity to be quiet, and respect for what she had been to Ren. Her skin was slick with hot blood, and shed of her clothes, her body seemed tiny in my arms.

I felt numb. It was the second life I'd taken in a day when I'd never had cause to do so before, and fuck, it had been Alta! Sweet, churro-loving Altagracia, yet infected with a power too great to permit when she'd already shown what she was capable of doing with it.

Was this even happening, or was I lying dead in the courtyard? I'd fallen from the walls six times — or at least, had Seen such a fate six times and had been able to avoid it by shifting my grip just in time, but perhaps one of them had been real? Maybe this was a vision in itself, a merciless promise of what awaited me if I managed to climb to the prince's open window. Commission of cold-blooded murder to protect the man I loved from a woman who loved him in turn.

Or I'd thought she had. But I'd heard Alta's words to Ren, and known there could be no more bargaining, no more convincing. She'd ignored Ren's pleas just as she'd ignored mine, and as much as I felt like a bastard for it, I hadn't seen another way to silence her in time.

There were probably dozens of other ways. I'd spend my whole life thinking of them, I knew that.

But now, here?

I'd done what I'd done.

The knife glinted dully from the floor, the gem in its handle winking at me half-heartedly. It had lost most of its edge from all those years spent buried in the orchard, a secret held by only Alta and Ren, but it had remained sharp enough to slice flesh. To take a life.

Brown eyes stared up at me accusingly, lifeless and horrified. I closed them with crimson-soaked fingers.

"Mat…"

I took Ren into my arms, feeling his shoulders shaking as he fought back the shuddering breaths that threatened to consume him. Blood drenched his face and clothes – a slit throat may have been quiet, but it was certainly not clean – and its iron tang bit the back of my throat.

"Mathias," he groaned, pulling out of my grip.

"It's okay," I said, having no idea whether the fuck it was or not. "It's over."

"No," he muttered, and shoved at me with such viciousness I was forced back a step.

I didn't say anything. I deserved his anger, his grief, everything he wished to inflict.

"No, Mat, her last command is still on me. I need you to…I need…"

"Oh, shit," I hissed as I realised what he was saying. What he was attempting to do as he knelt over Alta's body.

That was…fucked up, too sick to even think about.

I grabbed Ren under the arms and hauled him backwards even as he struggled against me.

"Nathanael, you fucker. You don't know how good it is to see you."

I winced as I caught a sharp elbow to the face. "Evidently."

"It's not me," he snarled, trying to pull away. "Hold me tighter, damn it!"

I did, and yet the slippery bastard still managed to slither halfway free before I took us both to the floor, dropping my weight onto his back to try to keep him still.

Yet the Voice compelled him to Alta, and even her death had not expelled the final order she'd given him. Ren continued to resist me, scratching at anything and everything within reach.

"But I stabbed you!" he said with audible bitterness, reaching out to clasp my hand affectionately even as he tried to claw the skin from my palm.

"You did," I agreed, grimacing when he slammed his fist against my hip in a further effort to escape. "It turns out you didn't do it very well. Starling was able to heal-"

"*What the fuck?*"

I glanced over my shoulder, startled by the unfamiliar voice, to find the bedchamber doors open and two palace guards in the doorway. They were staring at Alta's naked and bloodstained corpse, but their gazes quickly turned to me, accusing and cold.

It was only then that I realised how I must look: a foreigner covered in blood and wrestling a struggling – and also bloody – Quarehian royal to the floor.

Well, shit.

"It's not what it looks like," I began, hating those damn words, but the pair predictably ignored me, drawing their swords and advancing with murderous intent in their eyes.

I swallowed. "Ren?"

"Don't hurt him!" the prince shouted back from where he was pinned beneath me. "Let him be: that's an order!"

But the command was punctuated with more desperate struggles as he fought against my hold, and the elbow he managed to get up into my gut wasn't entirely consistent with what he was telling them. Unsurprisingly, the men looked unconvinced.

I swore, trying to drag Ren backwards to put more space between us and the guards who appeared determined to execute me for laying hands on their King and Queen Consort. The compulsion had to be wearing off soon – I just had to...

And then a third guard appeared between the others, stocky and familiar, hair drawn up into a careless bun on the top of his head. His face was cast into a deep frown, but his sword was still sheathed at his hip, and that was important. That was good.

Until the moment he took two giant steps towards us and hauled me bodily off Ren. I staggered backwards, catching myself on the windowsill before I could fall to the floor.

"Luis, no!"

My yell was mirrored by Ren's own startled shout. But mercifully, the guard didn't let the prince go, instead tightening his arms around him to encase Ren in a wall of muscle. My lover bucked against him, teeth bared, yet Luis held firm.

"Leave him," Luis told the other guards, who immediately backed off from where they were closing in on me with somewhat of a confused expression. They seemed only too eager to flee the room when Luis gave that order next, and even Ren grinned at the sudden bossiness of his guard's tone.

Sinking down the wall to the floor and not caring that I was getting blood everywhere, I drew in a long breath. And then another, because by the Blessed Five, I was *done*.

"You certainly pick your moments," I managed to get out, when I'd finally taken in enough oxygen to stop my head from swimming. "How did you know?"

"Elías," Luis said, looking amused as Ren tried to bite his forearm. "I had to rescue him from a misunderstanding with the palace guards as well. He told me…" The guard glanced over his shoulder at Alta's body. "He told me enough."

After another minute, the prince finally fell limp in the guard's arms. His face, framed by the tangled mess of his hair, looked pale and exhausted, but his brown eyes were bright as they sought out mine. "Mathias?"

"*Da?*" I crawled closer and took his hand. Luis released his prince tentatively, but I wasn't worried. The Voice wasn't sophisticated enough to utilise deception to fulfil its commands; the compulsion had apparently ceased.

"I need to sort out my fucking country," Ren whispered. "And then you and I are having words."

I swallowed. Of course I couldn't just…do what I'd done to Alta and hope all would be forgiven. What had I been thinking? He probably never wanted to see me again, would hate the very sight of me and what I-

"*Eres un estúpido, idiota imbécil,*" he hissed, practically spitting out venom with the words, and I couldn't deny that accusation. *Stupid, moronic idiot* summed me up quite well.

I tried to pull free to hide the dismay I couldn't keep from my expression, but his grip on my hand was too firm.

"Ren-"

He rolled his eyes and tugged me closer, crashing his lips against mine. He tasted of blood and home.

"You were fucking foolish to return here. Twice," he murmured. "But such terrible judgment makes you *you*, and I love you for it."

My heart raced at the words as he wrapped his arms around me and buried his face in my neck. Had he just said…

Luis seemed to suddenly find the ceiling very interesting.

*

Chapter Seventy-Five

Ren

"But His Majesty needs to-"

"I don't care," Mat hissed from behind me, his arms tightening fractionally around my waist as he spat out the words. "What he *needs* is his rest. Just tell them to deal with whatever it is by their fucking selves for once."

"I...yes, Your Highness."

A moment later, I heard a door shut.

"Who are you pissing off this time, Nat?" I murmured, not bothering to open my eyes. Everything was so comfy, and...no, it really wasn't. The cushion under us was hard, I had a splitting headache, and the large ballroom we'd fallen asleep in was far too draughty. But *he* was comfy, his warm body curled around mine, and that was enough to make me want to stay like this forever.

Being with Mat was different to every other lover I'd ever had. The gentle touches as well as the rough ones, the soft kisses along with those stolen from him in desperate lust. The time we spent together while still clothed, like now.

"More like they're pissing *me* off," Mathias grumbled into my shoulder. "That's the fourth time a guard has tried to bother you in the last half hour. Go back to sleep."

But I was awake now, unable to believe I'd slept through so much disruption even if I had been up until late in the morning trying to undo some of the mess caused by the Morenos' plotting. Discreet word had already been sent to Máros about the king's death, but I knew I had to control the public narrative before it blossomed into harmful gossip. Everyone in *la Cortina* had been ordered into silence until I had the chance to make an official statement, but there would always be leaks. And then there had been the arrangements that needed making for Alta and Ademar's bodies, the cleanup of the destruction to the palace, the initial preparations for my crowning, and of course, the time spent in the surgery at Jiron's bedside, praying for his recovery as the interim royal healer worked tirelessly on his wounds.

A WHISPER AND A BREATH

Jiron will make it was all I remembered being said before the guard blearily shooed me from the room, fussing about my own pallor and need for sleep. But as there was no way in hell I was ever returning to my bedchamber with Alta's blood still staining the grout between the tiles, I'd wandered the halls until Mat, with wet hair and fresh clothes, had dragged me into the ballroom and settled us down on one of the guest lounges.

I'd had just enough energy left to be up for something more than cuddling, but Mathias had refused to let me take it further with my guards in the room, and Elías in turn had declined to let me out of his sight, despite grieving for his brother. Of course I'd tried my luck with Mat anyway, only to receive an elbow to the face and a hissed *"I'm not a fucking exhibitionist, Ren,"* which was a darned shame. But my northerner had permitted me to lay my head on his warm chest, and the gentle stroking of his fingers through my hair had been the only thing that eventually allowed me to sink into sleep.

"Have I admonished you for your stupidity in climbing the tower wall yet?" I asked lazily, tugging his arm around me more securely to prevent him from doing anything ill-advised like attempting to leave.

"You have."

"Clearly not enough, if you can speak of it so casually. Dios, Mat what were you thinking? You could have broken your neck!"

"I did," he said, and my heart stopped at the admission. "Several times over. Each time, the Sight showed me how I fell and what to avoid. I got lucky, I guess."

I sent another quick prayer of gratitude to Him for keeping my wildcat alive, even if it felt like there had been a remarkable lack of judgment on both of their parts for letting him attempt something so foolhardy in the first place.

And yet I'd been the one to risk Mathias' life first, by keeping him in the palace longer than I should have, and then letting Alta force me into hurting him. I couldn't wipe from my mind the image of Mat's blood coating my fingers, the knife I'd twisted deep inside him. His horrified, betrayed expression as he stared back at me, and how I'd been unable to offer anything but an insincere-sounding apology in return.

I expected that would haunt me for the rest of my life.

Unaware of my dark thoughts, Mathias yawned and rolled away, stretching out on his back.

"Where's Starling hiding out?" I asked him. I owed her gratitude for saving Mat's life, but her absence from the surgery since the previous day had almost cost Jiron his. Without a healer, he might have bled out without ever regaining consciousness, and the little señorita could have fixed him ten times faster than the Martinezs' healer had done. I needed her back where she belonged, and I needed it yesterday.

My lover's eyes opened and came to rest on mine. He looked guilty as fuck.

"Um. Don't be mad," he said carefully, offering me a half smile that just made me extra suspicious.

"Funnily enough, those words are doing *nothing* to reassure me, Nat. Where's my fucking healer?"

"She's not yours."

I set my jaw. "What?"

"She's not yours," Mathias repeated stubbornly, although he visibly swallowed as he caught sight of my expression. "A woman can't be owned."

I narrowed my eyes, leaning over him until we shared breath. His eyes flickered to Elías nervously, but the man stared impassively forward, too loyal to me to consider intervening on his behalf.

"It's not because she's a woman," I told him. "It's because she's mine."

"She's n-"

I pressed a hand down over Mat's mouth, cutting off his inevitable protests. "Her magic is. It's the most powerful Touch in Quareh, perhaps even on the continent, and I *will* be getting it back."

He peeled my fingers away and smirked at me from under those long eyelashes of his. "Good luck with that. I expect she's already over the border."

Oh, he *hadn't*.

But of course he had. Nathanael Velichkov couldn't have just set Starling free...no, he had to go putting ideas in her head about the liberation and equality of women in the north, and send her fleeing to the parts of Riehse Eshan I couldn't follow.

"I'll find her," I promised, allowing dark threat to seep into my voice. "And every day between now and then, you'll pay for the inconvenience you've caused me." I shifted my hips onto his, pinning him down against the uncomfortable lounge. "Perhaps with things that you'll wish Starling was here to heal you from. Ever been caned, *mi cielo*?"

He jerked in my grip, startled, and I snickered. "Of course you haven't. You're far too innocent for such things."

He managed to get a hand free but I snagged it before he could push me off him, pressing it back against the cushions to hold him still. Mat's lips parted slightly and his eyes flared with lust as he lay beneath me; not still, exactly, but settled. It stoked my desire to tease, to hint at what I truly wanted from him and bring out all of his hidden sides as he did to me.

"Not any longer, Mathias," I purred. "That pale skin of yours is just begging to be bruised under my cane, and I expect you'll scream so beautifully at its touch. What do you think?"

"I think that if I find it at my back or ass, you'll find it around your head," he snarled up at me, and that made me laugh too much to keep a proper hold on him. He shoved me off, causing me to land on my ass on the floor, and then watched with quiet amusement as I heaved out the last of my chuckles.

"Mat," I said when I'd finally sobered. "She better be okay."

"She will be," he assured me. "Star's tough."

But the words, as true as they were, didn't seem to ease the worry in his brow at the thought of her being out there alone, and they didn't negate the fact that he'd potentially put one of Quareh's best assets into the hands of my northern enemies.

—

The afternoon was sombre, filled with the services for Alta and Ademar as they were each laid to rest in the royal *nicho* on my orders, their bodies wrapped in shrouds. El stood stoically at my back as *la Cortina's* priest spoke about his brother's life with a weariness born of having performed too many such ceremonies for Quarehian soldiers, despite Mat's efforts to convince the guard to take the day off duty.

Elías had simply raised an eyebrow and said that he didn't take orders from him. Muttering something about how that was clear because otherwise El would have *waited*, Mat had resorted to fussing over me instead. He'd plaited my hair three times before he was satisfied with it, suddenly seeming much more willing than before to have it in such a style, and somehow found us outfits appropriate for the funerals from deep within my vibrant wardrobes. Things Camila could have done in a tenth of the time.

But I well understood both men's need to keep busy, distracting myself with royal affairs right up to the moment the chapel's bells called us to the first requiem. Standing still was infuriating, *devastating*, bringing home everything that had happened and everyone we had lost.

No one but Mathias and my three remaining personal guards knew what Alta had done, and it would be staying that way. I'd ordered a hero's internment for her body, while her father's corpse was left out for the carrion to recognise the traitor he was. I was determined that Quareh would remember my late wife as the woman I knew her to be: brave and resilient, beautiful and kind, the unfortunate victim of a tragic accident on her wedding night. If there were whispers about the timing of her death, I ignored them, because the alternative – disclosing the truth – was unacceptable.

Mat, for once, had agreed without argument. He knew as well as I did that revealing what had occurred would damage the position of southern women further, lending support to those Quarehians who already deemed females power-hungry backstabbers. And then there were those who would attribute her actions to her sexuality, or her education, or a thousand other things that were entirely irrelevant to the complexity that was Altagracia and what she'd wanted from this world. The fuckers didn't get to do that to her.

In another life, she and I would have stood together and brought her dream for equality to fruition. But her desperation and fear had driven her down a path I was unwilling to follow, and I could only hope she'd now find peace in Dios' eternal embrace.

"*Padre nuestro, que estás en el cielo,*" I murmured, and even Mathias joined in with the prayer, although he mumbled his way awkwardly through most of the words. "*Amén.*"

"*Amén.*"

And then the niches were closed, flowers draped before them, and I found myself back on the terrace where Mat had fallen. But I wasn't here for that.

It was also a place of older memories, one where Al and I had spent so many of our afternoons whenever I'd had the time to escape my duties. I could almost see Ademar watching over us from the shadows, nearly as constant a presence to me as Jiron, with his initial reservedness that belied a dark humour only seen once he'd warmed up to you. Fuck, I missed them both as a physical ache in my heart.

"*Mi rey?*"

My king. Oh fuck, I liked Mathias calling me that. I liked it a lot. But saying so would deprive me of my chance to contradict and correct him, and that was by far the greater pleasure.

"I'm not the king yet, Nat, despite what they call me. Technically, I'm still a prince until I'm formally crowned in Máros. All going well, that should be in three days' time."

"We're going to the capital?" His tone was excited, but there was trepidation there too. And that was no surprise – the racism and disgust my people had shown him in *la Cortina* would only double in the grand palace, and he was braver than me for being willing to shoulder that.

"I travel tomorrow."

Mat looked at me with a question in his eyes at the word *I*.

I didn't respond, instead resting my head against his as he moved to stand beside me, and we both looked out over the citrus orchards beyond the walls.

"You see beyond that far row of orange trees, that set of hills there?" I asked instead of answering him, pointing them out. He nodded, glancing at me in silent question.

"In those hills is a vacant hacienda that we sometimes use for visitors for whom it is best not to be seen in the palace," I told him. "Less than two hours' ride."

"A hacienda?"

"Yes," I said. "A house."

"I know what a fucking haci..."

Mat closed his eyes and pinched the bridge of his nose.

"What I *meant*, Ren, is what's the significance of it?"

"Well," I said, suddenly feeling the need to fidget. "Haciendas have beds."

His expression abruptly changed from exasperated to sly. "That they do."

"Take Viento and Luis," I ordered.

"That's...not exactly the encounter I had in mind." Mathias wrinkled his nose, and I laughed, leaning in to kiss it.

"The horse, definitely not. Luis however, I could get behind. In *all* the ways."

Mat sighed in what I optimistically chose to believe was infinite fondness rather than irritation, shoving me away from him.

"Fine," I conceded. "Luis will stay strictly on guard duty."

"Why can't we just...here?" Mat asked, flushing in that adorable way of his as he edged around the words.

My laughter faded.

"Because two feet from us is where I almost killed you, Mathias," I said, my throat raw as I voiced it out loud. "The Throne Room is where I let Moreno maim you, my father's quarters are where he stole your breath, and my bedchamber..."

I trailed off. *Where I tied you to the bed and took my anger out on you. Where I almost took you against your will, not realising you were under the compulsion of the Voice. Where you had to do the unspeakable to save me.*

Clearing my throat, I looked back over to the hills. "Our first time will not be here, not in this accursed place. I will not fuck you until you are free of *la Cortina*, and I know you have the choice to refuse me without consequence."

Mathias blew out a long breath. "Fine. But is that a promise?"

"Nat," I said, refusing to look at him because there was something playful in his voice and I knew that if I saw that *come get me* look in his eye, I wouldn't be able to resist. Pulling a letter from my coat, I handed it to him. "I received this an hour ago. Your brother, Dios knows how, managed to negotiate a change to the terms of the northern treaty. Congratulations: you're no longer to be a Mazekhstani hostage, and nor will any other Temarian child."

"Fuck," he breathed, unfolding the parchment with reverence as if it held the secret to eternal life instead of Velichkov's detailing of currents in the Málacete Ocean that hid both his news and the usual threats to me.

I shrugged. "It means that if you want, you can take Viento and Luis to the Temarian border. Go home, be with your family. Reclaim the heritage you are owed, and be a prince in your own right."

Mat stiffened beside me and I took a deep breath, trying not to let my distaste for such an option get in the way. This was his choice to make.

"Or," I said, and he cocked his head, raising a perfectly infuriating eyebrow. "Or you could ride no further than that hacienda. And I…"

A second eyebrow joined the first.

"I, uh, will journey there myself tonight," I told him awkwardly. "And if you were there too, well we could see if we could make this work, you and me, where there's no Moreno, or my father, just us. We could decide if there's a future. To try this with you as you, and not…where you're not my prisoner." I swallowed. "But rather my guest. My lover. My friend."

Mathias didn't say anything for a long moment, folding the parchment in precise halves until it could go no smaller.

"Is this one of those tests where you let a caged bird fly free to see if it returns to you or leaves forever?" he asked, and from the corner of my eye I could see him watching me far too intently. I looked at my boots instead.

"You're not a bird," was all I said, and that seemed to amuse him.

"Very well, prince, I'll play your game." He raised his voice to be heard by the guards at the door of the terrace. "Luis, it seems you'll be joining me on a…" My northerner looked at me and smirked. "…on a ride of indeterminate length."

Oh, the asshole. He wasn't going to give me a single clue as to his intentions, was he?

*

Chapter Seventy-Six

Mat

"Your Highness?" Luis asked, and Ren nodded to confirm my words, his brow drawn tight.

"Yes," he muttered. "You'll accompany Mathias wherever he wishes to go. Tell Galo to saddle you both horses, including Viento."

Luis bowed and left El standing in the doorway as he departed. Ren tugged on my hand to pull us back out of earshot, but we were still well within the guard's sight when he kissed me deeply, his tongue exploring my mouth with an urgency that suggested he thought he'd never see me again.

"Trying to influence my decision, are you?" I teased when we finally pulled apart for air. He growled at that, sinking his teeth into my bottom lip and clutching me close, possessive and wild.

"Absolutely," Ren breathed against my mouth, his gaze alight. "Because despite all that shit I just said about being friends, I hope you know that the next time I lay eyes on you, Nathanael Velichkov, you're getting well and truly fucked."

An excited thrill shot through me at the promise, but I kept it from my expression, albeit with some difficulty.

Instead, I offered a casual shrug, knowing it would drive him crazy. "We'll see."

Ren bared his teeth at me, clearly frustrated, and I almost laughed at how easy it was to rile him. And then he seemed to catch himself, his eyes meeting mine with shrewd intelligence in their soft brown depths.

"We'll see," he repeated, but it was thoughtful, that dangerous calm only the prince possessed. I shivered.

"We'll *see* how much you feel like backtalking me when you find yourself stuffed full with my cock," he purred in that wicked, coarse way of his, leaning in for another kiss even as I lost the ability to breathe.

A WHISPER AND A BREATH

I let my lips linger a hair's breadth from his, not quite touching, before I pulled away. It was agonising but made worth it by Ren's desperate moan as I did so, the inadvertent sway forward as he chased what he couldn't have. I wanted him thinking of me for every damn second he made me wait for him at the hacienda, and I didn't care that he'd make sure I paid for my teasing when we were alone together tonight.

In fact, I was quite looking forward to it.

"Here," I said, unstrapping the leather cuff from my wrist and affixing it to his own. His stricken look made me take pity on him. "Means nothing, prince, except that I don't like the thought of you being here in the palace without a means of escape."

"Mat," Ren practically whined as I turned towards El. I paused. "Will you be there tonight?"

"Only Dios knows," I said to piss him off, and then because the prick deserved it, I ensured I caught his eye as I deliberately bit down on my torn bottom lip before making my way to the door. Soft cursing erupted behind me and I half expected him to jump me before I reached it, but it seemed the prince was trying very hard to be good, even if he was an idiot.

Because if Ren really thought it was a difficult decision for me, then he was a blind fool and I was quite happy for him to worry his little heart out for the next few hours. I'd made my choice when I risked my life for him in turning back to the palace when I'd had my chance for freedom…twice.

Now that the danger had passed and we had the chance to indulge in something more between us, did he really think I'd leave without at least trying?

—

I tiptoed down the hallway of the hacienda, holding my breath.

"Where are you going?" Luis called out, and I glanced over my shoulder to find he'd raised his head from the lounge in the receiving area where he'd been resting after not getting any sleep the night before. By the Blessed, I'd been damn near silent.

"Back to Temar," I said sarcastically, straightening up. "Where do you think I'm going, Luis?"

The guard eyed me and the shears dangling from my hand that I'd found in the hacienda's kitchen.

"I'd say you're planning on cutting some roses for His Highness," he guessed, surprising me with his astuteness. "Those ones out near the rear porch?"

Annoyed I'd been caught out so easily, I found myself moving into a defensive posture with my hands on my hips. Then I almost stabbed myself doing so, and quickly dropped the pose.

"Indeed," I said. "The thorns on those fuckers should upset his day quite nicely, don't you think?"

Luis chuckled and lay back down, draping a meaty forearm over his eyes. "Who knew you were such a romantic, Mathias?"

I contemplated stabbing *him*, but that might blunt the shears, and I really did need them for the roses. I wanted white ones and red ones, some for a vase and others with their petals plucked and strewn over the bed upstairs so they would cascade around us as Ren and I *finally* went all the way, and by the Blessed Five, what the fuck was I thinking? I didn't do *romance*.

I scowled at the shears, and then at Luis, satisfied myself with tossing a rude gesture in his direction which of course went unseen, and headed outside. There was a light drizzle in the air, the petrichor scent pleasant to the nose, and the sun had dipped low enough behind the horizon for the orange evening glow to cast everything in a hazy, barely-there light.

The roses shivered in the gloom, as if knowing their fates at my hand.

"Sorry," I told them, putting the neck of the blades around the stalk of the prettiest candidate and snipping it in two. I caught the severed flower with my bare right hand, no longer needing to hide it under a glove. "It's for a good cause. The best really, not that I'd ever tell him that."

There was a polite cough behind me and I spun, embarrassed at being caught talking to myself.

"It's not-"

My words died when I found it was not Luis standing before me, but a woman. Dark hair tied up around her head, a long scar stretching down the left side of her face, broad shoulders. Eyes that I could have sworn I'd seen somewhere before, a light blue reflecting the dying sunlight.

And yet I knew I'd never met this stranger before in my life.

And a stranger she certainly was, for her pale skin and attire – fighting leathers, trousers, and a sword at her hip – marked her as anything but Quarehian. What was a northerner doing so far south, so close to *la Cortina*?

"Nathanael," she said in a ragged, hoarse voice, the type induced by the continent's worst hangover.

I swallowed, lifting the shears to hold them as a warning in the air between us. Was she another of the Mazekhstani assassins that had dogged my steps since our return from Sesveko? Did she know that Ren had ruined those machinations by revealing my identity? Did she not realise that with the dissolution of the hostage exchange, I no longer belonged to Mazekhstam?

"Don't," I warned when she took a step closer.

The word seemed to anger her for some reason as she scowled, spitting into the dirt at her feet.

"Drop them," the woman ordered, matching my Quarehian with her own accented growl.

"No," I said, both because I enjoyed being contrary and because depriving myself of the makeshift weapon seemed like the stupidest thing I could do in that moment. "Not until you tell me who you are and what you want." I risked a glance over my shoulder, peering back into the hacienda for any sign of Luis. "I warn you, there's a six foot something – *blyat*!" I swore, as the blades were knocked from my hand and something pressed to my face.

Not a knife or a sword, which was a nice surprise, but the softness that I found against my lips seemed out of place.

Fuck me, I hadn't even seen the woman move. She was Blessed fast, and what the hell was she doing? The material she was holding over my mouth and nose smelled sweet, and it was-

Oh, double fuck me. I struggled, trying to rip the cloth away, but she had tight hold of me and had pinned my arms to my sides with a single one of hers. Despite my resistance, her breathing remained steady, but mine sounded inordinately loud in my ears, shallow breaths that sucked in the poison pulling me into unconsciousness.

Darkness clouded my vision, irresistible in its call.

A WHISPER AND A BREATH

My last thought, as the herbs on the cloth stole the remainder of my consciousness and breath, was of Ren. How he'd given me the choice of staying or leaving, and how it hadn't been a real choice at all. I'd taken joy in tormenting him with it, knowing for certain I'd be here when he arrived at the hacienda tonight.

But now, he'd find me gone.

And he'd believe I'd chosen to leave.

***

THE END

A WHISPER AND A BREATH

ACKNOWLEDGEMENTS

Thank you, reader, for sticking with me, Mat and Ren through two books (and yes, you're not imagining it – *A Whisper and a Breath* was 50% longer than *A Knife and a Blade,* and I know it wasn't a quick read. But I also couldn't bring myself to cut anything further from its pages). We're now halfway through the Riehse Eshan series, with books 3 and 4 scheduled for release in 2023.

The hardest step in becoming an author is accepting that no matter what or how you write, there will always be readers who don't like it…and for a self-acknowledged perfectionist and people pleaser, that's a fucking hard pill to swallow. Yet, a necessary one.

Still, it warms my heart each time I see a positive review or rating, so don't ever underestimate the power that *you* have over authors in leaving them reviews. It encourages, inspires, motivates…and makes us grin like utter fools when you reveal how much the characters have gotten into your head. Because trust me, Mathias and Ren seated themselves quite contentedly in mine over a year ago and haven't showed the slightest inclination to leave. And the things they get up to in there…well, all I'll say is that it's not *quite* the kind of thing I should be using my acknowledgements for. Maybe the next book, ay?

I'd like to thank my usual translation checkers – Ximena for looking after my Spanish (and making me laugh at her utter devastation when she thought she'd lost *Knife* in a park), and Diana and her partner for fixing up my Russian. As usual, if there are any errors in my languages, it's because I was too stubborn to listen.

To Neen, for our regular writing catch-ups at our favourite café, during which it *could* be said that we do far more talking than we do writing, but I'm certainly not saying any such thing because I'm too busy writing, see?

To Alethea Faust, this series' godparent, because they're just fucking awesome. I'm honoured to call this jousting, accident-prone, passionate author my friend, and I promise it has *nothing* to do with the filthy smut sent my way in return. If you've not picked up their *Sex Wizards* series…well good, because it blows every other book out of the water and you'll never be satisfied again, but at the same time: DO IT. Thanks Al, for your constant support and encouragement, and your chapter-by-chapter rants about Moreno.

To my husband, for still managing to respond enthusiastically after the thousandth time I squealed about the sale of another book or a good day for Kindle Unlimited page reads, his chuckles about my 'debauched' imagination (including whenever he caught sight of the not-so-subtle crossed swords cover image), and not complaining *too* much when I forgot I had been meant to do something like get dressed or go to work and he found me writing frantically in some corner of the room instead (which has also occurred approximately a thousand times).

Thank you to my beta and ARC readers for helping shape this book into its current form, including Drew for the sensitivity feedback, and to the welcoming M/M reader online community for everything you've done in promoting and sharing my books.

See you soon!

*and the café's proprietor, Tanya, for the caramel slices. She made me put this in.

*Join **Adelaide Blaike's Blades** in the author's reader group on Facebook to discuss this book, get teasers from upcoming work, and stay up-to-date with the latest releases.*

A SHADOW AND A STORM

The Riehse Eshan Series, Book Three

Devastated by Mathias' decision to return home, Ren knows he should be focusing on the challenges that ruling his country will bring. Yet a fateful encounter in the foothills of Quareh sees him fall into the hands of his enemy, and Valeri Velichkov is out for Aratorre blood.

Now it's Mat's turn to choose between his duty to his family and the man he loves. But if the devout north discovers the truth about his relationship with Ren, he risks losing a whole lot more than his newfound freedom.

Read on for an excerpt

Ren

I wriggled on the hard cot, trying to get comfortable. "Budge over."

"I fear I have *budged* as much as is physically possible."

"Are you denying me, Jiron?"

"Never, my king," he said, and somehow managed to fold his huge form into an even smaller space, pressing closer to the wall.

"Prince until I'm crowned," I corrected, almost something of a reflex now. "How do you feel?"

"Fine, Your Highness."

I grinned into the dusky gloom of the surgery. "Really? Not even a *little* squashed?"

There was a moment of silence as my oldest guard carefully considered his answer.

"Not even a little," he said eventually, apparently deciding that satisfying my sadistic inclinations was the wisest course of action.

"Good. Move over some more."

"...yes, my prince."

There was a knock on the door and a moment later Elías stepped through it, my travel cloak slung over the guard's arm. He bowed low, and I felt Jiron tense where his body was tucked snugly against mine on the narrow surgery cot.

"How are you feeling?" Elías asked, his brow folding as he took in my sprawled posture and Jiron's squished form. I raised an eyebrow of my own, daring him to object to my taking two thirds' ownership of Jiron's sick bed, but El was too well-trained for that. He simply met my gaze with a steady look of *I know what you're doing, and I'm not falling for it.*

Too bad. I was in a teasing mood and needed someone to torment.

"I'm well, thank you," I drawled, cutting over Jiron's murmurs of affirmation. "And as for him," – I gave the guard lying beside me a sharp elbow to the ribs, which he bore without protest – "Jiron was just telling me how he'd like to see the next person who walked through that door strip completely naked and go down on us both. You wouldn't want to disappoint a dying man, would you, El?"

He didn't even blink, and Jiron's soft sigh in my ear was barely exasperated.

Damn it. What did a prince have to do to get a rise out of someone around here?

"Alas, if we only had the time," Elías said dryly, "but I expect Your Highness wants to leave immediately now that night is falling?"

"Leave?" Jiron asked, and the tension I'd felt in his body when he caught sight of my cloak finally seeped through into his voice. "Where are you going?"

"Going? Absolutely nowhere," I lied. "Coming, on the other hand? Hopefully several times." I pressed a gentle kiss to his stubbled cheek and got to my feet. The guard shifted on the cot, as if making to rise himself, and I delivered a scathing glare back down upon him. "You lift one finger from that bed and I'll have you tied to it. You're meant to be resting and recuperating, remember?"

Even if he didn't, I remembered far too well. Every time I closed my eyes, I saw Moreno's dagger slide between Jiron's ribs, watched the huge man crumple to the floor of the throne room. Replayed how I was forced to abandon his too-still form on the tiles as Alta ordered me away with the compulsion magic of her Voice.

And when my fucked-up mind wasn't showing me images of *that*, it was entreating me to the sight of my own hand plunging a knife into Mat's gut, spilling his blood over the terrace and watching him fall out of sight over the walls, accompanied by that numbing feeling of true loss and despair. Or Alta's frozen horror as her throat was slit. Or how Ademar's fearless taunting of the Comandante had been silenced with a single swing of his sword, my guard's headless body etched onto the inside of my eyelids.

I swallowed. Mathias and Jiron, against all odds, had survived, holding onto life with sheer determination and the magical healing power of the Touch. But Al and Ademar were…now resting in Dios' embrace, and fuck, that didn't reassure me one inch. Because despite the wonders undoubtedly waiting for them in heaven, neither of them deserved their fates, and damn it, I needed them back with me, full of life and the quiet joy they each took from it. It wasn't fair, none of it, and I wanted to scream.

But I was also the awaiting monarch to the Quarehian throne, and I rather expected that *screaming* wasn't what my people were looking to me for. I had a shit ton of work to do to fix my father's mistakes, stabilise the politics of my country, and prevent what happened to Alta from driving any other woman to such desperate acts.

But first, I had one thing to do that was for me alone. One night of selfishness, to wholly lose myself in Mathias before the whirlwind of the next few weeks – funerals for my family, my crowning, the appointment of my Council and the restoration of Quareh – took over everything else.

If Mat was waiting for me at the hacienda in the hills.

If he hadn't returned home to his own family as I'd offered for him to do and provided him the means through which to achieve it. Freedom from the palace, a horse, a guard. Everything he needed to ride straight to the Temarian border and leave behind all the shit he'd suffered in the south, me included.

I scowled and tossed that thought away. He'd be there. Mat was…he was mine, and I was his, and if he felt *half* of what I felt for him in turn, he'd be watching the sun set as keenly as I was. Not that he'd admit it: I fully expected to be greeted with a fake yawn and a comment on how he just couldn't be bothered to ride any further than the house so I *shouldn't take it to mean anything, prince*, but his eager little sounds and fervent touches as I took him fully for the first time would tell a different story.

Our story.

"*Ren*," Jiron pressed, and the rare use of my name on his lips brought me out of my imagination.

"Hmm?"

"Where's Mathias?"

I waved a hand. "Around."

El blinked at that, but he didn't contradict me. Not that he could; *around* was a vague term that encompassed the remote possibility of 'waiting in the hills at a pretty little house for us to fuck away from this blood-drenched palace so he doesn't feel like I have power over him…except for the sexy kind of power where I have him on his knees before me', just as easily as it included 'still upstairs, such that I have no inclination to go anywhere at all, Jiron'.

But damn it, Jiron knew me too well to fall for such a ploy as ambiguity. "You're not leaving the palace. Not with everything that's happened."

"Prince," I reminded him sharply, pointing at my chest.

*

A WHISPER AND A BREATH

A WHISPER AND A BREATH

Made in the USA
Las Vegas, NV
18 February 2025